fierce invalids home from hot climates

TOM ROBBINS

BANTAM BOOKS

New York   Toronto

London   Sydney

Auckland

Fierce Invalids Home From Hot Climates

FIERCE INVALIDS HOME FROM HOT CLIMATES

A Bantam Book / May 2000

A signed first edition of the book has been privately printed by The Franklin Library.

BOOK DESIGN BY GLEN EDELSTEIN.

Library of Congress Cataloging-in-Publication Data
Robbins, Tom.
Fierce invalids home from hot climates / Tom Robbins.
p.   cm.
ISBN 0-553-10775-5
I. Title

PS3568.O233 F54 2000
813'.54—dc21
99-051683

Published simultaneously in the United States and Canada

Bantam Books are published by Bantam Books, a division of Random
House, Inc. Its trademark, consisting of the words "Bantam Books" and the
portrayal of a rooster, is Registered in U.S. Patent and Trademark Office
and in other countries. Marca Registrada. Bantam Books, 1540 Broadway,
New York, New York 10036.

PRINTED IN THE UNITED STATES OF AMERICA

BVG / 10   9   8   7   6   5   4   3

For Rip and Fleet and Capt. Kirk

I want God, I want poetry,
I want danger, I want freedom,
I want goodness, I want sin.
                    —Aldous Huxley

part 1

Sometimes naked
Sometimes mad
Now the scholar
Now the fool
Thus they appear on earth:
The free men.
　　　　　　—Hindu verse

Lima, Peru
October 1997

the naked parrot looked like a human fetus spliced onto a kosher chicken. It was so old it had lost every single one of its feathers, even its pinfeathers, and its bumpy, jaundiced skin was latticed by a network of rubbery blue veins.

"Pathological," muttered Switters, meaning not simply the parrot but the whole scene, including the shrunken old woman in whose footsteps the bird doggedly followed as she moved about the darkened villa. The parrot's scabrous claws made a dry, scraping noise as they fought for purchase on the terra-cotta floor tiles, and when, periodically, the creature lost its footing and skidded an inch or two, it issued a squawk so quavery and feeble that it sounded as if it were being petted by the Boston Strangler. Each time it squawked, the crone clucked, whether in sympathy or disapproval one could not tell, for she never turned to her devoted little companion but wandered aimlessly from one piece of ancient wooden furniture to another in her amorphous black dress.

Switters feigned appreciation, but he was secretly repulsed, all the more so because Juan Carlos, who stood beside him on the patio, also spying in the widow's windows, was beaming with pride and satisfaction. Switters slapped at the mosquitoes that perforated his torso and cursed every hair on that hand of Fate that had snatched him into South too-goddamn-vivid America.

Boquichicos, Peru
November 1997

attracted by the lamplight that seeped through the louvers, a mammoth moth beat against the shutters like a storm. Switters watched it with some fascination as he waited for the boys to bring his luggage up from the river. That moth was no butterfly, that was certain. It was a night animal, and it had a night animal's mystery.

Butterflies were delicate and gossamer, but this moth possessed strength and weight. Its heavy wings were powdered like the face of an old actress. Butterflies were presumed to be carefree, moths were slaves to a fiery obsession. Butterflies seemed innocuous, moths somehow . . . erotic. The dust of the moth was a sexual dust. The twitch of the moth was a sexual twitch. Suddenly Switters touched his throat and moaned. He moaned because it occurred to him how much the moth resembled a clitoris with wings.

Vivid.

There were grunts on the path behind him, and Inti emerged from the forest bearing, somewhat apprehensively, Switters's crocodile-skin valise. In a moment the other two boys appeared with the rest of his gear. It was time to review accommodations in the Hotel Boquichicos. He dreaded what he might find behind its shuttered windows, its double-screened doors, but he motioned for the boys to follow him in. "Let's go. This insect—" He nodded at the great moth that, fan though it might, was unable to stir the steaming green broth that in the Amazon often substitutes for air. "This insect is making me feel—" Switters hesitated to utter the word, even though he knew Inti could understand no more than a dozen simple syllables of English. "This insect is making me feel *libidinous*."

Central Syria
May 1998

trekking toward jebel al Qaz-az in a late spring rain, the nomads were soaked and nearly giddy. Behind them, at lower elevations, the grass was already yellowing and withering, fodder not for flocks but for wildfires; ahead, the mountain passes conceivably could still be obstructed by snow. Whatever anxieties the band maintained, however, were washed away by the downpour. In country such as this, hope's other name was moisture.

Even the sheep and goats seemed merry, lighter of hoof, although individual beasts paused from time to time to shake rainwater from their coats, vigorously, stiffly, causing them to look like self-conscious burlesque queens. Their leathery black muzzles, glistening with rain, were pointed—not so much by their drivers as by a migratory instinct older than humanity—toward distant pastures.

Switters was one of four men—the khan, the khan's eldest son, an experienced pathfinder, and himself—who traveled on horseback at the head of the procession. The rest were on foot. They had been on the move, dawn to dusk, for almost a week.

About two miles back, prior to beginning their gradual ascent, they had passed a large compound, an oasis, undoubtedly, completely surrounded by a high mud wall. The boughs of orchard trees rose above the wall, and the scent of orange blossoms boosted to a higher power the already intoxicating smell of the rain. From inside the compound, Switters thought he heard the wild sugary shriek of girlish laughter. Several of the young men must have heard it, too, for they turned their heads to stare wistfully at the remote estate.

The band pressed on. That is what nomads do. Forward the march. The burden and the bleating.

Switters, however, could not get the mini-oasis out of his mind.

Something about it—its mysterious walls, its lush vegetation, its auditory hint of young women splashing in the rain—had gripped his imagination with such steady pressure that eventually he announced to his hosts his intention to return and investigate the place. One might say they were shocked, except that his very presence among them was in and of itself so extraordinary that they were partially immune to further bewilderment.

The khan shook his head, and his eldest son, who spoke passable English, objected, "Oh, sir, we must not turn back. The flocks—"

Switters, who spoke passable Arabic, interrupted to explain that he meant to go alone.

"But, sir," said the eldest son, wringing his hands and screwing up his forehead until it looked like the rolled-back lid of a sardine can, "the horse. We have only these four, you see, and we—"

"No, no, good buddy. Assure your papa I had no notion of galloping off with his fine nag. Now, he can let his next eldest son hop up and take a load off *his* tootsies."

"But, sir—"

"I'll just zip on back there in my starship. If you boys'll be so good as to ready it for me."

The khan waved the procession to a halt. At that exact moment the rain stopped as well. Two of the tribesmen unfastened Switters's chair from behind the saddle, unfolded it, placed it on a reasonably level patch, and set its brake. Then they helped him off the horse and lifted him gently into the seat. They strapped his croc-skin valise to the chair back and laid his computer, satellite telephone, and customized Beretta 9-mm revolver, each wrapped in a separate plastic garbage bag, on his lap.

Elaborate farewells were exchanged, after which the nomads watched for many minutes in nothing short of awe as Switters, laboriously, precariously—but singing all the while—maneuvered the rickety, hand-operated wheelchair over the brutal rocks and ensnaring sands of a landscape so harsh in its promise that a mere glimpse of it would propel a Romantic poet to therapy or a developer to gin.

Slowly, he dissolved into the wilderness.

He seemed to be singing "Send in the Clowns."

Vatican City
May 1999

the cardinal ordered Switters and his party to queue up single file. The garden path was narrow, he explained, and besides, it would be unseemly to approach His Holiness all in a bunch. Switters was to go first. If his weapon had not been confiscated at the last security checkpoint, he might have insisted on bringing up the rear, but now it didn't matter.

Because of his "disability," Switters needn't feel obliged to kneel upon reaching the throne, the cardinal had generously conceded. Switters wondered if, nevertheless, he would be expected to kiss the pope's ring. *Only way I'm smooching that ring,* he thought, *is if they paste a crumb of hashish on it, or else smear it with pussy juice or red-eye gravy.*

As he thought that, he was remembering an actress he used to know, who, in order to entice a tiny trained terrier to follow her around during a movie scene, had had to have scraps of raw calf's liver stapled to the soles of her high-heeled shoes.

Thinking of that terrier magnetized by meat-baited slippers reminded him then of the old bald parrot that had waddled after its mistress in a Lima suburb many months before—and for a moment Switters was back in Peru. That's the way the mind works.

That's the way the mind works: the human brain is genetically disposed toward organization, yet if not tightly controlled, will link one imagerial fragment to another on the flimsiest of pretense and in the most freewheeling manner, as if it takes a kind of organic pleasure in creative association, without regard for logic or chronological sequence.

Now, it appears that this prose account has unintentionally begun in partial mimicry of the mind. Four scenes have occurred at four different locations at four separate times, some set apart by months or years. And while they do maintain chronological order and a connective element (Switters), and while the motif is a far cry from the kind of stream-of-consciousness technique that makes *Finnegans Wake* simultaneously the most realistic and the most unreadable book ever written (unreadable precisely *because* it is so realistic), still, alas, the preceding is probably not the way in which an effective narrative ought properly to unfold—not even in these days when the world is showing signs of awakening from its linear trance, its dangerously restrictive sense of itself as a historical vehicle chugging down a one-way street toward some preordained apocalyptic goal.

Henceforth, this account shall gather itself at an acceptable starting point (every beginning in narration is somewhat arbitrary and the one that follows is no exception), from which it shall then move forward in a so-called timely fashion, shunning the wantonly tangential influence of the natural mind and stopping only occasionally to smell the adjectives or kick some ass.

Since this new approach should render chapter headings (those that designate date and place) unnecessary, they will from now on be scratched. If the next chapter *were* to have a heading, however, it would read:

Seattle
October 1997

it was on a mist-bearded Saturday morning, gray as a ghoul and cool as clam aspic, that Switters showed up at his grandmother's house. En route from the airport, he had stopped by Pike Place Market, where he bought a bouquet of golden chrysanthemums, as well as a medium-sized pumpkin. Now, he was forced to juggle those items in order to free a hand with which to turn up his trench coat collar against the microdontic nipping of the drizzle. He had also purchased a capsule of XTC from a hipster fish merchant he knew, and as he walked from the rental car to the stately mansion, he managed to get it to his mouth and swallow it without benefit of liquid. It tasted like snapper.

He punched the bell. After a brief interval, his grandmother's voice crackled out of the speaker. "Who is it? What do you want? This had better be good." The woman refused to keep a downstairs maid, although she was eighty-three years old and had the wherewithal.

"It's me. Switters."

"Who?"

"Switters. Your favorite relation. Buzz me in, Maestra."

"Heh! 'Favorite relation' in your dreams, maybe. Do you come bearing gifts?"

"Absolutely."

He heard the electronic loosening of the latch. "I'm advancing. Brace yourself, Maestra."

"Heh!"

When Switters was less than a year old, his grandmother had stood before his highchair, her hands on her still glamorous hips. "You're starting to jabber like a damn disk jockey," she said. "Pretty soon you'll be having a name for me, so I want to make this clear: you are not to insult me with one of those déclassé G words, like granny or grams or gramma or whatever, you understand; and if you *ever* call me nannie or nana or nonna—or moomaw or big mama or mawmaw—I'll bust your cute little chops. I'm aware that it's innate in the human infant to produce M sounds followed by soft vowels in response to maternalistic stimuli, so if you find it primally necessary to label me with something of that ilk, then let it be *'maestra.'* Maestra. Okay? That's the feminine form of the Italian word for 'master' or 'teacher.' I don't know if I'll ever teach you anything worthwhile, and I sure as hell don't want to be anybody's master, but at least maestra has got some dignity. Try saying it."

Little more than a year later, when he was two, the child had marched up to his grandmother, pinned her with his already fierce, hypnotic green eyes, planted his hands on his hips, and commanded, "Call me Switters." Maestra had studied him for a while, had puzzled over his sudden identification with his none too illustrious surname, and finally nodded. "Very well," she said. "Fair enough."

His mother continued to call him Baby Dumpling. But not for long.

Maestra failed to greet him in the vestibule, so Switters wandered the ground floor searching for her. Nearly a year had passed since he'd been in the house, but it was as he remembered it: spare, elegant, and spotless (Maestra had a professional housecleaning service come in twice a week; her meals she ordered delivered from Chinese and pizza take-out joints), and a dramatic contrast to the dumps in which her offspring—and *their* offspring—had often resided. Maestra had done all right for herself. Above the living room fireplace was an Henri Matisse oil of a mountainous blue nude reclining, distorted limbs akimbo, on a jazzy patterned harem sofa. He was reasonably sure it was authentic.

He found her in the library, perched at a computer. Much of the library was jammed with electronic equipment, twice the amount as on his last visit. Her collection of great books was now double- and triple-parked at one end of the room, while at the other end there were two computers, an array of modems, printers, and telephones, a forty-inch television set into which a stack of black boxes was jacked, a fax machine, and a helmet with goggles attached, which Switters took to be some type of virtual reality device.

"Maestra! Surfing so early in the day?"

"Less traffic this time of morning. Switters! Are you alone?"

"Of course. Who'd I dare bring with me?"

Punching off-line, she swiveled to face him. "Well, I did intercept an e-mail message in which you promised little Suzy you were gonna take her 'all the way to grandma's house.' " Her affectionate gaze hardened into a glare.

Switters blushed so incandescently he could have hired out his face as a beer sign. It was one of those instances, rare in his life, when he was at a loss for words.

"Perhaps that expression has some different connotation for you. Eh? Something I'm not hip to?" Her smile was ironic and a tad malicious. "After all, you've always exhibited the good taste not to refer to *me* as 'grandma.' "

"Uh, er," Switters stammered, "Suzy? Suzy's in Sacramento, how in hell did you access her e-mail?"

"Heh! Easy as pie. Child's play. You of all people ought to know that." The edges of her smile softened some. "All right, Switters. Come here. Kiss these wrinkly old cheeks. It's a blessing to see you. A mixed blessing, but a blessing, nonetheless. Mmm. Boy. So what'd you bring me? Great, you know I'm crazy about mums. And a most fine pumpkin. Yes. Excellent damn pumpkin." Her disappointment in the presents was ill concealed.

From his jacket pocket, he fished a Bakelite bracelet, pinkish butterscotch in tone. "Found this in an antique shop in Paris. Guy claimed it belonged to Josephine Baker."

"Well, it's mine now!" Maestra was immoderately fond of bracelets, often wearing as many as ten on each thin arm. "That's so thoughtful of you, Switters. So sweet." She paused, adding the bracelet to her jumble and admiring it there. "But don't think this lets you off the hook, buddy boy. I don't have to tell you what a wicked degenerate you are."

"Oh, tell me anyway. I never tire of hearing it. Puts a spring in my step."

"You *are* a wicked degenerate. A rascal, a wastrel, a pervert. . . . Don't look so pleased with yourself. This business with little Suzy is not funny. It's sick. What's more, it's criminally prosecutable. You've always been the most irresponsible—"

"Now, now. How can you say that? I'm a dedicated, decorated public servant with a top-secret security clearance. Hardly the resumé of a slacker."

"I'm supposed to sleep better nights knowing the likes of you is guarding the henhouse? It amazes me you've lasted in that job."

"Over a decade now."

"It amazes me they ever recruited you in the first place."

"It was my firm jaw and air of tragic nobility."

"It was your academic record." There was an irrepressible yeast of pride in her voice when she said, "The dean of students at Berkeley told me personally they'd never seen the likes of you when it came to cybernetics and linguistics. . . ."

"Don't forget modern poetry. I had nine hours of modern poetry."

"He neglected to mention that. And the rugby fellow, that swarthy Englishman, he said you were the only American he'd ever coached who actually understood the game."

"Nigel was just buttering you up. He was consumed with desire for you. You drove him wild."

"Heh! Rubbish. I was a senior citizen even then. Rugby's barbaric. Worse than football. But there's no denying it, you hit the grade-point jackpot."

"Genes, Maestra. Abilities I inherited from you."

"Heh!" The old woman beamed in spite of herself. "You were clever, in *some* areas, but I'm still surprised they'd recruit you, considering your extracurricular activities and your weak moral fiber."

"It's government service, Maestra. Morality's scarcely an issue."

"You have a point there, unfortunately. So what monkey business has that agency of yours got your nose into now? What're you up to? What're you doing in Seattle? How long before you leave me?"

"Upon the rosy-fingered dawn."

"Tomorrow? No!"

"I fly to South America first thing in the morning—but I'll be back in a wink. Actually, I'm supposed to be starting a thirty-day leave, but the yard boss insisted I postpone it just long enough to dash down to Lima and back. Really, I'll probably only be there overnight."

He saw her eyes narrow behind her spectacles.

"Assassination?"

"I don't do windows. You've been watching too much TV. Company recruited a very promising young dude down there, indigenous operative, fronted him a new Honda as a signing bonus, and now he's backing out on the deal."

"You're going to terminate him with extreme prejudice."

"Get real. I'm gonna lobby him, try to talk him into staying aboard."

"Why you?"

"I guess because we have similar backgrounds. He earned a

double master's from the University of Miami. Computer science and languages."

"No modern poetry?" She was needling him.

"Methinks not, Maestra. But I bet he can quote a line or two from *Howl*."

"And what'll you do on your vacation? May I expect another intrusion?"

"Absolutely. Another bangle, too. First thing when I get back. Uh, I was hoping you'd let me use the cabin up at Snoqualmie Pass for a week or two. I've sucked way too much cement this year. Bad juju rising off them city sidewalks. I need to babble with a brook or two, inhale starlight, make friends with some trees. Then I may hop over to Sacramento briefly, regale the family."

"Including Suzy?"

"Uh, well, uh, Suzy quite possibly may be on the premises. I believe she's going to school."

"Of *course* she's going to school! She's a *teenager!*"

Maestra fell quiet and remained quiet for such a lengthy period that Switters wondered if she might have nodded off, as the elderly are wont to do. Either that or she was truly very angry. He cleared his throat. He cleared it again. Louder now.

"South America," she said abruptly.

"Yes."

"Nice."

"Not nice. No. South America holds a minimum of charm for this buckaroo."

"I suppose. The death squads, the poverty, the corruption, the destruction of nature."

"Hmm, well, yes, there's *that*." He scratched himself, as if thinking of South America made him itch. "And then there's the fact that it's just too goddamn vivid."

She regarded him quizzically, but when she spoke she asked not what he meant by "vivid" but to what country, exactly, was he traveling in South America?

"Peru."

"Peru. Yes. That's what I understood. Lima, Peru."

There followed another long silence, but this time he could tell she wasn't drifting in any geriatric ozone. Her eyes simultaneously narrowed and brightened until they looked like the apertures through which Tabasco droplets enter the world, and the *zing zing zing* of synaptic archery was very nearly audible.

"Jeez," he muttered eventually, shaking his head. "If J. Robert

Oppenheimer had thought that hard, he'd have invented video poker instead of the A-bomb."

Maestra smiled sardonically. "Prove to me," she said, "that chivalry can still eat lunch in this town." With a rattle of bracelets, she extended both arms. "I need to be excused."

Switters was taken aback at how light she was, how frail. Her body was a husk compared to the meaty pulp of her spirit and her voice. Yet once he had helped her to her feet, she left the room rather briskly, barely relying on the rustic mahogany cane that she seemed to sport mainly for effect. He heard her rat-a-tatting it along the banister posts as she climbed the stairs.

After tossing his trench coat over a modem (underneath, he wore a gray Irish tweed suit and a solid red T-shirt), he strolled to the library windows. Maestra's house sat high on the bluffs of the Magnolia District, so called because a botanically challenged early explorer had mistaken its profusion of madrona trees for an unrelated species that graced more southerly climes. Magnolia's cliffs overlooked the shipping lanes through which all manner of vessels, from warships to oil tankers to funky little salmon-snaggers, sailed from the Pacific to Seattle's docks by way of the Strait of Juan de Fuca and Puget Sound. Maestra's second husband had been a sea captain and owner of tugboats, and he liked to keep an eye on the tides. On this drizzly day, the captain wouldn't have seen very much. The sky and the water looked like separate panels of the same chalk-fogged blackboard. Nature had erased the diagrammed sentences and multiplication tables, leaving a view that was all pan and no orama.

Switters turned from the misty void and was instantly confronted with its opposite: namely, a well-defined object of lurid coloration. It was the pumpkin, only its orangeness had become so intense it seemed to be undergoing spontaneous combustion right there on the library table. Switters didn't know whether to reach for a fire extinguisher or fall down and worship. The thing was blazing—and spinning, as well. At least, it appeared to be, for a minute or two. He blinked and rubbed his eyes. Then he remembered.

He had forgotten about ingesting the XTC. It was starting to come on, and come on strong. Knowing that 150 milligrams of 3, 4-methylenedioxy-methamphetamine, to call it by its rightful name, would not produce hallucinations, he figured that his present-moment awareness must be substantially heightened. With that in mind, he pulled up a chair and sat directly facing the gourd. It was no longer afire, but it was *very* pretty and *very* friendly, and Switters felt compelled to caress its haptic contours.

"We search for the door in the side of the pumpkin," he whispered, "but unlike Cinderella's coach, it is drawn only by its own slow ripening." (Where was this coming from?) "Distracted by the toothy glitter of corn, mice leave it to round, to orange: a globe of lost continents, a faceless head, its true identity known only to the Halloween knife and certain deputies of the pie police. O pumpkin, pregnant squaw bladder, hardiest of moons, scarecrow's beachball, in the name of farmers' daughters everywhere, remove your hood and—"

"Switters!" Maestra had entered the room behind him. "What the hell are you saying to that poor fruit? Is this what nine hours of modern poetry does to a man?"

"My queen. You have returned."

"Christ, boy! I see the frost is off *your* pumpkin. Have you finally gone around the bend?"

He smiled at her sweetly. Shyly, he studied his white sneakers. "Maestra, would you mind putting on some music? I feel like dancing."

"Never mind the damn music. Sailor Boy and I want your undivided attention."

It was then that he noticed the parrot.

How his grandmother, in her fragility, had managed to fetch Sailor's cage from her upstairs sitting room, Switters could not imagine. Although airily constructed of wicker and copper wire, it was spacious, as birdcages go, and probably none too light. Normally a skeptic, Maestra had become convinced that pyramids possessed the power to refresh and preserve organic tissue, whether of a plucked apple or a fully feathered bird, and inspired by an article on the subject in a reputable science magazine, she had long ago commissioned a craftsman to build her parrot a cage in the model of the Great Pyramid, although whether its geometric shape added to or subtracted from its total weight was something that had never been considered. Its impact on Sailor Boy's health was likewise unproven, yet no observer could dispute the salubrious sheen of his plumage.

"I'm aware," she said, "of your antipathy toward animals."

"Why, that's slander, Maestra. I cherish all God's creatures, great and small." It was the XTC talking. The XTC grinning.

"Okay, pets then. I have it on good authority, namely you yourself, that you don't like pets. Why are you acting so goofy?"

He scratched his jaw in a pensive manner. "It's cages I dislike. Cages and leashes and hobbles and halters. It's the taming I dislike. I appreciate that a pet can be a comfort to one such as yourself, but domesticity shrinks the soul of a beast. If God had meant for animals to live indoors, he would have given them second mortgages."

"It's the wild kingdom that you fancy."

"Well, sometimes nature has a tendency to go over the top, lay it on a bit thick with the creeping and crawling and sliming and hissing and stinging and ceaseless reproducing. But generally speaking, yes, my respect is for the thing that sniffs its prey instead of sniffing my crotch, the thing that shits in the elephant grass instead of shitting in a box in my kitchen."

"Your phrasing is indelicate, but your meaning is clear. You prefer your creatures wild and free. That's good. That's very good."

"Is it good, Maestra?" His expression was that of a proud child who has just been praised for some trivial if heartfelt achievement.

"Yes, it's very damn good because it means that you're philosophically disposed to undertake the little mission I'm about to assign you."

Switters blinked. He was in a drug-induced neurologically based state of blissful benevolence, a state in which ego was softened, fear dissolved, and trust expanded, yet through it all he sensed that he was about to be conned.

It turned out that his grandmother wanted Switters to take Sailor the parrot with him to South America and release the bird in the jungle there. At her advanced age she faced the inevitable, and while its life expectancy was almost certainly greater than her own, the parrot, too, was no spring chicken. She wanted her pet to spend its remaining years flying free in the forest of its birth.

"But, but, uh," Switters sputtered, "you've had Sailor for about as long as I can remember. . . ."

"Thirty-four, thirty-five years. And he was at least that old when I acquired him."

"Sounds right. I'm thirty-six. So, why at this late date . . . ?"

"Don't pretend to be a knucklehead. You *know* why. I've always assumed that he was leading a good life, but that may have been a chauvinistic presumption. I mean, he's behind bars, isn't he? You might recall that he used to be loose in the house, but in recent years he's taken to ripping up the draperies with his beak and committing other disagreeable and destructive deeds. He's undergone a personality change. You're the one who's claimed that all pets eventually become anthropomorphically neurotic. Correct? Anyway, I've had to keep him locked up. You have no idea how guilty I've felt. So it's for my conscience as well as for his 'shrunken soul' that I want you to liberate him."

"But, but I thought Sailor was from *Brazil*. He's a Brazilian parrot. I'm going to *Peru*."

"Quit speaking to me like I'm senile. Brazil, Peru—the Amazon jungle's the Amazon jungle. Birds and beasts don't recognize national boundaries. They have better sense."

"Okay, but I'm not going to the Amazon jungle. I'm going to Lima." His voice was fuzzy, and muffled by faux nonchalance. "Lima's on the coast. There's desert around it. It's hundreds of kilometers from the Amazon." He turned to face the cage. Sailor was tearing at a bunch of grapes, but his head was cocked to the side, with one shiny orb trained on Switters, as if he could detect the man's abnormal state. "Sorry, ol' birdy, ol' pal, but if you expect to wing home to the emerald forest, you're gonna have to redeem your frequent-flyer miles."

Maestra was neither amused nor dissuaded. "Your tone disappoints me," she said. The pupils of his aforementioned fierce, hypnotic green eyes were so dilated they looked like the burners on a dollhouse stove. She stared into them without trepidation. "A quick detour, that's all I'm asking. It may widen the pinhole in your travel map, but you're going to have to do it for me."

"Oh, no. No, no. It wouldn't be anywhere near quick enough for me. If I'm not out of South America within forty-eight hours, I will have forfeited all claim to future happiness. Can't do it, Maestra. It's an ordeal in the making, and it's too much to ask."

She clapped her age-spotted hands together with such a sharp *pop* that it caused the parrot to start and flutter. "Then I'm no longer asking. I'm insisting."

Switters grinned. He loved the whole world at that moment, South America and a demanding old matriarch included, but he wasn't going to let himself be manipulated. "You forget, I'm the only member of our family you've never been able to intimidate or control. That's why you adore me. So, you might as well—"

"Heh! The reason I tolerate you, to the extent that I *do* tolerate you, is that you're the only one of us left with any tricks in his bag. In this case, I'm afraid, those very tricks of yours are your undoing." She paused briefly for the theater that was in it. "You see, buddy boy, I happen to have on file every e-mail mash note you've posted to Suzy in the past six months."

"No, you don't!" he blurted out confidently, but somehow he knew she wasn't bluffing.

"Want to bet?" She went directly to the smaller and older of her two computers, the Mac Performa 6115, and within a few minutes had pulled up a text. "All right, this one is dated thirty, September. Ahem. It reads, and I quote, 'I long to greet your delta like a rooster greets the dawn.' "

"Oh, dearie me." Blushing, he slumped in his chair and began to croon very softly, "Send in the Clowns."

In the discussion that followed, the word *blackmail* fell many times from Switters's lips. He said it without rancor, she responded without guilt.

"I can't believe my own grandmother would stoop to blackmail." He shook his dark blond curls. He was bemused.

"Nobody else will believe it, either. But they'll have no choice but to believe the sordid evidence of Suzy's e-mail. I ask you again: Do you want your mother and stepfather to read those messages? Want your superiors in Virginia to read them? Mull it over."

"Blackmail most foul. No pun intended."

"It's for a good cause. Don't take it so hard. And you know, I've been contemplating updating my will. The Sierra Club probably wouldn't know what to do with the cabin at Snoqualmie, so I'm now considering, only considering, leaving it to you."

"I . . ."

"Hush. Just listen. My Matisse that you've always been kind of gaga about? At present it's destined for the Seattle Art Museum, but I might be persuaded to keep it in the family. If Sailor was sprung free and my heart was at peace."

"Blackmail wasn't sin enough. Now you've added bribery."

"Yes. The old B and B. It doesn't get any better than that."

"You realized from the start that bribery alone wouldn't work."

"Materialism is one of the few vices you don't subscribe to. Yet, deep down, even you have a pitty-pat sense of self-survival."

He made a final effort to escape his fate. "Perhaps this hasn't occurred to you, Maestra, not being a traveler, but a person can't just take live animals in and out of foreign countries. Most countries have strict quarantine laws regarding pets. I'll wager Peru—"

"Switters! You're a CIA agent, for Christ's sake! Surely you have ways of getting any manner of restricted items through the tightest of customs. You told me once it was like diplomatic immunity, only better."

Defeated, he slumped further in his chair. In that position, he was at eye level with the pumpkin, and he imagined he could detect its seeds spiraling inside of it like stars in a galaxy or bees in a hive.

Conspicuously pleased with herself, Maestra strutted over, bracelets clattering, and gently poked his neck with her cane. "Sit up straight, boy. Do you want to be Quasimodo when you grow up?" From somewhere in her richly brocaded kimono, she produced a thrice-folded sheet of crumpled pink paper. "All this blackmail and bribery has given me an appetite. Let's do lunch." She slapped the cheap brochure and a cordless phone onto the table between him and the pumpkin. "There's a new Thai restaurant opened in the Magnolia shopping area. Why don't you order for us? Five years in Bangkok should've given you a modicum of expertise."

He ought to be hungry (except for a pint of Redhook ale at Pike Place Market, he'd had no breakfast) just as he *ought* to be furious with Maestra, yet thanks to the XTC, he was neither. "Like sedated spacemen conserving their energy for the unimaginable encounters ahead, the pumpkin seeds lie suspended in their reticulum of slime." Those were the very words he whispered, but luckily she paid them no heed, having already moved to the pyramid to speak to the parrot. Unlike those old women who coo baby-talk to their birds, Maestra spoke to Sailor exactly as she spoke to everyone else, which is to say, with language that was fairly formal and occasionally flowery, a self-amused, ironic eloquence that to some degree, though he might deny it, had influenced Switters's own manner of speech. (As for the parrot, on those rare occasions when it spoke at all, it would utter but a single sentence, and it was always the same. "Peeple of zee wurl, relax," is what it would say, as if giving sage advice in a raspy Spanish accent.)

Seeing no route around it, and aiming to please, he studied the menu and picked up the phone. As he requested such dishes as *tom kah pug* and *pak tud tak*, names that routinely sounded like a harelip pleading for a package of thumbtacks, the tricky tonalities of Thai didn't faze him. The waiter, in fact, mistook him for a fellow countryman, until Switters explained that despite his immaculate accent, he could not actually speak that tongue that in all probability had been invented by the ancient Asian ancestors of Elmer Fudd.

In less than thirty minutes, cartons of aromatic food were clustered, steaming, on the library table. Wafts of lemongrass, chili paste,
and coconut milk enlivened the technologized old room.

After about five torrid forkfuls of *pla lard prik*, Maestra dozed off in
her swivel chair and slept for hours.

Switters didn't eat a bite, but danced alone in front of the CD
player until deep in the dark afternoon.

the next morning he flew to Peru. Alaska Airlines to Los Angeles, then the 1:00 P.M. LAN-Chile flight to Lima, which stopped in Mexico City barely long enough for him to telephone a maverick philology professor he knew there.

Once he had gotten the parrot secured in the pressurized portion of the cargo hold that airlines set aside for passengers' pets, the departure passed smoothly. That was fortunate because the effects of the XTC had left him moderately fatigued. Settled into a business-class seat with a Bloody Mary on his tray, he began to feel consoled, if not actually buoyant, about the demands of the immediate future. In all honesty, he had to admit that the mission forced upon him by his crafty grandmother was a good deal less boring, potentially, than the mickey mouse assignment he'd been handed by Langley. Which was not to say it would be anything beyond an inconvenience, but it had the virtue, at least, of being an *out-of-the-ordinary* inconvenience, a kind of dead-cat bounce. A couple of extra days in South America wasn't exactly going to poison all the tadpoles in his drainage ditch. He would endure.

Yes, unquestionably, he would get through a sticky, buggy, rainy, much-too-vivid side trip to the Amazon jungle. The in-flight movie, however, was another matter.

It was one of those so-called action suspense pictures in which the primary suspense was the uncertainty as to whether there would be ninety seconds or a full two minutes between one massive explosion and the next. In those films the sky was seldom blue for long. Black billows, orange flame, and polychromatic geysers of flying debris filled the screen at irregular intervals, while on the soundtrack the crack, roar, and shatter of battered matter was as common as music, although not quite so common as gunfire and wailing. Both Maestra and Suzy sometimes watched such movies because they imagined that this was what his life must be like in the Central Intelligence Agency. Silly girls.

Switters endured a half hour of it before ripping off his headset, quaffing his drink, and turning to the passenger in the next seat, a tall, wiry, sharp-featured Latino in a blue-and-white-striped seersucker suit. "Tell me, amigo," said Switters in a voice just loud enough to penetrate the fellow's earphones, "do you know why boom-boom movies are so popular? Do you know why young males, especially, love, simply love, to see things blown apart?"

The man stared blankly at Switters. He lifted his headset, but on one side only. "It's freedom," said Switters brightly. "Freedom from the material world. Subconsciously, people feel trapped by our culture's confining buildings and its relentless avalanche of consumer goods. So, when they watch all this shit being demolished in a totally irreverent and devil-may-care fashion, they experience the kind of release the Greeks used to get from their tragedies. The ecstasy of psychic liberation."

The Latino smiled, but it was not a friendly smile; it was, in fact, the sort of quasi-smile one observes on small dogs in the backseats of parked cars just before they begin to bark hysterically and try to chew their way through the window glass. *Perhaps he doesn't understand,* thought Switters.

"Things. *Cosas.* Things attach themselves like leeches to the human soul, then they bleed out the sweetness and the music and the primordial joy of being unencumbered upon the land. *Comprende?* People feel tremendous pressure to settle down in some sort of permanent space and fill it up with stuff, but deep inside they resent those structures, and they're scared to death of that stuff because they know it controls them and restricts their movements. That's why they relish the boom-boom cinema. On a symbolic level, it annihilates their inanimate wardens and blows away the walls of their various traps."

Feeling loquacious now, Switters might have gone on to offer his theory on suicide bombers, to wit: Islamic terrorist groups were successful in attracting volunteer martyrs because the young men got to strap explosives on themselves and blast valuable public property to smithereens. Exhilarating boom-boom power. If they were required to martyr themselves by being dragged behind a bus or sticking a wet finger in a light socket, volunteers would be few and far between. "Incidentally," he might have added, "are you aware that there's no such thing as a smithereen? The word exists only in the plural." He said none of this, however, because the Latino had begun to grind his teeth at him. Yes, it's an odd concept, grinding one's teeth *at* another, but that's unmistakably what the fellow was doing: grinding them audibly, too, and so forcefully that his bushy black mustache bucked and rolled as if it were a theme-park ride for thrill-seeking tamale crumbs, leaving Switters with no choice but to pierce the grinder with what some people have described as his "fierce, hypnotic green eyes." He stared at the grinder so fiercely, if not hypnotically, that he gradually ceased to grind, swallowed hard, turned away, and avoided Switters's gaze for the rest of the journey.

Aside from that, the flight was uneventful.

He arrived at Jorge Chávez International at two o'clock Monday morning with a dull, dry headache. He was subject to moderate migraines, for which air travel was a definite trigger. Reading intelligence reports concerning Peruvian guerrilla activity while drinking Bloody Marys hadn't helped. The pain behind his eyes escalated as he went through the rigmarole of getting Sailor Boy cleared by customs. Had he not been carrying papers stating, falsely of course, that he was temporarily attached to the United States embassy, he might have been there until Christmas. Sometimes Langley was capable of marvelous efficiency.

Carrying the shrouded parrot cage in his right hand, he used the left to steer a luggage cart through clusters of surly men who wore brown uniforms and shouldered automatic rifles. These were the Policía de Turismo. Their duty was to protect foreign tourists from the pickpockets, purse-snatchers, bag-slashers, muggers, con artists, bandits, and revolutionary thugs who were as thick in Lima as seeds in any pumpkin. On occasion, the police themselves were the problem. (During his last trip to South America, he'd been forced to shoot a policeman in Cartagena, Colombia, who tried to rob him at gunpoint. The man lived, but Switters still had nightmares about it, hearing in his dreams the unbelievably loud echo of his Beretta as he shot the man in the wrist to disarm him, and the screaming as Switters pulverized both of the scumbag's kneecaps to insure that he would never again leap out at a victim from behind a badge. Switters believed that law enforcement officers who themselves broke laws should receive sentences twice as severe as civilians who committed the same crimes, for the criminal officer had not only betrayed

a sacred public trust, he or she had also undermined the very concept
of justice and fairness in the world. A crooked cop was every bit as
much of a traitor as was a seller of national secrets, and should be punished accordingly.)

At the Gran Hotel Bolívar, there were even Policía de Turismo in
the worn though still opulent lobby. Most were napping in faded overstuffed armchairs. One who was standing scowled suspiciously at
Sailor's cloth-covered pyramid, but he chose not to investigate and
Switters registered with no more than the typical delay.

Without bothering to unpack, he popped an Ergomar pill for his
headache and went straight to bed. It was four in the morning. The
hour when Madame Angst knits large black sweaters, and blood sugar
goes downstairs to putter around in the basement.

He awoke, groggy, at ten-thirty and opened the blinds just enough
to illuminate the telephone. First, he called Hector Sumac, the reluctant recruit, and arranged to meet him for a late dinner. He'd
keep his fingers crossed that Hector would actually show up. Then, he
phoned Juan Carlos de Fausto, a guide recommended by the hotel
desk clerk, and scheduled for midafternoon a tour of Lima's more
important cathedrals and churches. Switters was considering con-
verting to Catholicism in order to please Suzy, who was devoutly
religious. He'd make a terrible Catholic—he found organized religion
in general to be little more than a collective whistling past the grave-
yard, with dangerous political undertones—but he enjoyed ritual, if
it was pure enough, and certainly infiltration was a tactic not entirely
unfamiliar to him.

Ritual he liked, but compulsory routine he hated. Thus, he resented every minute that he now had to surrender to showering, sham-
pooing, shaving, and flossing and brushing his teeth. If mere men
could devise self-defrosting refrigerators and self-cleaning ovens,
why couldn't nature, in all of its complex, inventive magnificence, have
managed to come up with self-cleaning teeth? "There's birth," he
grumbled, "there's death, and in between there's maintenance."

Having said that, he went back to bed and slept for three more
hours.

Before leaving on his tour, Switters contacted the housekeeping staff
to warn them that there was a parrot in his room. Sailor was quite jet-

lagged, so disoriented he wouldn't eat, and it was unlikely he would cause any commotion, yet all it would take would be a screeching "Peeple of zee wurl, relax!" as an unsuspecting maid came through the door, and Switters could find himself in a situation similar to that experienced by his grandmother a dozen years ago.

At the time Maestra had had in her employ a normally competent servant named Hattie. One day, while Maestra was away at an all-day computer workshop sponsored by North Seattle Community College, Hattie added to her list of chores the cleaning of the pyramid birdcage. In the process, she scrubbed Sailor's water dish, which, admittedly, was rather funky, with a popular household cleaning product that went by the brand name of Formula 409. Parrots, alas, are unusually sensitive to chemical odors. Perhaps it was the solvents in Formula 409, perhaps the 2-butoxyethanol, but when Sailor went to drink from his now immaculate dish, the lingering fumes, subtle though they were, overcame him, and he passed out cold.

Hattie thought he was dead. Desiring to spare her employer the trauma of dealing with a freshly deceased pet, she wrapped the comatose bird in newspaper and placed it in the trunk of her car. Leaving Maestra a sympathetic note, she then drove home to prepare an early supper for her semi-invalid father, after which she planned to dispose of the corpse. While Hattie was busy in the kitchen, her father hobbled out to the car, looking for something or other. When he opened the trunk, the parrot, now fully revived, flew out in his face, wings flapping furiously, and squawking like the mad conductor on the night train to Hell. The poor man had a heart attack from which he never fully recovered.

It took Maestra a day and a half to coax Sailor down from the fir tree in which he'd taken refuge, and as for Hattie, her reaction was that of the typical contemporary American: "I'm suffering. Therefore, somebody must owe me money. I'm hiring a lawyer."

Eventually the judge dismissed Hattie's suit as frivolous, but not before it had cost Maestra more than thirty grand in legal fees. She hadn't had a servant since.

Because Switters lacked confidence in his Spanish—he was considerably more fluent in Arabic and Vietnamese—and because he wished to make certain that the hotel staff understood that the object of his concern was a parrot, he pulled from his jacket pocket a Polaroid snapshot that Maestra had taken, using the automatic timer, moments before he departed the house on Magnolia Bluff. To the maids struggling to comprehend, he pointed out the cage and its gaudy occupant. It was there in the snapshot. Switters on the left, Maestra in the middle, Sailor on the right.

Or, as Maestra had written in a wavering hand on the lower border of the photo: the Slacker, the Hacker, and the Polly-Wanna-Cracker.

Inspecting his reflection in a full-length, gold-framed mirror, one of several baroque ornaments whose bombastic tendencies were rendered meek by the dramatic stained-glass dome atop the lobby, Switters commented, "Don't *look* like no slacker," and if the truth be told, he probably didn't. The saving grace of places such as Lima was that they afforded him an opportunity to wear white linen suits and Panama hats, which is precisely how he was attired at the moment. The suit bore the label of a famous designer, but for all of the pussy in Sacramento, he couldn't have identified which one. It had a yellowish tinge, due to lack of proper maintenance.

Completing the ensemble was a T-shirt, solid black except for what at first glance appeared to be a tiny green shamrock above the left breast, but which on scrutiny proved to be the spiderlike emblem of the C.R.A.F.T. Club, a secretive society with branches in Hong Kong and Bangkok, whose members met periodically to imbibe strange beverages and discuss *Finnegans Wake*. When asked about it later, members would answer, "C.R.A.F.T."—Can't Remember a Fucking Thing—and for the most part, they wouldn't be lying. Switters also wore black sneakers and chomped on a skinny black cigar that somewhat resembled an iguana turd. He liked the way he looked but knew better than to pretend it mattered.

With respect for fellow guests, if not the Policía de Turismo, he waited until he was outside before torching the cigar. No sooner had he expelled the first perfect smoke ring than he was approached by a stoop-shouldered, balding, middle-aged gentleman with kind eyes and a light dusting of mustache hairs above a sincere smile. The man introduced himself as "Juan Carlos de Fausto, English-speaking guide to all attractions and points of interest in this, the City of Kings." Señor de Fausto was the person who, for thirty-five U.S. dollars, would give Switters a tour of Lima's holy sites and who, free of charge, would give him advice that would indirectly, but severely and irrevocably, alter the course of his life.

From the Gran Hotel Bolívar, it was but a short walk along the Jirón de la Unión mall to the Plaza de Armas and Lima's main cathedral. The notorious coastal fog had burned off, and the afternoon had turned unseasonably hot. The mall was sizzling. It was also teeming. A pick-pocket stir-fry.

Juan Carlos, parting a surf of aggressive vendors, led Switters across the plaza and into the rather stark, dimly lit cathedral. He showed his client the coffin that held the remains of Francisco Pizarro, made sure he admired the intricately carved choir stalls, and described for him the earthquake that had flattened most of the building and dis-assembled Pizarro's skeleton (knee bone no longer connected to the thigh bone) in 1746. One thing he neglected to explain was why Lima's most important cathedral had no name. Silently, Switters chris-tened it Santa Suzy de Sacramento.

On foot, they visited the other churches in the Centro: Iglesia de la Merced, Iglesia de Jesús Maria, Santuario de Santa Rosa de Lima, San Pedro, San Francisco, Santo Domingo, and Iglesia de las Naza-renas, edifices in which myriad generations had schemed to catch the eye of God with gold leaf, carved wood, and garish tiles. Vaulted ceil-ings strained to scuff their lofty beams on the doormat of Heaven, only to be yanked back to earth by the leaden weight of statuary and a sad geology of catacomb bones.

Later, Switters and Juan Carlos pushed through the swarming vendors—Indians in rainbow ponchos peddling pottery, *mestizos* in Chicago Bulls T-shirts hawking pirated cassette tapes—to the guide's 1985 Oldsmobile, lovingly buffed but hopelessly battered, and drove to the Convento de los Descalzos, a sixteenth-century monastery with two lavish chapels; and to several outlying churches.

If cities were cheese, Lima would be Swiss on a waffle. Its avenues were moonscapes of potholes. After banging and bouncing over ubiq-uitous craters, as well as dodging traffic even more anarchistic than Bangkok's, the two men found Lima's religious buildings islands of peace. Glum, maybe, morbid, perhaps, but in contrast to the busted infrastructure, rackety commerce, and thievery-on-parade, nothing short of serene.

At one point during the tour, having observed that Switters never knelt nor genuflected and that he had to be frequently reminded to remove his hat and stub out his cigar, Juan Carlos could no longer restrain himself. "Señor Switter, I am suspecting that you are not being the Catholic fellow."

"No. No, I'm not. Not yet. But I'm thinking about joining up."

"Why? If you do not mind me asking."

Switters pondered the question. "You might say," he eventually replied, "that I have a special feeling for the virgin."

Juan Carlos nodded. He seemed satisfied with the response. Naturally, there was no way he could have guessed that Switters was referring to his sixteen-year-old stepsister.

The sun dropped into the horizon line like a coin dropping into a slot. The ocean bit it to make sure it wasn't counterfeit. Twilight softened the city visually but did not hush it. If anything, Lima became more raucous, more crowded, more menacing with the coming dark. Switters kept his wallet in his front pants pocket, kept his Beretta in his belt. He belonged to that minority who had yet to accept the rip-off as an inescapable fact of modern life.

Their tour completed, the guide and his client stopped at a working-class bar for a glass of pisco. Who would have thought that the juice of the grape could be transformed into a substance so near to napalm?

"Heady, no?" exulted Juan Carlos.

"Quintessentially South American," grumbled Switters.

In the course of conversation, Switters revealed to Juan Carlos his plan to repatriate Sailor Boy. For some reason, it struck the guide as a horrid idea. He warned his client that there was an unpublicized but widespread outbreak of cholera in the countryside and that the Marxist marauders known as *Sendero Luminoso* or "Shining Path," thought to have been eradicated in 1992, had come back to life and revived their campaign to murder innocent tourists as a means of improving the lot of the Peruvian poor. The American explained that he'd been inoculated against cholera and that he'd had run-ins in other countries with self-styled "liberators of the people" and they didn't scare him a bit. He said the latter in a whisper, however, well aware of the prevailing political climate in bars such as this one.

Juan Carlos countered that the cholera vaccine was only about 60 percent effective and that he hadn't realized that a dealer in farm equipment led such an adventurous life. (Switters had passed himself off as an international sales representative for John Deere tractors.) Furthermore, he would bet Switters another glass of pisco—"Not on your life, pal"—that his grandmother was already in remorse over her decision to return her longtime pet to the wild, and that if Switters went through with such a rash exercise, he eventually would join his dear relation in profound and protracted regret. Juan Carlos was adamant about his sense of impending tragedy, and to convince his foolish client, he begged him to come along on a brief drive. Switters agreed, if only to avoid a second pisco.

They motored to the posh neighborhood of Miraflores, parked, slipped through a hedge, crossed an overgrown garden—stirring up in the process a bloodthirsty billow of bugs—and tiptoed onto a patio, from where they might peer through the windows of an elderly, distant relative of Juan Carlos. This scene, naked parrot, merciless mosquitoes and all, has already been described.

If the guide expected that a peepshow of a feeble widow and her feeble bird, blinking and stumbling toward the grave in each other's company, expected that a stolen exhibition of enduring and everlasting owner-pet fidelity would melt his client's heart and move said client to facilitate a joyous reunion between grandmother and ill-advisedly emancipated parrot, then he was mistaken.

However, the first thing Switters did when he got back to the hotel was to go on-line and check his box. An e-mail message from a repentant Maestra canceling her instructions and insisting that Sailor be returned to her care with all due haste? No, not surprisingly, there was nothing of the sort. Maestra would never be counted among those millions who permitted loneliness to compromise their principles, their judgment, their taste.

The single message on the screen was a coded one from the spookmeister at Langley, reminding Switters to "obey protocol" and inform the Lima station of his presence and intent in the city. Well, he'd think about it. The word *obey*, from the archaic French *obéir* and the earlier Latin *obedire*, meaning "to give ear," entered the English language around 1250, the year in which the goose quill began to be used for writing—and to this day, should one give ear, one can detect the stiff scratch of the goose quill in its last syllable. For his part, Switters associated *obey* with *oy vay*, the Yiddish cry of woe or dismay, and while there was absolutely no etymological justification for it, it did provide a hint that *obey* was not the kind of word to make him glad.

"Sorry, pal," Switters said to Sailor as the bird watched him apply calamine lotion to a galaxy of mosquito bites. "I'd love to spend some quality time with you, but duty calls." No sooner did he exchange his C.R.A.F.T. Club T-shirt for a fresh one in solid violet, splash on some Jungle Desire cologne, and dilute the pisco aftertaste with a gargle of mouthwash than he was out the door.

A pothole-spelunking minicab carried him to a modest steak-house in the Barranco, a district popular with students and bohe-mians. Hector Sumac was seated at table, sipping a North American beer.

"You dig the Yankee brewski?" asked Switters.

"This Bud's for you," answered Hector.

Thus was mutual identity established.

Hector Sumac proved to be a nerdy-looking fellow, pale for a Peruvian, with a shaggy pageboy haircut (Beatles, circa 1964) and those dinky little wire-rimmed spectacles commonly referred to as "granny glasses." (Switters's granny, by contrast, wore an outsized, owlishly round, horn-rimmed pair that made her look rather exactly like the late theatrical agent, Swifty Lazar.) Even sitting down, how-ever, young Hector betrayed a fluid, athletic grace, and though he lacked bulk, he might be quick and tough enough, Switters thought, to give a good account of himself on the rugby field.

Switters ordered a Yankee beer as well, and the two men whipped up small talk, first about the unusually warm day and then about cyber-netics. Hector was surprised—even impressed and amused—when Switters confessed that he used a computer only when it became unavoidable for efficiency's sake.

"What interests me are the post-Newtonian, extrabiologic implica-tions of a human species able to think and act using clusters of elec-trons: *light*, in other words. If the opening act of the evolutionary drama involved a descent from light into matter and language, then it only makes sense that in the closing act, so to speak, we reunite with our photonic progenitor. The role that language—the word—will play in our light-driven metamorphosis is the furry little question that cranks my squirrel cage. Say, didn't the guinea pig originate in the Peruvian Andes?"

"But personally you do not boot up?"

"Sure I do, pal. E-mail's a wonderful convenience—even when it's goddamn hacked, but that's another story. What I'm saying is I'm not gonna sit around for hours every day having nonorgasmic sex with a computer or a TV set. These machines will fuck the life right out of you if you give 'em half a chance."

"I log on five or six hours a day," admitted Hector somewhat sheepishly. "But I am always happy when I have the chance to read a good book."

"Yeah? What do you read?"

"I am looking for the novelists whose writing is an extension of their intellect rather than an extension of their neurosis."

"Good luck to you, pal. That's a search these days."

For the third time, an impatient waiter cruised up to their table. "This place is good for meat," Hector said. "What is your favorite dish?"

Switters stared wistfully into space. "Spring lamb Roman Polanski," he said.

"It is not on the menu, I am afraid."

"Just as well. It's an acquired taste."

With gusto, Hector Sumac polished off a mixed grill of beef heart and kidney, a dish he had missed during his recent three years of scholarship in Miami. As for Switters, despite his professed hunger for baby lamb cakes, he was primarily a consumer of fish and vegetables, so he swam against the kitchen and ordered ceviche, picking warily at it, for, predictably, it was not the dewiest ceviche in town.

It was over dessert—fruited cornmeal pudding for each of them—that the two men got down to business. Having jumped to the conclusion that Hector had reneged on the arrangement with Langley due to late-blooming reservations about the CIA's history of illegal interference in Latin American affairs, particularly, perhaps, its heinous behavior in Guatemala and El Salvador, not to mention Cuba, Chile, and Nicaragua, Switters had come armed with a response, an argument that would neither defend nor condemn Langley's murderous hanky-panky but that would convince the recruit of the validity and necessity of his service. Ah, but when Hector explained his change of mind, his reason was of an entirely different tenor.

"Our federal administration is thoroughly corrupt . . ."

Yours and everybody else's, thought Switters, but he didn't wish to belabor the obvious.

". . . and even though I now am employed in its Ministry of Communication, I cannot support it. On the other hand, the Sendero Luminoso is brutal and self-serving, so I cannot support revolution. Your— what is your soft name for it?"

"Company."

"Yes. Right. Your 'company' has assured me that never would I be put in the position of betraying my people, my native land. . . ."

Heh! thought Switters, imitating, in his cranial echo chamber, Maestra's ejaculation of incredulousness.

". . . so I do not have the strong political objection to the surreptitious work for your 'company.' But, Agent Switter, I want very much to be completely honest in my dealing with you and your superiors, and the honest truth is, I, personally, could never fit in with your 'company.' I am of a different character."

"What character's that, pal?"

"Well," said Hector, a tinge of reddening in his cheeks, susurration in his tone, "the shameful but honest truth is, what I am most interested in in life is sex, drugs, and rock 'n' roll."

Thanks to various misunderstandings, rugby scrums, fender-benders, and occupational hazards, Switters was left with only eleven whole and healthy teeth. The inside of his mouth, in his opinion, so resembled a dental Stonehenge that he refrained from smiling broadly "for fear," as he put it, "of attracting Druids." Now, however, Hector's guilty admission elicited a wide, open-mouthed grin that no amount of self-consciousness could censor—although much of what might have been revealed was obscured by pudding.

"Perfect," he said. "That's just perfect, Hector."

The Peruvian was perplexed. "Please, what do you mean?"

"I mean that you'll have a great deal in common with your new colleagues. Sex, drugs, and rock 'n' roll are enormously popular in the CIA."

"You are joking with me."

"Not among the administrators, naturally, and not with *all* the agents in the field, but with the good ones, the brightest and the best. You see, unlike the U.S. Forest Service or the Department of Energy, just to mention two of the worst, the CIA is not entirely an organization of bureaucratic meatballs."

"But the 'company'—the CIA, if I'm allowed to say that now—does not actually condone—"

"Officially, no. But there's little it can do about it. Experienced recruiters understand completely what type of person makes the best operative or agent: a person who is very smart, educated, young, self-reliant, healthy, unencumbered, and relatively fearless. Well, a guy who's smart, educated, young, self-reliant, healthy, unencumbered, and fearless is a guy who, chances are, is going to reserve a big place in his affections for sex, drugs, and rock 'n' roll. It goes with the territory. And it's tolerated. Sure, from time to time there're cowboys who slip through the net. . . ."

"Cowboys?"

"You know: flag-wavers and Bible-thumpers. Trigger-happy patriots. They're the ones who create the international incidents, who're always embarrassing the CIA and the United States and getting innocent people killed. Of course, they tend to win promotions because basically they're the same kind of dour-faced, stiff-minded, suck-butt, kick-butt, buzz-cut, macho dickheads who oversee the company as political appointees, but anyone who truly understands the art and science of intelligence and counterintelligence will tell you that the cowboys mostly just get in the way. The gods dropped 'em in our midst to generate misery and gum up the works. You're aware, are you not, Hector, that the gods are tireless fans of slapstick?"

It was Hector's turn to smile. "You have a festive manner of speech, Agent Switter. If you are at all typical, and if you are not pulling my legs, I think I am going to enjoy very much my association with this CIA."

"Atta boy."

"And so, dinner is complete, yet the night is still ahead. Tell me, Agent Switter, do you like to dance?"

"Why, yes, I do. Just a couple of days ago, as a matter of fact, I danced for hours without a break." He neglected to mention that he was alone at the time.

Hector Sumac's drug of choice, at least for that October evening, was a clean, beige, relatively mild form of Andean cocaine. Switters wanted no part of it. "Thanks, pal, but I tend to avoid any substance that makes me feel smarter, stronger, or better looking than I know I actually am." There were, in his opinion, drugs that diminished ego and drugs that engorged ego, which is to say, revelatory drugs and delusory drugs; and on a psychic level, at least, he favored awe over swagger. Should he ever aspire to become voluntarily delusional, then good old-fashioned alcohol would do the job effectively and inexpensively, thank you, and without the dubious bonus of jaw-clenching jitters.

Nevertheless, Switters sat with Hector while he snorted a few lines. They sat in Hector's '97 Honda. The vehicle was still immaculate, but if Lima didn't hasten to allot a few billion *nuevos soles* to street repair—the tyranny of maintenance—it wouldn't be long before Hector's proud chariot would be shaken and beaten into a spring-sprung tumbleweed of automotive nerves. At present, however, it exuded that peachy, creamy, new-car aroma, and inhaling it, Switters was led to wonder if part of the appeal of young girls wasn't the fact that they gave off the organic equivalent, the biological equivalent—okay, the genital equivalent—of a new-car smell.

When Hector was sufficiently tootered up, he ejected the Soundgarden cassette to which they'd been listening, and the two men walked the block and a half to the Club Ambos Mundos, arriving shortly before eleven o'clock. Five nights a week, the Ambos Mundos, like most clubs in Lima, featured live Creole music, but each Monday it was taken over by a hipster deejay who played the latest rock hits from the U.S. and Great Britain. Blue lights apulse, the place was rocking to Pearl Jam when they made their entrance.

Switters's broad, tanned, big-boned face was at all times abuzz with an activity, a radiance, of randomly spaced scars, which, though delicate as sand shrimp and variable as snowflakes, created an impression of hard history; and which, when combined with the intensity in and around his emerald orbs, caused him to look potentially dangerous. That impression was offset, however, by the irrefutable sweetness of his smile, a smile that possessed the capacity to dazzle even when held in check to hide chipped teeth, which it usually was. (Since every time he had them fixed, it seemed his teeth just got abused again, he had made a vow to abstain from further dental work until his forty-fifth birthday.) So, perhaps *dangerous* is not quite the right word for his countenance. Maybe *disconcerting* or *conflicted* or *unpredictable* would be more accurate—although for some drab souls, *unpredictable* and *dangerous* are synonymous. At any rate, women did not find his appearance unintriguing, and when the muscular gringo stepped—jaunty, yet somehow dignified—through the door in his white suit and guarded smile, two or three bamboo-colored curls snailing out from under his Panama hat, there was a sudden quickening of more than one female pulse.

Over the next ninety minutes, Switters danced with an assortment of women, local and foreign, but by midnight—the hour when myth's black cat pounces on time's mechanical mouse—one in particular was in orbit around him. Her name was Gloria, she was Peruvian, and she was drinking too much too fast. Saucy and petite, Gloria wore her short hair in bangs, similar, in fact, to Hector; and her eyes were like chocolate-dipped cherry bombs with their fuses lit. In her mid-twenties, she was a tad old for his specialized taste, but when she pressed her pelvis against his during the slow dances, when she poked holes in his breath with a vodka-heated tongue, his body forgot about Suzy, and beer by beer, his mind followed suit.

He was experiencing a growing appetite for Gloriapussy, and he figured that her alcohol consumption was not dimming his prospects. Indeed, she had become so disheveled, wild-eyed, and flushed that she would have looked more at home in a tangle of sweat-soaked bedsheets than there on the crowded dance floor. Nevertheless, he was surprised when she whispered wetly in his ear, "I desire you to chew my nipples."

Dancing away from her, he executed a twirl. When they came face-to-face again she said rather loudly and with a giggle, "I desire you to eat my breasts."

Chew? Eat? Perhaps it was a language problem. Perhaps Gloria meant *lick* or *suck* or *nibble*—oral activities in which he might have been a willing participant—but lacked the English for it. "You have a festive manner of speaking," he said, borrowing a line from Hector, and led her back to their table.

Hector sat across from them, an urbanized, dyed-blond Indian girl on his lap. He seemed alert and under control. Langley would approve. Switters felt the urge to talk shop with him, to impart, perhaps, Switters's somewhat novel notion that the CIA was on the verge of evolving into a kind of autonomous secret society (a larger, better funded, better organized version of the C.R.A.F.T. Club), a reverse hierarchy whose fundamental function was to work behind the scenes to distract the powerful and covertly thwart their ambitions so that intelligence (true intelligence, which is always in the service of serenity, beauty, novelty, and mirth) might actually flourish in the world, and some shard of humanity's primal innocence be preserved. Alas, the music was too loud, and Gloria was tugging at his sleeve.

"Yes, dear?"

"I desire you to fuck me in the *culo*."

At first he thought she said "cooler," and he had a vision of them entwined on the frosty, bloodstained cement of one of those refrigerated lockers, with waxy yellow and red sides of beef swinging from iron hooks all around them, their exhalations condensing the instant they panted or sighed so that they kissed through a mutually generated cloud and could not see each other's faces.

"I desire you to fill up my ass," she elaborated.

Well, he thought, *that's South America for you.*

"With premium or regular?" he asked.

As Gloria giggled uncomprehendingly, he rose on an impulse, retrieved his hat, and gave Hector an affectionate squeeze of the shoulder.

"No! Please! You are not leaving?"

"Afraid so. It's getting vivid in here, if you catch my drift. Good luck, pal. *Ha sido estupenda.* I'll be in touch."

As he headed for the exit, he called, "Order Gloria there a pot of coffee. And don't forget to put it on your expense account. The company's a mile-high Santa Claus with an elastic sack."

On the taxi ride back to the Centro, he passed one of the cathedrals he had visited earlier that day. It was the one with the statue of the angel on its porch. Once while playing Ping-Pong with Suzy—one of the rare times he was left alone with her—he had asked her what language she thought the angels spoke. "Oh," she answered, without missing a stroke, "probably the same one Jesus speaks."

"The historical Jesus is believed to have spoken Aramaic. Of all the possible languages, why would the heavenly hosts choose to converse in a long-dead Semitic dialect from southwest Asia? Do you suppose."

She looked so puzzled that he regretted at once having broached the subject. Suzy was a "babe in Christ," as the Bible refers to them, and "babes in Christ" become quite unhappy when asked to actually *think* about their faith. "Whatever," she said cryptically, and smashed a shot past his outstretched paddle.

"I guess it wouldn't matter whether we could comprehend angel talk or not," he conceded. "They've got those trumpets and flaming swords, and glow-in-the-dark accessories, they'd find a way to get their point across. I'm multilingual, so I've been told, but I spend a lot of time in countries where I can't understand the language at all. And you know, Suzy, I'm coming to prefer it that way. It's uplifting. When you go for a while without being able to understand a word of what anybody around you is saying, you start to forget what banal bores our blathering brethren be."

Suzy found that highly amusing, and when they traded ends of the table for the next game, she allowed him a fleeting fondle—which, of course, assured her of victory in the match.

Incidentally, Switters and his friends lumped all CIA agents into one of two categories: cowboys or angels. They spoke the same language, the cowboys and the angels, but with different emphasis and to far different ends.

It was approaching 2 A.M. when he reached the Gran Hotel Bolívar, and the lobby was not surprisingly shadowy and quiet. No sooner had he walked in, however, than a figure shot from one of the overstuffed chairs and began walking toward him. His hand slid to the pistol in his belt.

The figure was stoop shouldered and a little gimpy.

"Señor Switter. Who do you find to buy your tractors at this late hour?"

"Why, Juan Carlos, I've been to midnight mass." He shook hands with the guide. "Didn't see *you* there. The priest was asking about you. He's worried you aren't getting enough rest."

"Do not joke, señor. I could not rest for the thinking of your situation. You have changed your mind about breaking the heart of your dear grandmama?"

"No, my plans are firm. But don't worry, pal. My grandmother's tough as a plastic steak. And she's adamant about giving that cracker-snapper its freedom."

Juan Carlos looked as downcast as a busted flowerpot. "If you take it to Iquitos," he said, "it will not be free for long." The guide explained that despite its romantic reputation as an exotic jungle town and the capital of Amazonia, Iquitos had grown into a city of nearly four hundred thousand residents, and logging and farming were pushing the rain forest farther and farther from its streets. "You must go fifty kilometers from Iquitos in any direction to find the primary jungle, and even there your bird may not be safe. The parrot market in Iquitos is very big, señor, very extensive. Your grandmama's friend will only be captured and put in another cage. Eventually, some stranger will buy it and take it away—perhaps to the U.S. again."

Well, that would never do. And Juan Carlos went on to warn of cholera germs that were currently careening through Iquitos like a soccer mob. "Your inoculation, I fear, will offer only minimal—"

"Okay. I get the picture. Iquitos is gonna wrinkle my rompers, gonna squeak my cheese. So, what's the alternative? I have the distinct feeling that there's an option up your sleeve."

"For your own safety, señor, and for the peace of mind of your grandmama."

"I understand, Juan Carlos. You're a good man."

"I have taken the liberty to cancel Iquitos and arrange for you the noon flight to Pucallpa."

"Pucallpa?!"

"Sí. Yes. It is the much more small city, and, guess what, do you know?—it is the more shorter flight from Lima."

"That may be true, but from what I've heard, Pucallpa's not exactly Judy Garlandville. And it hasn't been kind to the forest, either."

A couple of Policía de Turismo had stirred from their doze and were giving them the old law-enforcement stink-eye. Switters was hardly intimidated, but Juan Carlos nodded toward a space by the elevator, and the two men strolled over there to continue their talk more privately.

"Pucallpa is more rough but is also more gentle. Is that sounding crazy?"

"Not at all. Only the obtuse are unappreciative of paradox."

"Yes, but you will not wish to remain in Pucallpa, for, you see, it is a city also and is also having a parrot market."

Switters's intention was to fly into a jungle town—Iquitos had been his original choice, but Pucallpa would do—and hire a vehicle to take Sailor and him to the edge of the forest for the release ceremony. He thought of it as a ceremony because Maestra had stuffed her camcorder into his crocodile-skin valise and insisted upon his videotaping the event. Now, Juan Carlos was telling him that the parrot wouldn't be safe within miles of either city and, furthermore, that the outskirts of those jungle towns would not provide a scenic backdrop for Maestra's viewing pleasure, being littered with oil drums, lengths of abandoned pipe, and the rusting remains of dead machinery.

"This is the ideal," confided Juan Carlos. "You hire the boat in Pucallpa. Boat with the good motor. A boy named Inti has the good boat and a little English. This boat takes you up the Rio Ucayali. South is upriver. Before you reach Masisea, a tributary will branch off to the east. Is named Abujao, I think. These rivers in the Amazon basin are changing like the traffic lights, like the moon, like the currency. Inti will find it. If you come to Masisea you have come too far."

"What am I looking for?"

"For the village named Boquichicos. On the Rio Abujao near the Brazil frontier. Boquichicos was one of the new towns founded by our government for the oil business, but they founded it with the strict environmental considerations. The oil business did not prosper, but the town, she is still there. Very small, very nice. Remote."

"Yeah, I got the feeling you were talking serious boondocks. *How* remote? How long's the dream cruise from Pucallpa?"

"Oh, is merely three days."

"*Three days?!*"

"It is now at the end of the dry season. The rivers run low. So, maybe four days."

"*Four* days? Each way? Forget it, pal. I don't have that kind of time, and if I did I wouldn't spend it up some damn creepy river." Switters was about to lift his T-shirt to display the number of insect wounds he'd managed to suffer right there in metropolitan Lima, but a glance at the tourist cops made him think the better of it.

"Not for the happiness of a poor old woman who has so long sacrifice for you, who may soon be call to the side of Jesus . . ."

"Heh!"

". . . not for to protect and reward the old loyal pet?" Juan Carlos went on to explain that what made Boquichicos special was its proximity—an hour's walk—to a huge *colpa* or clay lick that was visited daily by hundreds of parrots and macaws. The guide could not imagine a more pleasurable or compatible retirement home for Sailor, and Switters had to admit that such a locale would provide video footage destined to win Maestra's personal Oscar. She'd be ever grateful. Briefly, he entertained a vision of himself lying on a bearskin rug before the Snoqualmie cabin's stone fireplace, the Matisse oil—now his own—pulsating like a blue chromosphere of massive meaty nudity above the mantel. (Dare he include Suzy in that cozy fantasy? Better not.)

"What about predators? You know, uh, ocelots, jaguars, big vivid serpents?"

"There are those, Señor Switter, and also the accurate arrows of the Kandakandero, these Indians who use the bright color feathers for to decorate their bodies. But with so many birds from to choose in the big, big forest, it would be like the odds of the national lottery."

"Lots of birds, but only one well-fed white boy from downtown North America."

Juan Carlos laughed. "Do not worry. The Kandakandero are the most shy tribe in all Amazonia. They will hide from you."

"Yeah? Too bad. I might interest 'em in one of our John Deere chicken-pluckers. I'm certain it'll do its job on toucans and macaws."

"So, you will go?"

Switters shrugged. There are times when we can feel destiny close around us like a fist around a doorknob. Sure, we can resist. But a knob that won't turn, a door that sticks and never budges, is a nuisance to the gods. The gods may kick in the jamb. Worse, they may walk away in disgust, leaving us to hang dumbly from our tight hinges, deprived of any other chance in life to swing open into unnecessary risk and thus into enchantment.

legend has it that Switters went into the Amazon wearing a cream silk suit, a Jerry Garcia bow tie, and a pair of white tennis shoes. To set the record straight, he wore a suit all right, he wore suits everywhere and saw no reason to make an exception for Amazonia; but his trouser legs were tucked into calf-high rubber boots, purchased for the occasion; while his one bow tie, leather, designed not by Garcia but by Eldridge Cleaver, and which he wore only to meetings and functions attended by aging FBI men who'd yet to forget or forgive Cleaver's Black Panther Party, was in the drawer where he'd left it in Langley, Virginia.

To further straighten the record, he hadn't, at that point, the slightest intention of putt-putting to Boquichicos in a riverboat. Once in Pucallpa, he'd simply hire an air taxi, fly in, release Sailor, fly out. It would dent his vacation funds but would definitely be worth every cent. With any luck, he'd be back in Lima the following morning. This he did not mention to Juan Carlos, being by nature and profession a secretive person, though it was unlikely the guide would have objected.

To the contrary, for all of his concern about the parrot and its mistress, Juan Carlos expressed equal concern for the safety and comfort of Switters. "I am happy, señor," he said as they parted company in the hotel lobby, "that you have not the big enthusiasm for our jungle."

"Why's that?"

"Because of danger. No, it is not anymore like the Amazon you see at the cinema, not so wild and savage along the big rivers, not so many animals anymore, not the headhunters or cannibals. If you are staying on the river, walking the short walk into the colpa and returning the same route, then you will be perfectly safe. More safe than Lima, to be frank. But some Norteamericanos they want to leave the river, leave the trail, run into the forest like the movie star, like the Tarzan. Big mistake. Even today, the jungle she have a thousand ways to make you sorry."

"Don't worry, Juan Carlos, it's not my scene," Switters said sincerely, having no inkling of what lay in store for him.

In bed, he tried to pray because he thought it might connect him in some way to Suzy, but he wasn't adept at it, being overly conscious of the language, perhaps; not wishing to bore whoever or whatever was on the receiving end with hackneyed phrases, yet wondering whether ornamentation and witticisms might be inappropriate or unwelcome. Before he could get a rhetorically satisfactory prayer on track, his mind wandered to Gloria—many of Lima's women were cultured and sophisticated, as he suspected Gloria might be when she wasn't rendered crude by excessive alcohol—and he experienced a pang of regret, in his heart and his groin, that he hadn't fetched her there beside him. It was his own fault, of course, for being so finicky.

The irony of Switters was that while he loved life and tended to embrace it vigorously, he also could be not merely finicky but squeamish. For example, what else but squeamishness could account for his reluctance to accept the existence of his organs and entrails? Obviously, he knew he had innards, he was not an imbecile, but so repulsive did he find the idea that his handsome body might be stuffed like a holiday stocking with slippery, snaky coils of steaming guts; undulating meat tubes choked with vile green and yellow biles, vast colonies of bacteria, fetid gases, and gobs of partially digested foodstuffs, that he blocked the fact from his cognizance, preferring to pretend that his corporeal cavity—and that of any woman to whom he was romantically attracted—was powered not by throbbing hunks of slimy, blood-bathed tissue but by a sort of ball of mystic white light. At times he imagined that area between his esophagus and his anus to be occupied by a single shining jewel, a diamond the size of a coconut whose brightness rang in all four quadrants of his torso.

Really, Switters.

He was up by eight and on-line by nine. (In between, he packed, grudgingly committed acts of bodily maintenance, and ordered room service breakfasts: poached eggs and beer for himself, a fruit platter for Sailor.)

At the computer he dispatched an encoded report to the economic secretary at the U.S. embassy, who happened also to be Langley's station chief in Lima. Switters's report was entirely professional, devoid of literary japes or sarcastic references to the irony of an "economic secretary" being ultimately devoted to undermining the host economy, the Peruvian economy being a sickly system whose sole vitality, top to bottom, was generated by the very coca drug trade the CIA was commanded to help eradicate. To the chief, a cowboy through and through, Switters merely reported that the lost sheep had returned to the fold, adding, for what it was worth, that in his opinion Hector Sumac (he used his code name) probably could be relied upon to engage in second-level espionage and assist in enforcement operations, but that it might be wise to wait several years before permitting him to run any Joes of his own.

The line between cowboy and angel could be no wider than an alfalfa sprout—Switters, himself, occasionally zigzagged that line—and while Hector gave promise of impending angelhood, Switters was wary of the Latin temperament, suspecting it to be unnecessarily volatile, and thus was hesitant to trumpet too loudly on Hector's behalf before the fellow proved to him that he actually had wings.

Duty accomplished, and still at his deluxe, state-of-the-art, military quality laptop, Switters set about the task of worming his way into Maestra's home computer. A trifle rusty at such maneuvering, it took him the better part of an hour, but eventually he crashed her gates, jumped over the guard dogs, and landed in her files, where he proceeded to delete each and every one of the e-mail notes that *she* had hijacked from Suzy's mailbox. Assuming that she hadn't printed it or downloaded it onto a disk, and he was pretty confident she had not, written evidence of his heat for his young stepsister had now been swallowed by an uncaring, nonjudgmental ether.

In its place he left the following announcement: "Don't fret, Maestra, I'm still escorting Sailor into the Great Green Hell for you—only now I'm doing it out of love."

And mostly he meant it.

Pucallpa was the Dead Dog Capital of South America. Quite likely, it was the Dead Dog Capital of the world. If any other city lay claim to that title, its mayor and Chamber of Commerce were wisely silent on the subject. Pucallpa did not boast of it, either—but Switters had eyes, had nose. He recognized the Dead Dog Capital when he saw it and smelled it.

Smell alone, however, wouldn't have tipped him off. There were so many noxious odors, organic and inorganic, in Pucallpa—spoiled fish, spoiled fruit, decaying vegetation, swamp gas, jungle rot, raw sewage, kerosene stoves, wood smoke, diesel fumes, pesticides, and the relentlessly belched mephitis of an oil refinery and a lumber mill—that, on an olfactory level, mere dead dogs could hardly hope to compete.

Still, they were there, on view, concentrated along the river-front but also in midtown gutters, shanty yards, vacant lots, unpaved side streets, outside the single movie theater, and beside the airport tarmac. It might be fanciful to imagine many varieties: a dead poodle on one corner, a Saint Bernard locked in mammoth rigor mortis on the next, but, alas, the canine corpses of Pucallpa invariably were mongrels, mutts, and curs and, moreover, seemed mainly to come in two colors—solid white or solid black, with only the intermittent spot or two.

To Switters, who cared even less for domestic animals dead than alive, the question was, What was the cause of so much doggy mortality? In his halting Spanish, he posed the question to several residents of that on-again, off-again boom town, but never received more than a shrug. In boom towns one paid attention to those things that might make one rich and, failing at fortune, to those things that made one forget. Since there was neither profit nor diversion in dead dogs, only the vultures seemed to notice them. And for every dead dog, there was a full squadron of vultures. Pucallpa was the Vulture Capital of South America.

"This is a baneful burg," Switters wailed to Sailor. "I don't like to complain, you understand, whining being the least forgivable of man's sins, but Pucallpa, Peru, is polluted, contaminated, decayed, rancid, rotten, sour, decomposed, moldy, mildewed, putrid, putrescent, corrupt, debauched, uncultured, and avaricious. It's also hot, humid, and disturbingly vivid. Surely, a fine fowl like you is not remotely related to those hatchet-headed ghouls—no, don't look up!—circling in that stinking brown sky. Sailor! Pal! We must get us out of here at once."

Easier said than done. As Switters learned from a booking agent

soon after completing a walking tour of the town, a contingent of
resurgent Sendero Luminoso guerrillas had attacked the local airfield
three days earlier, destroying or damaging nearly a dozen small planes.
Only two air taxis were presently flying, and both were booked for
weeks to come, ferrying engineers, bankers, and high-stake hustlers
back and forth between Pucallpa and the projects in which they had
interest.

Sorely distressed, Switters was pacing the broken pavement outside the booking office, sweating, swearing, barely resisting the urge to
kick a power pole, a trash pile, or the odd dead dog, when, from inside
the pyramid-shaped parrot cage that sat with his luggage, there came a
voice, high as a falsetto though raspy as a pineapple. "Peeple of zee
wurl, relax," is what it said.

It was the first time the bird had spoken since leaving Seattle. Thirty
minutes later, in an overpriced but blessedly air-conditioned hotel
room, it spoke again—the same sentence, naturally—and while there
are those who may find this silly, the words lifted Switters's spirits.

The flight over the Andes, the poison air of Pucallpa, the brain-
boiling heat and pore-flooding humidity had combined to give him a
migraine; and the headache had combined with the disappointment
over the unavailability of air taxis to make him depressed. Fortunately,
when Sailor squawked his signature line, Switters was instantly
reminded of something Maestra had said almost twenty years before:
"All depression has its roots in self-pity, and all self-pity is rooted in
people taking themselves too seriously."

At the time Switters had disputed her assertion. Even at seventeen,
he was aware that depression could have chemical causes.

"The key word here is *roots*," Maestra had countered. "The *roots*
of depression. For most people, self-awareness and self-pity blossom
simultaneously in early adolescence. It's about that time that we
start viewing the world as something other than a whoop-de-doo
playground, we start to experience personally how threatening it
can be, how cruel and unjust. At the very moment when we become,
for the first time, both introspective and socially conscientious,
we receive the bad news that the world, by and large, doesn't give a
rat's ass. Even an old tomato like me can recall how painful, scary, and
disillusioning that realization was. So, there's a tendency, then, to slip
into rage and self-pity, which, if indulged, can fester into bouts of
depression."

"Yeah, but, Maestra—"

"Don't interrupt. Now, unless someone stronger and wiser—a friend, a parent, a novelist, filmmaker, teacher, or musician—can josh us out of it, can elevate us and show us how petty and pompous and monumentally *useless* it is to take ourselves so seriously, then depression can become a habit, which, in turn, can produce a neurological imprint. Are you with me? Gradually, our brain chemistry becomes conditioned to react to negative stimuli in a particular, predictable way. One thing'll go wrong and it'll automatically switch on its blender and mix us that black cocktail, the ol' doomsday daiquiri, and before we know it, we're soused to the gills from the inside out. Once depression has become electrochemically integrated, it can be extremely difficult to philosophically or psychologically override it; by then it's playing by physical rules, a whole different ball game. That's why, Switters my dearest, every time you've shown signs of feeling sorry for yourself, I've played my blues records really loud or read to you from *The Horse's Mouth*. And that's why when you've exhibited the slightest tendency toward self-importance, I've reminded you that you and me—you and I: excuse me—may be every bit as important as the President or the pope or the biggest prime-time icon in Hollywood, but that none of us is much more than a pimple on the ass-end of creation, so let's not get carried away with ourselves. Preventive medicine, boy. It's preventive medicine."

"But what about self-esteem?"

"Heh! Self-esteem is for sissies. Accept that you're a pimple and try to keep a lively sense of humor about it. That way lies grace—and maybe even glory."

All the while that his grandmother was assuring him that he was merely a cosmic zit, she was also exhorting him never to accept the limitations that society would try to place on him. Contradictory? Not necessarily. It seemed to be her belief that one individual's spirit could supersede, eclipse, and outsparkle the entire disco ball of history, but that if you magnified the pure spark of spirit through the puffy lens of ego, you risked burning a hole in your soul. Or something roughly similar.

In any case, Sailor Boy's squawky refrain reminded Switters of Maestra's counsel. He felt better at once, but to insure that he'd keep things in perspective, that he wouldn't again tighten up or inflate his minor misfortunes, he opened a hidden waterproof, airtight pocket in his money belt and withdrew a marijuana cigarette. Then, with a tiny special key that was disguised as the stem in his wristwatch, he unlocked the lead-lined false bottom that Langley had had built into his reptilian valise and unwrapped an even more secret piece of contraband: a compilation of Broadway show tunes.

After inserting the clandestine disk into his all-purpose laptop and cranking up the volume, he lay back on the bed, lit the reefer, and sang along zestfully with each and every chorus of "Send in the Clowns."

He found Inti down at the lagoon—the Laguna Pacacocha—where many Pucallpans moored their boats. Suppertime, Inti was aboard his vessel boiling a stew of fish and plantains on a brazier fashioned from palm oil tins. The boat was what was known on the Rio Ucayali as a "Johnson," meaning that it was a flat-bottomed dory, about forty feet long with a five-foot beam and low gunnels, driven by a seven-horsepower Johnson outboard motor. A quarter of it, amidships, was shaded by a canopy supported on bamboo poles. The canopy had once been all thatch but was now augmented by a sheet of blue plastic.

Switters was seriously questioning Juan Carlos's description of it as a "good boat" until he looked around at the other Johnsons in the lagoon and saw that most of them were even more dirty and battered than Inti's. What sold him on it, however, was its name: *Little Blessed Virgin of the Starry Waters.* Henceforth, we shall refer to *it* as *she.*

As for her captain, Inti was stocky, gap-toothed, bowl-cut, calmly pleasant if somewhat melancholy, and probably in his late twenties, though with Indians age can be difficult to judge. If Juan Carlos had slightly overstated the worthiness of the boat, he had wildly exaggerated the competence of Inti's English. Nevertheless, with a verbal and gesticular amalgam of Spanish, English, facial expression, and hand signal, the two men agreed on a voyage to Boquichicos, embarking early the following morning.

So, thought Switters, as he strolled back to the city center in the cherry-cola monkey-buttocks tropical watch-dial dusk, *I've got a date with a virgin, even if she does look like an old whore.*

In the hotel bar, the talk was almost exclusively about the raid on the airfield. The men who drank there were capitalists, connected to oil or timber interests (gold prospectors, would-be cattle ranchers, and dealers in exotic birds drank in the less expensive bars, workers in cheaper bars yet, while drug merchants drank in private villas, soldiers and policemen in brothels, and Indians in the street), and corporate sentiments ran hotly against the Marxist raiders. Because he was privy to classified CIA files, Switters knew that any number of the atrocities attributed to the Sendero Luminoso actually had been committed by government forces. In no way did this exonerate the guerrillas, for plenty of innocent blood mittened their hands as well.

Power struggles disgusted Switters, and usually his contempt for the combatants was distributed equally on either side. At the onset it was easy to favor rebellion because the rebels usually were struggling legitimately against tyranny and oppression. It had become a grotesque cliché of modern history, however, that every rebel success embodied a duplication of establishment tactics, which meant that every rebellion, no matter how successful, was ultimately a failure in that it perpetuated rather than transcended the meanness of man, and in that those innocents who managed to survive its bombardments would later be strangled by its red tape. (Czechoslovakia's "velvet" revolution, nonviolent and generous of spirit, was so far proving to be a notable exception.)

Where is Peru's Václav Havel? Switters wondered, although he supposed he might as well have asked, *Where is Peru's Frank Zappa, where is its Finnegans Wake?* He squashed any impulse to pose those questions to his fellows in the bar. He, in fact, refrained from making eye contact with others in the bar. It was part of his training, and though it was a part he regularly ignored, on that occasion he intuited it to be prudent. Quietly, he ordered another beer. As if unwilling to allow his mental focus to shift to fantasies of Suzy, however, he began to silently lecture an invisible audience on the sorrow and betrayal inherent in any insurrection led by the ambitious, the bloodthirsty, or the dull; but since none of the points he made were new to him, he soon grew bored and went up to bed.

In the hallway, around the corner from his room, he spotted a pair of calf-high rubber boots sitting outside a door as if waiting for a valet to give them a polish. They looked to be nearly new, and they looked to be his size. *I could sure use those babies where I'm headed,* he thought, but because he liked to fancy himself morally superior to both the appropriators in government and the appropriators seeking to overthrow government—he had, after all, just attended his own lecture—Switters left the equivalent of thirty dollars rolled up in a condom and knotted around the doorknob. He even uttered a polite *"muchas gracias"* under his breath.

Cigar soup. That's how Switters would have described the river.
Campbell's broth of stogie. It was the color of cigar tobacco, it smelled
like the butt of a cheap cheroot, and every now and then an actual
cigarlike entity would break the oily sheen of its surface to glide among
the citrus rinds, plastic cartons, and Inca Cola cans that dotted the
waters. These small torpedoes were, of course, neither waterlogged
double coronas jettisoned by a listing Cuban freighter nor a species of
blind Amazon trout but, rather, a sampling of the ocherous projectiles
fired into the river night and day from the fundaments of Pucallpa. "A
regular *turd de force*," muttered Switters, who was, characteristically,
repulsed.

No sooner were they upward of Pucallpa than the pollution
cleared, as if the city's garbage and sewage were thronging to a human
filth festival somewhere downstream: Dead Dogs Welcome. Like all
jungle rivers, the Ucayali was perpetually silty, though less so in the
so-called "dry" season (as Switters was soon to learn, it still rained
once or twice a day), and two hours out, he could see fish and turtles
and, occasionally, the bottom, for the Rio Ucayali was not especially
deep. It was wide, however; more than a mile wide in places. A flat,
broad, meandering stream, it bent, coiled, and doubled back on itself
again and again, causing its length to exceed, many times over, a
straight line drawn from its source in the southern Andes to the place
where it jumped in bed with River Amazon way up north at Iquitos. All
in all, the Ucayali was as great or greater than the Mississippi. The fact
that few North Americans had ever heard of it should not be shocking,
since a survey conducted in 1991 revealed that 60 percent of U.S. citizens could not find New York City on a map.

The knowledge that he could have flown to Boquichicos and back
in an active afternoon instead of chasing his tail in slow motion around
the loops of a giant liquid pretzel might have fattened his resentment
toward the insurgents, with their special talent (typical of such groups)
for lowering their boom-boom upon inappropriate targets, but by then
Switters was resigned to a magical mystery tour, going so far as to consider (influenced, perhaps, by his halfhearted flirtation with Catholicism) that it could be deserved punishment for a particular sin that he'd
rather not ponder.

Undoubtedly the heat was a salient feature of that hypothetical
retribution, offering as it did a foretaste of the afterlife steam-cleaning
promised in certain quarters to the morally gritty. (Surely there would
be humidity and plenty of it in Hell. Hard to imagine a condemned
sinner saying cheerfully, "Well, yes, it's two hundred and sixty degrees
down here, but it's a *dry* heat.") Switters lounged upon a cardboard

couch fashioned for him beneath the canopy, but though he was kept shaded, he was not kept cool. Off the gleaming surface of the river, heat bounced like vectors from a microwave oven, bounced right into the boat, shady spot and all. As the day progressed it grew hotter yet, and Switters could feel if not actually hear streams of sweat gushing down his legs and into his rubber boots. The following day he would travel as nearly naked as Inti and the crew. Or, he would until the black flies struck.

The gap-toothed skipper of the *Little Blessed Virgin of the Starry Waters* sat in the stern, his hand on the tiller/throttle arm of the outboard motor, his eyes rolled so far back in his head he might have been inspecting his own brain. *Spot anything interesting or unusual, Inti? Frontal lobe seems a tad distended from here.*

In the bow were two other Indians, boys of about fourteen. Or twenty-four. During rainy season, when the Ucayali was more often than not at flood stage, there were limbs, stumps, logs, entire trees (branches, bird nests and all) in the water, not to mention sudden rapids, and whirlpools mammoth enough to swallow a Johnson and not spit it out until closing time. Now, however, with the river as sleepy and sullen as pupils in ninth-grade algebra, there wasn't a whole lot to look out for—only rarely did the *Virgin* meet another boat—but the crew stood its watch anyway, practicing, maybe, for more lively excursions.

Lashed in the stern with Inti were several cans of gasoline, the proximity of which seemed to have no bearing on the captain's practice of chain-smoking misshapen hand-rolled cigarettes. Up front with the crew were such items as fishing gear, machetes, a tin of palm oil, a brazier made from empty tins, a couple of pots (heavily blackened, as if for a culinary minstrel show), and woven food baskets containing corn, beans, and plantains. There also were three bottles of pisco, and as Switters looked from the booze to Inti and back again, a dark puff of worry scudded his inner sky. Likewise mildly troublesome was the manner in which one of the food baskets rocked and jiggled. Switters hoped that it contained nothing more vivid than a chicken or two.

Under the canopy surrounding his cardboard chaise longue, was Switters's luggage, consisting of a king-sized garment bag and the croc valise, as well as his electronic equipment and Sailor's unusual cage. There was also a roll of mosquito netting, in which, to his dismay, he thought he could detect holes broad enough to admit the prima donna mosquito of the entire world and most of her entourage.

When, an hour out of port, one of the boys lifted the lid of the rocking basket to disclose a baby ocelot, Switters forgot his concerns for a moment and begrudgingly gave legs to a smile.

Except for the outboard motor, pushing the *Virgin* upstream at about six knots per hour against a seasonally flaccid current, there was little or no sound on the river, so when a loud, extended, imploring rumble issued from Switters's stomach, all aboard, including the ocelot cub and the parrot, cocked heads and took notice. "Lunch bell," announced Switters hopefully, to no immediate effect.

Ostentatiously he rubbed his abdomen. *"Comida?"* he suggested simply, not wishing to wax pleonastic. Again, there was an absence of response.

Taking squinting measure of the sun's position, he reckoned the time to be 11 A.M., and his customized watch confirmed it. That meant they had been underway for nearly six hours, without so much as a coffee break. Small wonder his colon was singing arias from tragic third-rate operas. Apparently, however, the Indians had a rule against lunching before high noon, and Switters, ever sensitive about being tagged a soft, coddled Yankee, was disinclined to breach it. He'd swallow his juices and wait.

In terms of distraction, the landscape didn't bring a lot to the table. Along the east bank (the west side was too distant to examine), the jungle had long ago been cleared to make way for cattle ranches. Alas, the forest-born, rain-leached soil was too thin to sustain grass cover for more than a couple of years. When their pastures expired, the cattle-men cleared more jungle and moved on, leaving the failed meadows to bake in the tropic sun, where they hardened into wastelands so lifeless and ugly they would have caused T. S. Eliot to start over and perhaps shamed the Up With People people into revising their slogan— although human events in Bosnia, Rwanda, and Beverly Hills hadn't done much to temper their enthusiasm for the species. He'd attempt to describe this scene to Suzy the next time she petitioned to be whisked to McDonald's. (Arrggh! Neither Suzy nor McDonald's—in both cases he favored the fish sandwich—was something he wanted to be reminded of at the moment.)

Now and then they would pass an operative ranch: a few acres of temporary pasture dotted with beef, a hastily built hacienda, and off to one side, a cluster of thatched huts where Indian workers lived. What would it be like to reside in such a place? Did anyone think of it as "home"? *Homeless* and *houseless* may not always be synonymous. *Home,* for example, wasn't a word Switters often employed when referring to the apartment in northern Virginia where he closeted his numerous suits (his sole extravagance) and armoired his plenteous T-shirts (not a syllable of product promotion on any of them), which was understandable, considering he rarely slept or ate in the place. The CIA had hired him as an analyst, chaining him to a desk at Langley, but after his supervisors reviewed his rugby tapes they granted him his wish to dive into the derring-do tank: three years in Kuwait, during which time he made frequent phantom forays into Iraq, earning a decoration for an act of valor that he was sworn never to discuss; five years in Bangkok, during which time his off-duty activities, above and beyond the C.R.A.F.T. Club even, had so incensed the U.S. ambassador there that the envoy managed to get him transferred; two years now trotting the globe in a role the company called "troubleshooter," but which to Switters's mind was not much more than an international errand boy.

The nomadic life had its drawbacks, but Switters would be the first to cheerfully admit that it cut way down on maintenance. When he considered that he had not one blade of lawn to tonsure nor brick of patio to patch; when he considered that no overly friendly stranger had ever tried to sell him storm windows, aluminum siding, or a *Watchtower* magazine; when he considered all of the condo association meetings he'd avoided (thereby sparing his poor brain from being quibbled right down to the stem), he had little choice but to rejoice. And additional joy ensued when he realized that the sun must now be directly overhead since no fragment of *its* aluminum siding any longer extended beyond the ragged edges of the *Virgin's* canopy. Indeed, the hands of his watch were rendezvousing at the top of the dial for a midday quickie (the big hand chauvinistically on top as usual, as it was even on women's watches).

"Noon!" he exclaimed, in case the others had missed it. He pointed to the sun. He pointed to the larder. "Who's the chef on this tub? The sous-chef? The pâtissier?" His glance took in the three bottles of pisco. "I doubt I need inquire about the sommelier."

At neither end of the boat was there movement or acknowledgment, so Switters stood up, the better to attract attention.

"Lunch," he said. His tone was even, rational, devoid of any knuckle of bellicosity. "That's what we call it in my country. L-U-N-C-H. Lunch. I'm fond of lunch. I am, in fact, a lunch aficionado. Give me liberty or give me lunch. Breakfast comes around too early in the day, and dinner can interfere with one's plans for the evening, but lunch is right on the money, the only thing it interrupts is work."

His voice rose slightly. "I require lunch on a daily basis. I'm insured against non-lunch by Blue Cross, Blue Shield, and Blue Cheese. Finicky? Not this luncher. I eat the fat, I eat the lean, and I lick the platter clean. Normally, I do shun the flesh of dead animals. Live animals, as well: bestiality is not a part of my colorful repertoire, although that is really none of your business. But in the dietary arena, pals, I have nothing to hide, and would at this juncture gladly masticate and ingest Spam-on-a-stick if you served some up. All I'm asking is that you serve *something* up, and speedily. I become grumpy when denied my noontide repast."

A hint of the histrionic now entered his delivery, and he pumped up the volume a decibel or two. "A hearty lunch is essential for growing bodies. Beyond that, it's a many-splendored thing. Man does not live by deals alone. Lunch is beauty. Lunch is truth. The Rubenesque beauty of chocolate pudding soaking up cream. The truth embodied in the Brechtian dictum, 'First feed the face.' Butter the bread, boys! Split the elusive pea! Hop to it! Lunch justifies any morning and sedates the worst of afternoons. I would partake. I would partake."

Inti and the boys stared at him, to be sure, but their expressions were closer to indifference than curiosity or appreciation. Inti's face, in particular, seemed glazed by those smooth sugars of inscrutability that are widely, if incorrectly, believed to flavor certain ethnic types. Frustrated that his rhetoric had inspired not a twitch of culinary action, Switters, stomach growling all the while, sat back down to reason things out.

It could be coca leaves, he reasoned. A cud of coca was reputed to keep a Peruvian Indian chugging from dawn to dusk and kill his appetite for lunch in the process. *Another reason*, thought he, *to eschew the toot tree*. He had missed one lunch already in the past few days due to XTC. Coca was to dining what late-night television was to sex, and he was about to say as much, to no one in particular, when he noticed a stalk of midget bananas partially protruding from under a roll of tattered mosquito netting that lay alongside the provisions. Well, eureka, then!

Tossing aside the netting, he reached for the bananas, only to yelp and jump backward in alarm as his fingers came within an inch of the ugliest spider he'd ever laid orbs on. Now *that* got a reaction from his stoic shipmates. Their faces contorted, their bare feet stamped, and they issued strange hissing sounds that must have been some Amazonian equivalent of laughter, persisting in such demonstration while he backed steadily away from the stalk and its inhabitant, a blondish creature that resembled, in size and hair-cover, an armpit with legs.

It wasn't a tarantula. Switters was familiar with tarantulas. No, this living emblem of evolutionary perversity wasn't merely hairy, it was sprinkled with purple spots—an armpit with a rash—and its pupilless white eyes rolled about the brow of its cephalothorax like mothballs in a lapidary. Yes, and it was rearing back on its hindmost legs in a most unfriendly presentation.

As Switters continued to retreat, finally reseating himself on his cardboard divan, the Indians continued to express amusement. *Maybe I should open my own comedy club in Pucallpa,* mused Switters. *Call it Arachno-phobia.* Instead, he opened his valise. Rummaged among his shorts and socks and handkerchiefs. And fished out the automatic pistol.

"Nothing personal," he said, as he stood facing the stalk. "I respect all living things, and I'm aware that to you, I, myself, must appear a monstrosity. But you've got my goddamn bananas, pal, and this is the law of the jungle!"

With that, he fired off about a dozen ear-splitting rounds, blowing bits of spider and banana all over the bow. "Anyone for fruit salad?" he asked politely.

Indeed, when the smoke cleared there wasn't much left of the bunch. Green shreds, yellow dollops, hairy confetti. Digging around in the organic debris, he did, however, find four and a half survivors. The half-banana, he presented to Sailor. The remainder he calmly peeled and devoured, one after the other, smiling with humble satisfaction.

"Now," he said to the Indians, who had become very still and very respectful (even the ocelot looked upon him with awe when it finally came out of hiding), "how about a soupçon of after-lunch conversation? It's my opinion—expressed before the C.R.A.F.T. membership in Bangkok on February 18, 1993, and reiterated here for your consideration—that the syntactic word-clusters in *Finnegans Wake* aren't sentences in the usual sense, but rather are intermediate states in a radiating nexus of pan-linguistic interactions, corresponding to—"

He broke off abruptly and did not continue. There were two reasons for this:

(1) Despite experiencing an acute craving for some intellectual stimulation, even if he had to supply it himself—and from Maestra he'd inherited a tendency to become periodically enraptured with the wheeze of his own verbal bagpipes—it did not long escape his notice that his monologue was not merely masturbatory but condescending.

(2) He couldn't remember a fucking thing.

About that time the rain came.

A rank of ample black clouds had been double-parked along the western horizon like limousines at a mobster's funeral. Rather suddenly now, they wheeled away from the long green curb and congregated overhead, where, like overweight yet still athletic Harlem Globetrotters, they bobbed and weaved, passing lightning bolts trickily among themselves while the wind whistled "Sweet Georgia Brown."

Then they merged into one sky-filling duffel bag, which unzipped itself and dumped its contents: trillions of raindrops as big as butter beans and as warm as blood. His protective canopy notwithstanding, Switters thought he might drown.

In twenty minutes or less, the downpour was over. It took the boys twice that long, using Inti's cooking pots, to bail out the boat.

If, during the interval in which it was obscured from view, the sun had seized the opportunity to do something un-sunlike, there was no lingering evidence. The sun was pretty much in the same position as where they'd left it a deluge ago, and it rapidly resumed wilting them with its nuclear halitosis. The sun, however, might generate radiation until it was red in the face, might stoke its furnace until it reached twenty million degrees Fahrenheit, it still could not begin to demoisturize the Amazon. Switters wouldn't be truly dry again until he was back in Lima, and even there he would find himself dampened—from the exertion of muscling a wheelchair.

That night, after a surprisingly delicious dinner of corn and beans, Switters slept in the *Virgin*. She had been beached on a sandbar. The sand would have made a softer mattress, but it was subject to visitation by reptiles. There was even worry that a myopic or excessively lonely bull crocodile might try to mate with his valise.

The stars were as big and bright as brass doorknobs, and so numerous they jostled one another for twinkle space. Because the mosquito population was equally dense, Switters spent the night rolled up in his netting like a pharaonic burrito, a crash-test mummy who couldn't see the stars for his wrapping. Visual deprivation was compensated for by auditory glut. From the sewing-machine motors of cicadas to the beer-hall bellows of various amphibians, from the tin-toy clicks and chirps and whirs of countless insects to the weight-room grunts of wild pigs, from the sweet melodic outbursts of nocturnal birds (Mozarts with short attention spans) to the honks and whoops and howls of God knows what, a rackety tsunami of biological rumpus rolled out of the jungle and over the river, which stirred its own sulky boudoirish murmur into the mix.

An additional sonic contribution was made by Inti and his crew, who, following dinner, took a bottle of pisco, threadbare blankets, and the banana-splattered mosquito netting and disappeared into the bush. Off and on for hours, the younger boys issued loud, primitive cries, as if Inti were beating them out there. Or . . . or . . . or something else. Something South American.

(As opposed to, say, Utahan. Recently, a Mormon gentleman in Utah had been shocked silly by the discovery that his wife was actually a man. They had been married three years and five months. It was an oversight that never would have occurred in South America, where the prevailing Catholic ethic seemed to stimulate rather than suppress vividity.)

When at dawn Inti gently shook him awake, Switters was surprised that he'd been sleeping, and even more amazed that he felt reasonably rested. As Inti helped with the unwinding, Switters emerged from the swathes of netting like a butterfly escaping its cocoon. "Free at last, oh, free at last!" he exulted, hopping onto the sandbar, where he danced a little jig. The Indians regarded him with a mixture of fondness and fear.

Throughout bathing and breakfast, the air around them was torn by the chattering, shrieking of monkeys, and as the darkness faded Switters could see parrots in the treetops, parrots in the air, parrots and more parrots. Keenly alert, in a heightened state of awareness, Sailor was bouncing up and down on his perch.

"Hmmm. You know something, pal? I could spring you right here, couldn't I? We're seventy miles from Pucallpa, the jungle's starting to jungle in earnest, you've got cousins by the dozen out there. I could open your door, record your exit for posterity, and get my poor South Americaed butt back to somewhere cool and clean and crispy. You'd be happy, Maestra'd probably be happy, and God knows I'd be happy. Shall we go for it? What do you say?"

Sailor didn't say anything, and in the end Switters resisted temptation. Why? No sound reason beyond the fact that Juan Carlos de Fausto had presented him with a harebrained scheme, and for harebrained schemes Switters was known to have something of an affection.

Inti pointed to the orange frown of sun that was grumpily forcing itself
above the distant Andean foothills. Then he pointed directly overhead. He rubbed his belly and shook his bowl-cut. Switters got the
message. "Okay," he sighed. "No *comida*."

"*Si, señor. No comida. Lo siento.*" Inti was apologetic. Even a bit ashamed.
Lunch was simply not a tradition aboard the *Little Virgin*. Ah, but there
was a lunch substitute. Shyly, Inti held out his hand. In his palm was a
folded packet of green leaves, about the size of a matchbook. Inti was
extremely nervous, giving Switters the impression that the Indian had
never offered coca to a white man before. Switters made it clear that he
was honored, but he politely refused. He'd already decided that the next
time he felt hunger trying to kick-start its motorcycle, he would still the
shudders and silence the rumbles with meditation.

He was out of practice, having meditated with increasing infre-
quency since he left Bangkok. He was also well aware that meditation was
intended neither as a diversion nor a therapy. Indeed, if he could believe
his teacher, ideal meditation had no practical application whatsoever.
Sure, there were Westerners who practiced it as a relaxation technique,
as a device for calming and centering themselves so that they might
sell more stuff or fare better in office politics, but that was like using
the Hope diamond to scratch grocery lists onto a bathroom mirror.

"Meditation," said his teacher, "hasn't got a damn thing to do with
anything, 'cause all it has to do with is nothing. Nothingness. Okay? It
doesn't develop the mind, it dissolves the mind. Self-improvement?
Forget it, baby. It erases the self. Throws the ego out on its big brittle
ass. What good is it? Good for nothing. Excellent for nothing. Yes,
Lord, but when you get down to nothing, you get down to ultimate
reality. It's then and exactly then that you're sensing the true nature of
the universe, you're linked up with the absolute Absolute, son, and
unless you're content with blowing smoke up your butt all your life,
that there's the only place to be."

Obviously Switters's meditation teacher was no Thai monk or
Himalayan sage. His guru, in fact, was a CIA pilot from Hondo, Texas,
by the name of Bobby Case, known to some as Bad Bobby and to
others as Nut Case. He was Switters's bosom buddy. The U.S. ambassador to Thailand, who sported a bitchy wit, referred to the pair of
them as the Flying Pedophilia Brothers, a nickname to which they
both objected. When Switters complained that it was slanderous and
unfair, Bobby said, "Damn straight it is. I don't mind being called a
pedophile, but *your brother*?!"

As a CIA agent who "sat" (that is, meditated), Bobby Case wasn't the rarity the uninformed might suppose. Thirty or forty years earlier, Langley had exposed a relatively large number of its field hands to meditation, yoga, parapsychology, and psychedelic drugs in a series of experiments to see if any or all of those alien potents and techniques might have military and/or intelligence applications. For example, could LSD be employed as a control mechanism, could meditation counteract the attempted brainwashing of a captured U.S. agent?

The experiments backfired. Once the guinea pigs had their veils lifted, their blinders removed by their unexpected collisions with the true nature of existence, once they gazed, unencumbered by dogma or ego, into the still heart of that which of which there is no whicher, they couldn't help but perceive the cowboys who bossed them, the Ivy League patricians who bossed their bosses, as ridiculous, and their mission as trivial, if not evil. Many left the company, some to enter ashrams or Asian monasteries. (One such defector wrote *The Silent Mind*, a premier book on the subject of sitting.) A few remained with Langley. They performed their duties much as before, but with compassion now, and in full consciousness. No longer "blowing smoke up their butts," as Bobby Case described *maya*, the folly of living in a world of illusion. They continued to meditate. Sometimes they taught meditation to promising colleagues. Awareness was passed along, handed down. Thus was angelhood expanded, perpetuated.

Bobby, who had been the recipient of an older agent's wisdom, saw the angel in Switters the moment he met him. Not every angel meditated. Some even shunned drugs. The two things they all had in common were a cynical suspicion of politico-economic systems and a disdain for what passed for "patriotism" in the numbed noodles of the manipulated masses. Their blessing and their curse was that they actually believed in freedom—although Switters and Bad Bobby used to speculate that belief, itself, might be a form of bondage.

Incidentally, this angel vs. cowboy business: didn't it smack rather loudly of elitism? Probably. But that didn't worry Switters. As a youth, he'd been assured by Don't-Call-Me-Grandma Maestra that the instant *elitism* became a dirty word among Americans, any potential for a high culture to develop in their country was tomahawked in its cradle. She quoted Thomas Jefferson to the effect that, "There exists a false aristocracy based on family name, property, and inherited wealth. But there likewise exists a true aristocracy based on intelligence, talent, and virtue." Switters had pointed out that either way, aristocracy seemed to be a matter of luck. Maestra responded tartly, "Virtue is not something you can win in a goddamn lottery." And, years later,

Bobby had told him, "What shiftless folks call 'luck,' the wise ol' boys recognized as *karma*." Well, if the CIA angels were a true elite within a false elite, so much the better, true being presumably preferable to false. It didn't really matter to Switters. What mattered was that he could taste a kind of intoxicating ambrosia in the perilous ambiguities of his vocation. Angelhood was his syrup of wahoo. It made his coconut tingle.

In any event, that day on the vivid South American river, Switters stripped down to his shorts. They were boxer shorts, and except for the fact that they were patterned with little cartoon chipmunks, they weren't much different from what Inti and the boys were wearing. He sat with crossed legs, his hands resting palms upward on his shins. Maestra, his lifelong influence, didn't know the first thing about meditation, while ol' Nut Case, his inspiration in that area, would have chided him for sitting so pragmatically, so purposefully, using *zazen* as a surrogate tuna sandwich. "Hellfire," Bobby would have snorted, "that's worse than drinking good whiskey for medicinal purposes, or some unhappy shit like that." Switters didn't care. He straightened his back, lined up his nose with his navel, cast down his gaze, and regulated his breathing; not tarrying, for it was only a trial: taking the damp and dirty folds of cardboard that would serve as his *zabuton* on a test drive, so to speak. Everything clicked, in a clickless way. He was ready. When all echoes of breakfast faded and his gastric chamber orchestra struck up the overture to lunch, he would lower himself obliviously into the formless flux.

What he hadn't counted on were the demons.

The demons came in the form of flies. Black flies—which, technically, are gnats. *Simulium vittatum*. The bantam spawn of Beelzebub. There must have been an overnight hatch of the tiny vampires, for suddenly they were as thick as shoppers, thirsty as frat rats, persistent as pitchmen. Switters swatted furiously, but he was simply outnumbered. No matter how many he squashed, there was always another wave, piercing his flesh, siphoning his plasma.

One of the Indians gave him a thick yellowish root to rub over his body. Combining with his perspiration to form a paste, the root substantially reduced the pricks of pain and drainage of his vessels, but a dark gnat cumulus continued to circle his head, and every five seconds or so, an individual demon would spin off from the swarm to kamikaze into his mouth, an eye, up one of his nostrils.

The attack continued for hours. Meditation was out of the question. Concentration, meditation's diametric opposite, was likewise impaired.

At approximately the same time that the black flies descended, the river narrowed. Perhaps there was a connection. Up to that point, the Ucayali had been so wide Switters felt as if they were on a lake or a waveless bronze bay. Now, he could have thrown a banana from midstream and hit either shore. Or, he could have were he in shape. He was barely thirty-six, and his biceps were losing their luster. He'd tried to shame himself into logging some gym time, but any way you sliced it, working out was maintenance and maintenance was a bore.

At any rate, there was a strong sense of riverness, now, and that much was good. Rivers were the primal highways of life. From the crack of time, they had borne men's dreams, and in their lovely rush to elsewhere, fed our wanderlust, mimicked our arteries, and charmed our imaginations in a way the static pond or vast and savage ocean never could. Rivers had transported entire cultures, absorbed the tears of vanquished races, and propelled those foams that would impregnate future realms. Everywhere dammed and defiled, they cast modern man's witless reflection back at him—and went on singing the world's inexhaustible song.

Switters guessed that they had left the Ucayali and entered the Abujao. Inti confirmed that they were on a secondary river, but Abujao was not a name he recognized.

The last signs of cattle ranching had petered out. The forest, thick, wet, and green, vine-snarled and leaf-tented, towered to nearly two hundred feet, walling them in on both sides. An impenetrable curtain, menacing, unrelieved, the jungle vibrated in the breezeless heat, dripped in the cloying humidity, and except for flights of parrots and the occasional flash of flower—a cascade of leopard-spotted orchids, a treeful of red blossoms as big as basketballs—grew quickly monotonous.

The river, on the other hand, was agurgle with antics. In exhibitions of reverse surfing, flying fish and freshwater dolphins leapt from the water to catch brief rides on shafts of sunlight. Then, putting a spin on that feat, cormorants, wings folded like a high-diver's arms, would plunge beak-first *into* the water, presumably, since they rarely speared a fish, for nothing but cormorant kicks. On benches of gravel, heavy-lidded caimans did Robert Mitchum imitations, seeming at once slow and sinister and stoned. Cabbage-green turtles that must have each weighed as much as a wheelbarrow load of cabbages slid off of and onto mud banks and rocks, while frogs of various hues and sizes plopped on every side like fugitives from mutant haiku. ("Too damn vivid," Bashō might have complained in seventeenth-century Japanese.) Around a bend, three tapirs, the mystery beast from Kubrick's 2001, waded the stream. According to Juan Carlos, most of Peru's tapirs had been killed off by hunters, depriving the animal of its right to inhabit the world and depriving the world of living proof of what would result were a racehorse to be mated with Porky Pig.

Because low water had exposed many rocks that in the rainy season would be well submerged, Inti was forced into almost constant maneuvering, and the *Little Virgin* could no longer average her customary six knots per hour. The slower pace, combined with the Abujao's more abundant attractions, afforded Switters the opportunity for an unusual riverine interface. Despite his distaste for the incessant teeming that characterized tropical South America, he was by no means insensitive to natural wonders, and he felt he ought somehow to take advantage of this opportunity. There was a fly in the ointment, however. *Simulium vittatum.*

His attentive powers were blunted by the persistent need to throw wild punches at the proboscises of the diminutive Durante-esque devils—and to fend off larger, unidentifiable insects who kept trying to crash the party. In the entomological kingdom, the quest for lunch was ongoing. Switters could empathize.

No comida.

No concentración.

And *meditación* was out of the question.

The next morning, when Inti and the boys returned from the bush with their second empty pisco bottle and facefuls of sheepish expression, Switters held out his hand.

"Gimme coca," he said.

Externally, day two on the olive Abujao mirrored day one. For thirteen more lunchless hours, they zigzagged among mossy boulders and through sopping streamers of feverish heat, attended by squadrons of black flies that refused to quit them until a late afternoon downpour literally drowned the biting bugs in midair.

Internally, the furniture had been rearranged. Switters was booming with vim. Impervious to hunger, he was possessed of such a quantity of unvented vigor that he longed to leap into the river and race the boat to Boquichicos. This he could not do, due to caimans, spiny catfish, the odd swimming viper, and the fact that he'd put his silk suit back on in order to expose less of his flesh to those South American things that would feed upon it.

Energized yet strangely at peace, he reclined on his rapidly moldering cardboard couch, his face, hands, and feet impastoed with the root goo that caused him to resemble a comic-book Chinaman (in real life, Asians were no more yellow in complexion than Caucasians were truly white), the wad of leaf in his jaw beckoning—reaching out!—to the massive green rampage of forest spirits along either bank. Or so it seemed. At some point he commenced to play with the baby ocelot.

That Switters was no pet-lover has been established. For days he'd paid keener notice to the wild parrots in the trees than to poor Sailor in his nearby cage. Yet, the truth was, he had sort of a soft spot for very young animals: for puppies, for bunnies, for small kitty cats. If only they wouldn't grow up! He'd sometimes wished there was a serum with which one might inject pups and kittens, a drug that would arrest their growth and retard their descent into adulthood. Oddly or not, his liking for domestic animals was restricted to those months when they were still frisky, spunky, and playful, before they became cautious and staid, before their spontaneity was genetically assassinated and their sense of wonder crushed by the lockstep rigors of the reproductive drive and the territorial imperative.

During the period when Switters and Bobby Case were under fire in Bangkok, tattletale embassy personnel having observed them on more than a few occasions in the company of what the ambassador referred to as "underage" girls, Bad Bobby had addressed their alleged misbehavior. "It's only natural," he'd said, "that I chase after jailbait. I'm a midlife adolescent, I can't make commitments, I'm scared of intimacy, and last but not least, I'm a piece of south Texas white trash who likes his pussy to fit tighter than his boots. But with you, though, Swit, it's something different. I get the feeling you're attracted to . . . well, I reckon I'd have to call it *innocence*."

Unwilling to flatly deny it, Switters had asked, "Attracted to innocence in order to defile it?"

Bobby hooted and threw up his hands in mock horror. The girls in the Safari Bar all tittered because he was crazed Bobby Case and he was drinking with his crazed friend Switters. "You're not fixing to feign a guilt trip on me, are you? 'Cause if you are, I'm going on home and read *Finnegans Wake*."

"You desert me in my hour of need, I'll follow you home and read *Finnegans Wake to* you."

"Oh no you don't!" Bobby exclaimed, signaling frantically for another round of Sing Ha. The girls wanted to join them—the Safari girls *loved* Bobby and Switters—but the men bought them champagne and shooed them away. They were under fire and needed to talk.

"There's folks," said Bobby, "who think sex is filthy and nasty, and they're spooked by it and mad at it and don't want anything to do with it and don't want anybody else messing with it, either. And there's folks who think sex is as natural and wholesome as Mom's apple pie and they're relaxed about it and can't get enough of it, even on Sunday."

"Personally," said Switters, "I think sex *is* filthy and nasty—and I can't get enough of it. Even on Sunday."

"Uh-huh. Yes indeedy. And it's particularly nasty when it's all sweet and fresh and innocent. Isn't that how it strikes you, Switters? I believe you lingo jockeys refer to this as *paradox.*" He yelled "Paradox!" at the top of his lungs, and the girls laughed merrily. "Or, we could say that innocence and nastiness enjoy a symbiotic relationship. Symbiotic! For the connoisseurs among us. Also for young folks, who're just busting with nastiness night and day, and have a completely innocent kind of awe of it."

"You're a troubled man, Captain Case. There're dark forces at work in you, and I will neither sanction them nor be a party to their rationalization."

"Yeah, well, don't forget who your employer is. If you and me didn't rationalize our butts off, we couldn't look in the mirror to shave."

"You haven't shaved in a week."

"Beside the point. What I'm trying to get at here—and I'm doing it on your behalf and in your defense, since I'm not fit to be defended—is that consensual, non-abusive, good-hearted fucking is not in and of itself defiling, not even to the very young."

"It's often a matter of cultural context."

"There you go. Look at the ladies in this very room." Bobby gestured wildly at a gaggle of chic bar girls huddled around the jukebox. They giggled and waved back at him. "At least half of 'em are as innocent as rosebuds."

"Because their minds are still curious and their hearts are still pure."

"There you go. Sure, the shadow of the big A is hovering over 'em like Death's own helicopter, and they have to put up with the bedside manners of snockered Sony executives and unhappy shit like that, you know, and sleeping with jerks can definitely numb a person's heart, but frequent fucking hasn't traumatized 'em or even cheapened 'em, not these ladies or anyone else, except maybe in those unfortunate blue-nosed societies that are uptight about the body in general. It's a matter of attitude."

"Cultural context."

"There you go. I read somewhere that in the olden days, when a girl reached a certain age—puberty, I reckon—she'd be initiated into sex by one of her uncles. Same with a boy, only an aunt would do the job. Sauce for the goose, sauce for the gander. It was considered a highly important learning experience, the uncle and auntie were teachers, and it was a serious though evidently smiley-faced family duty. And the thing is, you know, there's no evidence that this hands-on brand of sex education was anything but beneficial or that it ever left even the most itty-bitty psychological scar."

"Well, that was then and this is now. Today, it'd land the kids in therapy and the adults in jail. For decades in both instances."

"Different cultural context, if I can coin a phrase. And precisely why we should avoid America like the mumps. Thailand is perfect for an ol' boy like me, who's into sitting and hankers to be every niece's uncle; and it's perfect for a cat like you, who's got this deep secret Jones for innocence."

"Yeah, so deep and secret even I don't know about it. Maybe you ought to consider, pal, that you might be indulging in a simple-minded supposition."

"Supposition!" hollered Bobby, eliciting the usual amused response. "Okay, son. Forget it. You don't appreciate my support, I withdraw it. I wouldn't want to sully the Patpong night with any supposition."

They went quiet for a while, pulling on their frosty Sing Has. Then Switters said, "In regards to my personal proclivities, you're generating considerable flapdoodle." Immediately he bawled, "Proclivities! Flapdoodle!" in a voice more thunderous than Bobby's. He nodded at his friend and said softly, "To save you the trouble."

"You're a gentleman and I thank you. The ladies thank you, too."

"However," Switters resumed, "I have to say you're correct when you suggest that loss of virginity is in no way equivalent to loss of innocence. Unless, of course, *innocence* is defined as *ignorance*."

"In which case," put in Bobby, "every sum bitch in the state of Texas is innocent as a snowflake. I share this with you as a fellow Texan."

"You won't find the term 'Texan' on a single document in my resumé."

"Only because you've doctored your damn files. All-region line-backer at Stephen F. Austin High School. Or do I have you confused with some other, more studly, guy?"

"We only lived in Austin two years. And I spent both those summers with my grandmother in Seattle."

"Well, let's see: factoring in your age, that makes you one-eighteenth of a Texan. Woefully inadequate, I admit, but it probably accounts for your good looks."

"And my appreciation of red-eye gravy."

"Praise the Lord!" Bobby called for more beer. "By the way, I been meaning to ask you: how come you never went on to play football in college?"

"Oh, I don't know. Seems every campus I visited on those, uh, recruiting trips, all the players ever talked about was money. Football was a business to them, even at the college level, and the lone dream they had in life was to be let loose in the NFL gold mine with an agent and a shovel. So, I decided to give rugby a whirl. Rugby's every bit as rough and every bit as challenging, and a lot more fun because in America, at least, there's never been a chance anybody could make a nickel on it. I guess I liked it because it was beyond the reach of commerce and hype. In rugby you were just a guy laying his teeth on the line for the sport of it, you were not a commodity."

"Uh-huh!" Bobby crowed, with a triumphant smirk. "There you go. Attracted to purity. Switters, I rest my case."

"Case, I rest my Switters," countered Switters, and the pair convulsed with such silly, stupid laughter that even the bar girls shook their heads and looked the other way.

Bobby Case was soon to be reassigned to a U2 base in Alaska. It was rumored that upon his departure, the gutters of Patpong (Bangkok's "entertainment" district) had run with women's tears. Incidentally, despite Bobby's description of himself as a "midlife adolescent," he was several years Switters's junior, a fact underscored by his twenty-seven-inch waist and boyish shock of skunk-black hair, and contradicted by the purplish crescents beneath his glint-and-squint aviator's eyes. His last hours in Bangkok were spent in deep meditation at a Buddhist shrine, although in balance it should be reported that the evening prior, he'd addressed the C.R.A.F.T. Club for forty minutes on the first sentence of *Finnegans Wake*, which happened to be the only sentence of that book he'd ever read.

Switters was called home to Langley. He spent *his* last hours in Bangkok in the company of an actual adolescent. He bought her a new silk dress, jeans, and a compact disk player. Then he put her on a bus back to her native village with six thousand dollars in her pink plastic purse, her brief career as a whore at an end. She would rescue her family financially, and—since sexual shame was nonexistent in Thailand and he'd seen to it that she was free of disease—eventually marry her childhood sweetheart in a jolly public ceremony beside a field apop with ripening rice. The six thou he'd won from some Japanese businessmen in a *baka bachi* game that nearly sparked an international incident. As for Switters's farewell presentation to the C.R.A.F.T. Club, his lecture on the *Wake* went on until nearly daybreak and is said to have concluded with him bleeding, in the nude, and crooning "Send in the Clowns," a song the membership was shocked to learn he knew.

Switters was not much given to self-analysis. Perhaps he sensed that it forced the dishonest into even deeper deception and led the candid into bouts of despair. Consequently, he'd given little thought to Bobby's characterization of him that Bangkok evening as a seeker after purity. And now, two years later, aboard a dory in the Peruvian Amazon, rolling a spotted cub back and forth on its spine and pondering, what he pondered was not so much any alleged attraction to innocence on his part but his indisputable attraction to Suzy, reasonably confident they were not the same thing.

Like many modern-day sixteen-year-olds, Suzy was at a juncture where innocence and sophistication converged, much as the olive-colored Abujao converged with the cigar-colored Ucayali, mingling, chaotically at first, their contrasting hues and oppositional currents. The time, no doubt, had passed when it might have been effective to inoculate Suzy with his hypothetical adulthood-prevention serum. Quite likely, it would have been a mistake at any stage. Human beings were not well served by permanence or stasis. Obviously, if individuals were progressing, they were undergoing a series of presumably *desirable* alterations, but in a universe where flux is fundamental, it can be argued that even change for the worse is preferable to no change at all. Isn't fixity the hallmark of the living dead?

At any rate, to enumerate the ways in which Suzy had changed, he was obliged to picture how she'd been at the beginning. Initially, he had to strain to recall the details of their first meeting. Then, he had to strain to stop recalling them. All this Suzy straining was amplified, magnified, and possibly provoked, by the coca.

It had been four years. On leave and destined for Seattle, he'd stopped off in Sacramento at his mother's request, to meet her new husband and stepdaughter. The husband, a well-to-do hardware wholesaler, had admitted him and after a minute or two of small talk, directed him to his mother's sitting room. The door was ajar. Switters could hear voices. He rapped once and was charging into the room when his mother squealed and blocked his entrance. "No, you can't come in! She's trying on her training bra."

Switters froze in his tracks, momentarily startled, then curious and thoughtful. "Oh, really?" he asked with great interest. "What's she training them to *do*?"

There had erupted an unrestrained and altogether delicious giggle—really more of a girlish guffaw—and the slender figure that had been standing with her back to the door made a silky half-turn to look at him, swinging in the process a storybook pelt of straight blond princess hair. She was barefoot, he remembered, toenails twinkling with a pink-baby varnish. Her longish legs were bare to the brie-like thighs, at which point they vanished into white cotton shorts, stretched taut over a little rump so round Christopher Columbus could have employed one of its protuberances as a visual aid and bowled bocci with the other. Panty outline was in evidence. Above the waist she was naked, save for a dainty white harness, from which dangled shop tags of paper and plastic, and which she did not wear but, rather, clutched loosely at a distance of several inches in front of her chest. In that position it concealed only the nippled points of mammalian swellings, hard as quinces, that might have served as helmets for the marionettes in a German army puppet show—if the toy Huns were outfitted in winter camouflage. They were not quite in the *tits* category, but they had a running start at it.

Into view now, its prow piercing his reverie, came a dugout canoe, paddled by five loinclothed Indians with decorated faces and feathered coifs. These feathers had once been the exclusive property of individual parrots and macaws, a particular not lost on old Sailor Boy, whose reaction was anything but relaxed. "Come on, pal," said Switters to the agitated fowl, "practice what you preach." The wild canoers neither waved nor nodded at the crew of the *Virgin;* the Pucallpa clansmen ignored them as well. On the forest-shaded river, the boats passed in silence, twenty feet apart, as if the other did not exist. Switters looked imploringly at Inti, who shrugged and muttered, "Kandakandero."

Okay, where was he? Staring at Suzy, Suzy staring back, he was captivated to the extent that he failed to hear a word of his mother's prolonged greeting or to adequately return the maternal embrace; Suzy, openly curious, amused, and more self-conscious about her amusement than about her exposed breastlings, which she eventually covered almost as an afterthought. At twelve, modesty was a custom she had yet to fully assimilate. She stood there vacillating between poise and awkwardness, as if she were unsure just how much she had to protect.

The ghost of the guffaw still clung to her tumid lips, causing them to quiver, and in their quivering fullness they reminded Switters of one of those marine creatures that attach themselves to rocks and dare observers to guess whether they are animals or flowers. Her eyes were so large and moist and aqua they might have been scissored from a resort brochure, and her nose was fine, freckled, and slightly upturned, as if sniffing the air for hints of fun. Because she had experienced neither success nor failure in life to any appreciable degree, her countenance remained unwrenched by society's dreary tugs but rather was lit by the fanciful phosphors of the mythic universe. Or, so he imagined. It would be no exaggeration to say she struck him as a cross between Little Bo Peep and a wild thing from the woods.

If Suzy viewed her new stepbrother as a glamorous, witty man of the world, scarred of cheek and mesmeric of eye, Switters viewed his new stepsister as a freshly budded embodiment of the feminine archetype, equally adept at wounding a man and nursing his wounds. Her frank gaze and expectant smile, the blithe lewdness of her posture and the resolute piety symbolized by the plain gold crucifix that swung from a chain about her never-hickeyed neck, combined to suggest something timeless, some hidden knowledge, ancient and innate, well beyond her years. Did he perceive in her (or project onto her) a glimmer of primal Eve, parting the original ferns? Of salty Aphrodite, scratching her clam in the surf? Of a callow Salome, naively rehearsing a hootchy-kootch that would rattle a royal household and cost a man his head? Maybe he did, maybe he didn't go that far. Maybe he only appraised her with the dum-dum delight with which the GI Elvis must have appraised the pubescent Priscilla.

What is certain is that he liked her instantly, as she liked him. At that point—it should be said in his favor—his feelings were honestly platonic. (The flutter in his scrotum he attributed to the long flight from Bangkok.) Lust would come later, catching him unaware, intensifying slowly, a lump of hard lard in a skillet over coals, that melted almost imperceptibly, not reaching its current and ongoing maddening sizzle until that past Easter, five months earlier, when, attending a family dinner at a Japanese restaurant, he'd fondled her under the low table while she held a menu in front of her face, pretending to experience difficulty in choosing between the lotus cake and the green tea ice cream for dessert. Arrrgh! Jesus on a pogo stick! Her sea-anemone mouth had fallen agape, and he could still see the way the red neon from the Kirin beer sign had reflected off her orthodontic braces. "For crying out loud, Suzy," her dad had complained, as she struggled *not* to cry out loud, "why don't you just order both."

Emboldened by the coca, Switters unlocked the false bottom in his valise, an object to which the Indians still gave wide berth, fearing, perhaps, that it was inhabited by crocodile familiars, or at least impregnated with a magical essence. Pushing aside esoteric weapons, surveillance equipment, cryptography devices, and his aforementioned secret shame—the reproachful album of Broadway show tunes—he located and then withdrew an even more covert and humiliating item. It had yellowed a bit, and frayed, but was appreciably the same as it had been that day four years ago. (How surprised he'd been to later discover its friendly tail practically wagging from a hamper of unrecyclable clothing that his mother had condemned to the incinerator.)

For the next half hour or so, he dangled it just out of reach of the cub, who leapt in the air and swung at it repeatedly with its front paws. Then, on an impulse he'd prefer not to dissect, he pressed the skimpy article against his own face and held it there, as if some olfactory whisper of her might come wafting through the multitudinous stinks of time and space.

It turned out to smell like cordite.

The Indians watched him with complete acceptance. It was unlikely they had ever seen, or even imagined, a training bra and thus were immune to its implications. Moreover, they had come to treat Switters with a respect bordering on reverence. Perhaps that was due to the firepower with which he had dispatched the spider, perhaps it was his willingness to chew coca; or perhaps it was because, as they overcame their shyness and could finally look at him directly, they took notice of his eyes, eyes that it has become tiresome to again depict as "fierce," etc., but that in point of fact, quite possibly *could* have stared down John Wayne, unnerved Rasputin, and hypnotized Houdini.

About an hour before sunset, Inti guided the Johnson into an eddy and stalled her motor. This in itself was not unusual. They normally traveled from five in the morning until six in the evening, stopping while there was enough light by which to cook supper. However, the shore alongside this eddy was quite marshy, and caimans as long as coffins lumbered on wicked claws among the reeds. It seemed an unlikely spot for camping.

Inti motioned for Switters to join him in the stern. There, the Indian attempted to communicate something of a relatively complex nature. Not many years earlier, Switters would have spent his time aboard the *Virgin* learning as much as he could of Inti's language, a dialect of Campa, and with his linguistic talents, he might have picked up a fair amount of it. Nowadays, though, his interest in languages had shifted away from communicative utility; away, even, from revelatory rhetoric; had moved toward what he regarded as the future of language in the post-historical age: an environment in which words, relieved of some of their traditional burden, might be employed not to describe realities but to create them. *Literal* realities. Of course, he would have been as hard-pressed to define his proposed contribution to evolutionary linguistics as to define, with exactitude, his ultimate role in the CIA. He had ideas, he had plans, but they were as shadowy as the caimans that barked in the marsh.

Inti, nevertheless, managed to get his point across. The party was, at that moment, about three hours downstream from Boquichicos. They could find a suitable campsite for the night and travel on to Boquichicos in the morning. Or, they could just keep going, which would mean canceling supper (the boys had speared a fine mess of fish) and navigating the boulder-strewn river in darkness without so much as running lights.

Switters hesitated. In the reeds, the caimans rustled like drapery. In the air, thirsty mosquito clans gathered in great numbers, anticipating an uncorking of blood. Somewhere a monkey howled, and Switters's gut, no longer lullabyed by coca (funny how much noise a ball of mystic white light can make), followed suit. He turned to Sailor for guidance. As usual, the parrot said nothing, but the way it perched—its weight on one foot, one wing slightly forward, its head tilted expectantly—reminded Switters of a bellboy awaiting a tip.

So, "To the Hotel Boquichicos!" he cried, waving like a battle flag Suzy's peewee brassiere.

there were no bellboys at the Hotel Boquichicos. No bellmen, bell-women, bellpersons, bellhops, belloids, belltrons, bellniks, bellaholics, bellwethers, belles-lettres, or "bellbottom trousers coat of navy blue." Nothing of that sort. Inti and the lads were permitted to tote Switters's luggage into the lobby (spacious, though virtually devoid of furnishings), but once past the door he was on his own. A mammoth moth (described earlier) had attempted to follow him inside but was dissuaded by a swat from his Panama hat.

A mixture of Creole music and oddly Spanish static (come to think of it, all static sounds vaguely Spanish) trickled from a vintage, nicotine-colored Bakelite radio hooked up to an automobile battery behind the front desk, while the clerk, a haggard, graying mestizo, spent more time examining the gringo's passport than a pawnbroker might devote to a Las Vegas wedding ring. His scrutiny was illuminated by a pair of kerosene lanterns.

Spreading and flapping his thin arms, as if to encompass the vast jungle that lay outside, the clerk said in English, "You will find no buyers for your tractors here, señor." Switters had presented his "cover" papers along with his passport. "I think you come very wrong place." He issued a weaselly laugh.

With a weary sigh, Switters indicated the parrot cage and set about to explain, as succinctly as possible, his intentions in the fair city (he'd been unable to make out a bit of it in the darkness) of Boquichicos. Cautiously, but with surprising speed, the clerk handed him a rusty key and pointed to the staircase. The clerk wished to deal no further with what was obviously a madman.

"Electricity make from six to nine," he called out, as if that were information to which even a visiting *loco* was entitled. Presumably, he meant in the evening.

The stairs were adjacent to what must surely have been one of the world's longest bars. To walk its length in under nineteen seconds would no doubt qualify one for a place in some special Olympics. Had there not been a lamp flickering at its far end, it might have been perceived as extending into infinity. There were, Switters guessed, a minimum of forty barstools. Only one of these was occupied, it by a middle-aged foreigner. The man had sandy hair and a pink complexion, and wore pressed khaki shorts and a khaki shirt with military epaulets. Flip-flops dangled at an angle from his large pink feet, and a bottle of English gin kept him company. No bartender was in view. It took Switters two trips to lug his belongings up to his third-floor room (the third floor was the top floor: the second floor, Switters was to learn, was wholly unoccupied), and each time that he passed the solitary drinker, the fellow nodded and smiled encouragingly, hoping, it seemed, that Switters might join him.

Switters yawned ostentatiously, a signal that he was too tired for barroom conviviality. Indeed, he could barely wait for a hot shower and clean sheets.

The shower water, predictably, was tepid at best, and the sheets, while clean enough, were damp and smelled pungently of elf breath. Since the ceiling fan only rotated between the hours of six and nine (the river was presently so low that Boquichicos's tiny hydroelectric plant could operate no more than that), the air in the room was thick and still. The air was like a flexed muscle, the bicep, perhaps, of some macho swamp thing showing off for a female swamp thing, green in both cases. So heavily did it weigh down on Switters that he felt he couldn't have gotten out of bed had he wanted to. Despite the bed's slimy texture and toadstool aroma, he didn't want to. He reached out from under its mosquito netting and snuffed the bedside candle.

"Sweet dreams, Sailor Boy. This time tomorrow, if all goes well, you'll be a free Sailor Boy. In fact, you won't be Sailor Boy at all, you'll be a wild thing without a name."

Unable to decide whether or not he envied the parrot, Switters turned his thoughts, as he often did at bedtime, to the ways in which word and grammar had interfaced with action and activity during the day; had collided with, piqued, mirrored, contrasted, explained, enlarged, or directed his life. It so happened that something most unexpected, maybe even important, had occurred in the linguistic interface that very evening. To wit:

Athapaskan is the name given to a family of very similar languages spoken by North American Indians in the Canadian Yukon, as well as by tribes in Arizona and New Mexico, although the groups are separated by more than two thousand miles and have evolved various markedly different cultures. Now, astonishingly, it appeared that a dialect of Athapaskan might have migrated as far south as the Peruvian Amazon. As they parted company at the hotel entrance, Switters had first glanced hard at the pisco bottle in Inti's hand and then at the boys huddled shyly behind him. Showing his coca-ruined teeth, Inti had smacked the nearest boy on the buttocks and, turning away, muttered, *"Udrú."* It was intended as a private joke. Inti, in his wildest jungle dreams, could not have imagined that Switters would have recognized *udrú* as the Athapaskan word for "vagina."

Ah, but Switters knew the word for vagina in seventy-one separate languages. It was kind of a hobby of his.

He grinned in the dark at the scope of his own expertise.

In the morning he managed a cold-water toilet, donned a clean white linen suit over a solid green T-shirt (its hue matched the air in the room), and went downstairs. The sandy-haired, baby-faced gent from the evening before still sat at the bar. Although he was perched on the very same stool, he presumably had not been there all night, for he, too, looked freshly shaved, and the gin bottle had been replaced by a pot of tea.

"I say," he called to Switters in a decidedly British accent. "Searching for a spot of breakfast?"

"You, pal, have read my mind." He hadn't eaten since the previous dawn. "All those damned roosters crowing me awake before sunup, there's got to be an egg or two on the premises. And if not, fruit will do. Or a bowl of mush."

"Euryphagous, are we?" asked the man, instantly winning Switters's friendship on the strength of his vocabulary. "And a Yank, into the bargain! Last night I took you for Italian. Your suit was a frightful mess, but it *was* a suit. Then, just now, I thought you might be a fellow subject of the Queen. Never expected to run across a *Yank* in a *suit* in bloody *Boquichicos.*"

"Yeah, well, as for Yanks, the old colony's a variety pack, I'm afraid. You never know which or what is gonna show up when or where." Switters settled onto the next barstool. "Tell me something: Is it cool—is it acceptable—to ask for papaya around here?"

The man raised a pair of sandy eyebrows. "Why wouldn't it be?"

"Well, uh, in the dialect of Spanish spoken in Cuba, they refer to that particular fruit as a *bombita.* 'Little bomb.' Which makes sense, considering its shape and everything. But in Cuban Spanish, the word *papaya* means 'vagina.' Which has a certain logic, as well, I guess. However . . ."

"Oh, yes, I see," said the Englishman. "If one asks for a *jugo de papaya* in Havana, one gets a rather funny look."

"Or a glass of juice that'll put hair on your chest. So to speak." When the Englishman slightly grimaced, Switters added, "Gives a whole new meaning to 'bottoms up.' "

"Rather. And afterward, I suppose, a chap would want a cigarette." The man spoke dryly and without overt levity.

"Personally, I only got the funny look."

"I see. Well. Have no fear. Unless I'm much mistaken, *papaya* in these parts will give offense to none."

At that moment a disturbingly pretty mestizo girl, not much older than Suzy, emerged from the gloom with a tray of cornbread and tropical jams, which she set before the Brit. When she looked questioningly at Switters, he became flustered and blurted, "Bombita," simply lacking the nerve to ask for papaya in the unlikely event that here, too, it might possibly mean . . .

"You're wanting bombita, you better go see Sendero Luminoso," she said, giving him the kind of wary, patronizing smile one might give a known lunatic. He blushed and quickly ordered eggs. Sailor would have to wait for his breakfast fruit.

Apparently too well-mannered to commence eating before the other was served, the Englishman retrieved from somewhere on his person a fine leather case. Embossed in gold upon its lid was a coat of arms and the legend, Royal Anthropological Society. "Oh, bugger!" he swore, after opening the case. "I seem not to have a one of my bloody cards. A chap gets lax in a place like this." He wiped his large pink hand on his shirt and then extended it. "R. Potney Smithe," he said. "Ethnographer."

"Switters. Errand boy."

They shook hands. The hand of Smithe (it rhymed with *knife*) was neither as damp nor as soft as Switters had feared.

"I see. I see. And are you running an errand in Boquichicos, Mr. Switters?"

"Most assuredly."

"Contemplating a lengthy, um . . . errand run?"

"*Au contraire.*" Switters checked his watch. It was 6:13. "In about an hour, I'm scheduled to take a little nature walk. Then, provided I'm not overwhelmed by some aspect of the local fauna . . ."

"As well you might be. From this outpost to the Bolivian border, there exist twelve hundred species of birds, two hundred species of mammals, ninety or more frog species, thirty-two different venomous snakes—"

". . . or flora . . ."

"A most immoderate vegetative display, you may be sure."

". . . I expect to depart here in midafternoon. Tomorrow morning at the very latest."

"Pity," said R. Potney Smithe, though he didn't say why.

The girl reappeared with a plastic plate of fried eggs and beans. Switters worked his smile on her. If there was any reason to tarry in Boquichicos . . .

After they had eaten, Smithe lit a cork-tipped cigarette, inhaled deeply, and said, "No offense, mind you, and I hope you won't think me cheeky, but isn't it, um, *difficult* finding yourself an 'errand boy'? I mean, a chap of your age and with your taste in attire."

"Ain't no shame in honest labor, pal. You must have had the occasion to observe honest labor, even if you've never actively participated."

"And why wouldn't I have done?"

"Well, no offense to you, either, Mr. Smithe . . ."

"Oh, do call me *Potney*."

". . . but, first, your accent reveals that you probably spent your formative years knocking croquet balls about the manicured lawns of Conway-on-the-Twitty or some such pretty acreage, where the servants did all the heavy lifting; and, second, you're a professional in a branch of science that ought to be the most enlightening and intriguing and flexible and instructive of any branch of science— outside of, maybe, particle physics—and would be if the anthropologists had a shred of imagination or the dimmest sense of wonder, or the *cojones*, the bollocks, to look at the big picture, to help focus and enlarge the big picture; but instead, it's a timid, dull, overspecialized exercise in nit-picking, shit-sifting, and knothole-peeking. There's work to be done in anthropology, Potney ol' man, if anthropologists will get off their campstools—or barstools—and widen their vision enough to do it."

Smithe expelled a globe of smoke, and it bobbed just above them for a while like an air-feeding jellyfish or a rickety umbrella, slow to disperse in the cloying humidity. "Your accusation suffers, I daresay, not from lack of zeal but fact. Well spoken for an 'errand boy' but frightfully old-fashioned, I'm afraid, and from my point of view, more than a bit narrow in its own right. We ethnographers have a long history of direct participation in the everyday life of the cultures we study. We eat their food, speak their language, experience firsthand their habits and customs—"

"Yeah, and then you go back to your nice university and publish a ten-thousand-word monograph on the size of their water jars or their various ceremonial names for *grandmother* (*maestra* not being among them, I guarantee) or the way they peel their yams. Hey, the way they peel yams—clockwise or counterclockwise?—could be significant if it reflected some deeper aspect of their existence. Like, for example, if they use the same cutting motion in peeling a sweet potato that they use in circumcising a pecker, and that pattern consciously, deliberately replicates the spiral of the Milky Way or—and stranger things have happened—the double helix of DNA. As it is, you won't or can't make those connections, so all you end up producing is a lot of academic twaddle."

"All right, let me have a go at that."

"Hold on. I'm not finished. Surely, your knowledge of natural history is not so puny that you're unaware that extinction is a consequence of overspecialization. It's a cardinal law of evolution, and many a species has paid the price. Human beings are by nature comprehensive. That's been the secret of our success, at least in evolutionary terms. The more civilized we've become, however, the further we've moved away from comprehensiveness, and in direct ratio we've been losing our adaptability. Now, isn't it just a wee bit ironic, Potney, that you guys in anthropology—the study of man—are contributing to the eventual extinction of man by your blind devotion to this suicidal binge of overspecialization? Who're you gonna write papers on when we're gone?"

The girl returned to clear their dishes. Trotting out another of his seraphic smiles, Switters asked for papaya by its rightful name and was almost disappointed when she wasn't embarrassed or insulted or coy but, instead, inquired matter-of-factly if he wanted *mitad* or *totalidad*: half or whole. (Even Switters's nimble mind couldn't picture half a vagina.)

Potney Smithe, who had remained nonplussed throughout the Switters tirade, coughed a couple of times and said, "If you're talking about the need for more interdisciplinary activity in the academic community, I quite agree. Yes. Um. However, if you're advocating speculation, or a breach of scientific detachment . . ."

"Detachment, my ass. Objectivity's as big a hoax in science as it is in journalism. Well, not quite *that* big. But allow me to interrupt you again, please, for a minute." He consulted his watch. "I've got to dash off and meet a guide."

"Your nature ramble."

"Exactly. But first I'd like to pass along a short, personal story, because it might explain my hostility toward your profession and why I may have seemed rude. Aside from the fact that I'm a Yank."

"Oh, I say . . ."

"You're the second anthropologist I've ever met. The first was an Australian—met him in the Safari Bar in Bangkok—and he'd done a fair amount of field work deep in the interior of New Guinea. Big juju in there, you know, loads of spooky ol' magic. Well, this Ph.D. lived with one of those wild mud tribes for two years, and they sort of took a liking to him. So when he left, their shaman gave him a little pigskin pouch with some yellowish powder in it and told him that if he'd sprinkle the stuff on his head and shoulders, he'd become temporarily invisible to everyone but himself. He could go into the biggest department store in Sydney, the shaman promised, and help himself. Steal anything he wanted and nobody would see him. That's what the powder was for. The anthropologist is telling me all this, see, but at that point he just chuckled and went back to his cocktail. So, I said 'Well?' And he said, 'Well, what?' And I said, 'How did it work out?' And he looked at me kind of haughtily and said, 'Naturally, I never tried it.' "

"His response disappointed you, did it?"

"Potney, I'm not a violent man. But it taxed my powers of restraint not to slap him silly. 'Naturally, I never tried it,' indeed. I wanted to grab his nose and twist his face around to the back of his head. The prig! The spineless twit!"

Potney lit another cigarette. "I appreciate your candor in sharing this anecdote. It does cast your prejudice in a more favorable light. If rightly viewed, I suppose your peevishness over the bloke's . . . the bloke's *decorum* is somewhat understandable." He paused, staring into a bloom of smoke with a botanist's engrossment. "Sometimes, however . . . sometimes . . . sometimes it really doesn't pay to get too chummy with these primitive magical practices. If they don't actually do you physical or psychological harm, they can steer you well off-track. I myself am proof of that, sorry to say. Had I not allowed myself to become fascinated with one of those Kandakandero buggers and his bag of tricks, I wouldn't be back in this bloody place, waiting around for God knows what, mucking up my career and my marriage."

He shoved his teacup aside and in a loud yet plaintive voice, cried out for gin.

"I'd be interested in hearing more about that," said Switters, and he sincerely meant it, "but duty calls." He took the saucer of papaya slices and slid off the stool.

"Perhaps I'll see you later, then? I'd fancy an earful of errand-boy philosophy. An overview. The big picture, as you put it. Um."

"No chance in hell, pal. But I appreciate the chat. Tell the señorita I'll dream about her for the rest of my life. And hang in there, Pot. Ain't nothing to lose but our winnings, and only the winners are lost."

While Sailor pecked at papaya pulp, Switters, in his new rubber boots now, opened the shutters and parted the bougainvillea vines that nearly obscured the window. He was hoping for a view of town, but his room was at the rear of the hotel and looked down upon a clean-swept courtyard. There, white chickens scratched white chicken poetry into the sad bare earth, and a trio of pigs squealed and grunted, as if in endless protest against a world that tolerated the tragedy of bacon. Sudsy wash-water had been emptied in a corner of the yard, paving the area with soap-bubble cobblestones that glimmered in the morning sun. A couple of mango trees had been planted in the center, and though they were probably still too young to bear fruit, they produced enough foliage to shade the girl, who sat on an upturned crate, shelling beans into a blue enamel basin balanced on her lap. Her faded cotton dress was pushed up as far as the basin, affording a vista of custard thigh and, if he was not mistaken, a pink wink of panty. He sighed.

Tennessee Williams once wrote, "We all live in a house on fire, no fire department to call; no way out, just the upstairs window to look out of while the fire burns the house down with us trapped, locked in it." In a certain sense, the playwright was correct. Yes, but oh! What a view from that upstairs window!

What Tennessee failed to mention was that if we look out of that window with an itchy curiosity and a passionate eye; with a generous spirit and a capacity for delight; and, yes, the language with which to support and enrich the things we see, then it DOESN'T MATTER that the house is burning down around us. It doesn't matter. Let the motherfucker blaze!

Did those thoughts constitute an "errand-boy philosophy"? Possibly not. But for the moment they would have to do.

Boquichicos proved to be as different from Pucallpa as the dory *Virgin* was different from a tanker ship. It was considerably smaller, quieter, cleaner, more benign. Switters recalled Juan Carlos de Fausto's remark that Boquichicos was a planned community, founded by the government with "strict environmental considerations." Basically, that was true. Whereas Pucallpa sprawled in anarchistic abandon, mindlessly fouling, pillaging, and devouring its natural surroundings, Boquichicos had been assigned firm parameters beyond which it was forbidden to slop or tentacle. As a result, the numinous emerald breath of the forest lay gently against the town's whitewashed cheeks, while the river here serenaded the citizenry with an open-throated warble instead of a cancer-clogged rattle of death.

Laid out in classic Spanish style around a central plaza, every dirt street, of which there were only six, had been rolled level and smooth, every building except the church uniformly roofed in palm-frond thatch, giving it an Indian flavor. The walls of the edifices had been constructed with mud bricks and/or with lumber milled after clearing the town site, then proudly brushed with a blanching lime solution that had once made them shine but was now wearing noticeably thin. None of the structures, including the municipal hall, the hotel, and the church, was anywhere near as tall as the jungle trees that cast shade on their rear entrances, nor did their doorways match in breadth some of the trunks of those trees. Far and away the town's most significant structure, its crown jewel, its saving grace, was its modern waste treatment facility. (Were they wise, the inhabitants would float daily candles of thanksgiving upon the sassafras-colored waters of their nifty little sewage lagoon.) Certainly Pucallpa could boast of no such nicety, and quite likely Iquitos couldn't either.

There were perhaps a half-dozen trucks in Boquichicos—idle, scabious with rust, tires starting to sag: where was there to drive?—and not a single car. The town's short streets, every one a dead end, were enlivened by pecking chickens, rooting pigs, yapping curs, and naked children, all of them skinny and soiled, though neither a glimpse nor a whiff of recently deceased canine intruded upon the Switters sensibility. Nevertheless, there were vultures circling—patient, confident of the more certain, and tasty, of life's two inevitables—their necrophiliac radar sweeping the weeds.

And weeds there were aplenty. Egged on by fierce equatorial sunshine and soaking tropic rains, an amazing variety of plants invaded gutters and yards, threatening to take over the plaza, even, their bitter nectars slaking the thirst of Day-Glo butterflies and a billion humming insects of plainer hue.

Built to accommodate an oil boom that never materialized (geologists had vastly overestimated the potential yield of the area's petroleum deposit), Boquichicos blossomed briefly, then shriveled. It had lost at least half of its peak population. Half stayed on, however, because housing was pleasant and affordable, and because they believed a more reliable boom—a timber boom—was right around the corner. It wouldn't be long, the enterprising reasoned, before the Japanese had mowed down the great woods of Indonesia, Borneo, Malaysia, New Guinea, and possibly Alaska, and would be setting out in earnest to deforest west-central South America. In the Brazilian Amazon, they had already turned ancient majestic ecosystems into heaps of lifeless orange sawdust (one way to muffle vividity), and their buyers were becoming active around Peru's Pucallpa. Soon, it was predicted, chainsaws would be snarling monstrous money mantras within earshot of the Boquichicos plaza (where that morning all manner of birdsong rang), and once again those forty-odd barstools at the hotel would be polished night and day by affluent or, at least, ambitious backsides.

Incidentally, some might wonder what a relatively small nation such as Japan could find to do with so much timber. Switters knew. CIA reports confirmed that millions of imported logs had been submerged in bays all along Japan's coastline, salted away, so to speak, for that time in the not-too-distant future when much of the world had run out of trees. Switters also knew—and he thought about it with a mirthless smile as he strolled across the plaza lugging Sailor Boy's unusual cage—that a brother operative stationed in Tokyo was busily scheming to foil the Japanese gambit. Not under company orders but surreptitiously, on his own. This Goliath-hexing David was, of course, an angel.

Also incidentally, Switters had once been under the impression that the term *angel*, as applied to certain evolved mavericks within the CIA, was an entirely ironic reference to a dopey book by the evangelist Billy Graham, entitled *Angels: God's Secret Agents*. Not so, said Bad Bobby Case. Bobby claimed that the term referred to a little known scriptural passage recounting the existence of "neutral angels," angels who refused to take sides in the Heaven-splitting quarrel between Yahweh and Lucifer, and who chided them both for their intransigence, arrogance, and addiction to power. How a hotshot from Hondo knew such things (Case was graduated second in his class at Texas Tech, but that was aeronautical engineering), Switters couldn't guess, nor could he guess where the spy pilot might be that morning or what he was doing, but he would have given a vat of red-eye gravy to have Bobby with him there, sharing an early-bird beer in the somber little marketplace of far Boquichicos.

The market was right next to the plaza. It consisted of a dozen or so irregularly spaced stalls with thatched awnings, as well as several rows of unshaded tables covered with ragged, faded, roach-eaten oil-cloth. On display were a skimpy assortment of fruits and vegetables, dominated by plantains, chili peppers, and pale piles of yucca or cassava root; eggs, live poultry, smoked fish, animal and reptile hides; woven mats and baskets; dry goods and clothing (including shoddy cotton T-shirts adorned with unauthorized portraits of the most familiar face on the planet, more familiar, and perhaps better loved, than Jesus, Buddha, or Michael Jordan—the face of a bland, candy-assed cartoon rodent with a hypocoristic Irish moniker); and, at the stall where Switters currently stood, pisco, homemade rum, and warm beer.

Switters sipped slowly—the wise do not gulp warm beer—and looked around for Inti. The Indian was late. Maybe he'd had difficulty hiring a guide to escort Switters to the colpa, the clay lick where the parrots and macaws were said to gather every day to coat their tiny tastebuds with a nutritious mineral slick. Maybe he'd gotten into trouble over the noisy nocturnal fellowship he enjoyed with his lads. It wasn't feasible that Inti could have headed back to Pucallpa for the very practical reason that so far he'd only been paid a 40 percent deposit on his services. As unlikely as it was, however, the faintest fleck of suspicion that Inti might have abandoned him in this moldy, weedy, hell-for-lonesome outpost was enough to freeze the sweat on Switters's brow. He began to drink faster and faster, until the beer erupted in froth and its spume filled his sinus passages. Foam was still trickling out of his nostrils when, a minute later, he thought he spotted Inti at the opposite end of the market.

Some sort of commotion was in progress, and the captain of the *Virgin* seemed to be at the center of it. "Watch my beverage," Switters said to the parrot. "I'll be right back."

The argument proved to be between Inti and a sinewy, gold-toothed, young mestizo man in Nike basketball sneakers and a spooky anaconda-skin cape. Several of the mestizo's friends were supporting him, mainly with their physical presence, although they became vocally exhortative from time to time. Inti looked quite relieved to see Switters. Impressed by the latter's fine suit and hat, the mestizo jumped to the conclusion that he was an important señor, a lawyer(!), perhaps, and he, too, welcomed the intervention of a reasonable authority. Hope of an objective opinion in the mestizo's favor quickly drained, however, when Inti pointed to the Yankee, made a symbolic pistol of his fist and forefinger, and, jabbering aggressively all the while, fired a volley of imaginary shots into his adversary's sternum. Inti was urging Switters to obliterate the Boquichicosian exactly as he had the banana-hogging spider, and from the way the man stepped back, his face turning as gray as his wild snaky cloak, he obviously had some fear that Switters might comply.

"No, no, no," said Switters, shaking his head, forcing a big smile and trying to appear as genial as the toastmaster at a booster club prayer breakfast. He raised his arms in the universal peacemaker gesture and inquired conciliatorily, though in bad Spanish, what the trouble might be. This precipitated a dueling barrage of rapid-fire Campa-Spanish that sounded like stormy-night static on Radio Babel. It took a while, but eventually details of the dispute emerged, aided considerably by the fact that when cornered, the mestizo turned out to speak a surprisingly excellent brand of English.

Evidently, two weeks earlier, Inti had given Fer-de-lance (in order to enhance his reputation in one way or another, the mestizo had assumed the name of a deadly Amazon pit viper) a case of Lima's finest pisco in exchange for a baby ocelot. The animal could be expected to fetch a high price in Pucallpa. Later upon the very evening that Switters had hired Inti, the Indian had been caught trying to peddle the ocelot on the fringe of Pucallpa's semilegal parrot market. A game warden cited him for violating one of Peru's new wildlife protection laws and confiscated the cub, but Inti informed him that he was heading again into the upstream bush the following dawn and promised to release the cat in the forest near where it had been captured, if he could have it back. After much discussion, the warden agreed. A bottle of pisco sealed the bargain.

That would explain, Switters thought, *the potbellied guy in the shabby brown uniform who stood on the dock with folded arms and saw us off that morning. I wondered about that gentleman.*

What Inti had done instead, however, was to return the little ocelot to Fer-de-lance (for the first time Switters now noticed a lidded, jiggling basket off to one side) and demand his pisco back. Fer-de-lance was having none of that, if for no other reason than that the bulk of the brandy had already met its brandy fate, which was to say, it had been sucked into that black hole that yawns at the gates of human yearning.

Switters finally settled the matter by convincing the strange mestizo to return a single bottle of pisco to reward Inti for his trouble and save his face, while he, Switters, would assume custody of the ocelot. The idea wasn't to smuggle the cub home for Suzy, although that thought crossed his mind, but to release it on his way to the colpa to free the parrot. Ah yes. The Switters Pet Liberation Service.

That concluded, he stepped over to the gently rocking basket and stooped to lift its lid, intending to ascertain that the cub was not overheating in there, wondering, at the same time, if it might grow up with some animal memory of Suzy's amateur brassiere. The instant he touched the woven top, however, there was a rude cry, and Fer-de-lance seized his arm, gripping it in fingers as strong as steel pincers.

"Shit," Switters muttered. "I should've known it wasn't going to be that easy." He tried to relax his muscles and clear his mind, as he'd been trained to do in martial arts. "Here goes my glad morning. Here goes my nice fresh suit." Then, in one liquid motion, he sprang to his feet, whirled, *pak sao*ed Fer-de-lance's hand away from his arm, and unleashed a punch.

The punch was not as fast as it might have been (he was as far out of practice as he was out of shape), and before it could land, an amazingly agile Inti blocked it. Inti then grabbed Switters's right arm, and Fer-de-lance reestablished his steely claim on the left one. Solicitously, they turned Switters around. The basket, upended in the action, lay on its side—and from it there slowly slithered, flexing and reflexing, an anvil-headed snake as black and glistening as evil itself, death rays fairly shooting from its slitty chartreuse eyes.

The crowd cleared. Inti pulled Switters away. He pointed toward a second basket that sat in the shadow of a thatched overhang a few yards distant. He commenced to snort, hiss, and stomp, much as he had when Switters had been startled by the spider. "Yeah, I get the picture," Switters grumbled. "And I suppose a pathological sense of humor is better than no sense of humor." By the time he looked around, Fer-de-lance had somehow steered the viper back into its container.

"Okay, pal, your sleazy business deals have wasted a good half hour and nearly got me snake-bit. Let's get this circus on the road. Where the hell's our tour guide to the parrot spa?" Naturally, he had to rephrase the question. When he made his query intelligible to Inti, the skipper—ocelot basket (the correct basket) in his arms, pisco bottle stuck in his waistband like a pistola—assured him that his juvenile playmates had been sent to procure the finest guide available and would be showing up with that esteemed colpa connoisseur at any moment.

"Good. It's getting late. And it's getting hot."

Indeed, though it was not yet midmorning, the sun was looking down on them like the bad eye of a billy goat, jaundiced and shot with blood; and beneath its baleful glare, every living cell in every living thing seemed to slump like a Dalí watch. Switters felt his protoplasm turning into dry-cleaning fluid, and his suit, which soon enough would *need* a good cleaning, was glued to his body like a poster to a wall. The load of perspiration seemed to double his weight.

Breathing slowly, shallowly, as if the steamy air might choke him, he lagged several feet behind Inti while they traversed the marketplace. They hadn't gotten far before he became aware of another commotion of sorts. This one was occurring around Sailor's cage.

The pyramid cage was surrounded by a group of male Indians, five or six in number. Switters identified them as Indians not so much by their painted faces (geometrically arranged dabs of berry pulp), their features (long, flaring noses, chiseled cheekbones, sorrowful dark eyes), or their clothing (thorn-ripped cotton shorts and not much else) as by their haircuts.

Among the forest tribes of South America, countless languages were spoken, countless differing customs practiced. The one thing virtually all of them had in common was the unisex pageboy hairdo. It was as if in dim antiquity, back before time had really got its motor going, some primordial deity—the Great God Buster Brown, perhaps—had swept through the immense Amazonian woodlands with a clay bowl and a dull knife and administered to every early mortal the same bad coif. Hardly a unifying element—tribes that traditionally attacked each other on sight sported identical bangs—it nevertheless had persisted and prevailed. What Gaia the Hairdresser hath styled, let no man shear asunder.

Mixed blood South Americans tended to style their locks according to European fashion, allying in that manner with their countrymen of pure Spanish or Portuguese ancestry. In Lima, though, Switters had observed that certain of the youngish *blancos*—Hector Sumac and that girl, Gloria, at the club, for example—had begun to wear their hair in refined, upscale versions of the Indian crop. Switters wondered if there was a standardized Amazonian name for the style, if it had a different name in each tribal language or if it was something so taken for granted that it had no name at all other than each tribe's word for *hair*. Momentarily, he was tempted to ask Inti what he called his haircut, but on the off chance that the boatman might answer "Arthur," as Ringo Starr had responded to the same question in *A Hard Day's Night*, he held his tongue. There was some trouble even a troubleshooter didn't go looking for.

Little or no trouble, it turned out, was brewing at the beer stall. The group of Indians wasn't angry or rowdy, it was simply intrigued for some reason by Sailor Boy, excited just enough so that its members had transcended their usual reserve and were milling about his cage, pointing scarred brown fingers and stopping passersby to question them, or so it seemed, about the parrot inside. That was a bit bewildering because Sailor, while a handsome bird, even in advanced maturity, was by no means a rare or exceptional specimen. And just bringing a pet parrot to this part of the world was probably akin to bringing a Miller Lite to Bavaria.

"They shopping for antiques or something? The warranty on this cracker-burner expired years ago." Switters asked Inti, as best he could, what the attraction was, but Inti didn't know nor could he find out in any appreciable detail, for although Inti and the Boquichicos bunch both spoke varieties of Campa, the dialects lacked sufficient vocabulary in common to permit any but the most rudimentary exchange. And since Inti and Switters didn't have a lot of words in common, either, the most Switters could determine was that the Indians weren't actually interested in Sailor Boy, they were interested in his *cage*.

"Perfect," said Switters. "Can you inform your country cousins that this unique, custom-built aviary is about to be vacated in the next couple of hours and I'm prepared to make them a real sweet deal. What do they have to trade? A diamond bracelet, maybe?" Aware that rough diamonds were occasionally found in the gravel riverbeds thereabouts, he was thinking of Maestra.

The three-way language barrier proved insurmountable, however, and though the Indians' curiosity about Sailor's portable prison not only persisted but intensified now that its owner had appeared, Switters's interest flagged, and he began looking about for signs of the Pucallpa boys and the colpa guide. "They must be getting that guide from a mail-order catalogue," he complained, fanning himself with his hat.

When they did finally appear, the lads were accompanied not by a local tracker but by R. Potney Smithe.

"Hallo again," called the anthropologist brightly. Vapors of gin preceded him. "The news about town is that you're in requirement of a chap to lead you to the parrot wallow."

"Is that a problem?"

Smithe chuckled. "Hardly, old man. The trailhead's just behind the church over there. A straight shot, more or less, all the way. Follows the river. Unless you're achingly keen on contributing to the indigenous economy, you really shouldn't be wanting a guide. I'd be happy to tag along, though, if you feel the need for companionship."

"Ain't no shortage of that," said Switters, gesturing to indicate the captain and crew of the *Virgin* as well as the contingent of local Indians.

"I see." When Smithe acknowledged the Indians around the birdcage, they closed in and buttonholed him, speaking respectfully, although all at once. To Switters's surprise, the Englishman spoke back to them in their own language, and for a few minutes they carried on a conversation, often looking deliberately, meaningfully, from the parrot cage to the jungle and back again.

Smithe turned to Switters. "Blokes have a fascination with this bloody cage."

"Obviously. Why?"

Smithe pulled thoughtfully at first one of his fleshy cheeks and then the other. His jowls glistened in the heat and humidity like burst melons. "Symbolism," he said. "Homoimagistic identification or some such rot. Never mind that. It's simple, really. This is only the second, um, pyramid shape the Nacanaca have ever seen."

"The first one must have been a doozy."

"Quite." Nodding his big head, Smithe smiled mysteriously. "Assuming that *doozy* can be construed to mean 'impressive' or 'outstanding,' it was—and is—rather a doozy."

Briefly Switters entertained a vision of some lost pyramid, a ruin of ancient architecture hidden in the jungle out there. It would have had to have been Incan, though, and he knew that Incan pyramids bore but a passing resemblance to the Egyptian structures after which Sailor's cage was modeled. He scowled at the anthropologist, as if demanding that he continue, and Smithe appeared about to oblige when a sudden squawked command caused everyone within earshot to act for a split second as if they were shaking invisible martinis.

"Peeple of zee wurl, relax!" is what they heard. Just like that. Loud. Out of nowhere.

"Bloody hell!" Smithe swore.

"Aheee!" exclaimed Inti.

"Send in the clowns," muttered Switters, for reasons that were not entirely clear.

Although intimatcly accustomed to raucous bird cries, the Nacanaca had jumped more comically than any of them. When they recovered, they asked Smithe what the "magic" parrot had said, for they were convinced it had made a pronouncement, quite likely with supernatural implications. Smithe conferred with Switters, who replied, "You heard it right, Potney. The ol' green featherduster has bade us chill out, calm down, and lighten up; which, if you can forgive the parade of conflicting prepositions, is as sage a piece of advice as we're likely to get in this life—especially from an erstwhile housepet."

When Smithe succeeded in conveying the essence of Sailor's favorite saying, the Nacanaca's fascination seemed to escalate. They jabbered to Smithe and among themselves, going on at such length that Switters lost patience and broke in to announce that he was leaving at once for the clay lick. He motioned for one of the crew to carry the cage, since Inti was toting the ocelot and he, himself, was going to be occupied with taping atmospheric footage on the camcorder. Maestra might as well get a good show out of this.

Before the little safari could successfully embark, however, Potney Smithe halted it. "I say, Switters. I say. . . ." But he didn't say. He stammered indistinctly, searching for the correct wordage. He had the coloration of a conch shell and the bulk of a bear, so that a fanciful person could imagine him the offspring of a mermaid and a panda. "I say. I have something, I *may* have something, of consequence to impart."

"Then *im*part or *de*part," said Switters. "It's hotter than the soles of Dante's loafers out here." Immediately he regretted the remark, for he heard himself starting to sound like one of the petty mopers who wasted untold priceless moments of their brief stay on this planet complaining about its weather. Unless it was about to cause you bodily harm, rot your rhubarb on the stalk, or carry off your children, weather ought either to be celebrated or ignored, he felt, one or the other; although at times such as this, when it was steaming one's brain like a Chinese dumpling, it failed to inspire much in the way of celebration, while not thinking about it was even more difficult than not thinking about . . . Suzy.

Switters softened his tone. "I read somewhere that each second, four-point-three pounds of sunlight hit the earth. That figure strikes me as kind of low. What about you, Potney?" He mopped his brow. "I mean, I realize that sunlight is, well, *light*, but don't you suppose they meant four-point-three *tons*?"

Smithe smiled indulgently and wagged his cigarette. "You aren't exactly dressed for trekking in the torrid zone, old boy; now are you?"

"Why, that depends on—"

"Although I must say, the boots are sensible." He glanced at the chèvresque sky. "It's going to be raining soon."

Switters also glanced skyward. It didn't look like rain to him. He'd bet his bottom dollar it wasn't going to rain. "So what's your story, Pot? My little operation here is falling way behind schedule."

"You have your errand to run."

"That I do. You've hit the nail on the head."

Smithe cleared his throat vigorously, sending droplets of sweat flying off his Adam's apple. "A Yank in a business suit 'running an errand' in the Peruvian bush. A bit west of here, one would automatically think 'cocaine,' but there's precious little if any coca refined in the immediate vicinity, and the mineral wealth is negligible as well. Yes. Um. If it's exotic birds you're after . . ."

"Listen, pal . . ."

"None of my bleeding business, is it? No. None. However, if your errand at the colpa is such that it might endure a nominal delay, well, there's been a development." Switters tried to interrupt, but Smithe waved him off. "These Nacanaca blokes, you see, would like to borrow your parrot for a bit. They want to take it—and its cage, obviously—into the jungle a ways. Alarmed, are you? Of course you are. But you see, they'll bring it back. They only want to show it to a Kandakandero chap. A most remarkable chap, I assure you. The Nacanaca believe that this great Kandakandero witchman will be sufficiently impressed to grant you an audience."

"No, no, no, no, no. Thanks but no thanks. My social calendar is filled to the brim right now. Next time I'm in town, perhaps." He looked to Inti. "Let's round 'em up and head 'em out."

"Oh, righto. Absolutely spot on." Smithe had gone from pink to crimson. "I've boiled my pudding in this bleeding hole for five bleeding months, petitioning, pleading, flattering, bribing, doing everything short of dropping on all fours and cavorting like a Staffordshire bull terrier to win another interview with End of Time, and you come along on your bleeding errand, oblivious, unmindful, not caring a fiddler's fuck, and fall into it, just bloody stumble into it, roses and whistles; and, of course, it's not your cup of tea, it means nothing divided by zero to a bloke like you, you're wanting none of it. Well, brilliant, that's brilliant. Just my lot, isn't it? My brilliant bleeding lot."

Switters regarded him with astonishment. "Easy," he cautioned.

"Easy, pal. Heed the counsel of our Sailor Boy over there. Relax. You're acting like I'm some sort of spoilsport, and I don't have an L.A.P.D. clue what sport I'm spoiling. I'm only—"

"Oh, it's not your fault. Really. Sorry about that. It's just my bloody—"

"Stop whining, Potney. Whining's unattractive, even when your whine sounds like Kenneth Branagh eating frozen strawberries with a silver fork. Just tell me specifically what's on your burner. What's this 'end of time' stuff? 'Interviewing the end of time'? Sun got to you? Sun and gin? Mad dogs and Englishmen syndrome?"

Gradually Smithe was returning to his natural hue. A weariness moved into his smooth, shiny face like a retired midwestern farmer moving into a flamingo beach hotel. He shrugged his ursine shoulders and flicked, halfheartedly, his cigarette into the bug-gnawed weeds. "Never mind." He sighed. "Load of flapdoodle, that."

"Flapdoodle?!" Switters grinned incredulously, and with a kind of sarcastic delight.

"Yes. Bosh. Nonsense," explained Smithe. His tone was defensive.

"I know what flapdoodle means. I just wasn't aware that anybody under the age of ninety-five still used the term. Even in Merry Olde."

"Don't mock."

"So, flapdoodle, is it? Why didn't you say so in the first place? I happen to have a soft spot for flapdoodle. And if you toss in a pinch of the old codswallop or balderdash, why, you could get me really enthralled."

"Don't mock."

"Not mocking, Pot. Maybe we should find a patch of shade someplace and talk this over."

"If you're serious."

Switters was humoring the ethnographer, catering to his agitation, but at the same time he *was* a wee bit intrigued, he couldn't help himself. "Flapdoodle," he practically sang, as they made their way to the covered side entrance of the nearby infirmary. "Makes the world go 'round."

The Boquichicos infirmary's side entrance functioned, somewhat arbitrarily, as an emergency entrance. Bodies emptying from machete wounds or inflating from snakebite were admitted through it. The front or main entrance was reserved for those with aches, coughs, fevers, or one or more of the thirty or so parasites that could bore, burrow, squirm, swim, or wriggle into the human organism in a place such as this, and that contributed substantially to the region's reputation for vivid superfluity. (A time was approaching when there would be an argument over exactly which one of those entrances, side or front, was the proper one through which to admit an immobilized Switters, but that unpleasant quandary was still a few days away.)

A short path of flagstones led, from nowhere in particular, to the side door. Above the walkway was a narrow, thatched roof, supported by whitewashed poles. It was beneath that roof that Switters and Smithe took refuge, at first from the sun and, no more than five minutes later, from the rain; for scarcely had Smithe commenced to expound upon the Nacanaca, the Kandakandero chap, and the request to borrow Maestra's parrot, than a few guppy-sized waterdrops began to dash themselves against the dusty earth or splat with a timid thump against the platterlike leaves of thick green plants. Quickly there was a population explosion such as was entirely appropriate in a Catholic country, and the progenitor drops multiplied and geometrized into a blinding, deafening horde.

At the onset of the torrent, Switters pulled a scrap of cocktail napkin from his pocket, wrote upon it, *I.O.U. my bottom dollar,* and handed it matter-of-factly to Potney, who blinked at the message, folded it absentmindedly in a big rosy fist, raised his voice against the downpour, and went on with his narration.

On the pretext of keeping Sailor Boy dry, Inti had joined the two white men under the roof. The *Virgin* crew and the Nacanacan delegation remained out in the rain, which had grown so dense it turned them into silver silhouettes, though they stood but a dozen yards away. The Indians seemed nonplussed by the soaking they were getting, and Smithe, who admittedly had the more comfortable position, was virtually oblivious to the weather, as well. "Celebrate it or ignore it," Switters had maintained, and now he found himself surprised and somewhat shamed that others so easily practiced what he preached.

That, then, was the setting for Smithe's impartation, an unusual if not outright bizarre account, which shall be summarized in the paragraphs that follow; summarized because to re-create it, to reproduce it verbatim, isn't merely unnecessary, it could be construed as an abuse of both the reader's patience and posterior. That such abuse can sometimes be rewarding—consider *Finnegans Wake* or the church-pew ass-numbing that leads to genital excitation—is beside the point. Or ought to be.

R. Potney Smithe first came to Boquichicos in 1992. His aim had been to conduct ethnographic fieldwork among the Nacanaca, a wild tribe that had been "pacified" by Peruvian government anthropologists in the mid-1980s as a precautionary measure for the new town that authorities were about to establish, and then semi-civilized by contact with that town and its imported values. The Nacanaca were a transitional people, no longer feral but not quite tame, and were in danger of abandoning, forgetting, or being robbed of their traditional manners and ways. Christian missionaries were doing all they could, naturally, to assist in that dispossession. Smithe's purpose was to catalogue as many of the old customs and beliefs as possible before they disappeared. It was fulfilling work.

Alas, even while he immersed himself up to his skimpy beige eyebrows in Nacanacan culture, or what was left of it, he felt the hot point of his interest slowly, unintentionally, even unhappily, shifting to another tribe, a people with whom he had no direct communication; who, indeed, he'd never glimpsed except as shadows gliding silently among other shadows in the forest, a phantom race whose magic and indomitability held a great influence over the Nacanaca and, eventually, over Potney, himself. Kandakandero.

The principal Nacanaca village was a mile east of Boquichicos, on the opposite side of the river. It was on high ground, close to good fishing holes. However, its *chácara*—its garden—was located across the stream on the Boquichicos side, but several miles deeper into the jungle. Oddly enough, in an environment so relentlessly profuse in vegetation, good garden plots were few and far between. The jungle topsoil was as thin as varnish, and although immense trees had learned how to utilize it to staggering advantage, cassava, gourds, peppers, and other cultivated crops were there akin to orphaned children, whose thin gruel was watered down a bit more each year until it no longer provided the sustenance necessary for life. Biological and/or geological accidents sometimes produced rare pockets of fecundity, however, and such was the case with the Nacanacan chácara. It was quite possibly the largest, most perennially fertile garden patch in the Peruvian Amazon.

Some said this chácara had once "belonged" to the Kandakandero or, at least, that they had tended it for generations, only to abandon it when oil exploration and an influx of outsiders caused them to fade ever farther into the forest: the Kandakandero had not suffered Boquichicos gladly. Others claimed that the chácara had always been cultivated by Nacanaca and that the fiercer Kandakandero simply forced the Nacanaca to share its bounty, as if exacting tribute. In any event, Smithe knew from firsthand experience that once each month, on the new moon, a delegation of Kandakandero braves would show up at the garden to have their baskets filled with produce by compliant Nacanaca.

"Whether charity or extortion, I wouldn't know," said Smithe, "but I do know they come only at night, when there is little moon, and that there's a kind of 'way station' a few miles farther into the bush, a lodge where they remain overnight or occasionally longer in order to perform certain rituals having to do with the newly acquired produce. Nacanaca elders often participate in those ceremonies as invited guests, and finally, I, myself, after two solid years of jungle diplomacy. . . . Worth the bother? Well, it's a show that would strike any Christian as dreadfully malodorous, to be sure; but I'd already developed a tolerance for pagan proclivities; some such immunity is required in my profession. Yes. Um. What separates these jejune jollifications from others I've witnessed, either in person or on film, is that they're presided over by the Kandakandero's witchman, their shaman: a most remarkable chap."

"Yeah, so I've heard," said Switters. "That's the buzz. And what, pray tell, is so damned remarkable about him?"

Smithe didn't answer right away. He stared for a while at the rippling wallpaper of rain, and when at last he spoke, he could barely be heard above its din. "It's his head, you see."

"Did you say 'head'? What about his head?"

"Its shape." The Englishman abruptly, inexplicably, beamed. "His head," he said, louder now, almost triumphantly, "his head is a pyramid."

Switters had been around the block. He had even, one might say, been around the block within the block within the block within the block (depending upon his or her own experience, the reader will or will not know what this suggests). Aware that the world was a very weird place, he was no more prone to automatically scoff at unusual information than he was disposed to unquestioning acceptance. (The narrow, nononsense skeptic is every bit as naive as the breezy-brained New Age believer.) Nevertheless, Switters's open-mindedness was sorely tested by Potney's report, especially when the anthropologist insisted that the head he was describing did not merely suggest some vague outline of a pyramid, that it was neither a variation of hydrocephalus nor a particularly pronounced example of Down's syndrome, but actually *was* a pyramid (which was to say, a quadrilateral mass having smooth, steeply sloping sides meeting at a pointed apex), and in every other way except its shape, constituted a healthy, functioning human noggin.

"Entirely literal, old boy, I almost regret to say. Wretchedly literal." Smithe paused to light a cigarette, sending a plump pillow of smoke off to be drilled into feathery oblivion by the numberless bullets of the rain. "Yes. But if you knew your Peruvian ethnology and whatnot, you'd know that this chap's pyramid head is not completely without precedent. Not in the high Andes, at any rate."

Whereupon Smithe informed Switters of the occasional practice among certain Andean Indians of strapping boards to the soft heads of infants, molding them over time into cones that mirrored the contours of the volcanos that loomed on their horizons and that they worshiped as gods. Such sculpting of the skull—literally re-creating man in gods' image—was common enough to have been well documented, and while contemporary Kandakandero had no physical contact whatsoever with malformed Andean volcano-worshipers, one could not rule out an interchange in centuries past. Stories, moreover, had wings. Also, and Smithe would speak more of this later, the Kandakandero seemed to have the ability to access information, events, images, et cetera from great distances, a notion that failed to shock Switters because the CIA had once experimented with a similar psychic technique (under the term *remote viewing*), and several of the angels had become quite adept at it before opposition from irate Christian hillbillies in Congress had shut the project down.

There was doubt in Potney's mind, however, that End of Time's pyramid head was a copycat creation. At least, not entirely so. "I suspect DDT played a part in it. At the beginning."

"DDT? In the Amazon?"

"Oh my, yes. You Yanks mightn't fling your poison about at home any longer, but that jolly well hasn't stopped you from shipping it abroad. Especially to the unsuspecting undeveloped. Peru reeks of it. Even back here, I'm afraid."

"Ain't no weevils fattening they little selves on Nacanaca vegetables?"

"Wouldn't think so, although the chácara's entomological interlopers aren't the primary target, nor are malarial mosquitoes. DDT arrives here from Pucallpa in five-gallon drums. The government issues it to the Nacanaca, who trade it to the Ka'daks for hides and potents, or else the Ka'daks simply bully it from them. Whatever. Both tribes use it for fishing."

Smithe described a scene in which Indians pour five gallons of pesticide into a small river, just above a rapids or a waterfall, then stroll downstream to effortlessly scoop killed fish out of the eddies.

DDT as trade-good fish poison was finding its way into the jungle years before Boquichicos was settled, and congenital deformity was thought to have increased as a result, though there was no scientific proof of it. Smithe's theory was that End of Time had come into the world slightly mutated, due to maternal consumption of contaminated fish. The Kandakandero had taken his affliction as a sign of divine favor and a portent of supernatural abilities, and immediately consecrated him to witchwork. Before he began his active apprenticeship, while he was still a baby, the local shaman had placed his pointy little head in a series of progressively larger mahogany presses (Switters thought of that old-fashioned pressed tennis racket of his, heavy and wooden, that Suzy, with her modern lightweight graphite number, had made such fun of), deliberately and dramatically accentuating its pyramidal tendency.

It was only a hypothesis. It could have been something altogether different, altogether unimaginable. What did seem conclusive, however, was that by the time End of Time was a teenager, he had ousted his people's reigning shaman and assumed the man's duties. And now, at age twenty-five or thereabouts, he was regarded (by that handful of souls aware of his existence) as either the most feared and mysterious member of the most feared and mysterious tribe in that part of South America or as an addled medical oddity cashing in on the small-change benefits of primitive superstition.

If Switters's brow resembled the coils in an electric heater, it wasn't so much due to lingering doubt over the veracity of Smithe's story as to his effort to remember what his grandmother had told him about pyramid power. According to Maestra, and she had it on good authority, there was something about the configuration, the dimensional relationships of a pyramid's angles, the way it crystallized in static form the essence of dynamic geometry, that caused it to focus, laserlike, an electromagnetic or other atmospheric force (perhaps that energy the Chinese called *chi*), concentrating it in a relatively small, prescribed area. Switters recalled something about razor blades being sharpened and fruit kept from spoiling by pyramid-focused rays. That, come to think of it, was the rationale behind Sailor's customized cage. He supposed that if a pyramid really could hone steel and preserve peaches, a pyramid-shaped head might have a pretty entertaining effect on the brain inside it—and it would probably be no great exaggeration to describe as "most remarkable," a "chap" with such a brain.

"So," said Switters, "these Nacanaca boys believe their ferocious cousins would get a kick out of Sailor's cage because it's shaped like the head of their grand boohoo?"

Smithe nodded. "Something like that, yes. Far be it from me to speak for the atavistic mind." He paused to inhale and exhale a blue-tinted wad of smoke. "There *is* a bit more to it. When your bird blurted out that number about people needing to relax—clever turn, that: your tutelage?—it struck a chord. This End of Time chap, he has some novel ideas. A philosophy, one might be tempted to call it. Something beyond the usual mumbo jumbo, at any rate. Relaxation, at least in the Nacanaca understanding of the concept, fits rather neatly with it, I suppose. So, you see, our blokes here have concluded that End of Time must have a supernatural connection with this cage and its occupant, and while that's a load of bosh, I daresay he *would* be impressed. It's likely he'd grant you an audience, which would provide you with scrapbook fodder of the most exotic order, and me with the possibility of riding in on your coattails."

"You've socialized with him previously?"

"Yes. Three years ago. At the way station, for thirty-six hours. Bloody bugger really put me through it. Can't imagine why I'd want to go back—except that it's, well, *haunted* me ever since. And there's the chance I might turn it into something. Original yet academically rigorous. That first encounter went rather awry, I'm afraid. Crossed the line. Um. I'm no Carlos Castaneda."

Switters grinned. "Of course you aren't." *You're one of those people,* he thought, *who want to go to Heaven without dying. Cowardice in the name of objectivity is fairly characteristic of academics, especially in Merry Olde.* But he didn't wish to get into that. Instead, he inquired as to the nature of the living pyramid's so-called novel ideas. Considering the young shaman's name—an inexact translation by Smithe and Fer-de-lance, it turned out, of a virtually unpronounceable Kandakandero word—he guessed his notions must have something to do with eschatology, with apocalypticism, with time.

"Oh, there may be a bubble of that in the keg. I didn't bung into it. Not my end of the field, you see. Not that. Nor the other, either, honestly, though it may be yours. Our chap, you see, is rather obsessed with . . . with gaiety."

Gaiety? Potney Smithe's explanation was a rickety trellis of sober anthropological observations, lathed in the fine mill of British understatement, but rattled by occasional gusts of alcoholic verbosity, and, of course, splintered here and there by cracks from Switters. Once again, we shall attempt summation.

Kandakandero had always referred to themselves as "the Real People." Theirs was ethnocentrism in its unadulterated form. Other tribes, other races were not merely deemed to be inferior humans, they were relegated in the Ka'dak mind to the status of animals or ghosts. Then End of Time came along. It's very true, he told his clan, that we are superior to other Indians because we have stronger magic and purer ways. As for white men, they are so helpless and stupid they could not survive in the forest for a single moon. Yet the white man can do wondrous things that we cannot.

Fly, for example. For decades, air traffic between Lima and Belém or to and from Europe had passed over that area of the Peruvian jungle roamed by the seminomadic Ka'daks, and more recently, small planes out of Pucallpa had been buzzing around. White men also had shiny boxes that they attached to the sterns of their canoes to make them swim faster than dolphins, and they possessed weapons so powerful and accurate they reduced hunting and warfare to child's play. In Boquichicos they had motionless boxes that churned out more music than a tribe could make, other boxes that cooked meat and yucca without a spark of fire. (The Ka'daks were well informed about what transpired in Boquichicos, though whether they spied on the town from the forest, accessed it psychically, or simply relied on Nacanaca gossip, Smithe wasn't prepared to say.) End of Time recognized that white men were a threat to his people's habitat, that eventually these pale weaklings with their noisy magic would dominate the forest world and all within it, including the heretofore invincible Ka'daks. White men were the new Real People, the spirits obviously were favoring them. Why?

Over and over again, End of Time drank his potions, snorted his snuffs, entered his trances, rubbed his portable pyramid. He questioned sundry Nacanaca and once sat for five days in a treetop observing, undetected, goings-on in Boquichicos. What was it about these men (aside from a hideous complexion that no god could possibly find pleasing) that made them so different from the older and once wiser Kandakandero? (No fool, End of Time could distinguish between superficial and fundamental differences.) Roughly speaking, they ate, drank, smoked, and slept the same. They shat, pissed, and fucked the same. So what was the white man's secret?

Finally, one day, it hit him like a blow dart. The big secret was laughter.

Amazonian Indians, in general, tended to be somber, and the Ka'daks were especially severe. Kandakandero did not laugh. They did not even smile. Moreover, they had never laughed or smiled. The very concept was alien to them. Smithe suggested that for "the Real People," life simply might be too "real": too terrible, too short, too arduous, too . . . vivid. Whatever the reason, you might as realistically expect a Ka'dak to shout "$E=mc^2$" as to chuckle. No giggle had ever, in all of history, chased its tail around one of their campfires, no smirk had ever cracked their war paint, no guffaw had ever taken up where a belch left off, no titter or tee-hee had scratched for them its crystal fleas. The roar of civilized laughter might strike them as ridiculous, but it wouldn't strike them as funny. The Ka'daks didn't know from funny.

In a radical break with both instinct and inclination, End of Time tried to teach himself to smile. He practiced alone, monitoring his progress in a reflecting pool. The first time he smiled for his gathered clansmen, he left them so astonished, so awestruck that half fell, trembling, to their knees, and the rest ran away and hid in the bushes. When he commenced to experiment with laughing, nobody was able to sleep for months. And when he insisted that others learn the art of grinning and chortling, the whole tribe nearly had a nervous breakdown.

The shaman persevered, however, even as it occurred to him that his glee was hollow, mechanical, and contrived. He sensed that an attitude adjustment must be required, that the perpetually piercing level of intensity that characterized the Kandakandero might need to be softened, toned down. (Real People of the world, relax!) Around the occasion of Potney Smithe's visit, End of Time was just coming to the realization that white men didn't laugh as a chore or on schedule or to please the gods, that the mystical hee-haw was not self-induced but had to be provoked; that some external happenstance, frequently invisible, aroused laughter in them.

At their initial meeting, with Fer-de-lance as interpreter, Smithe labored to help the medicine man comprehend the concept of humor. "Nothing approaching the subtler moods of irony, naturally, but the more direct, earthy approach of juvenile mockery. Of course, much of juvenile humor is sexual and scatological, and to the Ka'dak mind there's nothing the least bit funny about bodily functions. Their taboos are of a different order. You might as well ask them to snigger at the sky."

Still, Smithe felt, End of Time made some progress in the area of lightheartedness, though he doubted there was any such thing as a joke comprehensible to him or his fellows. "The same could be said of the religiously fundamental and the politically doctrinaire," piped in Switters.

In repayment for Smithe's having assisted him in his uphill pursuit

of gaiety, the misshapen shaman offered to meet with him again the following day, and this next time Smithe could ask the questions. Moreover, Smithe would be allowed to actually look at him, face-to-face: during their first encounter, the witchman had concealed himself behind a woven grass screen. Not surprisingly, there was a catch. Before Smithe could be permitted to gaze upon the fabled pyramid head, the impure Englishman would have to prove himself worthy to a collection of guides, overlords, supervisors, kibitzers, and hecklers from the Other Side.

"I was recklessly unscientific, but it was a lapse I believed I could turn to good account. Um. I knew a thing or two about Amazonian hallucinogens, yage, ayahuasca and the lot, but my objective knowledge fell lamentably short of the subjective experience. Oh, Christ, yes!"

"Pot! You modest old fox. Congratulations. You're a Castaneda, after all."

Reddening and sputtering, the anthropologist seemed to swallow a bellyful of smoke. "No, no, far from it. I sampled the sorcerer's wares, but I didn't sign on for an apprenticeship. Nothing of the sort. I'm prepared to admit that I may previously have been suffering an unjustifiable complacency concerning the limits of reality, but that territory of . . . of terrors and senseless beauty is not any countryside I long to tramp. As it was, I indulged in behavior of which my colleagues strongly disapprove, and, in the end, I defeated my own purpose."

"How so?"

It had been an extended ordeal of vomit and hallucination, a long night spent surfing alternating waves of horror and ecstasy—and in the shaky morning when End of Time had finally showed himself, pyramid head and all, Smithe (less overwhelmed by the sight of that capitate curiosity than he might normally have been) found himself somehow disinclined, even unable, to interrogate the medicine man along the lines that he had so carefully prepared. "I was a disgrace to my profession," Smithe contended. "I asked all the wrong questions."

"What sort of things did you ask?"

"Never mind. Cosmological questions, you might call them. Issues that swam to the surface as I was being dashed about on that *yopo* ocean. Load of bosh, really."

And that was all he would say.

Five months prior to Switters's arrival, Smithe had returned to Boquichicos at his own expense, hoping to get another crack at the

phenomenally pated Indian. Repeatedly rebuffed—End of Time refused to encourage an atmosphere of familiarity with any outsider—
Smithe now dumped his eggs in Switters's basket. Should the Yank be
granted an audience, maybe, just maybe, Smithe might tag along; and
if not, then at the very least, Switters could put in a word on his behalf.
Both his university and his wife were vexed with him, but he couldn't
turn back. Not just yet. He gave indications of being, over End of
Time, in a rough equivalent of the amorous stupor that Switters was in
over Suzy. Thus, out of empathy as much as curiosity, and against that
paralyzer, that strangler of enlightened progress known as "better
judgment," Switters consented to let a ragtag gaggle of Nacanaca carry
off Sailor Boy into the jungle.

It was still raining, but halfheartedly now, and in a matter of minutes a hard shock of sunshine would blast their eyes and zap newly
formed mud flows into charcoal dust and solar cement. They stepped
out from under the infirmary awning. A straggler, a solitary traveler,
the last and final raindrop of the morning—unapologetically tardy,
even arrogant, as if on an independent mission its meekly conforming
confederates could not possibly appreciate or understand—landed on
the back of Switters's neck and rolled languidly, defiantly down his
spine. He took it as an omen, though of what he was not precisely
clear.

There had been a new moon on the previous evening, and both
Smithe and the Nacanaca held the opinion that End of Time would
still be at the way station, the ceremonial lodge. As they watched
the Indians scamper onto the forest trail with the pyramid cage and
its somewhat bewildered occupant, Smithe rubbed his hammy paws
together and said, "Smashing! A smashing turn of events. One dares to
nourish one's hopes, whether vainly or not one will soon enough find
out. It would take the likes of you or me the better part of a day to huff
and puff our way to that squalid lodge, but these blokes can cover the
distance in a couple of hours. They'll be back by dusk, I'll wager. By
the way, old man, what's the meaning of this I.O.U. you've thrust upon
my person?"

Leaving R. Potney Smithe to his customary stool in the hotel bar,
Switters climbed to his room, where he activated his computer in satellite mode. It was guilt and little else—guilt over the strange turn he'd
permitted the parrot assignment to take—that prompted him to want
to e-mail Maestra. Alas, he couldn't think of what he might say to her.

Certainly not the truth. Awaiting inspiration, he checked his own mailbox, the personal not the official one. There were three messages there, the first from his grandmother, herself.

> How come no progress report? Shouldn't you be home by
> now? I have a gut feeling you're up to no good. The
> museum's director of acquisitions came by today to see our
> Matisse and nearly peed his pants. Word to the wise, buddy.
> Get in touch.

The second message was from Bobby Case, apparently still in Alaska, piloting the spy plane known as the U2 and a more recent version called the TR1.

> The 49th state is a harsh environment for salty dogs. Girls too old, too
> grungy, or their daddies too well armed. Company continues to ignore my
> requests for transfer. O whither, O dither. I must be demented but I miss
> you, podner. Trust you're up to no good.
> Bababadalgharaghtakamminarronnkonnbronntonnerronn-
> tuonnthunntrovarrhounawnskawntoohoohoordenenthurnuk!

That last was the only real news in the message, implying as it did that Bobby had now gotten as far as the fourth sentence in *Finnegans Wake*. He deserved a congratulatory note on his headway—provided, of course, he hadn't skipped.

E-missive No. 3 proved to be from—be still, dear pulse!—none other than the baby-fatted skeleton in his closet, the hormonal soprano in his choir stall, the lollipop Lorelei on his river rock, the moon over his barnyard, the puss up his tree, the baba-toohoohoo-denenthurnuk! of his heart. And it read:

> Don't forget you promised to help me with my term paper.
> Jesus loves you.
> Suzy

A libido torpedo? Not by any means. Some men, true enough, would have been discouraged by Suzy's note, devoid as it was of the faintest blush of romantic undertone, but its very simplicity and pragmatic directness, its very *chasteness*, if you will, served only to amplify Switters's ardor. Suddenly dizzy with desire, he toppled onto the bed and commenced to moan.

Likewise amplified were his misgivings about having permitted a befuddled anthropologist to entangle him in some highly unpromising business involving a deformed witch doctor. If only he had discharged his duty as planned, had delivered Sailor to a suitable retirement community and taped the procedure as the parrot crossed the threshold of geriatric autonomy, he might, in a few hours, be making his way homeward to skittish teases, furtive squeezes, and who could guess how much more. Moans of inflamed appetite were interspersed with moans of regret.

In contrast to so many of his contemporaries, however, Switters failed to find in prolonged lamentation an appealing form of recreation. It wasn't so much that Switters was above self-indulgence but, rather, that he preferred to indulge himself in merrier ways. Thus, in not much more time than it took a gecko to circle the walls of his room, disappearing finally into the rust-streaked, concrete shower stall, he had willfully relieved himself of the burden of remorse (by simply refusing to shoulder it: *people of the world, relax*), and shortly thereafter, lightened his erotic load, as well (by means that shall not here be discussed).

He lay, naked and perspiring, upon his bed, watching an inactive ceiling fan use electricity deprivation as an excuse not to knock its brains out against the heavy air of the room; and, with a calmer mind, he conceded that it might well be for the better that he was delaying his reappearance in Sacramento, although in temporarily substituting a visit to the Kandakandero for a visit to his mother's, he suspected that he was merely choosing the frying pan ahead of the fire. He smiled at this, as if recognizing in himself a familiar trait, a lifelong willingness to take risks in order to experiment with a different set of circumstances; and when he caught himself smiling, he tried to visualize what the smiling lessons of the wild Ka'daks must look like.

If End of Time's thesis, that civilized man's powers were attributable to laughter, failed to strike Switters as unduly outlandish, it was probably because it was not so far removed from a favorite idea of Maestra's: her theory of the missing link.

"What is it," Maestra had asked quite rhetorically, "that separates human beings from the so-called lower animals? Well, as I see it, it's exactly one half-dozen significant things: Humor, Imagination, Eroticism—as opposed to the mindless, instinctive mating of glowworms or raccoons—Spirituality, Rebelliousness, and Aesthetics, an appreciation of beauty for its own sake.

"Now," she'd gone on to say, "since those are the features that define a human being, it follows that the extent to which someone is lacking in those qualities is the extent to which he or she is less than human. *Capisce?* And in those cases where the defining qualities are virtually nonexistent, well, what we have are entities that are north of the animal kingdom but south of humanity, they fall somewhere in between, they're our missing links."

In his grandmother's opinion, the missing link of scientific lore was neither extinct nor rare. "There're more of them, in fact, than there are of us, and since they actually seem to be multiplying, Darwin's theory of evolution is obviously wrong." Maestra's stand was that missing links ought to be treated as the equal of full human beings in the eyes of the law, that they should not suffer discrimination in any usual sense, but that their writings and utterances should be generally disregarded and that they should never, ever be placed in positions of authority.

"That could be problematic," Switters had said, straining, at the age of twenty, to absorb this rant, "because only people who, you know, *lack* those six qualities seem to ever run for any sort of office."

Maestra thoroughly agreed, although she was undecided whether it was because full-fledged humans simply had more interesting things to do with their lives than marinate them in the torpid waters of the public trough or if it was because only missing links, in the reassuring blandness of their banality, could expect to attract the votes of a missing link majority. In any event, of the six qualities that distinguished the human from the subhuman, both grandmother and grandson agreed that Imagination and Humor were probably the most crucial.

The finer points of their reasoning were vague to him now. There was something, to be sure, about how only those with imagination could envision improvements and only those with a sense of humor could savor a good laugh when those improvements backfired or turned to crap. The idea of focusing on the laugh itself—on the grounds that of all our different expressions of beingness, only laughter was pure enough, complex enough, free enough, endowed with enough mystery of meaning, to accurately reflect the soul—surely did not occur to them. But now Switters could see that while it was extremely unlikely that End of Time would ever be able to differentiate between, say, wise laughter and the yuks of jackasses braying at refinements they were too coarse to comprehend, the young shaman, nevertheless, might have stumbled on to something. Wondering what Maestra would make of it all, and thinking, though not for the first time, how in the CIA, the terms *cowboy* and *missing link* could easily be interchangeable, he fell asleep.

He was awakened about three hours later by a politely urgent rapping at his door. Employing his Panama hat as a fig leaf, he cracked the door to find R. Potney Smithe, breathing hard from the two flights of stairs and bubbling over with gin and news.

Word had reached Boquichicos—whether by drumbeat, smoke
signal, or telepathy, Smithe couldn't discern—that the Nacanaca delegation was already on its way back from the way station. It had left the
parrot and its cage behind. Switters voiced alarm, but Smithe brushed
aside his protests.

"End of Time will see you," Smithe announced. "The bloody
bugger won't see me, but he'll see you. I say, old boy, you look enormously ornamental in that hat. Um. Yes. In relation to the matter at
hand, however, you'd best get clothed. He's sent for you. He wants to
see you *tonight*."

And so it came to pass that at approximately four o'clock on that sultry
November afternoon, Switters walked into the jungle. He was wearing
his last clean white suit (Potney could not persuade him otherwise)
and a tie-dyed T-shirt (Potney agreed that the Ka'daks might take to
its variegated colors). This garb was accessorized with rubber boots,
Panama hat, and a belt of khaki webbing, into which, hidden by the
jacket, the Beretta had been handily stuck. Completing the ensemble
was a day pack (Potney lent it) containing dry socks, a flashlight, mosquito root, salt tablets, migraine tablets, drinking water, a notebook,
pencils, the camcorder, matches, and a snake-bite kit. "And would
you fancy a tin of biscuits?" Potney had asked as they stuffed the little
rucksack, but Switters could not entertain the notion of a biscuit
unadorned by red-eye gravy.

In addition to the five tireless Indians who would lead and escort
him, he was accompanied by Fer-de-lance. The product of a Nacanaca
mother and a Spanish petroleum geologist, Fer-de-lance (then called
Pedro) had been removed by Jesuit missionaries at the age of nine from
the Nacanaca village where he was born and taken to Lima to be educated. The Jesuits had been correct in their assessment of the boy's
intelligence. Their mistake, perhaps, was in exposing such native keen-
ness to too much uncensored information, for in college, he began to
seriously question the Catholic faith, eventually dropping out of
classes to join the Sendero Luminoso. Gradually he had become disen-
chanted with leftist dogmatism, as well, and returned to Boquichicos
to reconnect with his roots.

"That's often a false path, too," muttered Switters, referring to a
contemporary U.S. penchant for tracking down one's ethnic identity
and then binding oneself to its trappings and traditions, no matter how
irrelevant, rather than, say, liberating and transforming oneself by
inventing an entirely fresh identity. Nevertheless, he welcomed Fer-

de-lance—animal trader and aspiring shaman—for his linguistic abilities: English, Spanish, Nacanacan, and even Kandakanderoan. "He
should make an ideal interpreter for me," said Switters, "as long as
he doesn't get sidetracked by any damn snakes."

The plan was for Smithe to hike in as far as the chácara on the
following day. From the garden plot, where Smithe had Nacanacan
acquaintances, they would return together to Boquichicos, unless Switters was able to convince End of Time to grant the Englishman another
interview.

"You *will* take good notes, won't you?" Smithe almost pleaded. "In
the event he continues to reject me. I must have something to show for
this folly, besides a possible sacking and a probable divorce." Sincerely, yet with a degree of embarrassment, as if it were comportment
upon which his peers might frown, he commenced to pump Switters's
hand. "Can't thank you enough, old boy. Can't thank you enough."

"Forget it, pal. Errands 'r' me. Just make sure my Pucallpa mariners
don't weigh anchor without me. I'm needed Stateside on the double,
help a young friend with her homework."

With that, Switters turned and strode into the rain forest, van-
ishing almost immediately in a sea of titanic trees, a jumpy mosaic of
light and shadow, a tunnel of filtered sunshine and violet penumbras, a
funhouse with dripping green walls and slippery linoleum, a leaf-happy
music hall set vibrating by sudden unpredictable animal soloists and
steadily thrumming insect choirs. He quickly became a minor figure in
a dense, tattered tapestry that was shagged with Shavian whiskers
of moss, loosely stitched with long, loopy threads of vine, and fluttered by spirits and unseen Indian sentinels; while here, there, and
sometimes everywhere this rank, spooky tableau visually popped with
blubber-lipped frogs, festive sparks of bird flitter, and orchids the size
of boxing gloves; with monkey shines, butterfly stunts, phosphors,
fruits, belted white worms that resembled the severed fingers of the
Michelin tire man, and lumps of suspect nougat that could be toad or
toadstool, either one. Yes, and as if layering on yet another dimension,
this whole scene seemed scented by syrupy petal pies and bubbling
ponds of decaying plant muck, a nose-puzzling mixture of contradictory aromas (floral to fecal) perfectly befitting an environment where
cure-all juices coursed alongside poisonous saps, where the gorgeous
and the marvelous repeatedly alternated with the hideous and the dire,
where brimming Life and pertinacious Death held hands at the chloro-
phyll cinema; where Heaven and Hell intermingled as they did at no
other place on earth, except, perhaps, in the daily emotions of poor
fools in love.

This wasn't quite what Switters had had in mind when he told

Maestra he needed to get away from cities for a while. Nevertheless, he went forward. With the air of a man trying to eat the coating off a chocolate-covered grasshopper, he walked into that very forest.

He would not walk out.

r. potney smithe was lounging in the shade beside the garden patch, swatting flies, smoking cigarettes, and attempting to coax residual gin molecules out of his own saliva, when he was summoned to the ceremonial lodge by a Nacanaca runner. It was midmorning, and he'd been at the chácara since the previous afternoon.

The summons surprised him. At first, Switters's lengthy absence had made him hopeful, but as the night passed, and then the morning, he'd lost faith. Whatever was transpiring at that crude structure he called a way station—a station on the way from a primitive yucca patch to Christ knew what—there was scant cause to believe it might advance *his* fortunes in any considerable direction. Both the mysterious American (Ediberto at the hotel said he was a tractor salesman: not bloody likely!) and the grotesque shaman had their own special approaches to existence, and in those approaches, neither the traditions upon which Smithe had been nurtured nor the discipline in which he'd been schooled held any sway. One of those blokes was as indifferent as the other. But now he'd been sent for, and if not to interview End of Time, then what? Hope swelled anew, it could be said, though to Smithe, the phrase "swelled anew" always suggested the recurrence of a hemorrhoidal tribulation.

The trail was overgrown, and in places, slick and steep. It took Smithe more than an hour to reach the lodge, a three-sided sort of raised longhouse, supported by poles and blackened by smoke. Upon his arrival, he found that End of Time was gone. The place, in fact, was deserted, except for Switters, who lay peacefully asleep in Fer-de-lance's hammock, slung between two poles, and a couple of Nacanaca bucks who seemed to be watching over him.

Disheartened and a bit perplexed, the anthropologist climbed the unsteady ladder to the main platform and seated himself on a mat beside the hammock. "Where are the Kandakandero?" he asked in Nacanacan.

"Gone," the Indians answered.

"Coming back?"

"No."

"Where's Fer-de-lance?"

"Went to see great snake." They were referring to an anaconda, reputedly forty feet in length, that was said to inhabit a pool a few miles from there. Fer-de-lance frequently went looking for it, though his intent—to capture it, kill it, or commune with it—had never been disclosed.

"Has Señor Switters been sleeping long?" Forgetting himself, he asked this in Spanish, then rephrased it in Nacanacan.

Before either Indian could reply, there came a grunt from the hammock. The device commenced ever so slightly to swing. "Meaningless question, Pot," said Switters. His voice was relaxed, and so thick with sleep he could barely be understood. He yawned. He stretched. The hammock pitched, as if upon a gentle tide. "You know as well as I that duration is naught but an illusion around this here juju parlor." He yawned again.

"An end to time, you mean?"

"There's that, for damn sure. Although Fer-de-lance is of the opinion that you two may have mistranslated our witchman's name."

"Oh?" said Smithe.

Switters didn't elaborate. Instead, he yawned yet again and rubbed his eyes. "Whatever his name is, he's some piece of work."

"Unique."

"The most misused word in the English language, *unique*, but I believe you've employed it immaculately. The dude is genuinely one of a kind. Even without his medicines."

"He gave you ayahuasca?"

"Yeah, and something extra in the bargain. Some kind of powder he blew up my nose with a reed."

"A wild turkey bone, actually. But long and hollow, in that respect like a reed."

"Okay. As an ethnographer, you'd know such things. But, Jesus . . . ! I'm no stranger to mind-altering substances, Potney—keep that under your hat if you don't mind—but the stuff your man dispenses takes the cake, the pie, the strudel, the whole damn pâtisserie. Whew! Baby! It just keeps peeling away layers, one after the other, for hours."

"Yes."

"I mean, deep meditation can do that, too, except in meditation, what's peeling away are your own thought patterns. Worries, anxieties, clichés, bright ideas, ambitions, plans, mental and emotional hangups, all that half-conscious brain litter. You strip the layers away, one by one, until the images grow fainter and fainter and the noise grows quieter and quieter, and *bing!* you arrive at the core, which is naked emptiness, a kind of exhilarating vacuum. But this shit! Each layer is a separate dimension, a new world. They're like landscapes, you travel around inside them. And you're not alone in there, they're *occupied.*"

Smithe nodded. "Did you . . . ? The bulbs?"

"Bulbs. Yeah. That's a good name for them. Shiny copper-colored bulbs. Orbiting the earth. Called themselves masters, overlords."

"Most disquieting. Told me they're in charge of absolutely everything. Run the show."

"Me, too. Afterward, I asked End of Time about it. He off-loaded one of those wicked homemade grins he's been working on and shrugged, 'Oh, they always say that.' Made it sound like they were just big blowhards."

"Boasting."

"Yeah. Mind-fuckers. But who . . . ? Or what . . . ?" Switters fell silent.

"Raises a great many questions, but they're devilishly difficult to formulate."

"Hard to talk about. The whole experience."

"Quite." Smithe produced a silver monogrammed case, from which he withdrew a cigarette. "Impossible to put into words."

"I know what you're saying. But it isn't because words are inadequate. I won't go that far."

"Certain things words can't convey."

"Oh, but they can. Because those things you're referring to are . . . well, if they're not actually made of words or derived from words, at least inhabit words: language is the solution in which they're suspended. Even love ultimately requires a linguistic base."

"All concepts are basically verbal concepts? Now that you mention it, I have heard that theory advanced." Smithe spoke disinterestedly and at the same time anxiously. He hadn't muddied and bloodied himself bushwhacking his way to the lodge in order to sit around arguing semiotics. Only genteel breeding was preventing him from interrupting Switters with an irritated bellow: *Tell me about End of Time!*

"Even if most of our best words have been trivialized, corrupted, eviscerated by the merchandisers, by the marketeers, by the. . . ." Switters broke off. He could feel a rant coming on, but was too tired and, although his outward manner scarcely betrayed it, too shaken to go through with it.

Smithe seized the chance. "Now, tell me about—"

"The point is—" Like James Brown, spent, limp, reeling to the microphone for just one more whoop, Switters momentarily revived himself. "Words can still handle anything we can throw at them, including the kitchen sink. *Finnegans Wake* proved that, if nothing else. It's a matter of usage. If a house is off-plumb and rickety and lets in the wind, you blame the mason, not the bricks."

"Um."

"Our words are up to the job. It's our syntax that's limiting."

"And what's so wrong with our syntax?"

"Well, in the first place, it's too abstract."

"And in the second place?"

"It's too concrete."

In the silence that greeted his pronouncement, Switters snuggled down in the hammock and shut his eyes.

Switters rested for about ten minutes, during which time the Nacanacas descended the ladder and laid some yucca to roast in the embers of the firepit, while Smithe, in agitation, paced the floorboards. When at last Switters reopened what Suzy called his "big-bad-wolf eyes," Smithe strode immediately to his side. "I say, was that a Broadway show tune you were humming just now?"

Caught off guard, Switters nearly let the *Cats* out of the bag. "That was . . . no, couldn't have been. Probably some—some riff from, uh, Zappa or else the, uh, Grateful Dead," he stammered, preserving a secret he shared not even with Bobby Case. "Speaking of which, End of Time—if we're going to persist in calling him that—would make the consummate Deadhead, don't you think? Skull shaped like an Egyptian tomb. Take one of those turkey bones and blow Jerry Garcia's ashes up his nostrils."

Potney Smithe's musical leanings listed sharply in the direction of Vivaldi, but he was grateful (if not yet dead) to find conversation returning to the Kandakandero shaman. "I've not been stimulated overmuch by what I've heard so far. Do tell me what happened when you turned up night before last to join your bird. What was said?"

A great deal had been said, much of it, no doubt, lost in translation, but essentially, as Switters related it, his encounter with End of Time was not greatly dissimilar to Smithe's. The shaman received him from behind a screen, a barrier that could not, however, conceal his delight with the pyramid cage or its occupant. Sailor Boy, for his part, was talking up a storm. Or was he? The customary admonishment, "Peeple of zee wurl, relax!" squawked from behind the screen at thirty-second intervals, and though the message hadn't varied from the familiar in either content or tone, its frequency of transmission was something radically new. Later, Switters realized that the squawks could have been issuing from End of Time himself, Amazonian Indians being famously adept at mimicking bird calls. Perhaps they took turns, even: a man and parrot duet.

"We yakked all night—that Fer-de-lance is a whiz with nuances and complexities—jabbering about the pitfalls of morbidity, about levity versus gravity, struggle versus play, me mostly mouthing other people's ideas, but your *curandero* man contributing some fairly engaging wrinkles of his own. He said, for example, that in order for his people to withstand the assault of the white man, they must fashion shields out of laughter. He means that literally, I think. Speaks of laughter as if it were a force, a physical force or natural phenomenon. And within the realm of laughter, he says, light and darkness merge, no longer existing as separate or distinct conditions. A people who could live in that realm would be free of all of life's dualities. The white man can't do the trick because he lacks the Kandakandero knowledge of the different levels of reality, and so far the Ka'daks can't do it because they lack the buoyancy of the white man's humor. The person who successfully combined the two would move through the world as a 'shadow of light.' Can you picture a shadow of light? A person in whom the luminous and the dark are inseparable? Reminds me a bit of neutral angels, if you're familiar with the term."

"Um. I daresay he's evolved intellectually since I had a go at him."

"For a dude whose brain is stuffed in a pyramid, that's hardly surprising. That laugh of his is starting to get out of control, though. Sounds a lot like Woody Woodpecker. Friend of mine used to cackle like that to amuse the bar girls in Bangkok."

"Indeed? Well, do continue. What else?"

"Ah, well, gee, I don't know. We just kicked that gong around all night, like I said. Then, for breakfast, we ate my grandmother's parrot."

Switters had not eaten Sailor Boy on purpose. At the time, in fact, he wasn't aware that it was Sailor Boy he was eating. The gourdful of thin gray stew contained, so he presumed, the rubbery flesh of an overage chicken. It wasn't until later in the day, after awakening from a four- or five-hour rest, that Fer-de-lance showed him the headdress that, prior to his departure, End of Time had woven from Sailor's feathers. By then, it was too late to retch.

The shaman had eaten the parrot to appropriate its magic. "You're lucky he didn't eat you as well," Fer-de-lance had snarled when Switters expressed outrage. "Who do you think you've been dealing with? Some quaint poseur from central casting?" The parrot stew was served to Switters as a test. "He wanted to see how strong you are," said the mestizo.

There were other tests in line. Fer-de-lance challenged Switters to don the headdress at sunset and go stand alone in the forest. That would be the signal for End of Time to return, whereupon he would reveal himself, pyramid and all, and personally administer to the *gringo blanco* the vision root.

"What was I going to do," asked Switters, "turn tail and run? I'd come this far. My courage was in question. And, besides, I'd yet to lay eyes on the guy. Before curiosity kills it, the cat learns more of the world than a hundred uninquisitive dogs."

Thus, he replaced his Panama hat with poor Sailor's plumage (How would *that* look on video?) and as dusk pressed the dimmer switch, transforming the verdant disorder of the diurnal jungle into a muscular monolith, an enveloping solid throb, a Stonehenge of whispers, a phantom colonnade, he walked gingerly away from the lodge to go stand alone in the gloom. He neither saw nor heard End of Time's approach. Switters was standing there, staring, listening, barely breathing, unable, for some reason, to remember a single lyric to "Send in the Clowns," when he felt something touch his shoulder, causing him to nearly jump over a treetop.

"How did he look?"

"You know how he looks. Like a youngish Amazonian Indian with the skyline of Cairo on his shoulders."

"His facial decoration? What color, what pattern? *Achiote* berry or *tinhorao* bark? His necklace? Bone, feathers, claws, seeds, or teeth? These details are significant."

"For Christ's sake, Pot!"

"You took no notes?" The tone was accusatory.

"Not after that turkey bone went up my snout. I spent the next eight hours riding the quark. Pursued by my own ghost down the Hallways of Always. Hobnobbing with giant metallic cockroaches and transgalactic jive bulbs. You've been there. What do you expect?"

"Yes, but you did agree. . . ."

"The Hallways of Always, pal. One dies in there and is reborn. One doesn't take notes. Come on, Pot. If not watched carefully, you could turn into another tedious anthropologist."

"Impaired while under the influence, but what about prior to and following?"

"Very little of either. And somehow I don't believe 'impaired' is the right word." He paused. "Listen, I'm quite aware of the sort of stuff you're after, and I'm sure that picturesque details by the dozen will come to mind eventually. Right now, my biocomputer's down. I'm. . . . Death and resurrection, not to mention breakfasting on the longtime family pet, can take a lot out of a guy. Okay?" Again, he closed his eyes.

Smithe walked away. Head bowed, nose pointed at the toes that, like fans of pink pickles, spread over the tips of his flip-flops, neck knotted, meaty hands clasped behind his broad back, he paced. *Aware of the sort of stuff I'm after?* he thought. *Not bloody likely.* Smithe, himself, was neither comfortably nor completely aware of the "sort of stuff" he was after. Direct testimony, certainly, yet something as far beyond ordinary field notes as End of Time was beyond Chief Sitting Bull; data that might fuel disquisition and exegesis of an academically pragmatic caliber, that might even make something agreeably quotidian out of the bizarrely exotic, yet would not conceal from the sensitive some flavor of the cosmological rites that had blown most of the patio furniture off his personal lanai. He supposed, in short, that he was searching for planks to bridge a rupture that had widened within him and without, ever since he had so unwisely . . .

"Do you have to sulk like that?" Switters's voice was tired but tough. "If word gets back to End of Time that you're deficient in the category of joie de vivre, he'll—"

"He'll what?" snapped Smithe testily.

"He'll cancel your damn rendezvous."

Smithe halted in mid-stride. His chin withdrew from his chest like a city slicker's hand from a branding iron. "What rendezvous?"

"The one I set up for you."

"Are you ragging me?"

"Potney! If you can't trust a Yank, who can you trust?"

"He's actually agreed to meet?"

"At the next new moon. Be here or be square."

"You're serious. How in the world? . . ."

"All in a night's work."

"For an errand boy?"

"Precisely. Although in the gastrointestinal aftermath of ingesting fricassee à Sailor Boy"—he winced and it was not at all contrived—"I watched the errand I was sent to run, run through me."

The bells of his own jubilation prevented Smithe from hearing this last, which was just as well, regardless that in his elated state he might not have found it egregiously offensive. He was positively thrilled. His pale eyes sparkled, and strong white teeth, heretofore unrevealed, came out of the lipwork. "Bloody marvelous," he crooned. "Bloody marvelous."

Smithe struck a match to the cork-tipped Parliament he'd removed from a case some minutes earlier but not yet lit. "My work concerns itself with what Linton has called 'social heredity,' which, as you might suppose, consists of the learned, socially transmitted habits, customs, morals, laws, arts, crafts, et cetera of whole cultures: tribes, bands, clans, villages. Groups of socially related people, in other words. To focus on a single individual within a group, even such an extraordinary individual as our End of Time, is virtually unprecedented. Unique in the annals. Um. The paper I intend to prepare will be controversial, surely, but if viewed in a broad light, could well, unless I'm rationalizing wildly, do my reputation a power of good." He said all this as if he'd just that moment thought of it. "Could right things with Eleanor, too," he added almost as an afterthought.

"Wouldn't be surprised." Switters smiled. "Nothing like a jolt of unexpected boldness to make a woman's nipples stiffen. Why, just before I left the hotel, I e-mailed a young Christian lady of my acquaintance that I was coming to palpitate her clitoris the way a worker ant milks its favorite aphid. That'll burst her buttons, I guarantee. Unless my aged grandmother intercepts and intervenes."

Smithe looked him over with active bemusement. The Englishman seemed incapable of judging when Switters was speaking earnestly and when he was merely being flippant. (The truth of the matter was, Switters could not always judge that, himself.)

In no way, however, did Smithe's confusion lessen his gratitude. He thanked Switters over and over for interceding on his behalf. Then, abruptly he stubbed out his cigarette on a blackened post and said, "It's barely noon. If we set out at once, I daresay we could reach Boquichicos by nightfall. What do you say, old boy? Shall we get cracking? Brisk march will do wonders for your condition. You can impart further detail over dinner at the hotel. My treat. Dinner."

"The haute cuisine of Boquichicos is a lovely prospect," said Switters, but he made no move to extricate himself from the hammock. Rather, he lay there looking troubled. He plowed his fingers through his badly tangled curls. He ran his tongue over his palate, tasting the bitter film left by parrot goulash and yopo vomit. He had to admit that he could do with a bit of bodily maintenance. "I can't . . . uh . . . End of Time said. . . . There's this. . . . Listen, I've been thinking that I might ask the Nacanaca studs to *carry* me back. In the hammock. Like a hunting trophy. A roll-up. Sedan chair sort of thing."

"Really, Switters! How imperial." Smithe laughed, but he, too, suddenly looked troubled, as if he had a premonition that things were about to go bad in a dramatic manner. "Are you that short on stamina?"

"No, but . . ."

"Then buck up, old boy. Show us some of the heralded Yankee spunk."

Switters propped himself up on one elbow but stirred no further. The hammock swung gently, to and fro. "This is absolutely silly, I'm aware of that, but . . ."

"Do go on."

"I'm under, I guess, a kind of taboo."

"Whatever do you mean?"

Switters sighed, and for a second he looked less anxious than sheepish. "Well, End of Time told me, right before he left, that I had to pay a price for having been shown the secrets of the cosmos. At first I thought he wanted money, like almost everybody else on this pathological planet, and I objected because I've got barely enough cash to pay my hotel bill and my river crew, and am counting on Mr. Plastic to take care of me back in Lima. But that wasn't the sort of price he had in mind."

"No?"

"No. He said that henceforth I must never allow my feet to touch the ground. I can stand on top of things, as I understood it, but I can't stand on the floor or the earth. And if I ever do, if my feet touch the ground, I will instantly fall over dead."

"The bleeding bugger."

"Yeah. So what do you make of it? He's playing with my head, right? I mean, it's silly, ridiculous."

"Oh, without question. Quite silly. Load of bosh."

"I was hoping you'd concur. As an experienced anthropologist, you must have come across this kind of thing before. I know, for example, that West Africa is crawling with curses and taboos—but there're also a lot of credible witnesses who swear that they're real, they've seen them work. That's why I was inclined to err on the side of caution, to be perfectly honest." He cloned the sheepish smile.

"Righto," said Smithe. He paused, as if pondering. "Fascinating, though. There's a quite similar prohibition in Irish folklore. Should a mortal ever stumble upon a fairy hill and be allowed to fraternize with the fairies, watch their dances and so forth, then the chap is warned that his feet may never thereafter touch the earth, under penalty of death. Evans-Wentz wrote of this, as I recall. Stories abound of pixilated Irishmen who, out of fear, spent the remainder of their lives on horseback."

"Superstition, of course?"

"Of course. The Irish."

"Flapdoodle?"

"Don't rag me. I've been told more than once that my manner of speech is a trifle old-fashioned. Blame it on my school. Eleanor does. But you're quite right. Flapdoodle. As a matter of fact, End of Time, that scalawag, placed a comparable taboo on me."

"No kidding?" For the first time in that conversation, Switters looked relieved. "The same taboo as my own?"

"Uh, no, not *precisely*, though promising identical consequences."

"And you're alive and ambulating. That bodes well for me." When Smithe didn't respond, Switters asked, "Doesn't it?"

"Um."

"Doesn't it?"

"Oh, it should. It should. Yes."

For reasons not entirely clear, Switters felt his heart sinking. He made an effort to nail Potney with his infamous glare. "Let's have it, pal."

"Sorry?"

"Your taboo, goddamn it! Let's have it."

Smithe's wan smile was even more sheepish than Switters's own. "A bit off the bean, I'm afraid." He shuffled his flip-flops.

"Never mind the fucking bean!" Although still basically on his back, he managed to look menacing.

"If you must know," said Smithe, clearing his throat, "and there's little reason why you shouldn't, End of Time warned me that as penalty for having journeyed with him to so-called secret places, I would face instant death—in much the mode you, yourself, described—were I ever to touch another man's penis."

Switters didn't know whether to laugh or cry. He lay there, mute, listening as the creak of the hammock twine blended with the rustling of jungle foliage on all sides of them.

"Rubbish, obviously," said Smithe, trying to sound blasé. "One must contend with a sometimes maddening lack of rational—"

"You've tested it?" Switters interrupted.

"When dealing with the primitive mind—"

"So, you've tested it?"

"Why, no, no," Smithe almost sputtered. "Naturally, I haven't actually put it to the test. That's silly."

"But you're supposed to be a scientist. Were you *afraid* to test it?"

"Fear has had nothing to do with it. I might have tested it, probably would have, but, well, you know, the *nature* of the thing involved."

"You mean the penis thing?"

"Of course, I do. I jolly well do mean that. What do you take me for? I'm a married man. Christ!"

"Easy, big fellow. No inference intended. But you'll agree, will you not, that scientists must occasionally undertake experiments they find personally distasteful? You speak of rationality, yet how can you for a damn second rationally contend that this taboo is rubbish when you haven't subjected it to experiment?"

Smithe snorted.

"You've got to test it, pal. For your sake as well as my own—and I can't deny I have a stake in this. In the outcome, I mean."

"You're not suggesting? . . . Surely."

"Hey, it's not my cup of tee-hee, either. I'm as straight as you are. Probably straighter. From what I hear, your lads in the fancy schools of Merry Olde can get pretty chummy with one another when the lights are low."

"Of all the biased—"

"Okay, forget I said that. It's no big deal one way or the other. What's the big deal? Women don't have this problem. They're more evolved." He paused. "R. Potney Smithe. What's the R for?"

"I fail to see . . ."

"What's the R for?"

"Reginald."

"Reginald. Okay. You very easily could have gone by Reggie. Couldn't you have? Reggie Smithe. A moniker mundane by any standard. But, no, you elected to be called *Potney*. A fairly brave choice there, pal. I admire you for it. I'm serious. I mean it. Says something about your character. And here you are in this jungle juju joint when you could have been snapping petits fours with the vicar of Kidderminster or some damn such. You've got guts." (Switters spoke in the abstract, of course, since the image of *guts* as an actual physical mass was seldom permitted to invade his consciousness.)

"I fail to see . . ."

"Come on, Pot. Let's get it over with."

Smithe glanced around him, as if looking for support, but the long, narrow, platformed room was empty except for the two of them.

"Just a touch. One brief touch, that's it. You needn't grab hold of anything. I'd object if you did. Strenuously."

Smithe's hide, at all times richly hued, looked now as if it had been rolled in paprika. He seemed on the verge of spontaneous combustion. "Down there," he said, nodding his teddy bear head in the direction of the firepit and the Nacanaca. "They could easily notice. . . ."

"Not if you hurry. And so what if they did? Do you honestly believe anybody in this part of the world would be scandalized? We're in South America!"

With that, Switters unzipped the fly of his bedraggled linen trousers. The scratchy snickersnee *swoosh* produced by the swift separation of metal teeth was a sound more ominous to both men than any hiss or shriek or howl that might emanate from the unknown forest. Briefly, each of them froze, as if paralyzed by stun rays from an advanced technology.

Then, Smithe turned toward the hammock, a look of grim determination on his face. "Bloody good, then," he said. Childishly awkward in his flip-flops and quasimilitaristic tan tropical togs, he began to advance. "You're right. Let's be done with it."

"Uh," said Switters, hurriedly, "uh, now if you have any reason to suppose there's something to this taboo, that it might actually—"

"No, no." Smithe paused. "Oh, if a bloke were to accept such superstitious nonsense on faith, it's quite possible that he would be psychologically susceptible to whatever end the perpetrator of the malediction might have planted in his unsophisticated mind. But no civilized, sensible—"

"Okay, but what if you secretly believe in it, believe in it subconsciously and don't know that you believe?"

Smithe seemed not to hear. He was advancing again. Thus, wishing to avoid any clumsy, embarrassing, last-minute fumbling, Switters freed his penis from its confinement within the folds of cheerfully patterned boxer shorts and pulled it out into the open. Almost instantly, it commenced, of its own volition, to crane its neck and bob its head about, as if sniffing the air, sensing that something fun—something uplifting, even—might be in the offing. *Oh, Christ Almighty, no! This can't be happening!* In a panicky effort to quell the unwanted alertness, the independent impetus toward active participation, Switters strained to think of the most repulsive, unsexy things he could mentally conjure. He thought of an overflowing cat box and buckets of offal, thought of gift shoppes, TV game shows, and the time George Bush had addressed the employees at Langley. Just as he squeezed his eyes shut, the better to picture these anti-aphrodisiacs, R. Potney Smithe extended a forefinger and jabbed Switters's half-erect member the way a shy but righteously purposeful Jehovah's Witness might press an agnostic's doorbell. Switters felt an electric jolt, although later he conceded that he might only have imagined it.

Smithe took a couple of steps backward. All of the ruddiness drained from his features, and he commenced to pull and pick at his shirtfront, as if involved in floccillation. Then he swayed. Pivoted to the right. And toppled onto the scorched and pitted floor.

For quite a while—it may have been as long as five minutes—Switters swung quietly in the hammock, staring at the heap on the floor, searching for signs of life; signs, more precisely, that Smithe was, as the Brit himself would have put it, *ragging* him, putting him on, pushing to an extreme his occasional dry fondness for jest.

At that point a figure ascended the wobbly ladder, and Fer-de-lance climbed onto the platform. The aspiring witchman glided noiselessly across the room, like one of the creatures for whom he seemed to have such affinity, and looking, in snakeskin cape and Ray-Ban sunglasses, like a Hollywood Boulevard vampire. He knelt beside Smithe's form.

"*Muy muerto,*" Fer-de-lance whispered. "*Muy muerto.*" He glanced over his shoulder at Switters, who was struggling to inconspicuously fasten his fly. "This mister is very, very dead," said he.

part 2

Every taboo is holy.
    —Eskimo saying

except for one shortish but memorable visit to Sacramento, another to Langley, Virginia, Switters spent the next six months in Seattle. It was the strangest period of his life.

It was stranger than his cloak-and-dagger days in and around Kuwait, stranger than his strangest nights of pleasure in the brothels of Southeast Asia, stranger than the annual Bloomsday literary banquets at the C.R.A.F.T. Club of Bangkok (though of these he couldn't remember a fucking thing); stranger, even, than nine hours of modern poetry at the University of California, Berkeley.

Well and good, but surely, one must ask, was there nothing about that half year, passed largely idle, in Seattle that was not positively humdrum when compared to the calamitous craziness he'd recently undergone in South America or the beatific bumfuzzlements he was soon to undergo in Syria? Yes, as far as Switters was concerned, the Seattle sojourn would always be the stranger of the experiences or, at least, the period when his equanimity was most rigorously challenged. And he was, after all, the final authority on that sojourn, although others were unquestionably involved. These included Maestra, Suzy, and Bad Bobby Case, as well as an assistant deputy director of the Central Intelligence Agency called Mayflower Cabot Fitzgerald; and, indirectly, from afar, the Kandakandero Indian known, perhaps erroneously, as End of Time. (Fer-de-lance had concluded that the shaman's name could be more accurately translated to mean End of Future, or more explicitly yet, Today Is Tomorrow. Accent on the verb. Today *Is* Tomorrow.)

The oddness of those months back in the U.S. could be attributed not merely to the major problems implicit in adjusting to life in a wheelchair but also to his efforts to come to terms with the usher—the Ka'dak witchman or Switters, himself—who had assigned him to that

mobile yet restrictive seat. Compounding those predicaments, naturally, were the reactions of others, mainly but not exclusively, the
friends, relatives, and employers listed above.

During his first week back, he'd had to contend with no one but
Maestra. To her, he'd provided only the most ambiguous explanation
of his sudden confinement to a wheelchair, claiming that his disability
was related to activities that he was not at liberty to discuss; the same
activities, he said, that unfortunately had destroyed her camcorder
along with its heartwarming record of Sailor Boy's flight to freedom.

"Right," said Maestra sarcastically, rolling, behind the huge circular
lenses of her spectacles, a pair of bleary, beady eyes. "The old 'for reasons of national security' alibi. Heh! I'm a loyal American of long
standing, but that doesn't mean I'm so flag-addled I can't recognize our
favorite euphemism for 'governmental hanky-panky swept under the
rug.' Anyway," she continued, "there's a place where men disabled in
the line of duty can go to convalesce. It's called Walter Reed Army
Medical Center in Bethesda, Maryland. If you prefer to recuperate at
Chez Maestra instead, you'd better be prepared to spill some beans."

Switters put her off. "In a few days," he promised. "I'll be able to
talk about it in a few days." Thereafter, every time she attempted to
bring up the subject or even, in passing, shot him an imploring glance,
he'd wink, grin, and proclaim, "Women love these fierce invalids home
from hot climates."

Alas, Maestra was not the type to be charmed more than once or
twice by a line from Rimbaud memorized in a long-ago poetry class,
no matter how attractively delivered. Faced with her increasing impatience and growing suspicions—"I have to say, buddy boy, you look
pretty healthy to me; that camcorder cost twelve hundred bucks, I'm
privy to your wanting to milk Suzy's aphid, and you neglected to bring
me a bracelet"—Switters, already in a confounded state and not knowing what else to do, sent for Bobby Case.

"Switters! What the hell? What have you gone and done to yourself?"

The e-message Bobby received in Alaska had stated only that his
friend needed urgently to see him and supplied a Seattle address.
Having a couple of days off, Case hitched a ride aboard a military
transport plane out of Fairbanks bound for McChord Air Force Base
near Tacoma. Within twenty-four hours after reading his e-mail, he
arrived, noisily, at Maestra's door on a rented motorcycle.

"Bobby! Wow! Welcome. That was fast."

"Naw, man. That was slower than snail snot. Must be losing my edge. But you?! What the hell? Fall down the stairs in a whorehouse?"

Switters checked Bobby's black leather jacket for signs of moisture. "It's quit drizzling, hasn't it? Let's go out on the side deck where we can talk privately—although even the deck could be bugged."

"Company or offshore bug?"

"Maestra bug."

"Really? Your granny doesn't look like no ear artist, although she does appear to have a burr in her britches."

"She rude to you when she let you in?"

"Nice as pie. I even got the impression she was kinda flirting with me."

"That's Maestra. An Aphrodite type right down to the finish line."

"She took to me. It's *you* she seems to have a problem with."

"Well, she'll have to stand in line with the rest. Come on. Follow me."

"I'm right behind you, son. But what did she mean when she called you Mr. Worker Ant?"

"Never mind that." He all but blushed. "It's a pet name. Family thing."

"Oh. Like when my uncles and aunts used to call me 'little asshole.' "

Demonstrating his growing expertise with the chair, Switters wheeled down the dim foyer, past the living room—pausing briefly to ascertain that the Matisse was still there—and through a formal dining room permanently lacquered with the unsophisticated fumes from takeout food. From the dining room, French doors led out onto a spacious deck with a sweeping view of the cold and busy sound named for Peter Puget. Next to a potted evergreen there was a Styrofoam chest, which he circled three times rapidly before coming to a halt beside it, facing the water.

"You've taken to that chair like a worm to tequila," Bobby marveled. "How long's it been your mode of transport?"

Switters patted the blue Naugahyde upholstered arms of the lightweight, foldable Invacare 9000 XT, pride of Elyria, Ohio. He patted its plastic-coated, chrome-plated hand rims (used to manually propel it), kicked with the side of his foot its pneumatic "flat-free" tires, squirmed his rump about on the "contour plus" cushion that topped the "drop hook solid folding" seat. How such a brand-new deluxe-model wheelchair had ended up in the Boquichicos infirmary, he didn't know. Part of a foreign-aid package, presumably. He did know that he had failed to send it back with Inti as promised, and he felt a prickle of guilt over that omission, even though he'd wired the clinic a thousand dollars his second day back in the States.

"It's flame resistant."

"That's handy."

"And bacteria resistant."

"Smart. Furniture on wheels, you don't know where it's been."

"Oh, I keep a watchful eye."

"And lock it up at night, I hope. Person can't be too aseptic in this day and age." In a characteristic gesture, Bobby tossed a pompadour-like tussock of inky hair out of his eyes while simultaneously patting down the cowlick that coiled like a busted bedspring farther back on his head. Switters had recently turned thirty-six (his birthday had passed unheralded—except by the migraine-makers—on a flight from Paris to New York), which meant that Bobby must have been at least approaching his thirty-third year, but he seemed, if anything, to have grown more boyish—Huck Finnish in stance, Tiger Woodsish in build—since Switters had seen him last, and also more foredoomed. Small wonder Maestra or any other woman would find him worth a flutter. "Fine piece of engineering, but you'd think they'd figure out a way to plumb the damn things."

"To accommodate a wet bar or . . ."

"Naw," Bobby went on, shaking his raven mane as if rejecting his previous thought, "that'd never work. But I'll tell you, son, what'd throw my happy heart to the wolves if I was to have to park a bony Texas butt in one of these suckers every day is the trial and tribulation of just taking a whiz. I mean, don't you have to off-load yourself onto a customized throne and wee-wee sitting down like you was queen of the May?"

"Such unlucky gentlemen do exist," said Switters, "but behold the masculine ease with which I can perform the rite of the void." In demonstration, he bolted boldly upright and stood on the footplate as if before a public urinal. "Of course, you have to make sure the brake is set, and balance your weight, or you could pitch face-first into the fixture."

Bobby looked like a buffaloed rubbernecker at the Lazarus show. "You can stand?!"

Grinning, Switters hopped backward up onto the seat, where he then began to jog in place, raising his knees almost as high as the scarlet T-shirt he wore under his double-breasted navy pinstriped suit. The wheelchair shook. It teetered precariously. For an instant, he seemed to panic. He throttled the trot.

"What the? . . ." Bobby's face was changing expressions faster than Clark Kent changed underwear. He went swiftly from astonishment to relief to annoyance to amusement to imagined comprehension. "Okay. Alrighty. I get it. Even a maniac like yourself wouldn't go to all this trouble just to mock the afflicted or play a cruel joke on your ol' podner. So's I reckon you're fixing to go deep cover, and you'll be trying to convince some alleged bad guys somewhere that you've been crippled by the forces of imperialism. The CIA and Actors Studio: telling them apart has never been simple. Did you know Mata Hari's real name was Gertrude? But hey! Anyway. I'm gladder than shit you're not actually stoved in 'cause I was hoping we could hit a dance club or two this evening."

Switters reseated himself. "It's not like that, Bobby," he said quietly. "It's not a cover. I really am confined to this contraption. Indefinitely, if not permanently."

"Then what the? . . . You were bouncing around like a poot in a microwave."

"Why don't you take your bandanna, if you don't mind, and dry off one of those patio chairs." Switters lifted the lid of the Styrofoam cooler. There was a rattle of ice shards as he removed a pair of glistening bottles. Sing Ha. "For old times' sake," he said. "Only four of these in stock, I wasn't expecting you so soon. But there's a Thai restaurant a mile from here, and they deliver. Good. Have a seat. You're not chilly, are you?"

"I live in Nome," Bobby said. "Nome, *Alaska*. And in case your Langley-trained powers of observation have completely deserted you, I happen to be wearing my leathers. You're the one liable to get cold."

The sun had muscled through the oyster frappé for the first time in weeks, but a light breeze was blowing off the water, and it was raw around its edges. "The state I'm in, I'm impervious to climate. So make yourself comfortable. I've got a story to relate . . ."

"I should hope."

". . . and you're going to find it harder to swallow than a cat fur omelet. It's hard for me, too, so be patient, if patience is among your virtues . . ."

"You could fit all my virtues in Minnie Mouse's belly button and still have room for Mickey's tongue and their prenuptial agreement."

". . . because it's going to take me some time, even to get started. Maybe while I'm gathering my wits, as the maître d' used to say at the Algonquin Hotel, you could fill me in on what you've been up to."

Noticing Switters's untypical solemnity, Bobby said, "Sure. Take it slow if you need to. But you've got to tell me one thing up front. The question that's burning a hole in my tortilla is . . . well, is or is not the affliction that's landed you in this senior-citizen dune buggy the result of a sexually transmitted disease? I mean, I hate to be blunt, but if you've been bit by something of that nature two years after Bangkok, there's a chance that I might . . ."

Switters had to laugh.

"Well, we were plowing the same fields, you know. Extracting ore from neighboring shafts. So to speak."

The word *relax* was on the tip of Switters's tongue when the memory of Sailor intervened. Instead, he said, "Not it at all. Nothing remotely in that category, I promise." He removed a cell phone from the side pocket of the wheelchair and ordered a dozen Sing Has from the Green Papaya Café. Then, without waiting for Bobby to file his Alaska report, he began—first haltingly, bumblingly, then, gaining silver and fizz, dramatically, almost with heedless relish—to recount the events of the weeks just past.

The sun, as if wanting to listen in, as if there might be something new under it, after all, fought off the curdling stratocumulus and moved in closer. By the time Switters finished his hour-long account, the deck was awash in afternoon sunlight; mild, respectful, autumnal rays, bright enough but lacking any sear in their beam. The sea breeze persisted throughout, but so restrained, finally, it could give the impression that it, too, had been mesmerized by the tale.

If the sun was enticed and the breeze engrossed, Bobby Case was those things and more. The former Air Force officer was literally transfixed—whether with amazement, awe, disbelief, sympathy, or scorn, it was impossible to ascertain. Many minutes passed, however, during which he could not raise his beer to his lips. When at last he spoke, his voice was taut from the strain of trying to sound normal and unimpressed. "So, that ol' boy? That limey? He really bought the farm?"

"*Muy muerto.*"

"Damn shame."

"Yeah. Potney was a fine fellow. An aristocrat, I suspect, although the kind inclined to wear black business shoes and dress socks with Bermuda shorts."

"Every country club in the state of Texas has got a few of them. And you believe the Indian's curse killed him?"

"Well . . ." Switters, too, was making an effort to behave matter-of-factly. "I believe he chomped an apple he couldn't—"

Bobby's eyes narrowed. "An apple?" he asked archly.

"Yeah. Eve's apple. The fruit of the tree of knowledge."

"Oh? Thought for a second you were referring to the head of your—"

"Bobby! For Christ's sake! No, no tooth marks on *that* fruit, which, anyway, I would've modestly described as a crab apple or a plum. Jesus, pal! He only jabbed it. What I'm saying is that Potney took a bite out of the old forbidden Winesap and could neither assimilate it nor eliminate it. A cruel dilemma. As Hesse said, 'The magic theater is not for everyone.'"

"Bought a ticket to a show his rigid background hadn't prepared him to handle? But once seen, couldn't forget? Alrighty. How, exactly, did that kill him?"

Switters shook his head silently, slowly.

"More to the damn point, *you*? You're a horse of a different feather."

Switters just kept shaking his head.

Some gulls screeched by, sounding, as usual, in a state of barely controlled hysteria. Wondering if his friend wasn't close to being in the same condition, Bobby decided he ought to experiment with empathy. "If it was anybody but you, podner, I'd say you were haunting your own house. Like that uncle of mine in Jasper who still thinks Fidel Castro's hiding under his rose bushes. Raggedy ass roses, too. Never prunes 'em right. But knowing you're telling the truth, and after the crazy shit you saw down there, well, I'm trying to put myself in your place, and I have to say, if it was me who went through it and saw what you saw, I reckon I'd be lying on my back with my feet in the air like some upended June bug. At least, 'til I figured it all out."

Switters lit a Havana panatela, Cuban cigars being an occasional perk of CIA employment. On the out-puff (he never inhaled), he said, "Figuring it out is the rub."

"Yep, and I don't know if I can help you much with that end of it. For the time being, at least, I'm going to let you wrassle with the psychological aspects. As for me . . . we're in agreement that you've got good reason to be keeping your tootsies off the pavement. You got no choice right now but to scoot around in that wheelchair. The first order of business is to find a way to get you out of it."

"That would probably entail lifting the taboo."

"There you go." Bobby sucked on his beer bottle like a tot on a lollipop or a tout on a pencil. After a minute or two, he said, "We're both company men. Even if I am just a contractual flyboy and you're stuck below supergrader because of your personal proclivities. We're still company. So let's approach this problem like company. How would the geniuses back at the pickle factory deal with it?"

"Depends on the level of White House involvement."

"You got that straight, son. President's men the biggest damn cowboys on the planet, and we take the heat for 'em. Democrats bad as Republicans."

"Worse, maybe."

"Yep. That beloved JFK. More dirty tricks than a whore in a coal mine. By the time he supposedly ate acid and saw the evil truth about Vietnam, his karmic boomerang was already winging home to roost. Live by the cowboy, die by the cowboy, I reckon. But we digress. Now. The company. First thing, they'd dispatch some Joe to meet with that would-be giggle box of a shaman and buy him out. Bribe him to call off the bugaboo. Right?"

"Quite likely. But End of Time—or Today Is Tomorrow—has no use for money. In fact, I can't imagine what you might possibly bribe him with."

"Everybody has a price. 'Cept for you and me. On second thought, 'cept for you. I know all too well what mine'd be. But, alrighty, let's say we can't buy him off. Next thing, the company would send in some disinformation Joes, plant evidence, try to discredit him. Rile up the populace against him. Pressure him, blackmail him, get him run out of office."

"Near as I can tell, except maybe for a noninfluential outsider named Fer-de-lance, he has no rivals. If he ever had any, I suspect he may have eaten them."

Bobby burst out laughing.

"I'm not so sure that's far-fetched. You find it amusing?"

"Nope, nope," said Case. "I was just thinking about you eating granny's parrot." He grinned from sideburn to sideburn.

"Shhh," Switters shushed him, glancing around furtively.

"Sorry. But we did sweep for bugs. Which in itself is pretty funny. Anyhow, if all else failed, company'd dispatch an operative to smack the witchman. If the cowboys had a hand in it, they would."

"Well, they don't. And in the Amazon forest? I'm not sure they could. They couldn't even smack Castro. In seven attempts."

"All they had to do was go to Jasper, spray Uncle Jerry's roses."

"Besides, who would do it?"

Bobby didn't hesitate. "Me."

"You must be cartooning!"

"Nope. Not if it came to that. Not if it was the only way to release you."

Simultaneously touched and appalled, Switters asked, "You'd actually? . . ."

"If it came to that. As Krishna told Arjuna in the *Bhagavad-Gita*, it's permissible to—"

"I know what Krishna is alleged to have said in the *Gita*: 'If your cause is just,' et cetera. And like the 'eye for an eye' crap Yahweh is alleged to have thundered in the Bible, it's been twisted to excuse and justify every vile sort of opportunistic bloodletting. Anyway—and I sincerely appreciate your offer—the threat of death, or even death itself, is unlikely to produce the desired results. Today Is Tomorrow and his pals have a different slant on mortality than we so-called civilized types. The overly oxygenated who like to think all peoples are the same have never crossed paths with a Kandakandero."

"Hell, they've never crossed paths with a Frenchman. One-worldism is just a disguised brand of xenophobia. Even your cousin Potney from cousinly Merry Olde laid a bodacious cultural difference or two on the table. Otherwise, you mighten not be in this mess. Now, as for getting you out of it . . . I see your point. Eliminating the laughing shaman wouldn't necessarily eliminate the taboo."

"Not unless he died in some arcane manner that you and I couldn't even guess at."

"Hmm." Bobby filled his throat with Sing Ha. Switters followed suit. Out on Puget Sound, an aging freighter filled its stack with steam. The noise, long and mournful, set a neighbor's dog to yowling a canine version of a country western tune, which in turn set off the gulls, those graceful but grabby scavengers who wouldn't have hesitated to pick Hank Williams cleaner than a Cadillac full of agents and a courtroom full of ex-wives. Then, everything went quiet again, the sun let itself be bound and hooded by strato-terrorists, and Switters returned to shaking his head. As the ambience, sky and water alike, gradually turned a single shade of teal, Bobby slumped low in his patio chair, his battered boots propped on the ice chest. He appeared lost in thought.

Teal is an unfriendly color, and the air had an unfriendly feel. Chill, at last, found Switters's bones. He tapped the toe of Bobby's left boot with the toe of his own right sneaker. "Park Place, Illinois Avenue, and a Get-Out-of-Jail-Free card for your thoughts," he said.

"Make that a Boardwalk hotel full of blondes and fried chicken and you got a deal." He bolted upright and grinned his boyish hardpan grin. "I was thinking," he said, "that wheelchair or no wheelchair, I'm taking you dancing tonight."

They did go dancing. Even Switters danced, after a fashion, careening his Invacare 9000 around the floor of the Werewolf Club, more or less in time to the energetic rock of Electric Baby Moses, moving, more or less in concert, with one of the several young women Bobby had attracted to their table. Or, perhaps, Switters had attracted them on his own. "Women love these fierce invalids home from hot climates," he practically shouted at one point in the evening.

Even so, they taxied home alone. Alone, and more than meagerly intoxicated. So intoxicated, in fact, that an incautious Switters sang in the cab a medley of refrains from Broadway shows, included among them a seemingly poignant rendition of "Send in the Clowns." Bobby, fortunately, thought his friend was merely waxing ironic—and to a certain extent irony *was* involved. The stiff-witted and academic seem not to comprehend that it is entirely possible to be ironic and sincere at the same instant; that a knowing tongue in cheek does not necessarily preclude an affectionate glow in heart.

They awoke the next morning wound in the rusty anchor chains of hangover, but Maestra fixed them a delicious late breakfast of ham biscuits with red-eye gravy, surprising because they'd roused her noisily at 3 A.M., Switters lacking a key to the house, and because Maestra never had been what she contemptuously referred to as a "kitchen chicken." Bobby told her she made the Galloping Gourmet look like he was stuck in cement and kissed her on the cheek, and although she waved him off as if he were some kind of hopeless lunatic, Switters could tell she was pleased.

Arriving on the side deck just as the mist was lifting (they'd paused on the way to admire the Matisse), Switters suggested a tuft of hair of the dog. "Nope," countered Bobby, "nothing doing. First, we're gonna sit. I have a sneaking suspicion you haven't sat in a coon's age."

"However the hell long *that* is," said Switters. "I don't believe small arboreal carnivores are exactly famous for lavish longevity, not judging from the frequency with which they show up as road kill."

"Mock the folk wisdom of your ancestors if you must, ain't no concern of mine, but I can sense you haven't been sitting, son; and while meditation wasn't designed as therapy, it might do more for you than gravy does for biscuits—at this weird troubling time in your life."

They sat.

They sat for nearly two hours, in the course of which Switters lost himself so that his essence passed into what some are wont to call, perhaps unrealistically, the Real Reality: that realm of consciousness beyond ego and ambition where mind becomes a silver minnow in a great electric lake of soul, and where the quarks and the gods pick up their mail on their way from nowhere to everywhere (or is it the other way around?).

Afterward, tranquilized and centered by the meditation, and enheartened by the previous evening's coed recreation, Switters felt better than he had in a fortnight; felt so good that he came to an optimistic decision concerning his next course of action. His instinct, however, was not to share this with Bobby immediately. Instead, he focused on loosening the last remaining loops of hangover's iron turban. "Young buck like you might not notice," he said, decapping a beer, "but I find piper inflation to be on the rise."

"Yep. The bastard's been charging me twice the price for half the fun. When I avail myself of his services, that is. Since the excessive consumption of alcoholic beverages is the state sport of Alaska— they'd challenge for the gold at the Drunkard Olympics, but'd lose major points to Ireland in the charm category—I've been pretty much teetotaling, out of sheer contrariness, not wanting to be just another shitface in the crowd." Accepting a wet bottle from Switters, he examined it at some length. "Nostalgia's nice enough in little bitty doses, it puts personal peach fuzz on the hard ass of history, but I'd be lying like a cop in court if I was to tell you Sing Ha was anything but sucky beer."

Switters nodded. "It went down well enough in Bangkok, where there was hardly any choice, but here in the land of a thousand brewskies, it does come across as rather weak-kneed and effete."

"Tastes like butterfly piss. Of course, it's brewed by Buddhists. Guess it takes a Christian to put some muscle in a liquid refreshment."

"That's it. It's the fear and anger that's missing in Sing Ha. Bereft of those punitive and vindictive qualities we Christers have come to respect and love. No bops in the hops. No assault in the malt. But, Captain Case, if you're a no-show at Alaska's finer watering holes, how do you spend your time up there? Needlepoint? Laboring to reach page two of *Finnegans Wake?*"

"Fly more than you might think."

"Really? I wouldn't have thought. With our increased satellite capabilities, why do we fly manned spy missions at all?"

The crosshatched crinkles around Bobby's eyes stiffened slightly. "Can't rightly address that, son."

Caught off guard, Switters very nearly flinched. "Oh. Not my need to know?"

"There you go."

In the CIA, there existed a pervasive and perpetual rule that a company employee, no matter how light his or her cover, no matter if coverless, must never divulge to anyone—spouse, parent, lover, friend, or even fellow CIAnik—more about his or her job than that person had a need, not an abiding interest but an actual *need*, to know. With Maestra and to a lesser extent with Suzy, Switters had been somewhat lax in adhering to that rule, which was why he may have been so surprised to find Bad Bobby, flaunter of a fair number of society's more firmly held conventions and active critic of the multinational commercial entities to whose Muzak the company, with escalating frequency, now danced, strictly obeying it. Switters had long ago come to accept if not appreciate the fact that he himself was a study in contradictions, blaming the incongruities in his personality on his having been born on the cusp between Cancer and Leo, pulled in opposite directions by lunar and solar forces (that he maintained severe reservations about the reliability of astrology only reinforced the evidence). Now, he was starting to notice glaring inconsistencies in Bobby, as well. Maybe most people were fundamentally contradictory. The *real* people, at any rate. Maybe those among us ever steadfast and predictable, those whose yang did not intermittently slop over into their yin, maybe those were candidates for Maestra's subhuman category of "missing link."

"Well. Then. Forgetting your official duties, in which I was only feigning a polite interest in the first place, can I ask if you've got anything drawn up on the monkey wrench board, anything that might be causing John Foster Dulles to rotate in his sarcophagus?" Upon uttering the name, Dulles, Switters spat. Upon hearing it, Bobby spat as well. Two molten pearls of Dulles-inspired spittle shimmered on the tiles. (It may or may not be instructive to note that the Dulles who stimulated this derogatory salute was the so-called statesman, John Foster, and not his brother, Allen, the very first director of the CIA.)

"You mean angelic aces up my sleeve? Nothing new. Cook some books, so to speak; jam a few signals here and there, and then the usual archival stuff. Still collecting data on Guatemalan smack squads, on company drug running, the Manson setup, UFO coverups, et cetera. Not much corporate, which is where the dirt is nowadays. Got more than enough, though, to make 'em think twice about ever sacking me. Otherwise, I'm not sure when or if I'll play them cards."

"You wouldn't want to end up like Audubon Poe."

"Aw, ol' Audubon Poe's doing fine and dandy, for a man with a blue sticker on his head. Leading a more productive life than me or you. At this flaccid moment of our personal histories."

Before Switters could inquire after ex-agent Poe, Maestra appeared at the French doors to remind the two men that they'd promised to play her newest video games with her as soon as they'd finished their post-breakfast breather. It was now past noon, and Apocalyptic Ack-Ack was set up and ready to roll.

Bobby proved to be unbeatable at Apocalyptic Ack-Ack, but Switters was victorious at New World Order and Maestra creamed them both at Armies of Armageddon, so everyone was cheerful and devoured an extra large vegetarian pizza garrulously together before Maestra retired for a nap. The men peed, washed up, and changed clothes: Switters into his ginger Irish tweeds, Bobby into Wrangler jeans and a sweater so bulky and thick it must have taken a woolly mammoth and two Shetland ponies to make it. Then, after stopping once again to approve the brushwork of Henri M., they returned to the safety of the deck. There, in a grayish November glow that might have been filtered through frozen squid bladders, a kind of sunlight substitute invented by Norwegian chemists, Switters sat wondering how to broach the subject of his next move. It wasn't long before Bobby provided a segue.

"So, son, what're you gonna tell 'em back at the pickle factory?"

"Excellent question. My leave's up in ten days. I'll concoct something before I go rolling into the spookmeister's oracle. He certainly couldn't accommodate anything remotely resembling the truth. Not Mayflower Cabot Fitzgerald. Meanwhile, I have to decide on what to tell Maestra." He paused. "And Suzy."

"Suzy?"

"Yes."

"Your little stepsister?"

"Yes. I've decided to fly down to see her on Monday." (It was then Saturday afternoon.)

"To get in her pants?"

"To help her write her first high-school term paper." He paused. He smiled. "And . . ." He broke off.

"And what?"

"And get in her pants." Instantly, he regretted the statement, not because it was false—he had every intention of consummating their relationship and believed she felt the same—nor because he was especially embarrassed by sharing his intent with his best friend, but, rather, because the crudeness of the remark, the casual male baldness of it, misrepresented the depth of his feeling for her. His beach-blanket buttercup. His dewy wolverine.

As for Bobby, he failed to respond right away. He, in fact, gave every indication of being pensive. Lost not only in thought but in vastness of sweater, he looked as small as an offscreen movie actor,

and not many years older than Suzy herself. "Oh, you Switters,"
he said at last. "You poor bastard. Do you know what you're messing
with here? Do you know you're giving your address out to something
that'll make a shaman's curse seem like a get-well card from Mother
Teresa?"

Switters was mute, his beer arm stalled in midair between ice chest
and mouth, so Bobby continued: "Do you know you're messing with
the single biggest taboo in our culture? A taboo worse than taxing the
church and burning the flag rolled up in one, a taboo that'll get your
balls handed to you on a paper plate and every doctor in America'd
break his Hippocratic oath and three golf dates rather than sew 'em
back on?" He set down his beer and leaned forward toward the wheelchair. "I'm talking, of course, about the taboo against the sexuality of
adolescent girls.

"Yes, son. The taboo of taboos in the United States of America,
and I'm sticking my scrawny Texas neck out even to mention it. Good
thing we swept for bugs." Bobby retrieved his Sing Ha, took a long,
unsatisfying swig, and leaned back. "It's an indisputable, observable
fact that even infants have sex lives—purely recreational, mindless,
and self-centered, obviously: a simple matter of being pleasured by
genital stimulation—but it continues kinda marginally throughout
childhood until by the time puberty hits 'em full force, they're masturbating at such a rate it's a wonder they don't develop repetitive motion
syndrome. Girls as well as boys, *por favor*. In fact, because human
females mature faster, they get there first, and it's doubtful if we slow
boats to China ever catch up."

Half-closing his eyes, Switters, perversely, tried to imagine Suzy
masturbating, but it was beyond him, and, besides, Bobby was pressing on.

"The unadorned truth is, adolescent girls are horny as jackrabbits.
It's not their fault, nature designed it that way. For the protection of
the species. And there's nothing politics or religion can do to alter that
physical reality, short of drugging the girls with medical depressants or
siphoning off their hormones with rubber tubes. But because modern
society is by nature unnatural, we're in a state of absolute denial over it.
Absolute denial. That our daughters, granddaughters, nieces, and little
sisters might be highly charged sexual dynamos makes us so uncomfortable, so queasy, that we, men and women both, have to lie to ourselves and each other and pretend it doesn't exist.

"Well, that which you deny sooner or later rises up and bites you
in the ass. That ol' boy Miller dealt with this very subject in *The Cru-
cible*, but we applauded the play and pretended it was about witchcraft
or some such shit and went right on with our denial. And with our

witchhunts. It's the witchhunting that worries me. For Suzy's sake as much as yours."

"Uh-huh." Switters nodded dumbly, but his beer bottle remained stationary midway between the Styrofoam container that had lowered its temperature and the organic container that would empty its contents and warm them up again.

"We ain't in Thailand anymore, son. Remember that. It ain't Denmark or Sweden, neither. Here, a girl's got to sweep her natural biological urges under the rug. Keep 'em to herself and feel guilty about 'em. If not, she'll be charged a stiff price, socially and psychologically. Our girls are culturally unprepared for the . . . the, uh, emotional *intricacies* of fucking. Although, at sixteen, your Suzy'll be getting there pretty damn quick. In the meantime, though, I know you wouldn't want to muddy her sweet waters. Not you, who's got such a thing about innocence."

"That again," grumbled Switters.

"And you also have your own self to consider. Listen. Any adult male heterosexual who says he isn't never turned on by pubescent girls is a liar or a geek, and you can tell him Bad Bobby said so. But we're in denial over that, too. Serious denial. A man go Humbert-Humberting around in America, he'll find himself thrown into the volcano, a sacrifice to appease the gods who've blighted humanity with all these nasty, unwanted, upsetting transgenerational cravings. The morality police'll tar a romantically smitten fool like you with the same wire brush they use, justifiably, on the sicksacks and twisttops who actually prey on children and injure 'em out of a psychotic need to exercise power over somebody weaker than their own weak selves. The smut sniffers from the victimization industry are also into exercising power, remember, and drawing fair and intelligent distinctions has never been one of their long suits. Some of 'em, sad to say, are only seeking revenge for hurtful things that happened to *them* as children—but, then, the same could be said of the child molesters. Two sides of the same unlucky coin. At any rate, we got us a climate where normal men are scared to admit, even in the mirror, that they occasionally get bit by the lust bug whilst gandering at a junior miss. And I reckon society'll go right on lying about it until the day it reaches enlightenment." In one swift gulp, he finished off his beer. " 'Course, as long as it keeps lying to itself about itself, there ain't much chance of it ever becoming enlightened. Anyhow. Don't do it, Swit. That's my advice. For a dozen good reasons, don't do it."

When Bobby stood up and stretched, Switters said, "That was quite a speech, pal. Thanks. I'll chew every bolus of it many times I'm sure, and I'll carefully consider your counsel. But . . ."

"But?"

"But you haven't met Suzy."

"No, and I don't want to, neither. 'Cause every word I said, though true, was hypocritical to the core. If it was me in your place and she was willing, and I thought she knew what she was doing, I'd be in her pants quicker than she could bring 'em home from The Gap. But I'm white trash from Hondo and don't have the morals of a flea."

Like chip dip with a short shelf life, the imported Scandinavian sunshine had commenced to degenerate, reverting to the cod paste from which it was synthesized. Scud blew by close to the surface of the sound like dank puffballs of bacterial fuzz, and the men could almost taste mildew in the air. The atmosphere was leaden and thin simultaneously, as if composed of some new element that defied known laws of atomic weight and could be properly breathed only by lifelong residents of the Pacific Northwest. Feathery and innocuous on one hand, sodden and ill-willed on the other, it was the meteorological equivalent of Pat Boone singing heavy metal.

Switters was actually quite fond of Seattle's weather, and not merely because of its ambivalence. He liked its subtle, muted qualities and the landscape that those qualities encouraged if not engendered: vistas that seemed to have been sketched with a sumi brush dipped in quicksilver and green tea. It was fresh, it was clean, it was gently primal, and mystically suggestive. It was all those things and more—but it was never vivid.

The vivid excesses from which he recoiled in nature Switters found irresistible in language. Bobby's pointed rhetoric, the platitudinousness of its content notwithstanding (that teenage girls were sexual beings and society didn't like it wasn't exactly news), had left Switters lightly hypnotized. It was Bobby who broke the spell by abruptly asking, "You worried about how little Suzy's gonna react to finding your ol' butt stuck in a chair? Meals on wheels? Not the most virile of images, I wouldn't reckon."

"What? Oh. No. No." Switters smiled confidently. "Women love these fierce invalids home from hot climates."

"Heh! So I keep hearing. Sounds like a slogan from a recruiting poster." The voice was not Bobby's but Maestra's. She was standing on the threshold of the French doors, which she had managed to open undetected. How long she'd been there, how much she'd overheard, how an octogenarian widow with a walking stick had sneaked up on a couple of swashbucklers from the Central Intelligence Agency were questions of immediate concern. "What does a woman have to do to gain some attention around this place?"

"Dreadful sorry, ma'am," said Bobby, in his most courtly manner. "We've been pining away for your companionship but assumed you were enjoying a soothing respite from the likes of us two polecats."

"I was, indeed," she said, "until it reached the stage where I felt the two polecats were ignoring me."

"Never," Bobby assured her. "Impossible. Say, how'd you like to take a little spin?"

"A spin? Me? You mean on your motorcycle?"

Switters jumped in. "Not a good idea. It'll be dark before you know it." He was right about that. It was not yet five o'clock, but in Seattle in November, the diurnal house band played very short sets.

"Let's ride!" said Maestra, waving her left arm in the air until its bracelets rang out like an Afro-Cuban rhythm section in a bus wreck. "Unless Herr Alzheimer is playing tricks on me, I've got an old leather jacket in the hall closet."

There was no stopping them. She even refused to wear a helmet, not wishing to look like a wimp next to Bobby, who consistently violated the helmet law on the grounds that his head was his own affair, cowlick and all. With some misgiving, Switters saw them off, then wheeled into the living room and parked below the Matisse. The big blue nude rose like a mountain range, an azure Appalachia of loaves, humps, and knobs, a topographical maquette constructed from huckleberry jelly, a curvaceous cobalt upland where clumps of wild asters clung precariously to the hillsides and the bluebirds all sipped curaçao. Matisse's nude was nude but not really naked, which is to say, though she was beyond shame or embarrassment, she was far from brazen. Her purpose was not to titillate but to inspire awe at the infinite blueness of our finite world.

In her way, she was more innocent than Suzy, wiser than Maestra; a woman such as Switters had never known nor would ever know—or so he thought—and as such, perfectly suited to preside over his musings of the moment.

Bobby is correct, he mused. To deny that young girls were throbbing hives of sexual honey was to be both sexist and ageist. On the other hand, to steal samples of that honey or dupe them out of it, or to view them as *only* hives or even as *primarily* hives was an equal or perhaps greater wrong. The big blue nude seemed to nod in agreement. Taboos, however, were not good, either. Taboos were superstitions with fangs on them, and if not transcended, they punctured the brain and drained the spirit. A taboo was a crystallized knot of societal fear and must be unraveled, cut through, or smashed if a people were to set themselves free. Ancient Greeks had a concept they called "eating the taboo," and the *agorbi* sect in India took a similar approach. As a path to liberation, these golden Greeks and holy Hindus would deliberately break any and all of their culture's prevailing taboos in order to loosen their hold, destroy their power. It was an active, somewhat radical method of triumphing over fear by confronting that which frightened: embracing it, dancing with it, absorbing it, and moving past it. It was a casting out of demons.

Wouldn't it be to his betterment and, perhaps, to society's as well, to go on down to Sacramento and, in one way or another, stare that taboo in the eye? Wouldn't it? Or was this merely some elaborate Swittersesque rationalization? (The big blue nude gave nary a sign.)

At 6 P.M. he began to worry. At quarter past, he revved up the fret machine. It was darker than the clam beds of Styx out there, and a needle-nose rain had commenced to fall. Where could they be? Certainly, something had gone wrong. In her frail condition, Maestra might have lost her grip and fallen off. Bobby, hardly the most cautious of bikers, might have skidded them into a lumber truck. Or a driver, typically unmindful of motorcycles and further handicapped by the gloom and the rain, might have plowed into them or run them over a curb. There *must* have been an accident. What else would have delayed them? Switters dismissed any notion of hanky-panky. There were limits to Bobby's gallantry. She was a grandmother, for God's sake! She was older than salt.

He had just decided to give them ten more minutes before calling the police when the telephone burbled. A table was sideswiped and a floorlamp flattened on his way to the phone. Evidently he needed more practice in the Invacare 9000. He was not yet the starship commander he fancied himself to be.

"Bobby! What's happened? Is she all right?"

"All right? Yeah, she's fine—except for being stubborn as a frostbit fireplug. We're having a big fight, to tell you the truth."

"What are you talking about?"

"We're at the video store. I'm dying to see *Blade Runner* again—you know as good as me it's the best damn movie ever made—but your granny's got her mind set on some fou-fou flick about the expatriate art scene in Paris in the twenties. Guys with big noses sitting around in sidewalk cafés arguing over whether Gertrude Stein weighs more than Ernest Hemingway, or some unhappy shit like that."

"You must mean *The Moderns*. It's a delicious film. You'd lick your chops over it. Why don't you just rent them both?"

"Because, Solomon, in case you forgot, we agreed to play CD-ROM Monopoly with her later on, and that game takes longer than the lemonade line in Hell. I got to fly tomorrow night."

"In that case," said Switters, feeling like the vice president at a Senate deadlock, "I cast my deciding vote for *Pee-wee's Big Adventure*. Now come on home." He slammed down the receiver.

Bobby left the next morning. As he zipped himself into his leathers at the front door, he said, "We really didn't dig very deep into your situation. We talked about how to break the curse or whatever it is—and I'm still ready and willing to waltz down to the Amazon and seize any operational opportunity that should arise, you say the word—but we never got into the significance of the thing. What it means, where it came from. Was it a well-thought-out decision, that particular taboo? Is it traditional to ban interlopers and visiting firemen from touching certain things, in your case the earth? Is earth-touching symbolic in some cryptic way, or was it arbitrary, just a matter of a wily ol' jungle wiseguy having off-the-cuff sport with a city slicker? And how does it tie in with your yopo trip? What'd you see or learn on that trip that was so heavy or precious or privileged that you would have to pay for it by spending the rest of your life with your heels elevated? And just because some goofy limey bush professor keeled over from Kadockywocky juju, does that necessarily mean *you* would? Boy howdy! There's a fieldful of stones we left unturned."

"I've been flipping them like pancakes myself, and suppose I'll keep at it unless the company creates a major distraction for me."

Bobby chuckled. "I'd love to be a fly on the pickle factory ceiling when you report for duty in that hospital hotrod. At least travel for the disabled is easier nowadays. There a direct flight from Seattle to D.C.?"

"Probably, but I don't book it. I fly into New York and take the train down, so that I never have to patronize an airport named for John Foster Dulles." After saying "Dulles," Switters immediately expectorated, and Bobby did likewise. In such aesthetic harmony was their dual expulsion of salivary projectiles that they could have represented the U.S. in synchronized spitting. "Anyway, it doesn't matter that we didn't spend this all too rare reunion dissecting and analyzing my peculiar state of affairs. There'll be plenty of time to ponder End of

Time, even if today *is* tomorrow. And there're happenings in this life
that simply don't lend themselves to rational interpretation. To look at
them logically can be to look at them wrongly. Logic can distort as
well as clarify. What's important is—well, my psyche was a pregnant
mouse at a cat show when you arrived, I was in a fair amount of dis-
array, but you showed me a good time, gave me some laughs, got me
relaxed. Thanks to you, pal, I can now approach my prospects with a
relatively clear mind."

"Clear enough to stay away from little Suzy?"

"Well . . ."

Bobby shook his head reproachfully. "I sure hope Hell has wheelchair access."

"If not, I may have to settle for Paradise." (In his cerebral data base,
crammed as it was with etymological privity [some might say *pedantry*,
but there was nothing the least bit trivial about those underpinnings of
modern language that were by extension the underpinnings of modern
consciousness], he knew the word *paradise* to be derived from Old Persian for "walled garden" or "enclosed orchard"—but the significance of
this, while he was still many months removed from the Syrian oasis,
obviously would not have occurred to him.) "Heaven or Hades, as long
as Pee-wee Herman's on the premises I'll be content. Pee-wee may be
becoming my idol."

"I can appreciate that," said Bobby, thinking of the video they had
watched before Maestra bankrupted them both at Monopoly. "It's the
innocence."

"It's the joie de vivre."

They embraced in the manner that had raised more than a few
cowboy eyebrows. Bobby walked down the steps and mounted the
Harley. "By the way," he called, "you don't have to sweat anymore
about what to tell your granny. I talked to her last night on our ride.
It's all taken care of. She's cool as an ice worm in snow melt." He
roared away.

whatever story bobby had fed Maestra, it proved effective. As Switters wheeled about her spacious house at top speed, slaloming through an obstacle course of furniture, skidding around corners—practicing, honing his skills—she smiled knowingly, approvingly, almost with a wink. If only Capt. Nut Case had given Suzy a similar briefing!

Alas, as Bobby had hinted it might, the wheelchair had a dampening effect on Suzy's presumed and anticipated passions. When she came home from school (rather late, he thought) on Monday afternoon to find him chair-bound in his mother's parlor, she emitted a sharp cry of dismay and approached him tentatively, with grave concern. "Had a minor mishap in South America," he quipped, and she brightened. But when he, foolishly perhaps, confessed that his confinement might be long-term, if not permanent, her horrified frown reappeared.

Not that she was unsympathetic. *Au contraire.* From that moment on, she was solicitous and attentive nearly to a fault, but her ministrations were those of a nurse, not a nymph. His condition had awakened in her maternal and nurturing instincts, altogether admirable qualities in their place, but hardly the emotions for which he yearned. Although those big sea-squirt eyes of hers, poker chips in Neptune's deep casino, still regarded him adoringly, the coquetry in them had given way to pity. Pity. Lust's worst enemy.

There was something else. When on Tuesday, Suzy again was late from school, Switters inquired of his mother, Eunice, of her possible whereabouts. "Oh," said Eunice, "she's probably hanging out with Brian."

"Who's Brian?"

His mother smiled. "I think our little Suzy has a boyfriend."

It took every Asian breathing technique he'd ever learned, and one or two he improvised for the occasion, to rescue his brain from the Tabasco-filled birdbath into whose crimson waters it had suddenly fallen. When the searing and flopping finally abated, he felt a measure of relief at the way things were turning out. Almost concurrently, he felt a disappointment so profound he thought he might weep. It was similar to the mixture of relief and disappointment a moth must feel at the extinguishing of a candle.

If he thought he was free of the exquisite torture of obsession, however, if he believed fate had dictated he lay that shining burden down, he was mistaken. When, at about six o'clock, she came down the hall to his room with a can of Pepsi and a plate of brownies, came in her school uniform (pleated blue skirt and loose white blouse), came with her tiny gold crucifix twinkling like an eastern star above the twin mosques of her breasts (my, how they'd grown! that old training bra couldn't begin to corral them now), came with her round rump ticking like two casseroles in an oven, came with her smart smile and guile-less gaze, he could sense the want spreading throughout his organism like a cotton-candy cancer, and his mania once more had the wind to its back.

Suzy kissed him on the mouth, but without tongue or duration. "Don't eat all these brownies now, and spoil your dinner."

"Did you bake them?" In his mind he licked the spoon, her fingers, knuckles, wrists, forearms. . . .

"Yeah, but, like, not from scratch." She sat down on a hassock. "If you're going to hang in your room like this, you ought, you know, to be in the bed."

"No, I oughtn't. But I'd be delighted to jump into bed if you'd jump in with me."

She blushed, though only lightly. "Oh, Switters! You're so-oo *bad*."

"That isn't bad, that's good. Don't they teach you anything at your penguin academy?"

"Next year, I'm transferring to public school. Catholic school . . . I mean, I love the religious training and stuff, but a lot of the rules are just so *lame*." She closed her fingers around her throat to illustrate in some fashion the lameness of parochial regulations. "My dad doesn't mind, 'cause he got excommunicated for, you know, divorcing my mom and marrying your mom. Switters, has your mom been married lots of times?"

"Let's put it this way: my mother's on a first-name basis with the staff at several honeymoon hotels. I believe she may get a discount. Now, speaking of honeymoons, darling, don't you think it's time we started practicing for ours?" He inched the wheelchair closer to her hassock.

Giggling nervously, she shook her head. She had cut her hair and wore it now in a bob that, while better shaped and slightly longer, was not unlike a blonde version of the Amazon coif. The effect was somewhat childish, somewhat boyish. "You shouldn't even talk like that. You being injured and stuff."

"Nothing wrong with me that your pretty little sushi roll wouldn't improve."

"Switters! That's not what your grandmother says."

He blinked. "My grandmother? What did she say? When?"

"Last night. Remember when we were eating dinner and the phone rang? I ran to get it 'cause I thought it might be Bri . . . like, this friend of mine, you know. Well, it was your grandma up in Seattle. She told me how delicate your condition is and that, like, if I should ever be tempted to, like, let you do anything romantic or nasty, I should bear in mind that it could kill you. 'It'd probably be the death of him,' she said. So, you see."

Damn that Maestra! "That meddling old. . . . She's lying through her teeth, and even her teeth are false."

Suzy stood. "She's just trying to protect you."

"I don't need protection. I'm sturdy as a Budweiser draft horse."

"You are, are you? In that wheelchair? Hello?" She moved toward the door. "You behave yourself. I'll come get you when dinner's ready. We're both just trying to take care of you, you know. I think your grandmother's way cool." Suzy blew him a quick kiss and left the room.

"She cheats at Monopoly!" he called after her. It was all he could think to say.

This is ridiculous. I know life, the way humans live it, is absurd more often than not, and I don't particularly mind. I rather like the smell of absurdity in the morning. At the onset of a potentially dull day, a whiff of the genuinely ludicrous can be exhilarating. But this situation is too much. It's too much for me. It's stupid. I admit, I kind of enjoyed it at first, the sheer unexpected outlandishness of it, but now the novelty has definitely worn off, it's become a prime-time drag, it's drying up my syrup of wahoo.

I'm going to stand and walk away from this geriatric golf cart. I'm going to bound down the hall like an impala with a pack of hyenas on its butt and snatch Suzy up in my arms, which have toned up quite nicely, thank you, since I've been pushing these hand rims, I'm going to sweep her off her feet and chew the buttons right off her blouse, I don't care if the whole family sees me do it. I can't take any more of this. It's silliness worthy of the U.S. Congress, it's estúpido supremo.

Bracing the heels of his hands on the chair's Naugahyde arms, Switters lifted himself off its seat, extending and bending, simultaneously, his right leg until the tip of his black sneaker was a mere centimeter or less above the oval rag rug, one of many such carpets that contributed to the Early American decor of the rambling suburban ranch house. *R. Potney Smithe's death was undoubtedly a result of the power of suggestion—a kind of extreme version of the tactics of Hollywood and Madison Avenue—and only the mentally weak are susceptible to such psychological manipulation. Hey, even if Today Is Tomorrow possesses some cause-and-effect magical faculty totally unfamiliar to science, its reach surely is geographically restricted, it can't extend thousands of miles to north-central California.*

He wiggled his toes until he could almost feel the molecular interaction of foot with floor. Yet he didn't quite make contact. *Suppose it's real, the Kandakandero magic, suppose I touch this ugly rug and it strikes me dead: so what? I certainly can't go on in this manner for the rest of my life. Under such a cloud. It's oppressive. I'm a prisoner in an invisible jail. Worse, I'm an object of pity to the opposite sex. Rimbaud was wrong! I'm not putting up with it. Fuck your taboo and the snake it rode in on. I'm free! Kill me if you can, pal. Go ahead. I dare you.*

Although he pressed down harder on the chair arms, however, although he raised his buttocks higher and waggled his toes faster, he remained a quarter centimeter from actual contact with the floor. Chickpeas of sweat popped out on his brow, arteries popped out in his eyeballs. His Adam's apple turned into an Adam's grapefruit, and the ringing in his ears sounded uncomfortably like the whine Potney Smithe emitted immediately before keeling over. *Whew!*

His biceps started to quiver—perhaps he had misjudged the extent to which they'd recently firmed up—and his right leg quivered, too. Yet, like a model threatened with loss of employment, he held the pose.

The thing about death, though, is that it eliminates so many options. At least, in terms of the personality game. As long as I'm alive, there's always a chance that something extremely interesting will develop from all this. Who can guess where it might eventually lead or what I might learn from it? Doesn't the infinite emerge from the fiasco? And any time I want to test it or bring it to resolution, that option is only two inches away. What's the big hurry? There may be red-eye gravy for dinner.

And there may be other ways to woo the darling Suzy. Indeed, no sooner had he relaxed his posture and settled back into his seat, with a long breath and a frangible whimper, than he began to formulate . . . well, if not a cunning strategy at least a fresh approach. He would, he told himself, concentrate his energy upon assisting her with her term paper.

In the process, he'd open the charm taps, let her see how vigorous and entertaining he could be, treat her to displays of pith and pluck that would gradually dispel any image she might have of him as sickly or incomplete. He'd turn her pity inside out, kick it off its ivory perch, feed it to the foxes of ecstasy, and, while he was at it, feed Brian baby to the pterodactyls of oblivion. And if that course went awry, if it backfired, if the fact that he was no longer pantingly petitioning for consensual copulation succeeded only in confirming to Suzy that his "injuries" had rendered him feeble and fruitless, then he would consider telling her the truth. All of it: Sailor Boy to penis poke.

He sighed again, massaged his arms, and, like a railyard dick chasing hobos off a flatcar, swept the beans of sweat from his brow.

After dinner, under the semiwatchful eye of his mother, her stepmother, Switters and Suzy huddled in the den to discuss her paper, the subject of which was to be Our Lady of Fatima. Since there was a gap in Switters's erudition where this particular virgin was concerned, Suzy filled him in.

It seems that on May 13, 1917, three shepherd children from Fatima, Portugal, were visited (*allegedly* visited, though Suzy did not qualify it thusly) by a woman (Suzy said *lady*) in a white gown and veil while tending their sheep in the hills outside of the village. The children said that the woman—the *vision* of the woman—told them to return to that place on the thirteenth of each month until the following October, at which time she would reveal her identity. The kids complied, she dropped in on them briefly each month as promised, and on October 13, she spoke dramatically and at some length, disclosing, among other things, that she traveled under the name of the Lady of the Rosary. She bade the little sheepherders to recite the rosary every day and asked that a chapel be built in her honor. Switters suggested that this last smacked of raw egoism, but Suzy only frowned at him and went on.

Although the Roman Catholic Church never officially proclaimed the children's rosary-touting visitor to be a reappearance on earth of the Virgin Mary, it authorized devotion to her in 1932, and had a shrine with a basilica erected at Fatima, to which thousands of pilgrims were still attracted each year. "Maybe that's where I'll take you on our honeymoon," whispered Switters, and for a second he could have sworn he saw a flicker of excited expectation in her eyes.

The best was yet to come. At some point during the October visitation, the Fatima Lady issued to the children three sets of predictions and warnings, two of which she urged them to immediately make public. "Warnings! Predictions! This is more like it," said Switters. "You be nice and listen," said Suzy.

There wasn't a great deal more to hear, as it turned out. Regarding the Fatima Lady's prophecies, Suzy was short on detail. "Wars and big floods and, uh, famines and earthquakes and stuff."

"That figures." Switters nodded. "Death and destruction are a prophet's bread and butter. Nobody ever grabbed much ink predicting bountiful harvests, lovely spring weather, or that a good time would be had by all. Even the Second Coming is billed as 'Doomsday.'"

"She said that some great war was going to end in the next year. *That* was nice. But that if people didn't heed her words, another greater one would come along soon."

"Those would have been World Wars One and Two."

"Whatever. She was right, wasn't she?" In the Early American rocker angled next to his wheelchair, Suzy maneuvered a bare shin beneath the other knee so that she was balanced, more or less, on one of her lean, tanned legs, a position that thrust her upper body slightly forward until he could feel her breath upon his neck. She smelled both clean and dirty, sour and sweet, like a child. The reverie of childhood—its seamless daydreams, its gamelife and toylife, its timeless aura of magic happiness—was there in her aroma. Whatever that little bastard Brian might be doing to her (or she to him), she still smelled like the punch line in a nursery rhyme. "She *couldn't* be wrong," Suzy continued. "She was Mother Mary."

The precise logic of that declaration eluded Switters, but he thought he knew where it was coming from. Many human females, as they approached puberty, as the first hormonal waters—the precursor of the adolescent geyser—began to bubble up through their private earth, became enamored, to greater or lesser degrees, with horses and/or the Virgin Mary. Unlike human males, whose fixation on sports figures, explosions, horsepower, and vulgar comedy could muddle their minds into early middle age, and in hard cases, even beyond, the equine and Marian fantasies of healthy girls tended to wane and then peter out (so to speak) altogether once they became sexually active. The most cursory familiarity with Freudian psychology could explain the girlish preoccupation with horses; the infatuation with Mary, particularly on the part of non-Catholics, was more complicated, although he guessed it could be attributed to her status as Super Virgin: she conceived without coitus, gave birth without pain, commanded the affection and admiration of men without being corrupted by them; which was to say, she triumphed gloriously over the terrors, dangers, and uncertainties facing young females as they came "of age." The fact that Mary broadcast a monstrously mixed message—motherhood is divine, sex a sin—could not be underestimated for the damage it was capable of inflicting on a developing psyche, but given the discrepant nature of reality, the myth of the Virgin Mother might be said also to provide basic training in the acceptance of life's contradictions; and most girls did eventually escape her misogynistically generated web, though frequently secretly scarred.

That Suzy was bright and spunky, that she had an open heart and generous spirit, that she was physically attractive and therefore did not have to retreat into doctrine as a form of compensation, all indicated that she would soon outgrow Marianism. For the time being, however, especially as they prepared her term paper, he would accept it just as he accepted her limited vocabulary and imprecise speech. Hey, Mary might have been his own patron saint had not her innocence been commandeered as a front for a rapacious institution. He tried to picture what Mary (known then as Miriam or Mariamne) must have been like before she was hijacked and haloed by the patriarchs, back when she was Suzy's age, a dusty-footed, chocolate-eyed Jewish filly, swelling with a fetus of suspect origin—but the Virgin that unexpectedly filled his mind's eye was the *Little Blessed Virgin of the Starry Waters*, a scruffy dory bearing him ever farther up a steaming jungle river toward a destiny almost too queer to comprehend.

He shook it off. "Very well, cupcake," he said, "here's what we must do. First, we'll take the broad overall view. Research the subject generally but thoroughly. Then, we'll narrow our focus down to something manageable and particular and original. For example, the significance of the number thirteen in the Fatima visitations. We'll research that specific area with even greater thoroughness. Then we'll organize our material, make an outline of the salient points we want to cover. After that, we'll write a first draft. Submit it to ruthless scrutiny. Edit it to perfection. And bingo! Final draft. An A-plus paper. Scholarship to Stanford."

"Wow! Hello? Sister Francis didn't tell us all that. Sounds like a lot of work. Are you sure that's how people write term papers?"

"Absolutely. Some novelists even write books that way. The more dronish ones."

"Okay," she sighed. "You're the brain."

"You've got a brain, too, and don't forget it. If you develop it, it'll be around to enrich your life long after your tits and ass have declared bankruptcy."

"Switters!" His mother looked up from her fashion magazine and shook a crimson-nailed finger at him.

"It's cool," Suzy assured the older woman. "He knows what he's talking about. He's, like, the smartest person anywhere." She planted a vigorous kiss that very nearly slid off his cheek and onto his lips.

"I don't know about that," grumbled Eunice, although whether the source of her uncertainty was Switters's intellect or Suzy's kiss remained unclear.

Cranking up the search engine on the family computer, they commenced their investigation that very evening, discovering, to their mutual astonishment, twenty full pages of entries relating to *Fatima*. They failed to make a dent in the list, however, because when Suzy noticed that her Tweety Bird wristwatch read ten o'clock, she insisted that Switters go to bed. He protested energetically. "I was riding herd on these domesticated electrons before you were potty trained," he said. "As much as I loathe computers, I can drive them all night long. I mean it. I'm good until dawn."

"No, you're not," she responded. "You need lots of rest and stuff. I'm in charge here. I'm the nurse, and I'm going to take care of you, no matter what you say." She switched off the computer. "We can, like, do this tomorrow."

"All right, then, Nurse Ratchet. As long as you'll come straight home from school."

She frowned at this but agreed.

"Are you sure you can't tell your own family what's wrong with you?" his mother asked, not for the first time.

"He can't," snapped Suzy. "It's a governmental secret."

"That's correct, Mother. And if you don't quit prying, I'm going to suspect you of being in the pay of a foreign power. I'll bet Sergi is putting you up to it."

"Don't you dare mention that name in this house," she said, reddening. Sergi was one of her previous husbands.

Suzy pushed him out of the den. In the hall she asked, "Switters, there really is something the matter with you, isn't there? It's not some kind of, like, CIA trick?"

Oh, God! Here's my chance. I can just give her the whole story and be done with it. But he didn't. "It's no trick, darling," he said, agonizing as he said it.

"You promise you can't stand up and walk?"

Come on. Tell her the truth. Or have you worked for the company so long you're only comfortable when you're lying? He clenched his fists. He bit his tongue. "I promise," he said.

She rolled him into the bathroom. "Get ready for bed," she ordered. "I'll be back in a minute."

Not being in the right frame of mind for prolonged maintenance, he was already in bed when she returned, bearing a glass of milk and a bowl of oatmeal cookies. Having had his sweet tooth shattered by a rifle butt in Kuwait, he'd left her earlier delivery of brownies virtually untouched on the bedside table, but she pretended not to notice.

Suzy smoothed his covers. Then, very gingerly, so as not to disturb his "injuries," she lay down on top of him. "Here's your good night kiss," she said, but instead of one kiss there was a series, a staccato series, repeatedly stabbing, as it were, his mouth with the wet pink dagger of her little tongue.

Through the Early American patchwork quilt, through the floral patterned sheet, he could feel her rosy biological heat, a smokeless fire that enveloped the vestigial dollhouse and charred the residual mud pie; a soft, ancient, mindless burning emanating from a source oblivious to cultural conditioning; that neither knew nor cared that "civilized" girls no longer married at twelve, that unscrupulous older males might take advantage of its urgings, or that shrill neurotic voices might rage against it. Broiled by it, Switters centered himself and lay motionless, except to rest a cautious, non-probing, non-squeezing, rather avuncular hand lightly on her small, ripe rump.

"Tell me something about yourself," she demanded.

"Okay. Shoot."

"No, I mean, like, tell me something true about you that I don't already know. A secret fact. That nobody else knows."

He pondered this for a moment or two. Then he declared, "The more advertising I see, the less I want to buy."

For some reason, Suzy found this the most radical, outlandish, unexpected, and witty remark she'd ever heard. Giggling, and shaking her head in wonderment, she slipped carefully off him and moved to the door. "Gotta go now. Remember, if you need anything, just ring that little bell."

He glanced at the quasi-antique copper bell on the table beside the milk glass but said nothing.

"You're amazing," she said. "I only wish that—" She broke off abruptly and left the room.

He lay awake most of the night, trying to finish her sentence for her.

The California State Library was located in Sacramento, appropriately enough since Sacramento was the capital of that state. Glamorous, greedy Los Angeles had its Hollywood sign; picturesque, kooky

San Francisco had its Golden Gate Bridge; provincial, authoritarian Sacramento—in which the true pulse of America pumped a steadier beat—had its Capitol Mall. Within that mall, beneath the huge gold dome of the capitol building and at the end of a broad, tree-lined avenue, the state library sheltered its precious charge of books.

Although he anticipated—correctly, as it turned out—that the library would be home to a minimum of volumes pertaining to Our Lady of Fatima and that they must turn to the Internet for the bulk of their research, still he wanted Suzy to have the library experience, to undergo the sheer *bookness* of the place, to taste the "seepage," as he put it: the information and beauty that tended to leak from shelves of books even when the books went unread.

"Virtual reality is nothing new," he told her as she guided his chair up and down the rows of stacks. "Books, the ones worth reading, have always generated virtual reality. Of course, unless one can get past its cultural and sensorial levels, what is reality *but* virtual?"

Suzy was silent, but he imagined he could hear tiny luminous thought-worms chewing roadways in her half-green apple. DNA was certainly devious in that it ripened the body before the brain.

On the way back to the suburbs, feeling tome-toned and opus-pocused, Switters piloting his rented convertible, Suzy playing navigator, nurse, and tour guide, they debated whether the fact that Sacramento was noted for its manufacture of missiles, weapons systems, cake mixes, potato chips, and caskets did not qualify it as the quintessential American city. "Okay, but, like, Sacramento's also called the Camellia Capital of the World," she reminded him.

"A few weeks ago, I was in the Dead Dog Capital of the World. I have to say, camellias are an improvement." Sensing that she was trying to form some connection in her mind between a place so vile it was renowned for dead dogs and his presumed wounds and injuries, he sought to restore a more poetic and, he hoped, romantic mood by reciting a Buson haiku:

> "A camellia falls,
> Spilling out rainwater
> —from yesterday."

"Could you pull off over there?" she immediately asked, pointing not to a motel as he at first thought but to a gas station. "I really have to use the bathroom."

"Say *toilet*, would you, darling. I don't believe bathing is one of the services Texaco provides."

"Whatever."

"No, it's not unimportant. Intelligent speech is under pressure in our fair land and needs all the support it can get."

He spent the five minutes that she was absent trying *not* to picture her camellia spilling out yesterday's water.

She made him rest when they got home.

After dinner they went computerside and uncorked the Fatima jug. Quickly their cups runnethed over.

The children were Lucia, age ten, Francisco, nine, and Jacinta, seven. They were poor and completely uneducated. When they returned from the pastures that spring evening in 1917, they seemed to be entranced, almost in a state of ecstasy. Lucia ate her supper in blissful silence, and Francisco, too, was distracted and quiet, but little Jacinta was too young and excited to contain herself. The cat she let out of the bag, and which in time grew larger than a tiger, was that they had been visited on the northern slope of the Cova da Iria (where her uncle, Lucia's father, leased pastureland) by a beautiful woman enveloped in blinding light. She appeared to them, following several flashes of light-ning (it was a clear, sunny day) from a point some meters above their heads, in the top branches of a stubby tree. As Switters read aloud Lucia's later description of the woman, her dazzling white tunic that gathered at the waist without benefit of belt or sash, her graceful hands folded prayerfully at her breast and wound round with a pearl-beaded rosary, her exquisitely refined features, the sadness and maternal con-cern that showed in her countenance, the loveliness that exceeded anything to which a bride might aspire, the light that she radiated ("clearer and brighter than a crystal cup filled with purest water pene-trated by the most sparkling rays of the sun"), he noticed that Suzy herself was becoming enraptured. *For any number of reasons*, he thought, *this is probably not a good sign.*

He was tempted to suggest that they launch a botanical probe into the bush that the Lady had selected as her landing pad. In Portuguese, it was called *carrasqueira*, in English, holm oak. By any chance did it have psychotropic properties? Might the children have chewed its leaves or, perhaps, inadvertently inhaled its pollen? Alas, even were Suzy open to such an approach, Sister Francis would likely have a Sacred Heart attack, in which case an A-grade might be out of the question.

When, however, they learned that the Fatima children had twice in the previous year been visited by an angel, Switters couldn't keep quiet. "No television, no radio, and they were illiterate. Kids some-times have to provide their own entertainment. It was always Lucia, the eldest cousin, who saw these holy apparitions first, and it was with her that they spoke. Maybe little Lucia had an active imagination, a fantasy life fueled by Bible stories, the only extraordinary material to which she'd ever been exposed, and she pulled the younger kids into her fantasies, much the same way that Tom Sawyer pulled in Huckleberry Finn."

Suzy protested. "I don't know why you have to be so negative. Don't you believe in miracles and stuff?"

"Well, I know from first-hand experience that the universe is a very woo-woo place, and that so-called consensual reality is not much more than the tip of the iceberg. But my credibility alarm starts to jangle a bit when the Virgin Mary shows up speaking flawless Portuguese and looking like a Roman Catholic Sunday School portrait instead of the Middle Eastern Jewish matron she was at the time of her death. If I remember it correctly, rosary beads weren't introduced until more than a thousand years after Christ, so why—"

"Hello? God's time isn't the same as our time."

She had him there. Certainly he wasn't going to argue on the side of linear time, not after what he'd been through. Today *was* tomorrow, wasn't it? Or, at least, the future leaked into the present on a fairly routine basis. The past, as well.

"Anyway, like, what about all the people who saw the sun dance in the sky and stuff? On October thirteenth. They weren't Huckleberry Finns."

"Hmmm," hmmmed Switters. "That's interesting in itself. Of the seventy thousand people who joined the children in the Cova da Iria pasture for the Lady's farewell performance and prophecy session, roughly half claimed to have witnessed a meteorological light show of staggering proportions. The other half saw absolutely nothing. What does that tell us, darling? That fifty percent of humanity is susceptible to mass hallucination?"

"Or that fifty percent are pure enough to see God's miracles and the rest are like you."

"Fifty percent purity? Man, I wish the figure was even a fraction that high! As for me personally, I witness a divine miracle every time you enter the room."

"Oh, Switters!"

When she tucked him in a short while later—he wasn't tired, but he didn't object—she loaded a full package of tongue into their good night kiss.

Asked in an interview in 1946 if the Lady of Fatima had revealed anything about the end of the world, Lucia (by then Sister Mary dos Dores, a lay nun) responded rather like a CIA officer with cowboyish leanings. "I cannot answer that question," she said through tight lips. Lucia did not, as far as has been reported, add, "for reasons of national security."

Whether or not the Lady had been forthcoming about a possible final curtain ringing down on the Homo sapiens revue—and none but Lucia had actually heard her prophecies—she was not exactly a bubble of optimism in regard to our planetary prospects. For example, that spectacular celestial cha-cha that thirty-five thousand people claimed to have observed, along with Lucia and her cousins, on October 13, 1917, was executed, she said, not by the sun but by a preview of a flaming comet, a fireball that according to the Lady (and disputed by astronomers everywhere) would return someday to dry up oceans, lakes, and rivers and shrivel a third of the earth's vegetation. No, not precisely a planetary death sentence, but considerably more severe than a stiff fine and a hundred hours of community service.

If it was doom that intrigued them, however, the Fatima faithful got their money's worth. The white-clad apparition predicted straightaway that a plague would fall upon the land soon after the Great War ended and that two of the shepherd children would be among its victims. In 1919, first Francisco, then Jacinta succumbed to the influenza epidemic that killed twenty million people in Europe and North America. The Lady had hit a chilling bull's-eye with that one, and she was only slightly off center with her prophecy of approaching famine: almost on cue, a vine fungus spread through Europe, lasted more than three years, and left no grape unspoiled.

Her forecast in the second set of predictions that Russia would "spread its errors" throughout the world could probably also be considered a hit. Strongly disposed toward threats and scoldings—the Lady repeatedly warned that if people didn't amend their lives, beg forgiveness, and run marathons on their rosary beads there was going to be hell to pay—she was particularly hard on Communists, obviously viewing Communism as something more amplitudinously evil than a mere inherently flawed economic system. *Rather like John Foster Dulles,* thought Switters, but he didn't say as much for fear he might uncontrollably fire a saliva shot at the polished hardwood floor or the antique rag rug that lay upon it. Bobby would never have forgiven him if he hadn't.

It was Thursday afternoon, and Suzy, a shade less reluctantly than the day before, had come straight home from school. The two of them were in the den, sorting through the printouts of their Internet research, concentrating, at Switters's urging, on the Fatima predictions and warnings. Suzy had wanted to change into jeans and a sweatshirt, but at his request she remained attired in her school uniform. Whether his aim was to reduce temptation or to torture himself with it was probably debatable. In any event, he ceased counting her pleats long enough to wave a sheet of paper in the charged air that separated them. "This!" he exclaimed. "Right here. It's the only tidbit of information we've uncovered in three days that could spike the punch at the teddy bears' picnic."

"Hello?"

"Right here." The printout, which he now handed her, concerned Our Lady's third and final prophecy. At the time of its delivery, the children would say nothing of this last prediction except that it was of great consequence and would bring joy to some and sorrow to others.

Around 1940, some twenty-three years after it was supposedly issued, the nun formerly known as Lucia Santos wrote down the secret prophecy and sealed it in an envelope with instructions that it be opened in 1960, or upon her death should she die earlier than that date. The envelope was locked in the office safe of the bishop of Leiria in Portugal, where Church sources said it remained until 1957, when Pope Pius XII had it brought, under tight security, to Rome. Pius was itching to rip it open, but Lucia was still alive. In fact, Lucia was still breathing in 1997, whereas Pius XII died in 1958 without ever satisfying his curiosity.

While the Church would neither confirm nor deny it, highly placed Vatican sources claimed that at some point in 1960, Pius's successor, Pope John XXIII, did, finally, open the mystery envelope—and wept for three days over the "terrible news" it contained. Throughout the remainder of his life, John XXIII adamantly refused to discuss it with anyone, and the message was reputed to rest in a vault at the papal palace, unread by a soul save that sobbing pontiff nearly forty years in the past.

"Yeah," said Suzy. "That's pretty wild. But you know, how could I write about it when, like, I don't know what it says."

"We could speculate."

"You mean? . . ."

"I mean, extrapolating from her two published predictions, we could try to guess the content of the final and missing one. Might be fun. What possible prognostication from a controversial source could set a modern pope to blubbering for three whole days?"

"But bring joy to some."

"Exactly. Think about it."

From the way Suzy screwed up her face, she was thinking hard about it. "You're cute when you frown," said Switters.

She seemed daunted, perplexed by her stepbrother's proposal, and eventually she vetoed it. "No, I just want to tell the story. You know, tell about the children and Our Lady and all the stuff that happened. Even Sister Francis doesn't know much about it. She said she didn't. And the class is, like, clueless. It's kind of a beautiful story, so I just want to write it down for everybody. Okay?"

Switters shrugged. "It's your party. I'll help you organize the material if you'd like, and you can take it from there."

She lowered her eyes. "Switters? Are you disappointed?"

"Nein," he lied. "Only thing that disappoints me is that the authorities haven't locked you up somewhere. You're too damn cute to be at large. You're a public menace."

"Switters."

"I'll bet your armpits taste like strawberry ice cream."

She had just slid onto his lap and was tightening her tawny arms around his neck, her tongue muscles quivering like the hamstrings of a cheetah about to spring from its lair, when his mother made one of her periodic checks of the room. "Now, now, children," Eunice admonished.

"Can't I show my big brother some gratitude and affection?" Suzy asked. Her tone was defiant.

"You've been watching too much TV, young lady," said Eunice, somewhat inexplicably.

Reddening, Suzy stood, about to defend herself, but Switters intervened. "Mother's right," he said calmly. From an end table within his reach, he snatched up a cast-iron ashtray, fashioned to resemble an Early American hearth skillet, and used it to gesture at the forty-inch Sony across the den. "There's the problem right there," he announced. "Does it not possess the power of a totem pole and the heart of a rat? Die, demon box, die!" With that, he hurled the ashtray at the TV, badly cracking its plastic casing and missing the screen (purposefully or not) by a fraction of an inch.

As the ashtray, a souvenir of Monticello, caromed with a loud clanking onto the floor, his mother emitted a sound midway between a gasp and a shriek, and Suzy regarded him as if he were the most astounding entity to grace the earth since Fatima, Portugal, 1917.

Choosing to skip the family dinner, Switters slipped away and drove over toward Rancho Cordova, where he knew there to be a Kentucky Fried Chicken outlet with a drive-through service window. "I understand," he said to the clean-cut, if acne-peppered, hobbledehoy who dispensed his order (he imagined him to look a lot like Brian), "that KFC still uses the colonel's original frying recipe. Is that correct?"

"Uh, yes, sir, it is."

"Eleven secret herbs and spices. So I've heard."

"Yes, sir. I believe so."

"Would you identify them for me, please?"

"Huh?"

"The eleven secret herbs and spices. Tell me what they are."

Bewildered, the boy began blinking rather frenetically, as if during one of the lid closures, the customer and his cheeky red convertible might disappear.

"Don't play dumb," snarled Switters. "If you can't come up with all eleven off the top of your head, nine or ten will do."

The boy gathered his composure. "Uh, I'm sorry, sir. They're our secret recipe. Would you please pull forward?"

"I'll pay you forty dollars." He wagged two bank notes in the pustulated face.

"No, sir," said the boy, glancing over his shoulder with one of those half frightened, half irate I'm-going-to-send-for-the-manager expressions. "I don't. . . . You're gonna have to pull forward."

"What if I told you I have your girlfriend in the trunk of this car?"

His eyes widening until it appeared his pimples might pop, the young man seemed as if he were about to shout or retreat or both, yet he did neither for the simple reason that Switters had fixed him so forcefully with his fierce, hypnotic gaze that he was all but paralyzed. "I-I don't—" he stammered weakly. "I'm just a cashier. I don't know nothing about the—the cooking side of it."

"So, you won't betray the colonel for love or money? Not even to spare your girlfriend's life?" Switters abruptly relaxed his glare and lit up the boy with a smile that could paint a carousel. "Congratulations! You've done it, pal. You've passed the test." He held out his hand, but the boy was too stunned to shake it. "I'm Operative, uh, Poe, Audubon Poe of the Central Intelligence Agency. As you're doubtlessly aware, the CIA's main responsibility these days is protecting America's corporate interests, such as the colonel's eleven cryptic herbs and spices, from insidious foreign competitors. You play an important role in this struggle, pal. So, well done! Your government's proud of you, and I'm sure the colonel'd be proud of you, too—if the beloved old motherfucker weren't as dead as the gravy you counterfeit gastronomes slop on his unsuspecting biscuits."

Switters tossed the boy a twenty. "Take the night off," he exhorted. "Badger some phrontifugic adult to buy you a six-pack. Domestic, of course. Sacramento is, indeed, the quintessential American city, and you are a genuine American hero!" He gunned the engine. "I'll let your girlfriend out at the next rest stop!" he cried, and he squealed out of the KFC lot, laying down enough burnt rubber to blackface the cast of the *Amos 'n' Andy* show for most of a season.

With a Cajun-style drumstick between his oft-abused but still pearly teeth, he headed back toward the west, roaring into one of those lurid orangeade sunsets that could qualify as nature's revenge on Louis XIV.

Shortly before 10 P.M., as Switters sat propped up on the four-poster bed reading from *Finnegans Wake*, there was a soft knock at his door, and Suzy tiptoed in. "You missed dinner," she said.

"I dined out. How are things?"

"Daddy's been kind of gnarly. He wants to know why you, like, attacked his TV set."

"Yes. Good question. I've been wondering about that myself. I suppose you *could* say that these past few days in suburbia have roused my imp from its slumber."

"You mean," she asked, half frowning, half grinning, "the Devil made you do it?"

"Well, no, darling, that's not it at all. The Devil doesn't *make* us do *anything*. The Devil, for example, doesn't make us mean. Rather, when we're mean, *we* make the Devil. Literally. Our actions create him. Conversely, when we behave with compassion, generosity, and grace, we create God in the world. But all that's beside the point. I think probably the most truthful thing you can tell your daddy is that I attacked his TV set out of love of life."

"Love of life," Suzy whispered almost inaudibly, rolling the phrase around in her mouth and her mind, as if it were a concept so unfamiliar, so novel, it would take awhile to grasp it.

"What," asked Switters, "did my mother have to say?"

"Oh, she said 'Dumpling's'—sometimes she calls you *Dumpling*— 'Dumpling's a man of mystery, just like his father.'" She watched an odd, ironic smile bend his lower lip like a bartender twisting a peel of lemon. "So, like, what did your father do?"

"He was a man of mystery."

" 'Man of mystery,' " she repeated in a whisper, as though she were again ruminating on an exotic, esoteric but flavorful notion—and this time she watched the bedside reading lamp illuminate his spray of tiny scars, causing them to resemble a constellation projected on a planetarium ceiling. After a moment or two, she asked politely, "Uh, what're you doing tomorrow?"

"For one thing, I thought I'd sift through the Fatima detritus and get your outline started for you."

"Oh my God, Switters, you're just so fine! I was really hoping you'd do that. Like, I can't be here tomorrow. My dad's taking your mom shopping again in San Francisco, and they, I guess, don't want me to be home alone with you. So, I'm going with my girlfriend after school, and then Brian's taking me to his football game."

"Brian's an athlete, is it?"

"No, he doesn't play. He's a cheerleader."

Switters brightened. "A cheerleader. He doesn't by any chance moonlight at Kentucky Fried Chicken?"

She moved her buttercup bangs in a negative rotation. "Uh, I'm gonna try to leave early. Like, after the first quarter. I think I can, you know, get a ride home. The parental unit won't be back from San Francisco until ten o'clock. They told me."

"But you're leaving the game early and coming home?"

Lowering her filoplume lashes until they almost swept the blush from her cheeks, she said ever so gravely, "To be with you." She slid awkwardly onto the bed beside him, kissed him briefly but wetly, removed one of his hands from the binding of *Finnegans Wake*, and placed it in the general vicinity of her crotch. "I want to get naked with you," she said, blurting it out, softly but forcefully, like a jet of steam.

Switters swallowed hard, as though he were gulping down a goose egg. When his larynx stopped wobbling, he asked, "Are you sure?"

She nodded soberly. "I . . . think so. You're my . . . my. . . . But I . . . I'll be here if I can. I might not."

The next day Switters had the house to himself. He stayed in bed until he heard the Mercedes sedan pull out of the three-car garage, heading for the boutiques of Maiden Lane. Then he breakfasted on peanut butter and soy bacon sandwiches, taking them out by the swimming pool to eat. The pool had been emptied for the season and covered with a blue plastic tarp that for a zip of an instant transported him back to Inti's *Virgin* and the tattered canopy with which the dory had tried in vain to hold back the Amazon sun. In November, the Sacramento sun needed no such restraint, although it was certainly warmer there than in Seattle, and drier, as well. The golf course that bordered the stucco ranch house that Eunice had won in the marriage lottery was as green as Socrates's last cocktail, but everything between it and the coastal range to the west and the Sierra Nevada to the east was so amber, dusty, flea-bitten, and buff it reminded him of the lion population in a second-rate zoo. It was visual cereal that, milkless, crunched in his eyes, and he realized that were he to strike out across those stubble fields where wheat and barley had recently been sheared, he'd be better off in a wheelchair than on foot. Even the steely soles of Inti's feet would have been diced.

Done with breakfast, he decided to attempt meditation. It was never easy to commence—his internal river of thought and verbiage had a velocity that overflowed or crumbled Buddha's dams—and on that morning it was particularly difficult to get started. Bobby had taught him not to wrench the valves, however, so he sat passively, neither fostering thought nor trying not to think, and gradually the flow subsided—except for one unstemmable trickle, and that trickle's source was Suzy. After about an hour of that, he thought *What the hell!*, and gave it up. He hadn't made it into the medulla of the medulla, but he'd gotten closer to the Void than airports are to most major cities; he'd glimpsed its invisible skyline, breathed its odorless smokes; and since it was eternal, knew it'd be there the next time he bought a ticket. Just not today. Today, for better or worse, was a day to think about Suzy.

There is something so sweet about a young girl's sexual longings, he thought. *There's a sad and happy sweetness in them.* Her longing was not for orgasmic release: that would come with the years. Her longing was not even for an amplification of the genital quaver that her body for some time would have been softly trilling; nor was it strictly a longing for love and affection: in fact, the more love and affection a girl was receiving from her family and friends, the less that was a part of it. As much as anything else, it was a longing for *information*. There was information about men; about being with men, alone, in dark places, that she sensed she must access in order to navigate the mysterious vastness of her life-to-be. Her subconscious mind was signaling to her that such information was essential to her very survival in the adult world, and her hormones, for reasons of their own, were augmenting those signals with a barrage of swelling itches and tingles. Implicit in most sexual yearning was a deep-seated desire to connect somehow with the mystery of being, but the yearning of the young was overlaid with a scary yet optimistic desire to solve the smaller (though they'd hardly seem small at the time) mysteries of the adult universe, a universe in which the penis seemed to cast a long shadow and the vagina formed a gateway to both shame and salvation. If the longing of many older women lacked that sweetness, it was because they already had gleaned the information for which young girls were so shyly desperate, and may have found it disappointing and unsatisfactory, particularly where men were concerned.

Switters went back indoors and rolled about the house for a while, maneuvering around utterly obsolete churns and spinning wheels and uncomfortable wooden rocking chairs. Were he ever offered a voyage in a time machine, Colonial America would be far down his list of preferred destinations, although he suspected that Jefferson, Franklin, and the lot would be worthy drinking companions, maybe even deserving of C.R.A.F.T. Club membership, which was not something one could say of a single governmental leader of the past hundred and fifty years.

In contrast to the harsh pragmatism of the Early American decor, the contents of his mother's closets, which he examined now in some detail, were stylish and luxurious. Hanging there, bereft of the flesh whose silhouettes they mimicked, were soft, powdery pantsuits, slithery black cocktail dresses, and matte suede jackets trimmed with lamb, each flying an inconspicuous but haughty little flag emblazoned with an Italian name (Oscar de la Renta, Dolce & Gabbana) that he'd have recognized if he read *Vogue* or even *Newsweek* instead of *Tricycle* and *Soldier of Fortune*. Eunice did them justice, too, he had to admit, though he failed to find her, at fifty-seven, hair in a hennaed bun, face in a brittle tuck, to be as buzzy with allure as he remembered her mother, Maestra, to be at that age. Dwayne's closet, which he also examined, was filled with goofy golfing garb and shiny suits Switters wouldn't have worn to a Chiang Mai cockfight.

Gradually he made his way to the door of Suzy's room, but although he went so far as to grasp the knob, he just could not allow himself to violate its sanctity. He'd never been *that* kind of spy. He sat there for a long time, however. Thinking.

Suzy doesn't merely want to feel, she wants to know. She yearned to concretize the unsubstantial image of the "real" life that awaited her; to prepare herself, perhaps, for the transfiguration, the metamorphosis that would split her dreamy cocoon, discharging her, a wing-damp, unsure butterfly, into the leafy gardens of wifedom and motherhood. Well, would he not be the perfect teacher? He not only had the experience, he also had the devotion, the caring. If the male erection was the compass with which so many women, for better or worse, must get their bearings in the world, what finer instrument than his own? *Why, if Amelia Earhart had had my peepee on board. . . .* He recalled Bobby's story of how, in olden times, the uncles had initiated—

But no. He couldn't sell it to his conscience. The bedroom was not a classroom. There were some skills (if *skill* was the right word) that a person needed to develop, through trial and error, on their own. To "teach" Suzy about sex, from his well-burnished lectern, would be to deprive her of the follies and fumbles of teen romance: the embarrassment and awkwardness, worry and wonder, telltale stains and tangled-up limbs—all the gawky ecstasies and sticky surprises that jack out of the box of neophyte lust. What right did he have to streamline that process? What right to teach her *anything*?

He asked that question again late in the afternoon, when, after completing an outline of the Fatima story at the family computer, he found himself adding to it the following provocation:

The Virgin Mary, in her Lady of the Rosary guise, appeared to the kids at Fatima six times in 1917. Way back in 1531, she chose Guadalupe, Mexico, for the first stop on her tardy comeback tour, imprinting her image, so it's said, on a poor Indian's poncho and instructing him to have a church built outside of Mexico City. Next stop, Paris, three hundred years later (God's time is not our time), where a novice spied her twice in a chapel. This time, she wanted a medal to be cast with her image and regular devotions said to her. She was back in a relative flash in 1858, appearing no less than eighteen times in a grotto down the road at Lourdes and referring to herself as the Immaculate Conception. She must have liked the neighborhood because she turned up next before four children in Pontmain, France, and succeeded in getting another church constructed in her honor. In 1879 she hovered above a village chapel in Ireland; in the 1930s she did Belgium big time, appearing to various youngsters no fewer than forty-one times in several locations, referring to herself at Beauraing as the Virgin of the Golden Heart, and at Banneux as the Virgin of the Poor. It was in Amsterdam between 1945 and 1959 that she took off the velvet gloves, calling herself the Lady of All Nations and demanding that her contact petition the pope to grant her the titles Co-Redemptrix, Mediatrix, and Advocate. Starting in 1981, she touched down in two of the most screwed-up places on earth, Rwanda and Bosnia, wanting to be known as Mother of the World, no less, and Queen of Peace. And speaking of bad locations, her image affixed itself to the side of a finance company office in Florida a couple of years ago, though she didn't apply for a loan.

So, my steamy little kumquat, I'm forced to ask: where has Jesus been during all this? Mary makes multiple appearances, demands increasing recognition, assumes ever more grandiose titles, and insists on equal billing as the Co-Redeemer. Yet over those five centuries, and the fifteen that preceded them, not a peek of Jesus or a peep from him. What's going on here? In his time on earth, he didn't seem all that shy. Notice how Mary never mentions him in any of her pronouncements? God, yes, but not Jesus. She herself is hardly mentioned in the Gospels, and on those few occasions when she does make the scene, Jesus is less than enthusiastic about her, going so far, in Matthew, I believe, as to snub her, asking, "Who is my mother?" and answering that anyone who does God's bidding qualifies as his mother. Could there be a revenge motif here? Could Jesus be under house arrest, chained up in his mother's basement? Does she have something on him, is he being blackmailed? I suppose we could perceive all this Mary activity as a natural resurfacing of the feminine principle in society, a welcome reemergence of the goddess as the dominant religious figure. But might it also signal a palace coup of the sort that cost the brilliant upstart Lucifer his No. 2 position in Heaven—or else a public airing of a nasty little family feud?

As Switters read, then read again, the preceding two paragraphs, his forefinger hovered over the *delete* key like the meatless digit of the Reaper pausing above his black eraser. What right did he have to provoke her sweet mind, to litter with funky horse blossoms of doubt the aseptic, uncracked sidewalks of her street of bliss?

"Every right in the world," he heard a voice within him say. "Not only a right but a duty."

Around sunset, as a geranium and satsuma luminescence turned the adjacent golf course into the playboard of a pinball machine, an onslaught of nervousness sent Switters to the garage refrigerator where Dwayne maintained a supply of beer. He drained a can of Budweiser, popped open a second, stuck a couple extras in the wheelchair saddlebag. Then he propelled himself about the house some more, grimacing at the hurricane lamps and clunky tin candlesnuffers. At one point he announced loudly, as if to a straggling duffer out on the seventeenth hole, "This home has bad *feng shui*. I can sense it."

He'd had a similar feeling once about his apartment in Langley, and, as he was later to e-mail Bobby Case (with apparent embellishment), "I went to call some *feng shui* geomancers to take care of the problem, but I dialed Sinn Fein by mistake, and a bunch of Irishmen showed up with automatic weapons." To which Bobby responded, "You're just lucky you didn't dial Sean Penn."

As the daylight vanished, his agitation increased. He pictured banks of halogens winking on at the parochial school stadium, the zit-bejeweled gladiators (he was one once) lining up for kickoff; the high, thin squeals from the students in the bleachers, the coldness and hardness of the narrow boards beneath their buttocks, the shrill whistle of referees and cheesy deep-fried echo of the P.A. system; the spilled cola and missquirted mustard, puffs of dust and puffs of quicklime, the pumped-up adolescent wonder of it all. And then the first quarter drawing to an end . . . the sophomore cutie stealing away. . . .

Switters had been Siamese-twinning it most of his life, but for the dichotomy that bedeviled him now he was not quite prepared. For the spider bite of guilt, yes, but not the ice hook of doubt. One moment he craved to give her a bath in his semen, to rub it, warm and pearly, into her navel, her lips, the nipples that in his mind evoked the candy-coated lug nuts on Cupid's pink Corvette. The next, he wished simply to kiss her toes. No, no, not the toes: much too erogenous! To kiss her heel or, better yet, her left elbow. In its cotton sleeve. To kiss once, lightly, the top of her sweet head—and then to shield her, with every means at his disposal, from the slings and eros of adult rage and fortune; to deflect the poison bullets of the "real world," which is to say, the marketplace, so that not one would ever blast a hole in the magic tutu of her childhood.

Damn! Switters had always been a shade contradictory, but he'd never been neurotic. Like many robust people, in fact, he held neurosis in contempt. Yet, here he was, a fever flaming in his veins, a thunder in his pulses; his lungs ballooning, then deflating, his thoughts all over the map like a fast-food chain. And the alcohol, as was its evil genius, was only egotizing and adrenalizing matters, making them worse. Better the silly genius of hemp.

He proceeded to his room, where he raised a window for ventilation and then lit a joint. Following a husky toke or two, a semblance of calm was restored. He toked further, nodding, closing his eyes. Ahhh. His vision of the football game took on a softer focus now. Rather than a ritual parody of the primate territorial imperative, complete with nonlethal but often painful violence, colored at its margins with decidedly sexual overtones, and fouled in recent years by the stink of commerce, it became . . . well, no, it was still all that, but there was an innocent oomph about it, too, a playful, high-spirited, savage zest, and he envied Suzy being there and, moreover, wished he could have been on the field, performing for her, flattening running backs and cracking wide receivers nearly in half.

Seconds later, he giggled at the dumbness of that fantasy, and, slumping low in the wheelchair, soon forgot about the game altogether. Other, seemingly more profound, thoughts took over his brain, thoughts such as, *To what extent would a given quantity of catnip have affected quantum mechanics in Schrödinger's theoretical catbox?* and, *Why was C selected to symbolize the speed of light when Z is obviously the fastest letter in the alphabet?*

The chiming of two of Eunice's three ridiculously oversize, depressingly ugly grandfather clocks interrupted his reverie. He thought he counted eight *bongs,* and his wristwatch confirmed it. Hell's bells! The first quarter would have ended long ago. Suzy wasn't coming. She warned that she might not. She had her own set of fears, including her kind concern that a physical assertion of their love might compromise his "delicate condition."

She wasn't coming after all. So be it. It was for the best. He lit another joint and partway through it, realized he was famished. A classic case of the cannabic munchies. (If manufacturers of chocolate and peanut butter were half smart, they'd lobby relentlessly for decriminalization.) He was so hungry he reached under the bed and retrieved the plates of brownies and cookies he'd hidden there so as not to hurt her feelings. They were by this time entering the early stages of fossilization—crusty, dry, and stale—but he devoured them as though they were bootleg ambrosia.

Sucrose sugars from the baked goods linked arms, singing, with dextrose sugars from the beer, to form a near-riotous rabble in his bloodstream, a chemical mob whose march on his cerebral ramparts was mollified but not diverted by the more gentle, introspective (though hardly staid) tetrahydro-cannabinols from the marijuana. Provoked by these energies, he found himself rummaging in the secret compartment of his crocodile valise for his disk of Broadway hits, and when, moments later, the sailors' chorus from *South Pacific* began to belt out "There Is Nothin' Like a Dame," he was moved to dance.

He rolled to the bed and vaulted up on it. Dancing on a bed has intrinsic limitations, and his preliminary steps quickly evolved, or devolved, into ungainly bounces. Rather than fighting it, he went with it, and by the time "The Surrey With the Fringe on Top" from *Oklahoma* blared on (he'd cranked the amps to full volume), he was bounding like a rambunctious kid on a bedtime trampoline, the fritter-colored curls at the dome of his skull almost brushing the ceiling. The exertion provided a much-needed release. His wahoo was rapidly rising.

Midair, during one of the higher bounces, he thought he heard a voice in the hall exclaim, "Good God! What is that *sucky* music?"

He landed. Springs depressed, then recoiled, and without breaking his rhythm, he catapulted ceilingward again, and as he elevated he saw her. Standing now in the doorway. She'd rouged her mouth, a bit too thickish, and shadowed her eyes, a shade too bluely, and she was wearing one of Eunice's party dresses, a slinky charcoal sheath that he recognized from his recent inspection of his mother's wardrobe. It was a sophisticated little number, but although she and Eunice were approximately the same height now, it hung loosely on her, its effect anything but chic. It was Suzy's objective, apparently, to look womanly and seductive. In actuality, she looked like a child playing dress-up in her stepmother's clothing (which, to some extent, she was), an impression reinforced by the fact that she was barefoot. To the extent that the effect was comical, it was also overwhelmingly erotic.

Switters stiffened his legs and dropped his arms to bring the bouncing to a halt, but the springs continued to contract and expand in a gradually diminishing action that sent him stumbling and staggering about on the bed, largely out of control.

Suzy's mouth was agape, the expression on her face one of shock, disbelief, and horror. Abruptly she turned and fled.

"This was a joke!" he yelled after her. "I've got other music! I've got . . . Frank Zappa!" *Shit! She's probably never heard of Zappa.* "I've got . . . I've got Big Mama Thornton!" *Sixteen, living in suburban Sacramento, would she even know Big Mama?* "The Mekons! There we go! Mekons? Suzy!"

Then, perched on the edge of the bed like a stone cherub urinating into a fish pond, it occurred to him that music wasn't the issue.

Switters came within a muscle contraction of jumping down and running after her. He was a survivalist to the marrow, however, and instinct tempered his panic long enough for him to transfer his body into the wheelchair before setting off in pursuit.

Through the closed door of her room, he could hear her weeping.

Again and again, his mouth formed her name, but the sound stuck in his throat like a fake Santa in a crooked chimney.

For a full five minutes, he sat there, listening to her sob. Then he trundled slowly back to his room, packed his things, and left the house. At Executive Field he spent the night sitting up in the Invacare 9000, occasionally dozing, mostly not. For a fee of thirty-five dollars, Southwest Airlines allowed him to reschedule his departure date from Sunday to Saturday, and he boarded an early morning flight to Seattle.

when, three days later, Switters arrived back on the East Coast, a migraine arrived with him. A headache likewise had ambushed him between Sacramento and Seattle, sending him to bed for forty-eight hours and minimalizing his contact with Maestra. It wasn't until he was leaving her house that he thought to give her the bracelet of linked silver camellias he'd bought for her at the Sacramento airport. Maestra had been preoccupied, herself, attempting to break into the computer files of an art appraiser whom she suspected of deliberately undervaluing her Matisse. Intuitively, she'd steered clear of the topic of Suzy.

The cross-country migraine was neither milder nor more severe than the short-distance one. In both cases, there was the sense that in the space behind his eyes a porcupine and a lobster were fighting to the death in front of a strobe light.

At some juncture on the train ride from New York to Washington, one or the other of the prickly creatures prevailed and a neuro-optic gaffer switched off the strobe. Switters was feeling reasonably normal when the skyline of the nation's capital came into view. At the sight of the Washington Monument, wahooish bubbles formed in his spinal fluid. The excitement, needless to say, owed nothing to the monument itself, it having even less of a connection to him than to the dead statesman it was meant to honor. Aside from the fact that it was tall and white, what did the structure evoke of George Washington, the soldier, President, or man? On the other hand, since Jefferson described his colleague's mind as "being little aided by invention or imagination," perhaps the blandness of the monument was entirely fitting—and besides, what symbol would a designer have erected in its place: a surveyor's transit, a hatchet, a set of clacking dentures?

To Switters, the monument signaled that he was back on the job, and that was the reason for his tingling. Back on *what* job was another matter. He knew only that, armed with privileged credentials, he had reentered the maw of the beast, the power-puckered omphalos upon which all angelic mischief must sooner or later come to bear, the city where winning was absolutely everything.

And only the winners were lost?

That night he slept in his own bed. Such a cozy, comforting phrase: "in his own bed." Like many such sentiments, however, it was fallacious. True, he owned the bed and, under mortgage, the apartment in which it was situated, but in the two years since he'd acquired those things, he'd slept in them fewer than forty times.

Because he was born on the cusp between Cancer and Leo—which is to say, drawn on one side to the hermit's cave, on the other to centerstage—he both craved the familiarity of a private, personal, domestic space and loathed the idea of being fettered by permanence or possession. At least, astrologers would attribute the ambivalence to his natal location. Someone else might point out that it was simply an acute microcosmic reflection of the fundamental nature of the universe.

The apartment was sparsely furnished. Except for some of the suits and T-shirts, the few articles in it (including refrigerated food items in states of degeneration that brought to mind the special effects in Mexican horror films) had been purchased at least two years prior.

The more advertising he saw, the less he wanted to buy?

Depending upon their level of . . . what?—fear? alienation? vested interest? humanity?—people looked at the new headquarters building of the Central Intelligence Agency from varying psychological perspectives. Switters's perspective was fairly neutral. He was, by Bobby Case's definition, a "neutral angel."

Switters was even neutral about angels. Biblical angels, that is. On the rare occasion when he considered the subject, he was inclined to compare angels to bats. He could scarcely think of one without the other. It seemed perfectly obvious. They were two sides of the same coin, were they not? One winged anthropomorph the alter image of the other.

White and radiant, the heavenly angel represented goodness. Dark and cunning, the nocturnal bat was associated with evil. Yet, was it really that simplistic?

Bats, in actuality, were sweet tempered, harmless (less than 1 percent rabid) little mammals who aided humankind by devouring immense amounts of insects and pollinating more plants and trees in the rain forest than bees and birds together. Angels, conversely, often appeared as wrathful avengers, delivering stern messages, wrestling with prophets, evicting tenants, brandishing flaming swords. Their "pollination" was restricted to begetting children on astonished mortal women. Which would you rather meet in a midnight alley?

Angels had their worth, however. Creatures of wonder, they bore the ancient marvelous into the modern mundane. Skeptics who howled at the very mention of ghosts, space aliens, or crop circles (not to mention greenhouse gases) were not so quick to scoff at angels. According to a Gallup poll, more than half of all Americans believed in angels. Thus did the supernatural still influence the rational world.

Women tended to be afraid of bats. Even Maestra. As near as could be determined, it was not a subconscious fear of pollination, some sowing of bad seed. Women, rather, were afraid that bats might become entangled in their hair. Ah, but St. Paul had decreed that women's heads be covered in church "because of the angels." In Paul's era, words for *angel* and *demon* were interchangeable, and there was a species of angel/demon that was said to be attracted to women's hair. Angels in hair. Bats in hair. Once again, distinctions were not as crisp as they might have superficially appeared. At some point, then, angels and bats must converge. There, as in mathematical space, the coin would have only one side. But what point was that? Where or when was it that light and darkness combined? End of Time—or, rather, Today Is Tomorrow—might have answered: "In laughter."

Within the CIA, the opposite of the *neutral* angel was the cowboy. Cowboys believed themselves on the side of light (which they identified exclusively with goodness), but because they insisted on light's absolute dominion over darkness—and would stop at no dark deed to insure that domination—they ended up transforming light into darkness. It was strictly a transformation, though, not a merger. Laughter never entered the equation.

Thus, when critics looked at the CIA headquarters and saw evil, they were not entirely mistaken. What they failed to see, however, was what Switters (now climbing clumsily out of a taxi in front of the building) almost always saw: a factory unexcelled at manufacturing the very monkey wrenches that might be tossed into its own machinery.

After being cleared through a series of checkpoints, Switters eventually arrived at the offices of Mayflower Cabot Fitzgerald, assistant deputy director of operations. It was 10 A.M. Joolie, Fitzgerald's red-headed secretary, with whom Switters had enjoyed an ongoing flirtation of some years' standing, frowned speculatively at the wheelchair but did not inquire about it. One does not prosper at Langley by being nosy.

As for Fitzgerald himself, he pretended at first not even to notice. Mayflower, as he signed his memos and preferred to be addressed, never showed surprise at anything. A display of surprise would have been a breach of sophistication, a violation of ingrained principles.

"You're right on time," said Mayflower, when he'd shut the door behind them.

"That's only natural," said Switters, who had blown Joolie a kiss as he disappeared into the inner office. "I'm an operative, not a lawyer, a Hollywood agent, or a self-important bureaucrat."

If Mayflower took offense, his face did not reveal it. Perhaps he was accustomed to Switters, expected him by now to deport himself with cool effectiveness under certain field conditions, but at other times to wax florid, audacious, rascally. In any event, he stared silently, inexpressively, at his subordinate for quite a few seconds, stared through steel-rimmed spectacles whose assiduously polished lenses gleamed as brightly as his bald spot. Actually, it was a bit more than a spot. At fifty-five, Mayflower had just about enough left of his iron-gray hair to bewig a small doll. Chemotherapy Barbie. Steel glasses, iron hair, granite jaw, golden voice, and a mind like weapons-grade plutonium. To Switters, the deputy director seemed less animal than mineral.

It was Switters who finally broke the silence. "Errand boy," he said, "not operative. Sorry if I overstated my position."

Mayflower's thin lips twitched but stopped short of a smile. "Is the wheelchair a prop to dramatize some point?" he asked.

"Minor mishap in South America."

"Really? Nothing to do with our fellow Sumac, I hope?"

"Nein. To do with End of Time. Or, rather, Today Is Tomorrow."

Mayflower stared at him some more. Switters stared at the wall behind the desk. In many government offices, an official of Mayflower Cabot Fitzgerald's rank might have displayed a Groton pennant and framed diplomas from Princeton and Yale (all part of Mayflower's background), but at CIA, relics of personal history were discouraged.

Not so much as a photograph of wife, child, or dog graced the desk. There was, however, on one wall, a signed eight-by-ten glossy of Barbara Bush. The former first lady wore a turquoise dress in the photo, and Switters compared her image unfavorably—and, no doubt, unfairly—to Matisse's big blue nude.

"Have you ever wondered, Switters, why I've run you personally, rather than put you under the direction of, say, Brewster or Saltonstall?"

"Because Saltonstall's a dickhead and Brewster's a tiddlypoop. Either would have cramped my style."

"I'm flattered that you think I don't. You're aware, of course, that I officially disapprove of your *sans gêne* approach to both the company's affairs and your own. At the same time, however, you fascinate me. There are things about you I admittedly find intriguing. For example, there's a rumor you can refer to a woman's genitals in fifty languages."

"Seventy-one, actually."

"Mmm? And are there some words for . . . for that organ that you favor above others?"

"Oh, I like most all of them, even the Dutch. There's a Somali term, though, that only females are allowed to utter. It reeks of mystery and secret beauty."

"And that word is? . . ."

"Sorry."

"What do you mean?"

"Not your need to know."

Although Mayflower smiled bleakly and maintained an air of metallic cordiality, he buzzed Joolie and told her not to bother with bringing in coffee. He cleared his throat quietly, with formality. "I wanted to outline a possible next assignment, but first we'd better discuss your . . . your, ah, condition." He gestured at the wheelchair. "What's the story?"

And Switters told him.

Switters told him. An abbreviated version, not a third as long as the one Bobby Case received, but a truthful account, nonetheless. And Mayflower's reaction? Incredulity, primarily. But also anxiety, barely concealed anger, and a flicker of disgust. When he spoke, his golden tones burned with frost. "Unless you can assure me that this is some silly prank—even if it isn't—I'm placing you on suspension. The committee will decide whether or not it's with pay."

"I'm short on funds."

"Not my department."

"But I'm able to work. What's the assignment? I can handle it. Better than any of your gung-ho cowpokes." Switters rose and stood on the footplate. Then he hopped backward onto the seat, much as he had for Bobby, although he refrained from running in place. "I'm sure this looks crazy, but . . ."

"Yes, doesn't it?"

"Come on, Mayflower. You know my record."

"Yes, don't I?"

"I'm available for duty."

"Physically, maybe. There are other concerns. Would you please sit down."

"I could have lied."

"Pardon?"

"I could have lied about the witchman, the taboo, the whole jar of jam. I didn't have to spill a bean. I could have fed you a perfectly plausible, ordinary explanation. . . ."

"No. You would have had to be medically cleared before returning to duty. And when Walter Reed found nothing physically wrong. . . . But why didn't you—I'm curious—give me a more believable alibi? If you honestly want to remain with the company . . ."

"I want very damn much to remain with the company!" Switters paused, took a deep breath, and lowered his intensity. "I guess that in itself could be considered a sign of mental illness—but we're all in the same boat, aren't we?"

Mayflower didn't hesitate. "No!" he snapped through clenched teeth. "Not in the same boat at all."

In the silence that followed, Switters remained standing in the wheelchair. *What's happening to me now?* he wondered.

Seemingly, what was happening was that he was losing his job, and it staggered him to realize how much his identity had become dependent on that job. He'd meditated enough to realize that his true self—his selfless self, if you will, his essence—didn't know or care that he worked for the CIA; didn't, for that matter, know or care that his name was Switters. And by no means was he wedded to his title ("operative": what the fuck was that?), his desk (didn't have one), his duties (only occasionally exciting), or his paycheck (the more advertising he saw the less he wanted to buy). Moreover, he enjoyed a variety of outside interests.

What gripped him, nourished him, enlarged and thrilled him, and molded the contours of his ego was in actuality the job within the job: the ill-defined, self-directed business of angelhood, with all of the romantic elitism with which that exercise in quixotic, but sometimes effective, subversion was colored. It was so special and furtive, so nutty yet seemingly noble, so *poetic*, even, that he had gradually permitted it to define him to himself, although he was keenly aware that much of the time he was working closer to the bullshit than the bull.

So: if he was no longer an angel, so-called, who would he be? Perhaps it was time to find out. Perhaps it didn't matter. The one thing he now knew was that he couldn't lie to Mayflower Cabot Fitzgerald—not after he had lied to Suzy.

"You can lie to God but not to the Devil."

"What's that supposed to mean?"

Slowly Switters returned to a sitting position. Good question. What *was* it supposed to mean? "Lies may disappoint God or exasperate him, but ultimately his compassion dissolves them, cancels them out. The Devil, though, he grows fat on our lies; the more you lie to him, the better he likes it. It's an investment in his firm, it increases the value of his stock by fostering the practice of lying. Only truth can hurt the Devil. That's why honesty has been banished from almost every existing institution: corporate, religious, and governmental. Truth can be dangerously liberating. Did I mention that the Devil's other name is *El Controlador*? He who controls."

"That's news to me." Mayflower was looking at his desk clock. "But then I lack your background in theology." He parted his pale lips just enough to indicate he spoke facetiously.

"Oh, yes. And his other name is *El Manipulador*. He who—"

"I know what it means. And I suspect I know what you're getting at. If I felt it necessary to defend the company, and the national interests it serves, against your implied criticism—and I emphatically do not—I would point out that both manipulation and control are sometimes requisite in order to secure and insure stability. If that smacks to you of the satanic, then I suggest you think of it as us using the Devil to further the aims of God." He cleared his throat again in that self-consciously dignified way of his. "Now, if you'll excuse me, I have to—"

"Stability the handiwork of God? You've got to be kidding! If God's aim is stability, then he's a monumental, incompetent failure, the biggest loser of all time. This universe he's credited with creating is dynamic, in almost constant flux. Any stability we might perceive in it on any level is as temporary as it is aberrant. Symbiosis, maybe; even a kind of harmonious interaction, but not stability. The Tao is a shaky balancing act between unstable yin and unstable yang. The fact is . . ."

"I must call an end to—"

". . . neither God *nor* the Devil is the least concerned with stability. Human artifices such as fixity and certainty are a big bore to the immortals. Which is why it's so corny of us to try to paint God as absolute good and Satan as absolute evil. Of course, I resorted to that convenient, conventional symbology myself in my previous analogy, so you're right, Mayflower, I *was* blathering like a theologian, and a half-baked one at that. Maybe it's okay, after all, to lie to the Devil. But for reasons of my own, I refuse to lie to you or yours."

(Where was this coming from? Usually, he only went on like this when he was bent or stoned, and that morning he'd had but one beer with breakfast.)

"Happy to hear it," said Mayflower, pressing the intercom buzzer. "Joolie, would you show Mr. Switters out. I hate to terminate this fascinating discussion, but. . . ." Clenching and unclenching his hard, perfect teeth, he stood. "Perhaps we can resume it at some future date. During a round of golf or . . . no, I suppose you'll not be golfing, will you? Excuse me. I'm sorry."

"No problem, pal. Most American men secretly hate women and love golf. I love women and hate golf."

"Yes, you are a man apart, aren't you? Well then. The committee meets Friday. Check in with me on, uh, Monday, and you'll be advised of your status. Should we decide on suspension or dismissal, you obviously have the right to appeal. I should caution you, however, that the Civil Service Commission is quite reluctant to interfere in internal matters of the CIA."

Doing his best to pop a wheelie, though only half succeeding, Switters spun and followed Joolie out. Before the door closed behind him, he called over his shoulder: "I'll give your regards to Audubon Poe." He could have sworn he heard Mayflower sputter.

"Joolie, would it be considered sexual harassment if I—"

"Don't even think about it," warned Joolie. But like a miser making a night deposit at an inner city bank, she leaned over with a kind of fearful glee and planted a peck perilously close to his pucker.

Women love these fierce invalids home from hot climates?

That night he hit the bars in D.C.'s hotel district, wishing he were in Patpong as he zigzagged from one to another, slicing through knots of pedestrians like Alexander's sword, turning away at the door when he found a lounge to have a pianist in residence, for fear that, provoked by booze, he might erupt in song at the first tinkling rendition of a Broadway standard. Years earlier, he'd contemplated having a device surgically implanted in his throat to prevent any such musical indiscretion under the quickening of drink, and had gone so far as to contact a certain Hungarian clinic, only to have its administrator suggest he see a psychiatrist instead.

Bar patrons were swift to move aside for him, showing him the guilty, condescending respect reserved for the disabled. At Spin Doctor's, he was invited to wheel his chair up to a table occupied by five government workers: two male, three female, under thirty, reasonably attractive. After a round or two, he was entertaining them with an abridged, shaman-free account of taking his grandmother's parrot to the Amazon to reunite it with its origins. They seemed enthralled, but midway through his narration one of the men interrupted him to describe the difficulties he was experiencing trying to housebreak his new puppy, and soon all of them were telling their favorite dumb, boring pet stories. Raising his voice above the rest, Switters announced solemnly, "This morning, I received proof positive that my tabby cat is the reincarnation of a Las Vegas crime lord." The table fell silent, and once more all ears were his. He merely looked them over, however, removed his hand from the baby fat of the feminine knee to his right (a hard-won concession), finished off his tequila jackhammer, then sped recklessly to the door. *Jesus,* he thought as he rolled out onto the street, *I might just as well have sung "Memories."*

the next day he slept late, not surprisingly, and upon rising began quite mindlessly to pack. It was almost as if he were being directed by his welled unconscious, a wholly intuitive impulse that he did not think to challenge until he had cleaned out his closets. It was evening before he received confirmation that his intuition had been on the money. E-mail arrived from Bobby Case claiming that the angel grapevine was abuzz with rumors that Switters was about to be sacked.

Bobby offered assistance, hinting that he had enough embarrassing dirt on company activities to make Mayflower Cabot Fitzgerald a reluctant ally for life. Switters replied that he would think it over. Bobby e-mailed back, "Okay, think, but don't forget to sit."

So, over the weekend he sat. And he got stoned. And he thought some. And when on Monday morning Joolie telephoned to inform him he was in trouble—Mayflower wanted him in on Tuesday for a day-long debriefing session—he could actually sound nonchalant, though some of it was faked. Impressed, Joolie confessed in a tremulous whisper (fully aware that she was being recorded) that she wished she could have known him better.

"Yes," agreed Switters, "I can picture the two of us sharing a gypsy cave above a deserted beach with nothing on but the shortwave radio, a shaft of sunlight visually activating the coppery coils around your . . ." Joolie, a true redhead, hung up for fear she might swoon.

Switters then called a real estate agency and put his condo on the market. He had very little equity in the property, but any amount he might realize would help. He wasn't fully aware of it at the time, but the fact that he was about to disobey orders by refusing to be debriefed would end up costing him his severance pay.

Too antsy to wait for a train, he took that very night a red-eye flight (sans gravy) to Seattle by way of Los Angeles, greatly annoying the D.C. taxi driver when, after announcing Dulles as his destination, he spat on the floor of the cab.

Undoubtedly, there are those who would be inclined to sneer at Switters, judging him in word and deed to have proven himself immature, frivolous, or even zany (to employ that stale adjective—from the Italian, *zanni*, a would-be or untalented clown—that the leaden are so fond of applying to characters less stodgy and predictable than they or their friends). The psychoanalytically disposed, on the other hand, might detect in his behavior, particularly as described in recent pages, a classic, arguably heroic, example of despair refusing to take itself seriously. Well, maybe.

Sigmund Freud once wrote that "Wit is the denial of suffering," meaning not that the witty, the playful among us, deny that suffering exists—in varying degrees, everyone suffers—but rather that they deny suffering power over their lives, deny it prominence, use jocularity to keep it in its place. Freud may have been right. Certainly, a comic sensibility is essential if one is to outmaneuver ubiquitous exploitation and to savor life in a society that seeks to control (and fleece) its members by insisting they take its symbols, institutions, and consumer goods seriously, very seriously, indeed.

It's entirely possible, however, that Switters was merely exhibiting the tics that can show up in a spirited intelligence when it can no longer count on, as an outlet, periodic meetings of the C.R.A.F.T. Club.

switters was raised in Northern California, Colorado, and Texas, but whenever his mother's domestic life went topsy-turvy, as it seemed intermittently to do, he'd been sent for months at a time to Seattle, and it was in Seattle that he once again took refuge. It could not be said that during his youthful asylums under Maestra's roof she had ever mothered him, tending always to treat him as friend and equal, and she definitely wasn't going to mother him now. In fact, once he broke down and informed her of his predicament and the queer Amazonian incidents (he omitted the part about eating her Sailor Boy) that had rather directly occasioned it, it became plain that he could not remain in her house.

Accepting no blame for having set events in play—guilt, in her opinion, being one of the most useless human emotions—Maestra chided him repeatedly for what she termed his "disappointing display of ignorance and superstition."

Whacking her cane on floor and furniture until she set up an ominous rhythmic resonance evocative of the timpani in Greek tragedy, she accused him of a reaction worthy of primitive cave-bear worshipers or, worse (because they ought to know better), evangelical Christians. "You go down there and encourage Suzy to accept as fact the tall tales of dogma-crazed underage ignorant Portuguese hillbillies. . . ."

"I only encouraged her to fully investigate that thing that she found most compelling in life. Isn't that—"

"I was appalled when I heard you were aiding and abetting her dabblings in such harmful nonsense. Appalled. What I didn't know was that you yourself were in the dimwitted thrall of something even more ridiculous, more destructive. In all of my eighty-plus years I've never. . . . As far as I'm concerned, this millennium business is wholly bogus, but there must be *something* in the air that would cause you, of all

people, to surrender your spirit, to wreck your career, to turn yourself
into a craven invalid. . . ."

"*Fierce* invalid," he corrected her.

"I guess I thought you were one of the last of the torchbearers, but
as it's turned out, sad to say, you couldn't strike a match in an elevator."

Stung, he asked, "Do you want me to stand, then?"

"What do you mean?"

"Knowing what you know about Smithe, the anthropologist, what
happened to him, do you want me to get up and walk? Because I'll do
it. Right now. Right this second. Just say the word." He was already
half out of the chair.

Maestra couldn't. Or wouldn't. She stalked off, only to return ten
minutes later to chide him for passively accepting his dismissal from
the CIA without even requesting a hearing. "At the very least, you
could have gotten a mental disability pension. As screwy as you've
turned out, they still owe you something. Many times you gambled
your life for them."

"Never."

"You did!"

"No. I may have gambled my life, but it wasn't for them. It was
for—something else."

"What? Precisely."

"Precision doesn't enter into it."

"Heh!"

He wasn't kidding, though, nor being unnecessarily evasive. Switters had conducted his professional life in much the same way as
he made love to a woman: wholeheartedly, romantically, poetically, in
a frenzy of longing for the unattainable, the unknown; ladling onto
himself—and his partner or his mission—that mysteriously generated
concentrate of exhilaration that he sometimes referred to as his syrup
of wahoo, a kind of emotional extract produced by the simultaneous
boiling down of beauty, risk, wildness, and mirth. Delusional or not, it
was hardly a matter of precision.

When Switters took a room in an old building adjacent to the Pike
Place Market (he'd considered moving into the Snoqualmie cabin, but
there was already heavy snowfall in the mountains), both Maestra and
Bobby Case quizzed him about what he would do there. "For the time
being, my aim is to keep the oxygen from leaking out of my life,"
he replied, an answer neither they nor he found satisfactory. So, he
hinted that he might be embarking upon a scholastic bender.

Assisting Suzy with her term paper had dusted and oiled creaky academic reflexes just enough to convince him that the dissertation that stood between him and a Ph.D. degree—he'd long ago completed the course work—would not be all that painfully difficult to write. "How would you feel about calling me Dr. Switters?" he asked. "Hell, I'd probably get mixed up and call you Dr. Seuss," said Bobby. "You're just lucky I don't call you Baby Dumpling," said Maestra.

Joining them briefly at Thanksgiving, Bobby listened politely to Switters rant about the future of the word in cyberculture. "From the time of the invention of the alphabet, if not before, all technologies have originated in language, but in cyberspace, we don't see or hear information so much as we *feel* it. Technology may at last be outstripping language, not merely leaving the nest but killing the mother, if you will. You know, we don't really see darkness, or even light, we feel neurologically their effect on surrounding surfaces. The binary digital system—Brother One and Sister Zero—that makes computers possible is a kind of light/dark relationship to begin with, and when you start to factor in the electron rather than the word as the primary information link between the brain and the external world . . ."

And so on and so forth. Bobby got the idea that Switters didn't believe that language was doomed per se but, rather, was about to be transformed, much as it had been by the invention of the Phoenician alphabet; liberated, as it had been by the invention of the Greek alphabet; and then celebrated, as it had been by the advent of the Roman; yet suspected that he, nevertheless, felt protective of words, the stranger, more archaic the better, perceiving them as keys to some lost treasure. All very interesting, basically, but Switters, once he got going, was inclined to scoot off on tangents, to drive in the ditch. For example: "Why, our cosmology is a binary system, as well. God equals one, Satan, zero. Or is it the other way around? Whichever, we use that pair of digits only—eschewing numbers two through nine and the endless combinations thereof—to compute the meaning of life and our ultimate destiny. Ah, but in the beginning was the word. Before the division, before—"

"Yep, podner, you'll churn yourself a damn fine thesis outta that butterfat, I'm sure, but what ought to be sizzling on your front burner is a strategy for getting yourself back on your feet, and I don't necessarily mean financially. Pass the peas."

"Amen to that!" chimed in Maestra. "Have a drop more gravy, Captain Case. Sorry it isn't red-eye, but the caterer's led a sheltered life and didn't have a clue."

After dessert, as the two men smoked cigars in the living room, watched over by the Matisse nude, herself as blue as smoke, Bobby broached the subject of Suzy. "Forget cyberspace for a minute. You've been quieter than a Stealth potato about what went on in Sacramento. Come on. Did you deflower the 'wholesome little animal,' or did I manage to talk you out of it?"

"Talked myself out of it, I'm afraid. With my forked tongue."

"Lordy, Lord. And who said talk is cheap?"

"Some inarticulate man of action, I imagine; the strong, silent type who other males admire but who women secretly find a dupe or a dope." He expelled a dancing doughnut of smoke. Like every smoke ring ever blown—like smoke, in general—it bounced in the air like the bastard baby of chemistry and cartooning. "I'm unsure how or if it applies in this particular situation, but the poet, Andrei Codrescu, once wrote that 'Physical intimacy is only a device for opening the floodgates of what really matters: words.'"

Bobby looked skeptical. "Sounds like sublimation to me. Anyhow, I thought the verbiage was supposed to *start* the ball rolling. In the fucking beginning was the fucking word."

"So the Good Book informs us. What it neglects to tell us, and for which omission I can never forgive it, is which came first, the word for *chicken* or the word for *egg*."

Bobby couldn't make it down for Christmas—his little clandestine U2 unit was on some kind of alert—but he telephoned Maestra's manse on Christmas Eve, and once he'd stuffed the old woman's goose with flattery, got on the line with Switters, surmising from their conversation that the latter had cooled a bit toward the prospect of writing a dissertation, although he could and would, if given a chance, still get wound up over its thematic potentialities.

"The role of the computer in literature is limited to grunt work and janitorial services. Makes research easier and editing faster without making either of them any better. Where the computer does appear to foster genuine innovation and advancement is in graphics: photographic reproduction, design, animation, et cetera. Amazing development in those fields. But to what end?"

"More interesting TV commercials."

"*Exactement!* Marketing. Merchandising. Increasingly sophisticated, increasingly seductive. And sure, it's just a flashy modern version of the age-old bread-and-circuses brand of bondage—except that today the bakery's a multinational and the circus follows us home. Well, culture has always been driven to some degree by the marketplace. Always. It's just that nowadays the marketplace, having invaded every nook and cranny of our private lives, is completely supplanting culture; the marketplace has *become* our culture. Nevertheless—"

"Yeah," put in Bobby, "and wild ol' boys like you and me may turn out to be one of the last lines of defense against corporate totalitarianism and unhappy shit like that. That's why it's important that you . . . I know for a fact that the company would reinstate you if you'd—"

"Did I tell you Mayflower sent a pair of grim-faced pickle-packers out to debrief me? Right after Thanksgiving. Cornered me in my room, six o'clock in the morning; damned unsporting of them, me being groggy from the toils and impairments of the evening prior. Still, they had rather a thick time of it before I allowed them to take back some of their toys. I managed to keep my laptop, my Beretta, and my faithful crocodile, although the pistol remains an issue, and there's reason to believe they've put a Joe on my tail."

"That could be fun."

"Perhaps. But all that's irrelevant. What I was getting at a minute ago is that the real show, as usual, is taking place behind the tent, and neither the hawkers nor the ringmasters are hip to it. Forget the graphic-art gymnastics. What's really happening in cyberculture is that language isn't contracting, it's expanding. Expanding. Moving outside of the body. Beyond the tongue and the larynx, beyond the occipital lobe and the hippocampus, beyond the pen and the page, beyond the screen and the printer, even. Out into the universe. Bonding with, saturating, or even usurping physical reality. Let me explain."

"Ut! Swit? Whoa. Give me a rain check on that if you don't mind. All this brainstorming of yours is costing me MCI's holiday rates—and costing you what's left of your marbles, I wouldn't be surprised. I mean, if you're not planning to write your damn thesis, why? . . . The main thing is, you're still in that feeble-foot Ferrari, son, and it's been seven or eight weeks now. Jesus! You got to deal with this problem, bring it to an end, whatever it takes. If that involves tripping back down to the Amazon, so be it. You, me, either or both of us. Will you please just lock in on that target? Direct your fire toward getting well, getting free? Jesus!"

There was no immediate response, and in the absence of dialogue, the men could hear MCI's holiday meter running. Eventually Switters said, "Remember the story that monk told us?"

"Which monk? The one who hid us from the Burmese border patrol?"

"No, not him. The one we had tea with in Saigon. The—"

"You still won't call it Ho Chi Minh City."

"I refuse. Although I certainly mean no disrespect to the brave and honorable Uncle Ho. . . ."

"Betrayed, slandered, pushed into a corner . . ."

"By that ice-hearted, lizard-brained, sanctimonious Christian bully boy . . .

"John Foster Dulles!" the two men snarled in contemptuous harmony. Then, also in unison, they spat into the mouthpieces of their respective phones.

"I heard that!" cried Maestra, who, to the best of Switters's knowledge, had been engrossed in e-gab in a hackers chat room, a kind of on-line cybercryptic Christmas party. "Disgusting lout! Clean it off. Now."

Separately they each obeyed, chuckling softly as they wiped, the one with coat sleeve, the other with bandanna; and then Switters returned to the Saigon monk. "Remember? He told us about a great spiritual master who was asked what it was like being enlightened all the time. And the master answered, 'Oh, it's just like ordinary, everyday life. Except that you're two inches above the ground.' "

"Yeah," said Bobby. "I remember that."

"Well, it occurred to me a week or so ago that that's where I'm at. In this wheelchair, my feet are almost exactly two inches off the ground."

"Aw, come on. It ain't nowhere near the same thing."

"No, but maybe it *could* be. Maybe that was even ol' Pyramid Head's point. So to speak. He was oblivious to wheelchairs, presumably, but, still, maybe . . . In any event, I'm being forced to survey the world from a new perspective—you'd be astonished the difference two inches can make—and I'm loath to relinquish the vantage point quite yet. There may be other angles, other takes, whole phyllo pastries of existence I've yet to explore from this sacred height. So, patience, pal. Let me play it out for a while. Let me discover what it is that I've become: synthetic cripple or synthetic bodhisattva." He paused. "Merry Christmas, Bobby."

From the Alaskan end of the connection, there floated a huge sigh. "Merry Christmas, Swit. Here's wishing you a sleighload of eggnogged virgins in mistletoe underwear."

Switters did, indeed, maintain his vantage point. Throughout the long, wet winter he maintained it, his "starship in hover mode," as he put it, orbiting the earth from a height of two inches.

For several weeks in November and December, he had, every morning, propelled his chair eastward on Pike Street and south on Fourth Avenue to the downtown branch of the Seattle Public Library, where he sought to supplement his on-line research toward a dissertation that was to be entitled, "Speaking in Things, Thinking With Light," but near Christmas those academic forays dwindled, and by the first of the year he had abandoned both wood pulp and electron for a different kind of research.

Like some beggar or street performer, he would dock the wheelchair beneath the aged arcades of the labyrinthine Pike Place Market, and there, in the grotto light, protected from the rains that pounded the cobblestones and hissed beneath the tires of delivery trucks, he'd turn a keen eye on whiskered parsnip and hairless apple, and bathe himself in the multitudes.

The old market, worn half away by dampness and fingerprints, sweat drops and shoe heels, pigeon claws and vegetable crates; soiled by butcher seepage, sequined with salmon scales, smelling of roses, raw prawns, and urine; blessedly freed for the winter from the demanding *entertain-me-for-nothing!* gawkings of out-of-town tourists, the market bustled now with fishmongers and Vietnamese farmers, florists and fruit vendors, famous chefs and food-smart housewives, gourmets and runaways, flunkies and junkies, coffee brewers and balloon benders, office workers and shopgirls and winos of all races; with pensioners, predators, panhandlers, and prostitutes, and (to complete the p's) political polemists, punks, potters, puppeteers, poets, and policemen; with musicians, jugglers, fire-eaters (dry days only), tyro magicians, and lingering loafers such as he seemed to be.

Or did he? None of the market regulars, legitimate or illegitimate, were quite able to label him or find a reason for his daily presence among them. Just as shoppers would take one look at his stationary wheelchair and glance around automatically for a tin cup and accordion or the equivalents thereof, so denizens searched at greater length though equally in vain for some clue to his raison d'être. Occasionally, he tapped away at a laptop computer, but mostly, day after day, week after week, he merely sat there, observing the surrounding cavalcade or gazing into the rain. Rumors spread that he was an undercover cop, but when there was no increase in arrests, when it was noticed that he was periodically harassed by market security guards (usually for stationing himself in one spot for too many hours or days in a row), and when he took to carving tiny boats out of busted crate scraps, rigging them with lettuce leaf sails and launching them in rainswept gutters, that particular suspicion gradually faded.

Still, nobody was prepared to write him off as another lingering loafer: his presence was too strong, his demeanor too cool. While he never flashed wads of currency or sported gold jewelry, he dressed in well-cut suits over fine T-shirts and was wont to drape a black cashmere topcoat theatrically, rather like an opera cape, about his broad shoulders. He kept a cell phone in his saddlebag but spoke on it infrequently (Maestra preferred e-mail, the Sacramento contingent was incommunicado, and by February Bobby Case had been transferred to Okinawa), giving no indication when he did converse that any sort of business was being conducted. Reticent though hardly bashful, Switters had affixed to the back of his chair a neatly lettered sign that read I DON'T WANT TO TALK ABOUT JESUS OR DISEASES, this being necessitated by the countless well-meaning busybodies who were convinced that their New Age herbalist or their Sunday School Savior could provide succor if not remedy to whatever misfortune had denied his powers of perambulation. Preservation of wahoo demanded that they be discouraged.

There were those, chiefly women, who did talk to him, however. They couldn't seem to resist. Never in his life had Switters been quite so handsome. He'd let his hair grow long so that it framed his face, with its storybook of scars, in a manner that made it all the more intriguing. Enhanced by the moist climate, a predominantly vegetarian diet, and the liberty to do with his hours what he pleased, his complexion had the rich glow of a Renaissance oil, and his eyes were like jets of green energy. When he spoke, it was in grand syllables, moderated and warmed by a loose hint of drawl. He projected the air, falsely or not, of both a learned man and a rogue, innately exhibitionist yet deeply secretive, a powerful figure who habitually thumbed his nose at power—and thus might lead one, were one to fall under his spell, off in directions opposite those that one had been conditioned to recognize as prudent, profitable, or holy. To all but a missing link, then, he was an attraction.

Margaret, with the fresh baked piroshki she was fetching back to her desk at the law firm; Melissa, the Microsoft widow, with a basket of Gorgonzola and winter pears bound for suburbia; Dev, whose breasts in her cheap, fuzzy sweater were as heavy as the cabbages she sold in her stall; they and others, different and similar, would kneel hesitantly beside his chair, kneeling so they would be at eye level with him and so they would not be overheard, and say, with varying degrees of embarrassment, "I see you here a lot."

"Yes," he'd reply. "I've been watching you, too," and though that was not always the truth, the little lie didn't trouble his conscience, not even when he sensed a vibration travel down a spine to settle with an almost audible pang in a clitoris.

"What are you? No, I mean who are you? What do you do?"

"I'm Switters, friend of both God and the Devil." Then, getting an uncertain reception, "Taker of the stepless step." Then, "Two-inch astronaut."

That usually stopped them. Lightly dumbfounded, the woman would give him a long, perplexed though hardly rankled look, and as shyly and sweetly as she had knelt, she'd rise, muttering "Have a nice day" or "Stay dry" or some other genial inanity, and walk away, seldom without a wistful glance over her shoulder as she paused at the cobble-stones to unfurl her umbrella. Not infrequently, he'd spot one of them in the market again and exchange with her one of those futilely desirous smiles that are like domestic postage on a letter to a foreign destination. Did they approach him a second time? None save for Dev, who was much too undereducated and overburdened to be fazed by cryptic epigrams and non sequiturs; and who eventually followed him to his room, where, against his better judgment, she gladdened him unmercifully. Evidently he gladdened her, too, for afterward she claimed she needed a wheelchair more than he.

And she returned. Twice or thrice a week. Usually early in the morning, while her brothers were stocking the produce stand she would operate until dusk. When she unhooked her bra, it was like a farmer unloading a cart, and when she pulled down her panties, Switters thought he was back up the Amazon. Dev had meaty lips, chapped red cheeks, and walnut-shell eyelids beneath a prominent dark brow, and was as wide of hip as she was thin of guile. A strapping Eastern Orthodox milkmaid of Slavic descent, pretty in a coarse, uncultivated way, she was uncomplicated and honest in mind and emotion, complex and pungent in bodily aroma. She was always out of his room by five forty-five, but her musks hung around all day. Before long he was putting her on with his clothing, tasting her in his bread and cigars.

Wallpaper curled and stayed curled, windowpanes fogged and stayed fogged from Dev's humidity. Dev's cries spooked ledge pigeons into flight, and these were urbanized birds accustomed to every manner of human commotion. Dev's pubic mound was like the hut of a shaman. Fruit flies picnicked on her thighs.

They had virtually nothing in common, nothing whatever to talk about, but she seemed without agenda beyond the erotic, and, at twenty-nine (the oldest woman with whom he'd ever lain), fatalistic and juggy, there was not one thing about her to remind him of Suzy. Sometimes as he shook her—her vapors and her short hairs—out of his sheets, his eyes almost teared with gratitude. He did come to see, in time, that she perceived him as a dramatic figure of mystery and was as magnetized by that aspect (real or fallacious) of his image as, say,

Margaret or Melissa, but Dev was content to rub up against the mystery, wisely feeling no compulsion to probe or dispel it, which the others surely would have done. When he recognized that about her, his appreciation deepened into affection, and he took to awakening before five in cheery anticipation of her rapping—a coded knock he'd taught her so as to know it was her soft self knocking rather than one of Mayflower Fitzgerald's bothersome cowboys.

O Dev, unreflective Dev, you are the one who is the mystery. Despite the numerous clues, largely olfactory in nature, you scatter in your wake.

If Dev was an O-ring that sealed wahoo in his body, a gasket against the leaking of that emotional oxygen now in shortened supply as a result of his sacking, his break with Suzy, and the Kandakandero curse that precipitated those two events, so then were the Art Girls. No Art Girls, either individually or collectively, ever visited his room, and, in fact, not all of the Art Girls were girls, but their presence in the Pike Place Market and in his acquaintanceship helped him to sail through that strange season—literally as well as figuratively.

From his two-inch elevation, he'd watched them filter into the market almost daily from the art school down on Elliott Avenue, walking mostly in pairs, sometimes singularly or in threesomes, but never en masse, although they were classmates and dressed as if siblings or even clones: black berets, black turtleneck sweaters, pea coats on which were pinned buttons bearing messages of rude social protest (one alluded to CIA malfeasance and paid tribute to Audubon Poe), rings in earlobe, lip, and nose. They carried sketchbooks, mainly, but also paintboxes, cameras, occasionally an easel; and each according to her or his favored medium—pencil, ink, crayon, watercolor, or film— would set about to depict her or his favored feature of the market: people, produce, or architecture. They strove to be disconnected and cool, but their vitality and curiosity were difficult to suppress. Try as they might, the nearest they could come to the cynicism and ennui with which somewhat older artists advertised their genius was to strike the odd hostile pose or suck defiantly on cigarettes. Finding them charming, Switters flirted openly with the Art Girls, even when they turned out to be boys, and though they were too self-consciously hip to ever kneel by his chair, as did the Margarets and the Melissas, they demonstrated through knowing expressions and inclusive gestures their unpremeditated approval of him.

Approval was tested, shaken, and finally cemented one January afternoon when a couple of them, representing at least two genders, presented him with a photograph that the anatomically female of the pair had snapped of him without, so she believed, his knowledge. After briefly examining and complimenting the picture, Switters proceeded to give the astonished young woman the date and time of day it had been taken, as well as prevailing weather conditions before, during, and after the exposure, and a detailed description of the candy bar her friend had been eating while she aimed the telephoto lens—all routine for a company operative. Could she really think some callow amateur, let alone one as cute as she, could photograph him from any distance without being systematically registered and remembered?

To regain her composure, the girl informed him that her faculty adviser had complained that the sign on the wheelchair—prominent in the photo—might give offense to the religious and the afflicted, prompting Switters to respond that he was certain the student photographer had rejected that moralistic nudging toward self-censorship since no artist worthy of the name gave a flying fuck whether or not any special interest group—minuscule or multitudinous, benign or malicious—took offense at their heartfelt creations. "Humanity is generally offensive," he told her happily. "Life's an offensive proposition from beginning to end. Maybe those who can't tolerate offense ought to just go ahead and end it all, and maybe those who demand financial compensation for offense ought to have it ended for them."

If he had overstated his position a tad for the sake of shock value, it had worked: they retreated as though from a fiery chili they'd assumed to be merely exotic pimiento. Indeed, but a philter can blister the gums, and the most effective aphrodisiacs are often foul at first taste. In a matter of days, the pair and its cohorts were friendlier than ever, having debated his pronouncement vigorously and at length in classroom, studio, and coffeehouse (few among them were yet of tavern age), concluding that it made up in bravery and brio what it lacked in sensitivity, and that it had been issued, moreover, in defense of their own aesthetic rights. Besides, he had a *gorgeous* smile.

Where Switters and the Art Girls truly connected, though, was in the gutter.

For weeks they'd watched with ill-concealed fascination whenever he'd push one of his minute boats into a current of streetside rainwater, often wielding a wilted dahlia stalk as a wand to guide it past obstacles as it commenced its voyage into the unknown. Day by day, berets cocked, the girls edged closer to the launchings. Once, one of them returned a boat to him that she'd retrieved from the place it had finally run aground. "It made it all the way to Virginia Street," she said, dimples enlarging in both diameter and depth. It was only a matter of time before they started to make toy boats of their own.

From the start, their boats were lovelier than his. His, in fact, were pathetically engineered. How inept was Switters with tools? Had he been assigned to build crosses in Jerusalem, Jesus would have died of old age. The Art Girls, conversely, made lovely little vessels; clean, sleek, and well-proportioned, while his were decidedly otherwise. Yet, when they began to race them (human nature being what it is, racing was inevitable), his—lopsided, clumsy, cracked, splintery, wobbly of mast (often no more than a carrot stick)—always won. Always.

Challenged, the Art Girls fashioned increasingly finer craft. Forsaking those scraps of broken citrus crates that had provided shipwright fodder in the beginning, and that were now in short supply and deemed inferior into the bargain, they turned to the art school for materials, appropriating for hull and deck pieces of wood originally intended for stretcher bars, frames, maquettes, and the like, while making off with costly rice paper, parchment, and strips of Belgian linen canvas that could be cut into little sails. Rather quickly, spurred as much by artistic temperament and the human love of difficulty as by Switters's unexplained and undeserved success, they progressed from catboat to sloop to ketch to yawl to schooner. They spoke of jibs and mizzensails, added bilge boards, keels, and rudders. And being artists, they painted their vessels in brilliant blues, whites, and golds, often inscribing a well-chosen name on the bow such as *Shakti, Athena, Mermaid Lightning, Madame Picasso,* or *Madame Picasso's Revenge.*

Each and every one of Switters's boats was christened *Little Blessed Virgin of the Starry Waters* (scratched on the foredeck with a ballpoint pen), each was of the same primitive design in which he made no improvements beyond substituting a cabbage leaf sail for the customary lettuce leaf whenever the breeze was especially stiff or when he happened to accidentally produce a rat-trap-sized boat rather than the mousetrap size that was his usual limit. It wasn't that Switters eschewed beauty and grace. No, indeed. He was, in fact, a champion of the beautiful in an age when beauty had been voted out of office by philistines on both the right and the left. His boats remained raw and rudimentary because he was incapable of making them differently, the handyman gene having been recessive for generations in the males of his family (which might well account for their tendency to become "men of mystery," borrowing Eunice's droll phrase). And anyway, his dumb dinghies continued to triumph.

"Sorry, darlings," he'd apologize as, at the finish line, the girls would parade single file past his wheelchair to plant a victory kiss on his victory grin.

"I don't get it."

"He must cheat."

"Is it some kind of, like, *trick?*"

"Fuck!"

Into the shallow streams of their racecourse—streams that bore mum petals, sprigs of dried statice, seeds, spices, crab shell fragments and tossed latte cups; streams shoaled by squashed apples, rotting lemons, runaway brussels sprouts, and the occasional yeasty horse turd; streams drizzled with cloud water, tea, lemonade, soup, screwtop wine, and drool (avian, equine, and human), in addition to a half-hundred varieties of coffee; streams dredged clean by municipal workers every night only to be collaged the next day with lurid organic detritus shed by activities within the Pike, the belly and heart of Seattle—into those cobble-bottomed streams the girls commenced to shove brigs, brigantines, barks, frigates, and clipper ships: vessels meant not for sport but for cargo or battle. It was as if, having despaired of exceeding his vulgar *Virgins* in speed and endurance, they sought to overwhelm them with scope, intricacy, and grace.

Indeed, they were works of marvel, those nautical midgets, especially when the clipper ship decks were stacked with lumber, rum barrels, hogsheads, cotton bales, or sacks of grain; when the frigates were outfitted with cannon and beaked figureheads for ramming an enemy. Races were interrupted, delayed, or canceled altogether due to outbreaks of naval warfare. As the fighting raged around it—"Fuck the torpedoes, full speed ahead!"—a lumpish Switters *Virgin*, flying a crude Jolly Roger, would go careening by in awkward audacity and lurch its way (providing it didn't run aground on a half-submerged bagel) to the storm drain at the end of the street. Pretending to ignore him, the Art Girls made plans for a reenactment of the Battle of Trafalgar, deciding it might be a more interesting and authentic engagement if the warships were manned.

"Fruit flies," suggested Luna, one of the more innovative of the girls. "We could rub grape pulp and stuff on the decks and in the rigging, and next thing you know we'll have a crew."

"Hello?" countered Brie, who was Luna's heated rival in the talent department. "Did you happen to notice that it's winter? There aren't any fruit flies out."

"Are, too. There's always a flock of 'em flitting around that rosy-cheeked brunette who works in the stall over there."

"Yeah," agreed Twila. "Even when she walks down the street."

"You mean Dev?" asked Switters innocently. As one, to a woman, each of the girls swung like a beacon to face him, their eyes narrowed with suspicion, or rather, some psychic knowledge well beyond suspicion, a daunting display of feminine intuition in full efflorescence. He actually blushed.

When they'd had enough of broiling his marrow under their sarcastic smirks, they returned to preparations for Trafalgar. "Are we going to have critters aboard or not?"

"Darlings, please!" pleaded Switters, reclaiming his pallor. "*Critters?* Rarely has a linguistic corruption stunk so excrementally of willful hayseediness. It's the sort of ill-bred mispronunciation associated with barnyard sodomites and greeting-card wits, even exceeding in déclassé offensiveness the use of *shrooms* when *mushrooms* is the word intended."

"Life is offensive. Get used to it." They had him there.

"Bet Dev says *shrooms*." There, too.

Being as fundamentally nonviolent as they were artistically restless, the girls soon lost their taste for naval warfare. One day, to everyone's delight, a lowly garbage scow appeared in place of a windjammer, and the next day somebody launched an ark. These were followed by fishing trawlers, tugboats, barges, rafts, kayaks, houseboats, tankers, and ocean liners. And, as any art historian could have predicted, there eventually bloomed a period of stylistic mannerism, of art for art's sake. The girls began to bring in boats that bore little or no resemblance to boats: impressionistic boats, expressionistic boats, Cubistic boats, boats more closely resembling swivel chairs, toupees, bowling trophies, or poodle dogs than anything that ever plied the seas; boats that wouldn't steer correctly and in some cases wouldn't even float. Anti-boats. Suicides. Sinkers. Bangladesh ferry service. Then, Luna stopped the show with a miniature Christ who walked on water. Everyone was stunned, but two days later, during which time she'd neither eaten nor slept, Brie unveiled a Christ who not only walked on water but also towed skis. Apparently, the end was near.

Their little regattas had been attracting an increasing number of kibitzers, so it was hardly a surprise when a writer for the *Post-Intelligencer* mentioned them in her column. "Regrettable," bemoaned Switters. "Any day now we can expect the novelty-greedy snouts of TV cameras to come sniffing at our pleasures."

A product of their culture, the Art Girls could neither share nor understand his objection. An aversion to media exposure was as incomprehensible to them as would have been in earlier times an aversion to the favors of a king or the blessings of the Church.

There might have developed a quarrel, but (naturally enough, since it was well into April) the rains stopped. The sky went blue on them, the sun bounded on stage like a cut-rate comedian who doubled as his own spotlight, and within a day the market streets and gutters were as dry as rye. And dry they remained. With the dawning of spring, moreover, it dawned on the girls that their school year was drawing to a close, final exams were imminent, portfolios must be readied for grading; and, so, with a chirpy panic, they turned their full attention to the paintings, drawings, sculptures, and photographs that for months they'd been ignoring, to the faculty's supreme bewilderment, in favor of maritime models and nautical whirligigs.

On their rare forays into the market now, they did, singularly or in pairs, seek out Switters, always with just a trace of dreaminess in their perky hellos and good-byes. "What are you doing with yourself these days?" they'd inquire, implying that his life must be dreary without them.

"The house is on fire," he'd answer merrily. "I'm looking out the second-story window. In my case, that happens to be two inches above the ground. Perfect!"

Whereas in the past it had been an unspoken rule that no prying was permitted, now they'd ask, "But what are you doing here in the market? What did you do before? You know, like *before?*"

"Oh, I gave up a proctology practice to go live in the Ural Mountains. Or did I give up a urology practice to go work for Procter and Gamble? Hmm?"

"You can't remember whether you were a proctologist or a urologist?"

"Alas. All I know is that if you could sit on it, I was interested in it."

At least half the girls made it clear, largely through body language, that anything they sat on could be his for the asking. Yet, he did not ask. He was, in some oblique fashion, paying off a debt to Suzy, who, he kept reminding himself, was but three or four years their junior, and for whose sake he seemed to feel he owed more than a modicum of retribution. He lusted maniacally for the Art Girls, of course, and, in all frankness, might never have let remorse over Suzy stand in the way of getting to know them more intimately had not his sunrise visits from Dev been so carnally extracting.

It was spring. There was no mistaking it. The air had become like cotton candy, spun not from sugar but the sex glands of meadowlarks and dry white wine. In the Pike Place Market, green sprouts popped up between the cobblestones. When he ventured out of a morning, freshly if resentfully groomed, yet bearing Dev's funky signature like a laundry mark on a shirt, Switters left his topcoat at home.

Pale sunlight warmed the "starship," the "second-story window," the "throne of enlightenment" from whose eminence he kept watch on the world. Because spring brought with it, as it does each year, quiet spasms of longing that may be interpreted as *sad,* he found himself thinking of the sad-faced little mercado down in Boquichicos, so woe-fully wanting in goods and goods-buyers compared to the overstuffed market in which he parked his "one-man tilt-a-whirl." And because in the high stalls (including Dev's), oranges, onions, potatoes, and so forth were stacked in pyramid piles, he was repeatedly reminded of the shaman of the Kandakandero. Was it around Today Is Tomorrow's cranial apex that Sailor Boy's plumage had come to rest? And what of Fer-de-lance? The boy was out of vivid South America, but vivid South America was not quite out of the boy.

Bereft of Art Girl yachting parties, Switters again had lots of time to think, and while he thought often of Suzy and what he might have done to protect their relationship, thought of the CIA and what he might have done to preserve his job, he focused his thinking on his South American affliction, specifically on the question raised by Bobby Case, to wit: What had he been shown by the witchman's ayahuasca, his yopo, that was so privileged and precious that he'd be expected to pay for it by spending the rest of his life with his feet off the ground?

Was his predicament in any way a distant echo of Adam and Eve's? Had he, with a chit supplied by a creepy trickster, bought lunch at the Tree of Knowledge Bar & Grill, where only the cosmic elite were sup-posed to eat? If so, what forbidden information, exactly, had he ingested? That every daisy, sparrow, and minnow on the planet had an identity just as strong as his own? That all flesh was slowed-down light and physical reality a weird dance of electrified nothingness? That at a certain level of consciousness, death ceased to become a relevant issue? As did time? Today *is* tomorrow? Okay. But hadn't he known those things all along?

In Genesis 3:22, a peevish voice attributed to Yahweh said of Adam (caught with pip on his lip), "Behold, the man is become as one of us." *Us?* More than one god, then? Goddesses, perhaps: a Ms. Yahweh? Was Yah's collective pronoun meant to include his beaming lieutenant, Lucifer? Or, for that matter, the Serpent? How about the community of angels (an apolitical faction of which might already have been disposed toward neutrality)? Or might God possibly—and this was pretty far-fetched—have been referring to the bulbs? The coppery pods, the shiny, trash-talking siliques who had boasted that they were running the show? Ridiculous, maybe, but what *were* those damn bulbs? Were they intrinsic to the plants from which ayahuasca and yopo were derived, an example of an abiding botanical intelli-gence amplified and made comprehensible by an interfacing of vegeta-tive alkaloids with human neurons? Were they, rather, projected manifestations of his own psyche, hallucinated totems from the collec-tive unconscious? Or were they actual independent entities, a life-form residing, say, one physical dimension away from our own, reachable at a kind of supercharged Web site accessed through chemical rather than electronic means?

Well, whatever, he certainly hadn't become "as one" of them, or "as one" of the witchman's ilk, either. So, why was he being punished? Instructed? Initiated? Eighty-sixed, at any rate, from the garden of reason? The very terminology to which he was forced to resort in order to consider these issues was suspect, being at once alien and shopworn, the parlance having in recent decades been yanked from its arcane native contexts and incorporated into the vocabularies of popularizers, charlatans, and dilettantes. Ugh! Still, they were real issues, were they not, as challenging to science, which preferred to sweep them under the rug, as to Switters, who, for reasons personal and acute, lacked that timid luxury?

Thrilled by the strange implications of such questions and at the same moment embarrassed by them, he examined them repeatedly but sheepishly, like a forensic scientist sorting a collection of crime-scene lingerie. These private musings occurred mainly in public—on sun-smeared corners, in shadowed archways, or beneath the great car-toonish market clock—where the murmuring of unsuspecting throngs washed over him, and Florida grapefruit and Arizona melons, like the popped orbs of Buick-sized frogs, watched him without blinking.

It was in one of those places, toying with one of those riddles, that he was approached, too abruptly for his liking, by a blue-chinned, dagger-nosed young man with an excess of glower behind his spectacles and an excess of wrinkle in his suit.

If the fellow was Mayflower's Joe, coming out of the cold, something pretty serious must be up. At second glance, though, Switters would have bet this sulky slubberdegullion couldn't tail the Statue of Liberty. He was no Joe. The company still had standards. Of course, he might be a master of disguise. Lower lip like that could be a nice touch, provided he didn't trip over it.

"You Switters?"

"Who wants to know, pal?"

"I'm here to drive you to your grandmother's."

"Don't believe I rang for a car. My chauffeur's name is Abdulla, he's been known to patronize a dry cleaner, he calls me *Mr.* Switters, and unless I have him confused with the gardener, this is *not* his day off."

The man bristled, but any thought he might have had to rummage in his repertoire of rude retorts was dispelled by a look from Switters, hypnotic and fierce. Out of a jacket pocket unraveling at its seams, he drew a card that identified him as a paralegal at a downtown law firm that Switters remembered Maestra having mentioned once or twice in connection with her will.

"Guess there's some bad news," he said. "I'm parked around the corner on Pine."

In Maestra's foyer Switters was greeted by a doctor and a lawyer. Does it get any worse than that? Assuming that no decent person would allow a land developer in their home, only the presence of a cop and a priest was required (the Four Horsemen of the Apocalypse) to complete this roll call of damnation.

The physician was courteous and kind. He explained that Maestra had suffered a mild stroke, particularly mild when one considered her age, from which there were indications she would fully recover. There was no evidence of paralysis, although her speech was noticeably slurred. She was lightly sedated, and a nurse had been engaged to watch over her for the next seventy-two hours. Until she regained normal speech, she wished to see no one. "Switters would try to take advantage of my vocal impediment to win his first argument with me in thirty years." The doctor quoted her with a chuckle, gave Switters his phone number, and left the house.

It was now the lawyer's turn. She, too, was polite, though with her it seemed more a matter of professionalism than compassion. Uncommonly tall, she was as black of skin as many of her colleagues were of heart, and there was a trace of tradewind in her accent. "Barbados," she'd later explain. Her dignity, magnified by her height, might have been daunting to a man less reckless than he. In any case, since Ms. Foxweather had a couple of bombs to drop, her altitude was entirely appropriate.

"I don't suppose you've ever been apprised of your grandmother's indictment?" Foxweather inquired, opening the hatch and letting a big one fall. "No, I thought as much. Well, she was charged in January with computer trespass. Intrusion with mischievous intent. And it was mischief, I should stress. There was no evidence of larceny or social activism, per se. Nevertheless, it's a serious charge at an inopportune time since the government is attempting to clamp down in these cases before they get out of hand. The feds aim to send a message."

Whether in disbelief (though he shouldn't have been overly surprised), dismay, or a kind of admiration that was not far from delight, Switters just kept shaking his head. Foxweather couldn't be faulted for imagining that it was palsy that had landed him in his chair.

"Because of your grandmother's age, prison was never really a possibility and because, as far as can be proven, she didn't capitalize financially on her intrusions, there was. . . . Well, intentionally or unintentionally, she did bring down at least one computer network and destroy a fair amount of intellectual property, and while I did my best, the fine was steep. It was levied this morning, and I have to say, I'm convinced the judgment is what caused her stroke."

The attorney finally took a seat—Switters was getting a crick in his neck—and cut to the nougat. Maestra, even should she completely recover and suffer no further blockages, was going to require care. She threatened to cane-whip the tightwad who might try to move her into an efficiency apartment and gun down like a landfill rat the Nazi who would plant her in a nursing home (Switters and Foxweather exchanged glances that indicated they both knew the old lady wasn't joking), and home care was not inexpensive. The Magnolia manse was costly to keep up. Taxes were in arrears. There was a six-figure fine to pay. And, of course, legal fees. When all was said and done, Maestra, who'd donated generously over the years to some rather kooky causes, was staring into the hungry eyeholes of the lean white dog of bankruptcy.

"Now, I've agreed to accept her old cabin up at Snoqualmie Pass in exchange for my services. So that helps some. Ahem. Aside from this house, however, your granny has only one asset of any great value."

"The Matisse."

"Precisely. And it would fetch more than enough at auction to see her through. But she says she's promised it to you upon her demise and, therefore, doesn't feel she has the moral right to sell it."

Switters wheeled himself to the living room door and looked in. There it hung above the mantel, in all of its sprawling, life-affirming effrontery. How could anything so flat be so rotund, anything so still be so antic, anything so meaty be so spiritually contemplative, anything so deliberately misshapen be so gratifying? Upon patterned cushions that might have been honked, zig by zag, out of Ornette Coleman's horn, the odalisque exposed her flesh to a society that had grown frightened again of flesh. Without fear, inhibition, egotism, monetary motive, or, for that matter, prurience or desire, she loomed, she spread—as if she were both metropolitan skyline and wilderness plain: woman as city, woman as prairie, woman as the whole wide world. And yet, the longer he looked, the more removed she became from womanliness and worldliness, for in essence, she was but a song sung in color, a magnificently useless expanse of liberated paint. Owing nothing to society, expecting nothing, the painting bumped against the brain like a cloud against an oil derrick. It had the innocence and brute force of a dream.

Switters turned to Ms. Foxweather. "Matisse must not have had any damn heat in his studio. Woman went blue on him."

"Oh, but that's the way—"

"Sell it!" he snapped. "I never liked it anyhow."

You can lie to God but not to the Devil?

For at least two reasons, Switters had been planning to move into the mountain cabin as soon as the snow melted. First, he was ready for a sabbatical from the Pike Place Market, which, with the advent of warm weather, was becoming almost South American in its vividity; and second, if Maestra was staring the pale dog in its ciphers, Switters was already under its paws. With his unemployment benefits about to expire and his unsold condo facing foreclosure, he'd been steeling himself to approach Maestra for a loan. Now . . .

A lawyer's going to be weekending in my sylvan cabin whilst, in the glow of my beloved Matisse, some ruthless corporate raider will be plotting the hostile takeover of a pharmaceutical firm noted for the manufacture of mood-elevating laxatives. Along with appropriate details and his concern about his grandmother, Switters e-mailed the preceding to Bobby Case. When Bobby failed to respond right away, Switters figured he must be off flying a hazardous recon mission over North Korea (for, presumably, that's what his new assignment entailed) or else up to his knees in Okinawan pussy (Bad Bob was ecstatic to be in Asia again, boy howdy!).

In about twelve hours, however, the e-bell rang. *Damn! Why do those yellow-bellied fates always gang up on the elderly? How is she?*

In the mind and the body, where it counts, Maestra's doing remarkably well, Switters answered, *although, for the moment, her voice is unsettlingly reminiscent of her dear departed parrot. Financially, Sailor Boy may be the better off of the two. I had no idea. Turns out she's been donating large sums of cash to organizations whose names and objectives are not well known.*

Probably CIA fronts, every one of them, Bobby tapped. *But that Matisse, which a drifter like you never deserved in the first place, ought to bring in millions.*

Yes, millions. If it doesn't set off an alarm. Not only is its authenticity likely to be challenged, there's a possibility it could be stolen property. Maestra's first husband acquired it under somewhat foggy circumstances. In any event, I'm living by the temporary graces of Mr. Plastic and in dire need of gainful employment. I have to keep Maestra out of the nursing home, should it come to that, keep her in her own house with her wicked computers. Also, I've decided to go back and confront Today Is

Tomorrow in the autumn. One year should just about suffice for two-inch enlighten-ment. Wouldn't want to overdo it. Wear out my welcome in Nirvana.

Now you're talking, son! I'll get back to you if I have any bright ideas. Mean-while, give the old hacker my affection and admiration.

The very next day, Bobby was on-line with an intriguing proposal.

If you're able and willing to travel, You Know Who has got a speck of work for an ex-operative with your particular experience. April 30. Hotel Gül. Antalya, Turkey. Sit in the lobby and look innocuous—can you manage that?—until you hear somebody say, "Fuck the Dallas Cowboys." Pay: low. Risk: high. But you won't turn it down because the thrills are practically unlimited, and I know you're aching to get back in the game.

Was he? *Aching* (from the Old High German *ach!*, an exclamation of pain) to get back in the *game* (from the Indo-European base *gwhembh*, "to leap merrily," as in *gambol*)? Certainly, he had always looked upon his activities, official and unofficial, in the geo-political arena as a game: a combination of rugby, chess, and liar's poker, with a little Rus-sian roulette mixed in for good measure. While there were no conclu-sive victories to be had in that game beyond simple survival, a player scored whenever his acts of subversion thwarted or even delayed the coalescing of power in any single camp. In a sense, one won by making it difficult for others to win or, at least, to grow fat on the fruits of their triumph.

Six months in a wheelchair, however, had altered his overview slightly if significantly. When one was living two inches off the ground, one remained close enough to the earth to experience its tug, share its rhythms, recognize it as home, and not go floating off into some ethe-real ozone where one behaved as if one's physical body was excess bag-gage and one's brain a weather balloon. On the other hand, one had just enough loft so that one glided above the frantic strivings and petty discontents that preoccupied the earthbound, circumnavigating those dreary miasmas that threatened to bleach their hearts a single shade of gray. In short, one could be keenly interested in worldly matters yet remain serenely detached from their outcome.

Switters, if the truth be told, was as enthusiastic about geo-political monkey-wrenching as he'd ever been, but now, two inches removed, was no more attached to the end results than he'd been to the outcome of the rain-gutter boat races against the Art Girls. (Were he inclined—and he decidedly was not—he probably could have drawn several parallels between his passage through life and the careening of his unlikely little boats through the market's littery channels.) In fact, he'd reached the conclusion that the inertia of the masses and the cor-ruption of their manipulators had become so ingrained, so immense, that nothing short of a literal miracle could effect a happy ending to humanity's planetary occupancy, let alone the kind of game in which he played upon that slanted field. And yet, it was a game absolutely worth playing. For its own sake. For the wahoo that was in it. For the chance that it would enlarge one's soul.

So, perhaps he wasn't exactly *aching* to resume play, but he mustn't have been averse to it, for he wasted no time in twisting Mr. Plastic's arm until the card blubbered like a cornered snitch, surrendering a one-way ticket to Istanbul for Switters and a heavy silver bracelet in a Northwest Indian raven motif for Maestra. In one of the market's dimmer cul-de-sacs, he enjoyed a furtive farewell straddle from a drawers-down Dev, while yards away at her deserted stall, consumers edged across the narrow line of civilized restraint that separated shopping from looting, cleaning out the first of the season's Mexican strawberries. Switters reimbursed her from his undernourished wallet in order to keep her brothers from slapping her around. Then, he was off to meet, for the very first time, the archangel—

"Audubon Poe." The flannel-shirted, Mariners-capped man who spoke the name had been standing on the Pike Street curb poring over a bus schedule all the while that Switters was sliding into a taxi, folding his chair, and dragging it in beside him. He was a youngish, nerdy yet nimble Caucasian, not unlike Hector Sumac of Lima, Peru. As the cabbie signaled to pull into traffic, the stranger had suddenly thrust his face in the taxi window, uttered Poe's name, frowned one of those obligatorily disapproving frowns that is actually a smile with its pants on backward, and shook his head. "You know he's an arms runner," he said, making it sound more like a piece of hot gossip than an accusation or a warning. And just as quickly he was gone.

"Airport," said Switters.

"Where you fly today, sir?" asked the driver.

"Turkey."

"Ah? Turkey. Long way. Vacation there?"

"Run arms there," Switters replied matter-of-factly, wondering where that Joe had come from and what the hell Bobby had gotten him into.

part 3

Given a choice between a folly and a sacrament, one should always choose the folly—because we know a sacrament will not bring us closer to God and there's always a chance that a folly will.

—Erasmus

the land spread out before him like a pizza. Its topography was flat, its texture rough, its temperature hot, its hue reddish yellow, studded with pepperoni-colored rocks; and, at the moment, it glistened as if drizzled with olive oil. Water was absorbed slowly, very slowly, by the arid hardpan and tended to trickle toward any depression. Were the ground conscious, it would savor this unexpected rainwater, for it would see not another drop of moisture for a good seven months.

Behind him, where he'd separated from the band of Shammar Bedouins, the baked "cheese" bubbled up in low hills that grew progressively steeper until, farther west, they became a full-fledged mountain range with snowy peaks. Eastward, however, the "pizza" was unrelieved. This was the great Syrian desert that stretched into Iraq and Jordan and Israel and all the way across Arabia, and was the threshing floor upon which the human soul had been flailed free from the chaff of its long ripening, only to be ossified and shriveled by a degeneration into dogma of the very ideas that had nurtured it and winnowed it loose, in the endless granary of the desert, from its dark animal husk. Man's physical self evolved in the sea, and to the rhythms of the oceans our salty blood and waves of breath still moved, but it was here on the burning sands of the Middle East, where Switters now paused to rest, that the spiritual self emerged. There had been nothing to distract it.

Switters was left almost giddy by the realization that not only was he alone, he was also unseen. By anyone or anything. In the Amazon forest, by way of contrast, one never made an undetected move, for no matter how deeply one penetrated, how far removed one was from one's fellows and milieu, one was always of great interest to a hundred pairs of eyes: slitty eyes, bulbous eyes, multifaceted eyes, eyes bloodshot, chocolatey, or hollow; eyes that saw without being seen; a blinking, squinting, spying paradise of reincarnated Joes. Here in the desert, though, nothing watched but the gods. Small wonder that religion was born hereabouts or that, for better or worse, hereabouts it had thrived.

The coolness that had come with the rain was only a sweet memory now. Switters sweltered but didn't sweat: perspiration evaporated before it could pump out of his pores. The air that he gasped, due to the exertion of wheeling his chair over stony, pitted, thornbushed terrain, was so light and dry that it made but the weakest impression on his respiratory system and failed to inflate his lungs, although it tingled inside him in a faintly delicious way. For all its unsubstantiality, the air seemed as alive as the earth seemed dead. Massaging his wrists, he squinted through nets of rising heat at the oasis, still more than a mile away, and could not help but think how vastly different these bare, harsh, god-connecting surroundings were from the scene off the coast of Turkey, where he had yachted and sipped Dom Pérignon only three weeks prior.

"Fuck the Dallas Cowboys."

Switters had been expecting that declaration, had been nervously straining to hear it through a fog of jet lag and migraine and coffee-fueled Turk chatter all afternoon, but he hadn't expected to hear it issued so abruptly, openly, and emphatically by a denim-clad black man striding toward him across lush oriental carpets and speaking English with a Swedish accent.

"Fuck Notre Dame," Switters responded hopefully. Bobby hadn't supplied him with a countersign. "Likewise the Los Angeles Lakers and the New—"

"Steady, man," cautioned the contact. "You be speaking ill of the New York Yankees, you and me gonna have a problem. Ja, man, ya betcha."

"Oh, we wouldn't want that." With just a hint of fierceness in his grin, Switters had looked the man over. He was trim enough for someone of his age—late forties would be a good guess—but his shoulders were stooped, and his hands, from which long, sensitive fingers dangled like licorice whips, seemed uncallused and spongy. "However . . ."

"Ain't no however to it. You got luggage upstairs? Good. Tell the bellman to bring it to the yacht basin. And follow me." He paused. "I'd offer to push your chair, but if you can't get out of this lobby on your own, you sure as hell not be getting out of where Mr. Poe be sending you." For the first time, he smiled. "Go Yankees," he said softly. "Go Knicks. And by the way, man, nice suit."

The contact was Skeeter Washington, chief lieutenant to the legendary Audubon Poe and, in certain circles, a minor legend, himself. The son of a fairly well-known Harlem jazz couple (mother a singer, father played bass), Louis Mosquito Washington, about to be drafted, had enlisted in the army in 1969 after a recruiting sergeant assured him he'd be assigned to a military band. Instead, he'd been put in the infantry and shipped to Vietnam. He'd been wounded and upon recovery, ordered to return to battle once he'd enjoyed a week's R and R in Tokyo. At that point he deserted, threw himself upon the mercy of a group of radical Japanese pacifists, and a month or so later turned up in Sweden, where he resided for a quarter century, earning a living and a reputation as a bebop pianist. A couple of years back, still smoldering with resentment over the horrors wrought in Southeast Asia by America's savage wrong-headedness and his forced participation therein, he'd sought out Audubon Poe and volunteered his services—although neither Skeeter nor anyone else seemed to know exactly what Poe was up to, aside from providing the international news media with a steady source of information damaging to the "defense" industry and the CIA. It would have been unlikely, however, that the services of a jazz piano player would have been refused by a man born and reared in New Orleans.

"Uh, I should inform you," Switters had said as they waited on the dock for the hotel porter to arrive with his bags, "that the company seems aware of this."

"This?"

"My coming here. To meet with Poe."

"Aw, doesn't matter."

"But isn't there a price on his head?"

"Maybe, maybe not. Ol' Poe, he put out the story himself years ago that he was on a CIA hit list. After that, the government didn't dare to smack him. Not in no obvious, violent way, nohow. Could always try and slip him a heart attack pill or something, I guess. But Anna, she be sneaking and tasting his food before he eat a bite of it."

"Who is Anna?"

"His fifteen-year-old daughter."

Switters's Adam's apple flopped in his throat like an eel in a creel. *Good God!* he thought. *Why didn't Bobby warn me?*

Antalya's marina, one of the most beautiful on the Mediterranean, was built on the site of an ancient Roman harbor next to a restored Ottoman village. From its main dock, in the shadow of crumbling ruins, a motor launch had carried Washington and Switters out to a gleaming white ninety-foot yacht, *The Banality of Evil,* anchored about a half-mile offshore. The boat, flaring in the distance like a million-aire's teeth, belonged to Sol Glissant, a Beirut-based French national who had made a chunk of his fortune rebuilding Lebanon's swimming pools after the war and was known as the Pool Pasha of the Levant. For reasons of his own, Glissant had put *The Banality of Evil* at the disposal of Audubon Poe, who behaved as if it were his, which for all practical purposes it was.

Switters had been shown to a stateroom, given time to "freshen up" (code for *perform maintenance*), and then summoned on deck, where he was handed a champagne glass as large as a fishbowl by none other than Poe, himself. Like Washington, Poe was dressed all in denim, but his fine, sharp, birdlike features, his slicked-back silver hair, his efflu-vium of cologne that made Switters's Jungle Desire, in comparison, smell as cheap as its name, and the irony in his civil, confident quiver of a smile, produced an air of aristocracy that seemed to transform the egalitarian blue cotton into resort wear designed by a Riviera comte.

"So, you're Switters," Poe said, in an accent that managed to be both southern and refined. "The last I heard of you, you were hanging upside down over Baghdad."

Sloshing his champagne, Switters demurred. "I believe you may have me confused with my friend Case. While I've passed many a merry hour in fair Iraq, my peripateticism there has been limited to its terrestrial surfaces."

Poe regarded him curiously. "I see. Do please forgive my social blunder. But you are, are you not, the gentleman who knows how to refer to a lady's treasure in seventy-five different languages?"

"Seventy-one." *Good God,* he thought, *is this to be my only claim to fame? The lone thing by which men remember me? My other achievements—academic, ath-letic, and political—eclipsed by this frothy exercise in linguistic trivia? They'll probably engrave it on my tombstone, should I live long enough to get one.*

"Myself, I dig the Swedish for it," put in Skeeter Washington.

"Oh, yes," said Switters. "*Slida.* One of my favorites. For its onomatopoeia."

When Skeeter looked puzzled, Poe had said, "You must excuse Mr. Washington. He's been a long time away from English. Why, I had to teach him to speak Ebonics, and as you may have noted, he's not very fluent in it. Says things like 'Ja, ya betcha, motherfucker.'"

Laughing, he turned to his associate. "Skeet, *onomatopoeia* refers to a word that sounds like the thing it represents."

"*Slida*," said Switters, nodding. "And the Japanese for the organ in question is almost as onomatopoeic: *chitsu*."

"Yeah, man, that ain't bad, either."

"Preferable, certainly, to the Japanese for the male equivalent: *chimpo*. Makes it sound like a trained monkey in a traveling circus."

"Don't know about yours," said Skeeter, "but my dick behave like a trained monkey in a traveling circus most of the time."

"Let's change the subject, shall we, gentlemen?" said Poe. "Anna will be coming on deck momentarily with an hors d'oeuvre or two."

The men hadn't gotten down to business right away. In fact, nearly three days passed before Switters was taken belowdecks into the boat's storeroom and shown the contraband that Poe and Washington were running. In the meantime, they sailed Turkey's famed Turquoise Coast, slicing gracefully through waters the color of Suzy's eyes, from whose pellucid depths fairyland rock formations and playful dolphins rose. They sipped Sol Glissant's champagne, dined on fresh fish poached in grape leaves and served with capered sauces, and gazed at sunsets while Skeeter played on the salon piano, at Switters's tipsy request, amazing bebop renditions of Broadway show tunes. Occasionally they talked shop, wondering among themselves, for example, at the arrogance and uncharacteristic stupidity of Israel's Mossad in its recent bungled attempt to smack a revered Hammas leader inside Jordan.

"Goes to show you," remarked Poe, "that cowboys are cowboys, whether Jewish or—"

"Goyboys," suggested Switters.

"Cowgoys," offered Washington.

"More champagne, Daddy?" asked young Anna.

Anna proved to be a slender sylph, with a galactically freckled, waiflike face, brown hair braided in pendulous pigtails, and breasts scarcely larger than her fists. She was innocently flirty, and Switters, when not drinking with the men, divided his time between going to absurd lengths to avoid ever being left alone with her and spying on her voraciously as she sunbathed, topless, on the afterdeck.

Because he was on water, Switters assumed that the prohibitive taboo was not in effect and that he was free to move about the yacht on foot. However, since he didn't want to have to explain his situation to his hosts, he remained in the wheelchair. To honor the fates, he remained in the wheelchair even when no one was looking. He was heartened, nevertheless, for it occurred to him that should he fail to get the curse lifted, should worse come to worst, he possibly could spend the rest of his life aboard ship, be it a ship on the order of *The Banality of Evil* or one like *Little Blessed Virgin of the Starry Waters*. The latter type, he had to admit, was much more feasible, although it provided scant more space for walking about than had his double bed in Seattle.

In any event, in the early afternoon of their third day at sea, Poe had called him to the railing and pointed a manicured nail at a hazy, macaroon-colored horizon. "Hatay," he said. "On the Syrian border. A dismal, camel-gnawed area whose only distinction aside from it being the site of Alexander's victory over the Persians is that it was upon its uninviting beach that Jonah was supposed to have been coughed up by the whale. Nothing symbolic is intended, I assure you, but I regret to report that it's the very spot where we are coughing you up. Tonight."

"Hatay? Turkey? What's? . . ."

"How you get from Hatay into northern Iraq is your affair. Frankly, considering your physical liability, I have my doubts that you can manage it at all. People whom I trust, however, assure me you have excellent qualifications: the languages, the experience, the courage, the cunning. They couldn't vouch, of course, for your desire."

"Well, I'm plainly uninformed as to the nature of the mission, but I can tell you that I don't go to dances to sit on the sidelines nibbling fruitcake. I'm here to take the prom queen home. Moreover, I happen to be embarrassingly bereft of hard currency, and Mr. Plastic is pretending he doesn't know me. This gig has got to be preferable to selling used electrolysis equipment over the phone."

Again, Poe studied him curiously. Then he said, "All right. Come with me."

The silver-haired *précieux* (he could be foppish even in jeans) had unlocked the storeroom, shoved aside cases of champagne, crates of capers, and restaurant-sized jars of olives and pickled artichokes, to reveal a ton or more of . . . well, there were land-mine detectors and various devices for defusing or detonating mines, there were camouflage paints, gas masks, fire extinguishers, transmitters for jamming radio and radar signals, flares, bulletproof shields, water-purification kits, and a refrigerator stocked with serums for inoculation against anthrax, sarin, and other biological and chemical weapons.

"My goodness," said Switters, looking over the supplies. "You're a regular little elf."

Poe winced. "I've been called worse. 'Traitor,' for example. By the

President of the United States and the chairmen of the intelligence committees in both houses of Congress."

"Not to mention Mayflower Cabot Fitzgerald and swarms of racketeering locusts in the pulpits and the press. Congratulations. One man's treason is another man's valor. At Berkeley, where I was in grad school at the time your book was published, you were celebrated and revered. As a matter of fact, though I have to admit I only read the reviews and not the tome itself, it was your book that inspired me to sign on with the company."

If Poe had looked at him with curiosity before, those looks were nothing compared to the one he gave Switters now. "Pardon me? You joined the CIA because of a book that exposed it as an amoral, imperialist, bungling gang of money-wasters operating outside of and above the law?" He was starting to suspect that this man he'd been sent was crippled in mind as well as body.

"Why, yes. You made it irresistible. Because no other room in the burning house promised a more interesting view? Because every stand-up comic longs to play Hamlet? Because a big back has a big front? Because I believed my syrup of wahoo could sweeten its sulfur?" Switters shrugged. "It's a trifle hard to explain."

"Evidently." Poe's expression betrayed neither satisfaction nor confidence, and he enjoyed a long skeptical moment before shrugging, himself, and returning to the cache of—counteractives. "Those gas masks? There're approximately two thousand of them. Not fractionally enough, but they'll help. Your job is to get them to the Kurds near Dahuk."

"Which Kurds? KDP or PUK?"

"Should such a choice become necessary, I'd favor PUK for the simple reason that the KDP is sponsored by the Iraqi government and therefore is in less danger of being gassed by it. Like all political parties everywhere, however, they're both consumed with power and self-interest, so my preference is that you try to get the masks into the hands of those unarmed civilians whom both parties *claim* to represent."

In a parodying, theatrical gesture, Switters pounded his right fist against his left breast and exclaimed, "So it shall be written, so it shall be done!"

They had an early supper on deck, a leisurely meal in which Switters was restricted to a single glass of champagne. This was due to the fact that he would be needing his wits about him, but also because the last time he'd had his fill of the bubbly, he'd gazed into Anna's face and told her that her eyes were like a morning mist on the fur of a squirrel. Or something along those lines.

The sun was low but the air was still balmy, and the sea was the shade of blue that black could have been if it hadn't stepped over the line. After plotting the mission as best they could—it was a fly-by-the-seat-of-the-pants operation—they entered into a conversation about jazz, cinema, and literature, a dialogue that hit a snag when Switters began expounding upon "the mythological and historical echoes" that resonated in the most overtly skimble-skamble phrases of *Finnegans Wake*. "Nigh him wigworms and nigh him tittlies and nigh him cheekadeekchimple," for example.

After that, Audubon Poe talked of his boyhood among the gentry of New Orleans and how, to further his ambition to become a professional chess player, he had taught himself Russian at fourteen, thinking it might give him some advantage if ever pitted against the grand masters, who all seemed to hail from Mother Russia. At seventeen he became the youngest spy in the history of the CIA, which recruited him to dig for Cold War information at international chess tournaments, and although he blew his cover by having a love affair with the wife of one of the Soviet champions, he later became a full-time operations officer. In that capacity he served the company loyally for years, until he found himself gradually disillusioned and sickened by Vietnam, the secret war against Cuba, the gratuitous lying to the American public, the support of brutal dictatorships, the coziness with the Mafia, and, in general, the overly indulgent interpretation of the "such other functions and duties" clause in the agency's charter. Poe didn't blame company cowboys as much as he blamed the Presidents who used them, often illegally, as instruments of a foreign policy whose main objective was to enrich the defense industry and get them, the Presidents, reelected. Nevertheless, his exposé had badly dented the agency's fenders—and forced him into a precarious exile.

"The company's changed since your divorce," said Switters.

"I hear they let black men be agents now," said Washington.

"Black women, too. Only we call them 'African-Americans' these days."

"Ja, ja, that's right. I can't keep up with all our name changes, man. Back in Harlem, we was 'Negroes' or 'colored people.' Then it got to be 'blacks' and 'people of color.' But 'Negro' *means* 'black,' meant 'black' all along unless I'm mistaken; and maybe I'm thick, living among the Swedes all this time—I mean, America's a bouncy country whereas the

Swedes ain't got that much bounce to 'em, you know—but I fail to detect where they be a hell of a lot of *difference* between the terms 'colored people' and 'people of color.' Or between 'Afro-American' and 'African-American,' far as that goes."

"The distinctions are subtle, all right," Switters admitted. "Too subtle for the rational mind. Only the political mind can grasp them. I suspect there's a bid for empowerment behind it all, the power going to whoever seizes the right to coin the names. In a reality made of language, the people who get to name things have psychological ownership of those things. Couples name their pets and children, Madison Avenue names the products that dominate our desires, theologians name the deities that dominate our spirit—'Yahweh' changed to 'Jehovah' changed to plain ol' generic 'God'—kids name the latest cultural trends or rename old ones to make them theirs; politicians name streets and schools and airports after one another or after the enemies they've successfully eliminated: they took Martin Luther King's life, for example, and then by naming their pork barrel projects after him, took possession of his memory. In a way, we're like linguistic wolves, lifting our legs on patches of cultural ground to mark them with verbal urine as territory that we alone control. Or maybe not."

"Verbal wolf urine?" inquired Audubon Poe incredulously. He had tucked a polka-dotted ascot into the throat of his denim work shirt, accentuating the dapperness that seemed to originate from his hair. "Anna, you must promise me you'll never marry a man who uses phrases that picturesque."

Anna giggled in a manner that suggested she thought it might be good fun to marry just such a man. Switters averted his eyes, while Poe smiled ruefully and returned the conversation to the CIA. "You say the company has changed. For better, you think, or for worse?"

"It may be too soon to tell. About the company and about the world in general." Before Switters could say more—if, indeed, he had any intention of continuing—a crewman approached and whispered something in Poe's ear.

"Blow coming up," Poe announced when the sailor departed. "Radio reports there could be seven- to eight-foot swells throughout the night. Switters, I'm afraid we're going to have to dump you earlier than planned. There're likely to be Turks up and about, though they turn in early in these parts, but we can't wait until tomorrow night, as we've got a drop to make off of Somalia next week that we don't dare miss. Innocent lives at stake and so forth. If you'll just get your gear together . . ."

"Happily," said Switters, and he meant it, although it's debatable whether he would attribute his glee to the prospect of action or to the fact that he was about to escape without making a fool of himself—or worse—over Anna.

In any case, he had waved good-bye to the girl from a safe distance, shook the manicured hand that had nearly punched the breath out of the Central Intelligence Agency, and allowed the crew to lower him, his luggage, his chair, and the burlap sacks containing two thousand gas masks into a rubber raft. Skeeter Washington manned the oars (a motor might have attracted attention) and manned them well. The wind was already escalating, and between the darkened yacht and the rocky shore there was considerable chop, but Skeeter slid over the crests and attacked the troughs as if mastering a difficult composition by Thelonius Monk. Indeed, he was humming as he rowed.

"What's that tune, Skeeter?"

"Huh? Oh, that? Just something new I been working on. I thinking about calling it 'Slida,' thanks to you, man. Americans won't know what that mean nohow and the Swedes be broadminded about such matters. If my record company in Stockholm don't dig the reference, guess I could call it—what was your Japanese word for it?—'Chitsu'? Unless you got a better one."

The raft pitched to one side and caromed off a rock. Switters had to wipe spray from his eyes. "Well, you likely would want to avoid the Welsh. In Wales, they say, *llawes goch.*"

"Say *what?* You jiving me? That be ugly, man. Why, I wouldn't go near nothing with a name like that."

"A rose by any name would smell as sweet," Switters reminded him, then dug his left heel under the tubing to keep from being jolted overboard. They were entering the surf now, and despite Skeeter's skillful maneuvering, the raft was lurching violently. "Vietnamese is worse. In Vietnam they call it *lo torcung am dao* or *lo torcung am ba,* depending on whether a baby is coming out of it or a man is going in."

"And what about when it's not in use?"

Switters shrugged. He started to suggest that the Vietnamese term was so long that simply speaking it might constitute foreplay. However, he would have had to yell to make himself heard above the roar of breakers, and as they were then less than thirty yards from the beach, yelling was probably not a wise idea.

"I assume you got the Turkish in you repertoire, ja?" he thought he heard Skeeter say right before they slipped sideways again and a wave broke over them. (Good thing his computer and pistol were in plastic bags.) If he remembered correctly, the Turkish term for the vagina was *dölyolu,* but with the coast guard or a Jonah cult possibly nearby, he wasn't about to shout *that* into the gap-toothed chaw of the rock-biting waves.

The oasis didn't seem to be getting any closer. For a moment, he seriously considered that it might be a mirage, a faux tableau created by too much heat rising from too much sand into too much sky. True, the nomads had seen it, as well, but to Bedouins a mirage would have its own tangibility. Could it have been a shared hallucination, like the Virgin Mary's dancing fireball at Fatima? Well, whatever, it was all his now.

He was no longer singing. He still had the urge to sing, he had the wahoo in him—the hint of anxiety only boosted it, and its level had rarely been higher—but the exertion of propelling the chair robbed him of the breath to sing. Surrounded on all sides by an immense silence, the only sound he heard beyond his own shallow gasps was sand crackling beneath his wheels and thorny weeds brushing against the spokes like a tone-deaf witch trying to pluck a banjo.

That a person's elation seemed to be tightly bound to his or her unencumbrance was a detail generally overlooked by psychologists (not surprisingly, since psychologists tended to skirt the subject of elation altogether, except when describing symptomatic behavior at the manic extreme of bipolar personality disorder), but Switters's high spirits could be primarily attributed to the fact that he was . . . well, the word *footloose* did not really apply, not literally, considering his perambulatory injunction, but at large, certainly, at liberty, exempt, burdened neither with possessions nor duties; free in a wild, wide-open land, where he was consciously going against the flow (of reason, not of nature), deliberately choosing the short straw, flaunting the rule of "safety first" (surely one of the most unromantic phrases in the English language). However, it also had not failed to energize his coconut that the operation in Iraq had gone so swimmingly.

The hardest part of the mission had been the landing on Jonah's riviera. Once Skeeter had succeeded in beaching the rubber raft and helping him into his chair—a tricky, time-consuming task due to the surf, the rocks, and Switters's inability to disembark on his own or otherwise assist—it had been a piece of cake. They had stowed the gas masks in the ruins of an old stone net shed, where Skeeter rested while Switters got out of his soaked yeast-colored linen suit and into a dry, navy blue, pin-striped, double-breasted number of a sort that was not uncommon in Turkey. They talked briefly, shook hands (Switters imagined he could feel a current of pent-up music in Skeeter's fingers), and parted, Skeeter to buck the waves back to the yacht, Switters to trundle the four kilometers into the town of Samandaği, where, in a compound next to the marketplace, he had come upon a small contingent of Kurds.

Kurds belonged in *The Guinness Book of World Records* on at least two counts: they were the largest ethnic minority on earth without an independent homeland, and they had been double-crossed and betrayed by more foreign powers than any other people in history. For this last reason alone, Switters had expected it would take days if not weeks to win their confidence. The United States, after all, had been among the nations to use them as pawns. After that one night, however, spent smoking (cheap cigars provided by Switters), drinking (arrack, a date-based liquor furnished by the Kurds), and discussing (poetry and philosophy, in Arabic) around their headman's hearth, he had felt comfortable enough to confide in them, and they had agreed to participate, to the extent that they could, in his humanitarian escapade.

Because Iraq's border with Turkey was deeply troubled where Kurds were concerned, and abristle with Turkish troops, Switters thought it best to try to enter from Syria. His new friends agreed. If he would buy the petrol, a couple of their restless young men would drive him and his gas masks (they demanded thirty masks for themselves, though they resided far from the threatened region) across southeastern Turkey in one of their rickety old Mercedes trucks. Somewhere near Nusaybin, they would put him in touch with Syrian Kurds who would help him cross over into Syria. And so it came to pass.

The second Kurdish group, as colorful as carnival cavorters in their billowy trousers, embroidered blouses, and tablecloth-sized head coverings, had taken him along Syria's northeastern snout on camelback. It was while swaying to and fro atop one of those spitting, whining, kicking, loaf-lipped beasts that he had finally made contact with Maestra. He'd been afraid to e-mail her since, as evidenced by the Joe who'd seen him off in Seattle, the company was picnicking in his computer, and for reasons he hoped were just her characteristic orneriness, she wasn't answering her phone. As much to take his mind off his uncomfortable ride as to ease his worry about her, he'd punched her Magnolia number into the satellite phone one more time—and was actually startled when the line was picked up and a gruff voice bellowed, "This had better be good!"

"Did anyone ever tell you, Maestra, that you have the disposition of a camel?"

"Damn straight I do, so don't try to milk me or pile a load on my hump. Where are you, boy?"

"Are you aware that a camel's hump is naught but a lump of fat?"

"Really? Then it's the same as a woman's breast."

"Oh no, you must be mistaken. A woman's breast . . . why, a woman's breast is a miniature moon. It's made out of moon paste and warm snow and honey."

"Heh! You romantic ninny. Where are you?"

He dared not be specific, but she got the idea that he was in camel country, and, more important, he got the idea that she'd fully recovered from her stroke. She was, in fact, arranging to fly to New York to be on hand for the auction of the Matisse in late June. "I'm making sure those poufs at Sotheby's don't try to stiff me."

Thus it was with much lightening of heart that he slipped into Iraq, a country where it was as easy to get beheaded as to get a bad meal. Fortunately, he endured the latter and avoided the former. In a ruined mountain town southwest of Dahuk, he had bestowed the masks (minus the hundred he'd given his latest escorts) on a tearfully grateful mayor, whose constituents had been recently decimated with nerve gas dropped on them by the very Baghdad authorities who had promised them self-government in 1970. The mayor hosted a celebration in his honor that evening, with lambs on the spit, hookahs on the rug, and belly dancers on the balcony. Because these Kurds were more strict in their adherence to Mohammed's commandments than was the isolated group in Samandaği, it proved a nonalcoholic affair, a condition that actually suited Switters since his digestive tract found arrack as combustible as pisco and since sobriety could be a useful ally in a hasty getaway.

Knowing full well that Baghdad would have informants in the town (there would have been a minimum of two or three at the party) who'd waste little time in reporting his presence to the nearest military garrison, Switters excused himself early on in the festivities and, instead of visiting the outhouse, as advertised, ducked into the small room he'd been given and retrieved his belongings. He rolled out the rear entrance, rattled across an adjacent courtyard dotted with stones and tethered donkeys (belly dance music drowning out the clatter), and on through a gate onto a dark side street. The neighborhood was as empty as a Transylvanian blood bank, most of its inhabitants being at the party, but outside PUK headquarters a block down the street, he found a battle-hardened old militiaman leaning against the battered hood of a Czech-made version of the Jeep. The guard spoke little Arabic, while Switters's Turkish vocabulary was pretty much limited to dölyolu. In Kurdish, even the word for that revered orifice was absent—temporarily, he trusted—from the tip of his tongue; yet, somehow the message was conveyed that Switters desired to be driven to the Syrian

frontier, a hundred miles away. The request had been stubbornly
refused, even after Switters flashed the wad of deutsche marks that Poe
had provided to see him through (the rest of his pay, about nine thousand dollars plus airfare, was being wired to his Seattle bank). So, for
the first and only time in the operation, he drew his pistol. He cocked
it with an ominous click and snuggled its barrel up under the guard's
floating rib. "To the opera!" he called. "And five gold guineas if you
catch the king's carriage."

The emaciated PUK grenadier wept openly when Switters flung
his rifle out of the moving Jeep, and Switters, tears gathering in his
own eyes, felt such shame that he had the warrior turn the vehicle
around, and they went back and picked it up. "Jesus, pal! Your attachment to your symbolic manhood could get me killed." The teeth the
Kurd showed when he smiled made his abductor's seem a textbook
example of the rewards of dental scrupulosity. They clasped hands in
the Islamic manner. And—

Wham, bam, thank you, Saddam! Nigh him wigworms and nigh
him cheekadeekchimple! They were out of there.

The distance between Switters and the oasis at last began to shrink.
Quite suddenly, in fact, the compound seemed to enlarge, as if, cued
by a director and strictly timed (ta da!), it had burst out on stage. It was
no mirage. But what was it? It had better be good because all around it,
in every direction, as far as his eyes could see, the world was as empty
and dry as a mummy's condom.

He was wondering if he shouldn't have remained with the
Bedouins. They were a marvelous people to whom travel was a gift
and hospitality a law. The Kurds had been gracious enough, but he
preferred the Bedouins, for they were less religious and thus more
lively and free. Kurds were essentially settlers who roamed only when
forced from their villages by strife. Bedouins were nomadic to the
bone. Whereas Kurds were in a constant state of bitter agitation
over their lack of an autonomous homeland, Bedouins had no use
for such paralyzing concepts. Their homeland was the circle of light
around their campfire, their autonomy was in the raw sparkle of
the stars.

In almost every nation in the Middle East, Near East, and Africa,
nomads were under strong governmental pressure to plant themselves
in established settlements. Whatever the socio-political, economic reasons given, underlying it all was that great pathetic lunatic insecurity
that drove men to cling to various illusions of certainty and perma-

nence. The supreme irony, of course, was that they clung to those ideals because they were scared witless by the certainty and permanence of death. To the domesticated, nomads were an unwelcome reminder of instinct suppressed, liberty compromised, and control unimplemented.

The fires of this particular band of wandering herdsmen had been noticed by Switters only a few kilometers inside Syria, along the isolated, seasonally fertile wadi down which he'd been driven, headlamps off, to avoid both Iraqi and Syrian border patrols. Knowing that they would be honor bound to receive him hospitably, he ordered the commandeered Jeep stopped about three hundred yards from their encampment, gave the driver a fistful of deutsche marks, and sent him back to his Kurds and fray. "Thanks for the lift, pal. Good luck to you and your homeboys. And if you don't mind me saying so, you ought to switch brands of toothpaste. Give Atomic Flash or Great White Shark a try."

Initially, he'd planned to make his way back into Turkey, where an American with a properly stamped passport and no gunnysacks of gas masks in his possession would have aroused not the slightest suspicion. He might expect to reach the Istanbul airport within the week. But he was full of himself after his little caper, and soon he was full of the Bedouins, as well.

Despite the fleas that prickled him nightly the way stars prickled the desert sky, he loved sleeping on their musky carpets inside their big black tents. (*The universe is organized anarchy,* he thought, *and I'm lying in the folds of its flag.*) He loved their syrupy coffee, earthenware jars, silver ornaments, tilted eyebrows, and the way they danced the *dobqi,* their bare feet as expressive as a ham actor's face. Yes, and he loved it that they were as wild as bears and yet impeccably neat and polite. Their good manners would put a Newport socialite to shame. Every country had a soul if one knew where to look for it, but for the stateless Bedouins, their soul *was* their country. It was vast, and they occupied it fully. It was also portable, and he felt compelled to follow it awhile.

Should he not have stayed with them indefinitely, devoting his skills and energies to preserving their way of life? The khan, after all, had offered him one of his daughters. "Take your pick among the five," the khan had said, ever the perfect host, and Switters could sense them blushing behind their thin white veils, while the gold coins they wore strung around their heads jingled slightly, as if vibrated by hidden shudders of nuptial anticipation. Their chins were tattooed up to the base of their noses, and at mealtime each would squirt milk from a ewe's teat directly into her teacup. He tried to imagine marriage to such a girl. His hypothetical adulthood-prevention serum would be superfluous, for they already had been inoculated with an ancient genetic Euro-Asian plasma that kept them soft and fiery and curious and frisky to the grave. Imagine romping with a two-legged patchouli-oiled bear cub every moonlit evening on the carpets she would have woven for his own black tent! How primal, how lurid, how timeless and funky and mysterious and frank!

Yet . . .

She would never serve anything but yogurt for breakfast, beer and biscuits and red-eye gravy stricken from his diet forever.

She would never discuss *Finnegans Wake* with him, not even on Bloomsday eve.

And neither she nor her kin would get his jokes: for the rest of his life, every bon mot, every wisecrack, destined to fall on disregarding ears.

They wouldn't get his jokes even if he told them in Arabic. The Bedouins weren't stiff and somber by any means. They smiled when pleased, which was fairly often, and they laughed as well, but it was a kind of harmlessly mocking laughter, almost invariably directed at an act or an object—his undershorts with the cartoon pandas, for example—that they considered ridiculous. Unintentional slapstick might delight them, but a deliberate witticism was as alien to their sensibility as a fixed-rate mortgage. Comedy, as such, was not an aspect of Bedouin consciousness, nor of the consciousness of many other archaically traditioned, non-Western peoples.

Begrudgingly, Switters was starting to think that Today Is Tomorrow might be on to something. That goddamned pyramid-headed, grub-eating, drug-drinking, curse-leveling savage from the Amazon bush could have been right on the money when he concluded that it was Western man's comedic sense—his penchant to jibe and quip and pun and satirize and play humorous games with words and images in order to provoke laughter—that was his greatest strength, his defining talent, his unique contribution to the composite soul of the planet.

Conversely, civilized man's great weakness, his flaw, his undoing, perhaps, was his technologically and/or religiously sponsored disconnection to nature and to that disputed dimension of reality sometimes referred to as the "spirit world," both of which were areas to which the Bedouin, the Kandakandero, and their ilk related with ease and understanding, a kind of innate genius, and harmonious grace. Today Is Tomorrow had suggested that if civilized man's humor (and the imagination and individualism that spawned it) could somehow be wed to primitive man's organic wisdom and extradimensional pipeline, the union would result in something truly wondrous and supremely real, the finally consummated marriage of darkness and light.

An interesting idea, the shaman's proposal, but probably even less likely to be achieved than the happy marriage of a Berkeley-educated former CIA agent to a tattooed, teat-squeezing daughter of the khan.

Those were the things Switters was thinking as the nomad band moved deeper and deeper into the distant, slowly rising hills, and he, in the opposite direction, moved closer and closer to the mud walls of the small oasis.

Three of the khan's daughters—yes, he was still thinking of them— had blue eyes, betraying their ancestral origins on Asia's northern steppes. Theirs was not the Sol Glissant swimming-pool blue of Suzy's eyes, however, but a sapphire blue, almost an anthracite blue, as if hardened into being by millions of pounds of chthonian thrust. Their hair was so black that it, too, was nearly blue, and in a dozen other ways they were antithetical to Suzy. Yet, the oldest of them was no more than seventeen, so . . . so what? Seriously. So what? He had certainly not hooked up with the nomads because of young girls, and if they played any part in his impulse to leave, it was due neither to fear nor guilt (emotions quite irrelevant in that milieu) but rather because he had detected something in the girlish laughter wafting from the oasis during the downpour that had seemed glutinous, pulpy, and quilted, as if textured with layers the fleecy Bedouin titters lacked.

However, to what extent those stratified peals had influenced his sudden urge to explore the place, he couldn't honestly say. As mentioned, he was quietly crackling with an emboldened abandon in the aftermath of the Iraqi caper, there was wahoo in his tank, and that was quite likely a more accurate explanation for his whim than the curiosity aroused by distant laughter. In any case, the oasis was decidedly silent now.

It sat there, almost loomed there, like a mud ship becalmed in a rusty bay. Its contours, its lines, were simple but sensuous, organic but intrusive, utilitarian to a fundamental degree yet somehow oddly fanciful, like a collaboration between Antoni Gaudí and a termite colony. The walls, which enclosed an area of about seven or eight acres, were rounded on top, and the single tower that rose above the flat roofs of the two principal buildings inside was also round and bulbous, creating the effect that the whole compound, architecturally at least, had been formed in a gelatin mold. All that was lacking was a dollop of gritty whipped cream. The air around it was so awiggle with heat that one could almost hear a soft shimmering, but not the smallest sound escaped the compound itself. It seemed, in fact, deserted.

The gate—and there was only one—was arched, wooden, and solid. High on the gate was an area of latticed grillwork, but even when standing on his wheelchair, Switters was unable to quite peer through it. From the outside, the compound was as blank as it was hushed. Hanging from a wooden post beside the gate was an iron bell about the size of a football, and beside the bellrope a sign hand-lettered in Arabic and French. It read: TRADESMEN, RING THREE TIMES/ THOSE IN NEED, RING TWICE/THE GODLESS SHOULD NOT RING AT ALL.

Switters considered those options for quite a long while before giving the bell exactly one resounding gong.

After several minutes, having received no response, he next gave the bellrope *four* strong yanks. He waited. The sun was barbecuing the back of his neck, and his canteen was running on empty. What if he was not admitted? Left out in the heat and desolation? Those responsible for the laughter couldn't have vanished in so short a time. Were they deliberately ignoring him? Hiding from him? Trained, perhaps, to respond only to three rings or two, might his unauthorized signals have bewildered them or blown some pre-electrical circuit inside? Switters was always nettled when expected to choose between two modes of behavior, two political, social, or theological systems, two objects or two (allegedly) mutually exclusive delights; between hot and cold, tart and sweet, funny and serious, sacred and profane, Apollonian and Dionysian, apples and oranges, paper and plastic, smoking and nonsmoking, right and wrong. Why only a pair of choices? And why not choose both? Who was the legislator of these dichotomies? Yahweh, who insisted the angels choose between him and his partner, Lucifer? And are tradesmen, as implied here, never in need? Did the bell instructions infer that any visitor who believed in God would, per se, either be needy or have something to sell?

His skull-pot, fairly boiling inside his crumpled Panama hat, was not cooled by this cogitating. He was on the verge of swinging from the bellrope like a spastic Tarzan when he heard a scraping noise, like dog shit being scuffed from a jogging shoe, and looked up to see that the grill had slid open and was framing a human face.

As near as he could tell, the face was female. It was also European, homely, and either middle-aged or elderly, as it was lightly wrinkled and sprigs of graying hair intruded upon its margins. The owner of the face was either standing on a box, or Switters had stumbled upon a nest of Amazons about which University of California basketball recruiters ought to be apprised, for she was staring down at him from a height of more than seven feet.

"*Bonjour, monsieur. Qu'est-ce que vous cherchez?*"

"What am I looking for? The International House of Pancakes. I must have taken the wrong exit."

"*Pardon?*"

"Ran out of gas out past the old Johnson place, and I'm gonna be late for my Tupperware party. Can I use your phone to call Ross Perot?"

"*Mais, monsieur . . .*"

"I'm looking for this very establishment," he said, switching to his best French, which had grown as moldy as Roquefort from lack of use. "What else would I be looking for in this. . . ." He paused to search for the French equivalent of *neck of the woods*, though even in English the expression was irrelevant here, there being no woods within hundreds of miles, indeed, not a single tree in any direction except those embosomed by the compound walls. "I was in the neighborhood and thought I'd drop by. May I please come in?"

The hospitality so prodigious in that arid corner of the world was not immediately forthcoming. After a time, the woman said, "I must consult with . . ." At first she said something that seemed to translate as "Masked Beauty," but she quickly corrected herself and uttered, "the abbess." Then she withdrew, leaving him wondering if this desert outpost to which he had been drawn was not some kind of convent.

His suspicion would prove to be well founded, although the kind of convent it was, exactly, was not something he ever could have guessed.

A quarter hour passed before the slot in the gate reopened. The face in the grill reported (in French) that the abbess wished to know more specifically the nature of his business. "I don't have any business," Switters replied. It was dawning on him that he might have made a dumb mistake in coming here. "I'm a simple wayfarer seeking temporary refuge from a stern climate."

"I see." The woman removed her face from the grill and relayed his words to party or parties unseen. Behind the gate there was a low murmur of voices in what seemed both French and English. Then the face returned to inquire if he was not an American. He confessed. "I see," said the woman, and again withdrew.

A different face, noticeably younger, rosy as a ham hock, and congenial of smile appeared in the aperture. "Good day, sir," this one said in lilting English. "I don't know what you're doing here, but I'm dreadfully afraid we can't let you enter at the moment." Her accent seemed to be Irish. "I'm the only one here now who speaks English, and I haven't got any bleeding authority, if you'll please excuse my coarse speech, so Masked Beauty or rather the mother superior's sent word that your request can't be properly considered until Sister Domino comes back. I'm sorry, sir. You're not from the Church, are you, sir? That would be a different matter, naturally, but you're not from the Church, now are you?"

Switters hesitated a moment before responding, in imitation of R. Potney Smithe, "Bloody well not my end of the field." He was encouraged when the new face seemed to suppress a giggle. "I'm Switters, free-lance errand boy and all-around acquired taste, prepared to exchange hard currency for a night's lodging. And what's your name, little darling?"

The new face blushed. Its owner turned away, engaged in brief discussion with the unseen voices, then reappeared. "Sorry, sir, you'll have to wait for herself."

"Wait how long?"

"Oh, not more than a day or two, sir. She'll be coming back from Damascus."

A day or two! "Wait where?"

"Why, there's a wee shade over there, sir." She rolled her eyes toward a spot along the wall where an overhang of thickly leaved boughs cast a purplish shadow on the sand. "Bloody unaccommodating, ain't it? I can talk like this because only you and God can understand me, and I don't believe either you or God gives a pip. I'd like to hear how you got here in that bloody chair, but they're pulling at my skirts. Good-bye, sir, and God bless."

"Water!" Switters called, as the grill slid shut. *"L'eau, s'il vous plaît."*

"Un moment," a voice called back, and in about ten minutes the gate creaked open a few inches. In the crack there stood not the Irishwoman but the Frenchwoman to whom he'd spoken first. She shoved a pitcher of water and a plate of dried figs at him and quickly shut the gate.

"Oh, well," he sighed. He trundled the twenty feet or so to the shaded place, where he spread his blanket and lay down, his heels propped on the chair's footrest, two inches above the ground. The water in the pitcher was cool. The figs had a faint taste of *slida*. He fell asleep and dreamed of woolly things.

When he awoke it was night. Above him, all around him, the sky was a bolt of black velvet awaiting the portrait of Jesus or Elvis. Stars, like grains of opium, dusted it from edge to edge. In one far corner, the moon was rising. It looked like the head of an idol, a golden calf fattened on foxfire.

Why was the air so torrid? It was his experience that the desert cooled quickly after dark. And summer was yet a month away. Not that it mattered, any more than it mattered that his muscles seemed loosened from his bones or that his bones were swimming in gasoline. He felt like the Sleeping Gypsy in Rousseau's great painting, asleep with his eyes half open in a night alive with mystery and fever.

Fever? It gradually occurred to him that it was he who was hot, not the air. The sweat drops on his brow were like tadpoles. They migrated down his neck as if in search of a pond. Still, he didn't care. A night such as this was worth anything! His aching only gave pitch to its beauty.

The stars hopped about like chigger bugs. The moon edged toward him. Once, he had the sensation that it was licking him with a great wounded tongue. He smelled orange blossoms. He was nauseated. He heard himself moan.

His brain, lit as it now was by an unearthly radiance, accepted the fact that the fever that sickened him also protected him. It spun a cocoon around him. *I am the larva of the New Man*, he thought. But then he added, *Much as the paperclip is the larva of the coathanger.* He cackled wildly and wished that Bobby Case were there.

Moonlight enveloped him like a clown suit—voluminous, chalky, theatrical—into which he was buttoned with fuzzy red pompons of fever. Inside it, his blood sang torch songs, sang them throughout the night, as he drifted in and out of dream and delirium, unable to distinguish the one from the other. When he vomited, it was a fizzy mixture of bile and *dölyolu*.

At some point, he realized that the sun was beating him between the eyes like a stick. He covered his face with his hat and grieved for the enchantments of evening. Another time, he was sure he heard female voices, cautious but caring, and sensed that figures were gathered around him like the ghosts of dead Girl Scouts around a spec-tral weenie roast. *I'm hot enough to toast marshmallows.* He chuckled, pleased with himself for no good reason. The voices faded, but he became aware of a fresh pitcher of water beside him and a silk pillow under his head.

Then, it was night again. He uncovered his face in time to see the moon spin into view like a salt-encrusted pinwheel. Although he couldn't explain why, the night sky made him want to meow. He tried meowing once or twice, but it hurt his gums, which were swollen, and his throat, which felt like a scabbard two sizes too small for its sword. Oddly enough, it never occurred to him that he might be dying. For his composure he could probably thank fever, which nature had pro-grammed to weave illusions of invincibility, and End of Time, whose yopo had dissolved boundaries between life and its extreme alter-native (lesser alternatives being conformity, boredom, sobriety, consumerism, dogmatism, puritanism, legalism, and things of that sorry ilk). He realized, nonetheless, that he was in a kind of trouble for which he had not bargained.

It was on the second afternoon—or, perhaps, the third—that he emerged from deep torpor to find his forehead being sponged by a vivacious, round-cheeked nun. He studied her face only seconds before blurting out, weakly but passionately, "I love you."

"Oh, yeah?" she replied in American English with a faint French accent. "You're out of your cotton-picking mind."

That's true, he thought, and shut his eyes, though he took her smile with him into stupor. The next time he awoke, he was inside the oasis.

Whether an Amazonian germ colony had been insidiously incubating in his mucous recesses since Boquichicos, or whether he'd taken aboard a more overt yet equally malevolent family of microorganisms while in the company of the Bedouins or Kurds, he would never know. His nurse, the vivacious nun, had no name for his sickness, either in English or French, but she had a cure: sponge baths, sulfa drugs, and pots of herbal tea. Or else it simply ran its course. In any event, after a week of pain, fever, nausea, coma, and phantasmagorical rapture, his lids sprang open one morning like mousetraps in reverse, and he found himself, feeble yet curiously refreshed, upon a low cot in the tiny, blue-walled room that served the convent/oasis as a rudimentary infir-mary. Sister Domino sat, as she had almost continually, on a stool at his side.

She wore now a typically Syrian long cotton gown instead of the habit in which he'd first seen her. In truth, he had little or no recollection of their first meeting, and when informed later of his impromptu declaration of love for her, he was understandably embarrassed, although disinclined to deny he'd made such an avowal.

Domino had opened the louvered door and thrown back the curtains on the glassless window, and in the strong sunlight, he saw that she was older than her voice and mannerisms had led him to believe. Older, but no less sparkling of eye. And her pert little nose would have been an apt protrusion from the most popular face at any teen queen dairy bar. As for her mouth (what the hell was he doing evaluating her mouth?), it was one of those perpetually rubicund embossments that resembled a plum squashed half out of its jacket and seemed always on the verge of a pout or a pucker—but only on the verge, for it was a strong mouth, there was a firmness and resolve in it, even when it almost pursed, even when it modestly smiled. She could smile from six o'clock to doomsday, and nobody would ever see her gums. She exuded warmth and tenderness, but on her own terms.

Her complexion was Mediterranean of hue and thus seemed incongruous with her more northerly nose. Around her eyes the skin looked as if it had been trampled by sparrows, a tracing that caused him to put her age at forty. She was forty-six. Or would be in September.

In shadow, Domino's hair was dark brown; in sunlight, reddish tints shone through in streaks, like claw marks on fine maple furniture. She wore it straight, at medium length, and it had a tendency to swing free and half cover one or the other of her rotund cheeks. The cheeks were not fat, exactly, but each might have concealed a bishop's golfball—with a couple of Communion wafers thrown in for good measure. Her breasts and buttocks were also quite round, but Switters didn't notice that. He would have sworn under oath that he didn't notice. Why would he have noticed? She was a middle-aged nun.

"Well, hello," she said cheerfully. "You appear to be on the mend."

"Thanks to you, I'm sure."

"You must thank God, not me."

"All right. I may do that. But I sincerely doubt that any Divine Almighty worthy of the name is going to beam if I gush or grumble if I don't."

Much to his astonishment, she nodded in agreement. "I suspect you're right," she said.

"Don't you find it a bit batty that people believe God—the

absolute epitome of perfection and enlightenment—could be so puffed with petty human vanity that he'd expect us to sing his praises at every opportunity and twice on Sunday?"

She smiled. "Have you traveled by wheelchair to the middle of the Syrian desert in order to debate theology, Mr.—?"

"Switters," he answered, without the addition of the usual malarkey. "And no, I have not. I decidedly have not."

She laid a hand gently but authoritatively on his brow. "Naturally, we need to learn why—and how—you did travel here, but I don't wish to interrogate you until you're stronger, so . . ."

"Oh, thank you! Please, no interrogation. I'm only insured for fire and theft."

If she detected a facetious note, she elected to ignore it. "We must get you strong so we can send you on your way. Your fever has broken"—she removed her hand, somewhat to his disappointment— "but you look *la tête comme une pastèque*, as we say in France."

"Aren't you American?"

"No, no. I'm French. Alsatian French, by heritage, which is why I've been denied the grand Gallic nose."

"But—"

"When I was four, we moved to Philadelphia so that my father could oversee a famous collection of French art in a private museum there. I lived in the U.S. for the next twelve years and became very Americanized, as children will, and although I haven't been back since, I've worked hard to keep my English pure, so that I don't sound like Jacques Cousteau describing zuh most 'andsome craytures zaire are in zuh sea."

She laughed, and though it jiggled his sore gut, Switters found himself chuckling with her. "So, you're a Philly *fille*. What's your name?"

There was a pause. A long pause. For some reason, she was pondering the question, as if she lacked a ready or definite answer. "Around here, I'm called Domino," she said at last. "More formally, *Sister* Domino—but I'm not so certain I can be called that any longer." A troubled look dimmed the lights in her eyes. "Before Sister Domino, I was Sister somebody else, and before that I had my christened name, and in the not so far future I may have a different name yet." She paused and deliberated some more. "I think it's okay if you just call me Sister."

"I'd be honored to call you Sister, Sister." Then, thinking of Suzy, he added, "Fate has sought to compensate for the shortcomings of my parents in the sister production department by supplying me with the sweetest, loveliest sororal surrogates."

"Kind of you to say that, Mr. Switters, but I hope you don't think you can butter me off and get me to extend your stay here. You really must leave just as soon as you're healthy enough to travel."

Switters ran his hand over his face. A week's growth of stubble rasped his fingers. *I must look like a werewolf's bedroom slipper,* he thought. "I find it difficult to believe that someone who spent her formative years in the City of Brotherly Love could be so callously chomping at the bit in her desire to kick me out into the cruel wastes."

"Yes, but you mustn't take it personally. Or doubt our Christian charity. You see . . . well, no, you couldn't see because you haven't looked around, but the Pachomian Order has itself a regular little Eden here. But it's an Eden for Eves only. We cannot allow even one Adam to intrude, I'm afraid." She stood up to leave.

"Hmm? An Adamless Eden? I'll have to mull that over." Turning to face her, he heard the ponderosa music his whiskers made as they scratched the silk pillow. "What about a Serpent?"

"A Serpent?" She laughed. "No, no Serpent here, either."

"Oh? But there has to be. *Every* Paradise has a Serpent. It goes with the territory."

"Not this one," she said, but there was something about her denial that was patently unconvincing.

All day Switters lay on the cot, listening to the sounds of activity in the compound. There was work going on. He heard the spray of sprinklers, the clang of garden tools, the *whisk-whisk* of brooms, the rattle of buckets and pots, the *ech-zee ech-zee* of pruning saws, and the simple grunts of labor (so different in their coloration from the loaded grunts of love). A couple of times he stood on the cot to peer out the window at the adobe buildings, the orchards, and the vegetable plots, but he grew quickly dizzy and lowered himself to a prone position. Laments (there had been an unusually long, coolish winter, and the orange trees had bloomed so late that there was danger the fruit would cook on the boughs), complaints (evidently there was some kind of dispute between the convent and the Mother Church), and snatches of French songs (no hymn among them) drifted into the little room, where they were tossed in an auditory salad with the work noises and the cackle and bray of beast and fowl.

Every hour or so, Sister Domino would stick her head in to check on him. He'd wave to her helplessly, and it wasn't entirely an act. Midday, she brought him a warm vegetable broth but departed when satisfied that he was capable of spooning it himself between his fever-cracked lips. Midafternoon, she stopped by, to his supreme embarrassment, to empty his chamber pot.

Toward dusk, as she delivered a fresh kettle of tea, he apologized for being a burden to her. "I'm interfering with your duties," he said sincerely, "and it's making me feel guilty, an emotion my grandmother warned me against."

"Well," she sighed, "you must be carefully attended to for a few more days, and nobody else here has good English. Except for Fannie, our Irish lass, and I wouldn't trust her alone with you."

"Is that a fact? And which one of us wouldn't you trust?"

She looked him over. He was physically disabled, he was recuperating from fever, and yet . . . "Neither," she said. "Frankly."

"But what do you think might go on? If we were left alone together?"

Domino headed for the door. "I don't sully my mind with such details."

"Good," he congratulated her. "But, please, one more question before you go."

"Yes?"

"Who undressed me?" He nodded at his clothing, which—suit, T-shirt, cartoon shorts, and all—hung from a peg on the wall.

She turned as red as a blister and sailed out of the room. And it was the older nun who'd first answered his ring at the gate who showed up with his supper tray, removed it a half hour later, and tucked him in for the night.

"*Faites de beaux rêves, monsieur,*" she called as she put out the light.

Switters had always loved that expression, "Make fine dreams." In contrast to the English, "Have sweet dreams," the French implied that the sleeper was not a passive spectator, a captive audience, but had some control over and must accept some responsibility for his or her dreaming. Moreover, a "fine" dream had much wider connotations than a "sweet" one.

In any event, his dreams that night were neither good nor sweet, for he was made fitful by the notion that toward Sister Domino, with the intention of being playful, he may have behaved like an insensitive boor.

How oddly delighted he was (though he tried to conceal it) when she turned up the next morning with his breakfast! It was a fine breakfast, too: scrambled eggs, grilled eggplant, chèvre, and toast. Before he dove into it, however, he found himself apologizing once more. "I'm sorry if I embarrassed you. It's just that I come from a country where there are prudes on the left, prigs on the right, and hypocrites down the middle, so I sometimes feel obligated to push in the other direction just to keep things honest."

"No problem," she said. "What you don't understand is . . . well, there's a deep undercurrent of sexuality flowing through every cloister. That may be especially true of the Pachomian Order because we are merely a centimeter above a lay sisterhood, no pun intended. In the hierarchy of sisterhoods, we are not especially great, and we have accepted members who a few of the more esteemed orders might reject. Of course, a Pachomian sister must adhere to vows of chastity just like any nun, but prior to taking up the cloth, she need not have been a virgin. So, among us, we have women with some experience, and that makes men and carnality a more tense issue, perhaps, than in certain orthodox convents. But when I get so cotton-picking *coincée* about it, it is I, myself, who is acting the hypocrite."

Naturally, Switters had to bite his tongue to keep from asking Domino if she could be counted among those sisters with "some experience." What he asked, instead, after a lacerating lingual nip, was a question about the role and features of the Pachomian Order.

"Maybe we can discuss that at a later time," she said. "Right now, before I go to my work, we must talk about you. Who are you? What are you? What are you doing here? How did you get here? So far from the beaten track."

"May I assume my interrogation is off and running?"

She smiled, and it was a smile, he thought, that could raise roadkill from the dead or turn a lead mine into a Mexican restaurant, yet a smile made more with the eyes than the lips. "You seem to be much improved, Mr. Switters, although you still look like—how do you say it?—a thing that the cat has brought home. I don't mean to pressure you. If you don't feel well enough . . ."

"It's all right," he assured her, "although should I die in your custody, you'll have to answer to Amnesty International." Then, before she could protest, and holding to his vow to stop lying, he jumped right in with the truth, or, at least, an abridged version of it. "Until six months ago, I was a CIA operative. Central Intelligence Agency."

"Really? I know, of course, about the CIA. It has an unpleasant reputation."

"And largely deserved, I assure you." He might have added, "Thanks to corporate-owned politicians and their cowboy dupes," but he did not.

"Then why were you? . . ."

"Its unpleasantness, as you put it, had a purity, a spice, and anarchy that simply didn't exist in the academic, military, or corporate sectors, and I hadn't enough talent for art or poetry. Besides, it offered an unparalleled, world-class opportunity for corrective mischief: subverting subversion, if you will, although I won't pretend my motives were ever entirely altruistic. But all that's immaterial now. I had to drop out of the game last November."

She glanced at his wheelchair, folded in a corner, and he knew what she was assuming. He decided not to correct the assumption. Instead, he told her how he'd recently become involved in a private humanitarian mission inside Iraq, his old stomping grounds, and how, when it was over, he, feeling adventurous and having no particular place to be, joined a band of nomads driving their flocks to summer pasture in the mountains. "We passed by your Garden of Eden here, and for some crackpot reason I felt a magnetic attraction to the place. The rest, as they say, is histrionics." He shrugged, as if to emphasize the pristine logic of it all.

Whether or not she bought his story he could not tell. She was quiet, thoughtful, her countenance vacillating between serenity and fret. "Finish your breakfast," she said at last. "I'll come back for the tray. A supply truck will be arriving in a few days, bringing petrol for our generator. It can take you to Deir ez-Zur, but I can't see how you will depart Syria without the proper papers."

"Don't worry about it, Sister," he called after her. "Impropriety is what I do for a living."

Fortified by his first regular meal in more than a week, Switters attempted a few push-ups and sit-ups on the cot. It was a wimpy, pathetic display. After lunch, delivered by a French nun who introduced herself as ZuZu (she was Domino's age but lacked Domino's radiance), he tried again, with greater success. Mostly, however, he rested. He meditated, he dozed, he read, he drank in the farmyard sounds and orchard smells of the oasis. Once, a black goat wandered into his room. Almost immediately, ZuZu and another middle-aged nun arrived to shoo it out.

"That Fannie," ZuZu clucked. "She should pay more mind to her animal."

"Yes," said her companion. "Instead of to the animal in her mind." They laughed and departed. It was probably funnier in French.

In midafternoon, he tried telephoning Maestra. When she didn't answer, he pulled his computer up onto the cot. Now that Audubon Poe was far away, it shouldn't matter if the company read or even traced his transmission. Mayflower had little reason to be interested in him, per se, and even if he was, what could the cowboys do to him? Tip off Syrian authorities that he was in their country illegally? Intimate that he was a spy? Get him imprisoned or executed? In the old, crazed Cold War CIA, that might have been a possibility, but these days the company had a different censure and different methods. It had other fish to fry, its own bare asses to cover. Unless it believed he could help it get at Poe, whose whereabouts it doubtless already knew, he would be regarded as no more than a loose cannon with minimum firepower and no direction. He said a prayer to the satellite gods. He e-mailed his grandmother.

In less than an hour, she responded. Maestra was well. There was some unspecified trouble about the Matisse. She was glad he was enjoying his vacation in "Turkey," and understood that the Turks made fine silver bracelets. Was he finally out of that stupid wheelchair?

It was Domino who brought him his supper. "I'm sorry to be ignoring you," she said.

"I'm sorry, too."

She tested his forehead for signs of fever, and in her hand he sensed a current not unlike the throb of pent-up music he'd felt in the fingers of Skeeter Washington, only what was pent up in Sister Domino was of a different order: spiritual, physical, emotional, or a mixture of the three, he wouldn't venture to suppose.

"Can we talk?" he asked.

"Later tonight, or tomorrow," she said, glancing out the window at the purpling dusk. "Now we have a special vespers. And, oh, we won't be turning on the generator for a while, so, I'm sorry, you'll have to make do with candlelight if you want to read." She picked up the copy of *Finnegans Wake* from its place on the bedside stool. "It's an Irish book, isn't it? Fannie would be thrilled."

"Only a dozen souls in Ireland have actually read this tome," he said, "and I'd bet a crock o' gold and a barrel o' Guinness that your Fannie is not one of them."

About an hour after dark, as he lay digesting his thin goat stew, he heard singing. This time the song *was* a hymn, and more than a couple of voices were joined in its vocalization. "Vespers," he said to himself. At almost that same moment, he became aware that an orange glow had commenced to flicker, snap, and waggle against the drawn curtains of his little window. Inquisitive, he stood on the cot, down near its foot, and parted the rough cotton fabric. For the next half hour, he was to gawk at an extraordinary spectacle. The psychedelic porthole aside, no window he'd ever peered through looked out on a more memorable scene.

The convent chapel, identifiable by its stunted steeple and crude stained glass, was located at—and connected to—the far end of the building that apparently served as living quarters for the sisterhood. The chapel was a good seventy yards, maybe more, from the infirmary, which was situated near the compound gate. In front of the chapel, from whose open door the singing floated, there was a small flower garden, and in that flower patch, amidst poppies and jasmine bushes, a bonfire had been built.

As Switters watched, nuns—eight of them in all—filed, still singing, out of the chapel. Each wore her traditional nun habit, rather than the Syrian dresses in which he'd become accustomed to seeing them. Joining hands, they formed a circle around the fire, circumnavigating it several times, both clockwise and counterclockwise. Then they suddenly ceased singing, broke the circle, and began to disrobe.

Initially, a startled Switters jumped to the conclusion that the sisters were practicing witchcraft, that he'd stumbled upon some arcane sect that was combining Catholicism with Wicca. However, as the nuns, one by one—some eagerly, even vehemently, others with obvious reluctance—hurled or gently dropped their habits into the bonfire, he realized that something of a different nature was transpiring here. He couldn't guess what the ceremony was about, but it was no eye-of-newt sabbat.

As the heavy habits smoked and slowly ignited, the women watched in their underwear. Most wore knee-length bloomers, the sort of ultra-baggy shorts that might have outfitted a low-rent hip-hop ghetto gangster basketball team, and stiff old-fashioned prototype brassieres that could have harnessed pairs of boudoir oxen. One was in modern bra and panties. From that distance, he couldn't clearly recognize faces, but he thought (or hoped?) she must be Domino. The last of the eight wore bikini underpants and nothing else, and as firelight twinkled on her far naked nipples, he thought, *Fannie?*

His attention was diverted from Fannie's (?) breasts by the appearance in the residence hall doorway of yet another figure, a tall woman, whose silhouette had a certain majesty. She was immediately greeted by two sisters, who took her arms and led her, very gingerly, for she appeared to be old, to the fire. *Masked Beauty?* Switters wondered, although as far as he could tell, she wore no mask.

Two other nuns had gone inside the residence hall and lugged out a kind of wooden settee. A third went inside and fetched cushions. Masked Beauty—it *must* be her—stood in front of the settee and, assisted by the shapely one he believed to be Domino, undressed. With surprising vigor, she likewise flung her habit into the flames.

After Domino arranged the pillows for her, she reclined upon the settee, propping herself on one elbow, the better to view the conflagration, and the pose she then struck was so strangely familiar to Switters that it gave his spine an electrical shock.

And just then, as Masked Beauty's doffed habit erupted into full blaze, he, still tingling, saw by its light that the thin shift she wore as an undergarment was an equally strange and familiar shade of strangely familiar—blue.

silence is a mirror. So faithful, and yet so unexpected, is the reflection it can throw back at men that they will go to almost any length to avoid seeing themselves in it, and if ever its duplicating surface is temporarily wiped clean of modern life's ubiquitous hubbub, they will hasten to fog it over with such desperate personal noise devices as polite conversation, humming, whistling, imaginary dialogue, schizophrenic babble, or, should it come to that, the clandestine cannonry of their own farting. Only in sleep is silence tolerated, and even there, most dreams have soundtracks. Since meditation is a deliberate descent into deep internal hush, a mute stare into the ultimate looking glass, it is regarded with suspicion by the nattering masses; with hostility by business interests (people sitting in silent serenity are seldom consuming goods); and with spite by a clergy whose windy authority it is seen to undermine and whose bombastic livelihood it is perceived to threaten.

However, when Domino returned to the infirmary to find Switters propped up in bed, his arms folded, palms upward, across the rough sheet, a thick aura of quietude around him, she attributed it to the fact that he was in recovery from illness and would not have guessed that he might be trying to steady himself after witnessing, an hour and a half earlier, Masked Beauty's startling impersonation of his grandmother's painting.

As far as that goes, Domino might not have registered her patient's meditative air at all, so absorbed was she by her own cares. Her eyes resembled a serving of salmon sushi, and while their puffy redness could conceivably have been caused by bonfire smoke, Switters guessed that she had been weeping. She knew he wanted to talk (though she couldn't have known how badly), but she begged off, claiming fatigue.

"*À demain,*" she promised, and then apologized that exhaustion had made her lapse into French.

"Tomorrow's fine," he said.

"It's Sunday, so I will be free all the day, after chapel."

"You'll still have chapel?"

She was momentarily puzzled. "Oh, you mean after? . . . *Mais oui,* yes, of course we will have chapel." She paused. "You watched our brazen ceremony, didn't you? I saw your silhouette at the window."

"I wasn't intending to spy."

"Ah, but you couldn't help yourself: you're CIA." Sensing instantly that she might have yanked a sleeping dog's tail, she issued a retraction. "No, please, I'm only making a joke. It would have been impossible not to notice our. . . . We should have waited until you had gone away. Tell me, did you find our display to be tasteless?"

"No, on the contrary, it struck me as rather tasty. But, then, I have an appetite for bold gestures and burned bridges." To himself he added, *And blue nudes.* "I don't much savor pain, however, and I detected a sharp hickory of hurt in the fumes from your little barbecue."

She looked him over slowly, as if seeing him in a new light. "You are not an entirely stupid fellow," she said, and she smiled.

"Thanks, Sister," he replied. "Your own mental prowess has also proven to be significantly superior to that of the average pecan. Nevertheless, what I am most taken with are your eyes."

"Ooh-la-la," she protested, brushing her fingers across her lids. "Tonight they are ruined. But as a rule, they *are* my nicest feature."

How refreshing, he thought. *A woman who knows how to accept a compliment.* "It's like they were congealed from nitroglycerin and mother's milk. I can't tell if they're about to nurture me or crack my safe. And your mouth has a sneaky habit of getting them to do most of your smile-work."

"Yes, I admit it. I have such a round face that my father told me when I make a big grin, I look like a, how do you say, jack-in-the-lantern."

"Nonsense," he objected. "I know my pumpkins, and you're not of their race. If your cheeks are a little full, it's because they're packed with secrets and mysteries, like the moon."

Domino snorted, and her snort sounded surprisingly like Maestra's *Heh!*—an exclamation that usually suggested that what he'd just uttered was a load of bunkum, though a not uninteresting load of bunkum as loads of bunkum go. "I warned you, Mr. Switters, don't be trying to butter me off." She then left the room so abruptly he wondered if she might actually be peeved.

When she returned the next morning, however, she wore a
starched white dress, an affable aspect—and a sprig of orange blossoms behind her ear.

Switters, for his part, was freshly shaved, brushed, and dressed in
a yeast-colored linen suit (the one he'd soaked in the landing on
Jonah's beach) over a black T-shirt with the discreet C.R.A.F.T. Club
emblem above the left pectoral. The cologne that he liked to call
Jungle Desire, but which, in fact, was simply Old Spice, had been
splashed recklessly about his face and neck. He sat, for the first time in
more than a week, in his starship, and she seated herself on the stool
opposite him.

"Mmm. Mr. Switters. You clean up very nice."

"Don't be trying to butter me off."

She didn't mind that he mocked her but, rather, seemed amused
by it, though she put on an insulted face. He liked it that she was
amused, and he liked it that she pretended otherwise. There was something of Maestra in her, and something of Suzy, as well, but he didn't
dwell on those similarities. No heart-shaped blip could be said to have
formed on his radar screen. Sister Domino was as charming as she was
kind, as fresh as she was wise, but she was too old and too religious,
and, besides, he'd be gone in two or three days: whenever the supply
truck showed up. Meanwhile, he had an industrial-strength curiosity to
satisfy.

"This woman you call Masked Beauty—"

"Yes," Domino interrupted. "We should begin with her, because
everything that we are in this place is a result of her. I'm unsure what
you know of nuns. . . ."

"Well, *nun* comes out of Egypt, an old Coptic Christian word
meaning *pure.*"

"There's much disagreement over that, but I'm pleased and impressed that you've connected the nun to the Middle East, to the
desert. That's very important to us here. But let me go on to Masked
Beauty, who is our founder and leader, and who, in the secular realm,
also happens to be my aunt. Before I can say much about her, however,
I must say a little about the famous French painter, Henri Matisse."

Like the helmeted heads of an itty-bitty army springing from the
trenches, goosebumps appeared along the length and breadth of Switters's epidermis, where they marched in place, as if, intent on pillage,
they were preparing to advance on his brain.

Although Domino might have been loath to make such a claim, Switters gathered from her description of Matisse that he owed much of his greatness as an artist and as a man to the fact that he was simultaneously epicurean and pious, hedonistic and devout; that he made little or no distinction between his love of wine, women, and song and his love of God—an attitude that struck Switters as entirely sensible.

At any rate, as Domino's account went, Matisse, in the early 1940s, had painted several large pictures of his nurse at the time, a Dominican novice named Sister Jacques. Matisse loved to paint the contours of the female body, lush, rhythmic volumes that were shown to their best aesthetic advantage when undisguised by garb. Naturally, Sister Jacques could not pose nude. However, knowing the genius to be honorable, ailing, and elderly (in 1943, Matisse was seventy-four years old), and hoping to persuade him to decorate a chapel (which he did for her in 1948 at Vence), she didn't mind encouraging another girl to sit for him.

For generations, Domino's family had been deeply involved in both French art and the Roman Catholic Church, so when Sister Jacques set out to find Matisse a suitable model, the logical first choice was that family's voluptuous seventeen-year-old Croetine, the girl who would, at Domino's birth slightly less than a decade later, become her aunt.

Switters whistled. "Well, boil my bunny in carrot oil!" he exclaimed. "I can't believe it."

"You can't believe *what?*"

"That I'd wander into the middle of goddamn nowhere and stumble upon my actual, original, flesh-and-blood blue nude."

"Matisse painted a variety of blue nudes," she cautioned, "dating back to 1907. And what do you mean, *yours?*"

"Nothing," he said. "It's not mine. But she's the one, all right. You've got to let me meet her."

Domino would agree to nothing until he'd explained, and even after he had, she informed him that Masked Beauty was not receiving visitors. Moreover, while she found the blue nude coincidence remarkable—Domino couldn't help but be amazed that he'd grown up around that particular painting—she saw no need for Switters to get so carried away. Maybe she was right. More than she might realize. A man immobilized by a pyramid-headed Indian's curse was not a man who ought to be overreacting to a dollop of synchronicity, even when it involved an object of much sentimental wahoo.

"Okay," he said. "Forget it. I've been ill. Get on with your story. Excuse me. I mean, *please* get on with your story. *S'il vous plaît.*" At the same time, however, he was vowing to himself that he would not leave the oasis without having met Masked Beauty, and thinking, also, what a kick it was to be sitting there listening to the blue nude's niece.

Croetine posed for Matisse for more than two years, at Cimiez and later at Vence, and having fallen in love with the artist's paintings, photographs, and souvenirs of Morocco, made plans to accompany him there as soon as the war was over. When V-E Day arrived, however, Matisse was not hardy enough to travel, and at the encouragement if not outright insistence of her uncle, a well-known archbishop, Croetine made the decision to enter a convent.

Because of her background as a nude model, Croetine was forced to spend an extraordinarily long time as a novice before being allowed to proceed to final vows. Her physical beauty was so unnerving to the Church fathers that her uncle advised her to find ways to make her face and figure more godly, which, assuming that God is inclined toward plainness, she did, stopping just short of grotesque disfiguration. By the time she was finally permitted to formally "marry" Christ, an ovule of rebellion had been planted deep in the sod of her sanctimony.

The solemn vows were still rippling in her saliva when she began to petition for assignment to Morocco. Not wishing to be too accommodating, they sent her to Algeria, instead. She worked in a mission there and liked everything about it; liked it so much, in fact, that her mother superior feared she was going native, and, citing such disturbing activities as "long solitary walks in the desert," had her transferred back to France. It was in Paris in the mid- to late fifties that she formulated and promoted her ideas for the Order of St. Pachomius.

"Since I have a snakelike fascination with examples of extreme human behavior," said Switters, "I really ought to have paid more attention to the lives of the saints. But I confess I've never heard of good St. Pachomius."

"Pachomius was an Egyptian Christian ascetic. Around the year 320, he founded the first religious community for women, the very first convent. He built it out in the desert. So, Pachomius is the father of all nuns, and nuns had their beginnings in the desert. Today, the Middle Eastern desert countries are Islamic, and while there are small Christian minorities in these lands, those are almost exclusively Eastern Orthodox. It was my aunt's idea, back when she was Sister Croetine, that an order of desert nuns be formed that would both honor St. Pachomius and give the Roman Church at least a token presence in the region. Pretty smart, don't you agree?"

The Vatican had agreed. Up to a point. Which is to say, it liked the general idea but was sorry that it had come from Croetine, who not only had once posed for naked pictures but who, on at least two occasions, had openly expressed reservations about Rome's prohibition against birth control. The Church never rejected the Pachomius idea, it simply dragged its velvet slippers when it came to implementing it.

"Then, something happened. I can't tell you what it was. It was in 1961, and Croetine's uncle—my great-uncle—had been appointed to a cardinalship and was then stationed at the Vatican. He had come into the possession of an item—a document, let us say—that he wished to conceal in the safest way possible. So, our cardinal used his influence with Pope John the Twenty-third to get the Order of St. Pachomius approved. Quarters were procured for it in Jordan. Croetine was named as its acting abbess, and when she went to the desert, she took the cardinal's secret document with her to safekeep it there."

"What kind of document?"

Domino shook her head, causing her cheeks to wobble like puddings on a pushcart.

"Does she still have it? Are you privy to it?"

"You're pretty cotton-picking nosy, Mr. Agent Man."

He touched her wrist. "You know, Domino"—it was difficult to call her "Sister" when she was in white lace and orange blossoms—"you know, Domino, I hate to have to tell you this, you trying so hard to be hip American and all, but the euphemistic expression, *cotton-picking*, left the idiom about the time you left Philadelphia. Or even sooner. Nobody says *cotton-picking* anymore."

Domino looked as if a scorpion had stung her, and Switters felt as low and venomous as any one of those arachnids. However, she quickly recovered her composure. "If *I* say it," she announced haughtily, "then somebody still says it."

And as she took a sip of tea before resuming her story, Switters thought, *Now here's a woman who would stick to your ribs.*

When it had been proposed that Abbess Croetine be permitted to personally choose the nuns who'd serve with her in Jordan, one prelate objected on the grounds that she might stock the new order with those who shared her radical views. "Of course she will," said another, "and what better way to get them out of our hair." The area of Jordan where the convent was to be located was not only remote but also dangerous. Moreover, it was chartered as an *enclosed* convent, one in which the sisters, fully isolated from the outside world, would be expected to seek their salvation and that of others through a regimen of worship, prayer, and contemplation, rather than providing health care, education, or social services.

For several years, while they adjusted to the enclosure and the climate, the Pachomians stuck to that blueprint, but eventually Croetine and her twenty-two hand-picked sisters began—through epistolary campaigns and journal articles—to take public issue with the Holy See's inflexible stand against birth control. From the peeling wastes east of Az-Zarqā, there came a faint but persistent cry, a cry to dam the flood tides of semen, to leash the sperm packs running wild in the sheets, to zonk the zygotic zillions and mitigate the multitudinous milt, to garrote the gullible glorification of gamete, forsake the foolish fidelity to fecundity, and wrest free from a woman's shoulders the boa of spermatozoa that the Church had draped there like a weighty shawl and that pulled her ever downward into sickness and servitude, while at her skirts her too-many children went hungry, went bad, or just went.

"Rome tolerated it for quite a while," said Domino, "but after Croetine's uncle died in 1981, they finally erupted against her."

"Naturally," said Switters. "Isn't it the sacred duty of the Catholic masses to increase geometrically the number of true believers in the world, just as it's a secular duty to provide merchandisers with more and more little consumers?"

"Pachomians don't look for ulterior motives. That's too cynical. We petition for free will and common sense and compassion, and avoid casting blame on the guardians of the doctrine. After all, they were divinely commanded to 'go forth, be fruitful, and multiply.'"

"You mean their tribal antecedents were so commanded. Four thousand years ago. Before a person had to stand in line for an hour and a half just to get a whiff of fresh air. It's tough to say who's a greater threat to the world, an ambitious CEO with a big ad budget or a crafty cleric with an obsolete Bible verse."

In the ensuing exchange, Domino made it clear that while she might be estranged from the Church, she would no more brook criticism of its mediators than Skeeter Washington, in exile from New York, would accept insult to the Yankees. In the absence of an urgent ax to grind, Switters was happy to shut up and let her get on with her chronicle.

The Vatican fathers did not officially abolish the Order of St. Pachomius—an act that might have engendered bad publicity—but in the hope of drying it up, they quietly reduced its budget by two-thirds. A necessary economic move, they said. Then, they sold the Pachomian compound to the Jordanian military. If the sisterhood was to survive, it would have to arrange private subsidy. Amazingly enough, it did, although by the time Croetine found the Lebanese businessman who offered her a small oasis in neighboring Syria (he'd scored it as part of a real estate deal but could make scant use of it himself, the oasis being quite out of the way and he being quite Jewish), most of her sisters had moved on to other places, other orders. Undaunted, she returned to Europe, recruited a handful of new members, including her niece, Simone Thiry, and led them to the Syrian desert in 1983.

"We've been here ever since. Nine of us in all. Nine mavericks. Once we were settled, my aunt informed us that she was henceforth to be called 'Masked Beauty' and that each of us was also to be renamed. She asked us each to remember the name that as a child we would have preferred to the one our parents had given us. Most children have such a wish name, do you know? Well, we got five Marias and three Theresas—and Masked Beauty shouted, 'No no no! Not the name of your heroine, the woman you were taught to most admire, but your dream name, your whisper name, the one you called yourself when you pretended alone in your room to be somebody else.' Okay, we tried again, and we still got a couple of Marias. So, we have Maria Une, who first spoke to you at the gate, and Maria Deux. We have also Pippi, ZuZu, Mustang Sally, Fannie, and Bob."

"Bob?"

"You'll have to ask her."

"What about Domino?"

"I was lazy and just remembered my nickname from high school in Philadelphia."

"Domino Thiry. I get it, though I wish I didn't. That phrase was used to hoodwink the American public into supporting our criminal war against Vietnam, and it was popularized if not coined by the pus-brained pluto, John Foster Dulles." Hesitant, he held the pellet of spittle against his gum for several seconds before at last discharging it as daintily as possible toward a target area beneath the cot. His restraint notwithstanding, the act caused Sister Domino to look at him askance.

Once they had assumed, in ceremony, their new names, Masked Beauty showed her sisters the document she had been hiding for her

uncle, the late Pierre Cardinal Thiry. He'd never retrieved it, perhaps preferring that it be lost. But just as certain cloisters are built
around a relic—the middle finger bone of a saint, for example, or the
charred trouser cuff of a martyr—the Pachomians allowed their tiny
community to coalesce around the document. This, even though the
document's text had relevance neither to St. Pachomius nor to any
particular canon to which the sisterhood adhered, except maybe a
tenuous connection to the desert lands, and the nature of that connection was not for Switters to know. Yet, the Pachomians were the
document's guardians and protectors; they made it both their charge
and mortar, their onus and distinction, a symbolic yet tangible secret
fulcrum at the center of their turning and toiling for humanity and
Christ.

"Caravans used to travel by here," said Domino. "Camel caravans
as well as motor convoys, but in the past ten years or so, we see only
the rare band of nomads, such as the one that left you on our doorstep,
and a truck that passes every few weeks carrying passengers, freight,
and mail between Damascus and Deir ez-Zur. There's no road, of
course, only what nature has left of the old caravan trail."

Because of their isolation and the meagerness of their ecclesiastical stipend, the Pachomian sisters had had to make their oasis as self-
supporting as possible. For at least a decade, the compound had been
used as a training center and command post for officers of the Druse
militia, and its agricultural aspects had been neglected. It took the nuns
several years of hard labor to restore productivity. They cleaned,
cleared, tilled, planted, pruned, and husbanded, and in between, transformed the Druse mosque into their chapel. During that period, neither the Church nor society heard any noise from them, and they were
largely forgotten.

Toward the end of the eighties, however, letters, essays, and
articles bearing the signature or byline of Masked Beauty began to
appear in publications both religious and secular, and while they
sometimes ranged far and wide, the core of these writings was an
unabashed appeal for papal sanction of birth control. In addition to the
misery that unlimited procreation caused women and children, Masked
Beauty argued that much of the poverty, violence, addiction, ignorance, mental illness, pollution, and climate changes plaguing humankind in general had major roots in careless or coerced reproduction. It
would not be mega-weapons, asteroids, earthquakes, or extraterres-
trials that destroyed the earth, she wrote, but excessive population.
The prophetic "fire next time" referred to loin heat that, if not properly
banked, could only lead eventually to cataclysmic global warming.

"A foregone conclusion," said Switters, "what with six billion gobbling gullets and an equal number of squirting anuses. But religious fundamentalists—and New Age fluffheads, I should add—can barely *wait* for the earth to be destroyed. Doomsday is the jackpot on their golden slot machine, the day they'll be allowed to dig their quivering fork into all that pie in the sky. And have you considered, Sister D., that the afterworld is likely to be even more crowded than our little ball of clay because if every Christian who ever lived is camping there . . . well, that's a lot of pie-gobbling, although I can't imagine there'd be squirting anuses in Heaven. Can you? Wouldn't God have some alternative system?"

For an answer, Domino shot him a look of pity, scorn, and revulsion. It was deserved, he thought. He'd spat on her floor and made crude remarks; she must think him an absolute lout. How could she understand the exorcisement explicit in the expectoration ritual or know that he used a phrase such as "squirting anuses" only in the abstract? Were he actually to picture one such opening—let alone billions—performing that base function, he'd be more revolted than she. After all, she was a woman who could ferry the chamber pots of the sick, whereas he thought of the rectum, on those very rare occasions when he thought of it at all, as a receptacle for white light, the intake valve through which that mystic energy that Bobby Case's wise ol' boys called kundalini entered the body to slither up the spinal column in radiant coils, like the Serpent bringing divine knowledge to the unsuspecting bumpkins of Eden. Enlightenment or excrement: O anus, what doth thy truest purpose be?

"I'm sorry about the scatological undertones," he said. It was the third time he had apologized to her in as many days, and sensing that he was a man unaccustomed to apology, she was moved to forgive him. "Overtones," she corrected him, with a tolerant smile, and then concluded her story.

The Vatican eventually figured out that Masked Beauty was Abbess Croetine. It ordered her to cease and desist. She refused. Other Pachomians, including Domino, began to publish letters as well. The sisters agitated. The Church complained. And threatened. It was a battle that raged slowly for years. Then, a fortnight ago, it had come to a head. Masked Beauty was summoned to Damascus to face charges at an ecclesiastical hearing presided over by a trio of bishops dispatched from Rome. Citing poor health, the abbess sent Domino in her stead. The tribunal proved immune to the sisterhood's arguments and Domino's charms. It officially dissolved the Order of St. Pachomius and commanded its members back to Europe for discipline and reassignment. On behalf of Pachomius, father of all nuns, on behalf of overbooked wombs around the world, Domino told the bishops to go fly a cotton-picking kite.

"They couldn't evict us. They don't own this property. We took a vote and decided to stay on. Only Fannie was of a mind to flee, but she relented. Afraid, perhaps, of Asmodeus, her incubus. Then, yesterday after lunch, while you were resting, a courier arrived here from Damascus. He brought the news that we most feared, that we never thought would really happen. We had been excommunicated. Every single one of us. Thrown out of the Church. Forever."

"So you're not a nun anymore," Switters said, hoping he didn't sound too pleased about it.

She tightened her lips. The defiance in her eyes was like the fizz in a fuse. "I will always be a nun. And we'll carry on with our worship and our work just as before. Only now there will be no—how do you call it?—man in the middle. No intermediary. We'll report directly to God. And God alone."

"Well," said Switters, searching for words of comfort or support, "maybe that's the way it was always meant to be. In the Koran, Mohammed says that direct, personal, one-on-one contact is the *only* way to Allah, not that the mullahs, imams, and ayatollahs paid him much heed. It's also written in the Koran that, 'The gates of paradise open wide for he who can make his companions laugh,' but in all of Islam only the Sufi seem to have gotten the message. Of course, there're no comedians whatsoever in the Christian scheme of things. If a single giggle ever fluttered the lips of Our Savior, the Gospels neglect to report it. I'm guessing that the gene that disposes people to be true believers may render them immune to wit."

He was on the verge of bringing up Maestra's missing-link theory and maybe a word or two about Today Is Tomorrow when it occurred to him that he'd gone tangential, which was accepted, even expected, at a C.R.A.F.T. Club donnybrook but generally unappreciated in ordinary company. He smiled sympathetically and shut his mouth.

"And what is *your* faith, exactly, Mr. Switters? What do *you* believe in?"

"Umm. Well. I try not to."

"You try not to believe?"

"That's right. I'm on the run from the Killer B's."

"Pardon? What have killer bees to do with? . . ."

"B for Belief. B for Belonging. The B's that lead to most of the killing in the world. If you don't Belong among us, then you're our inferior, or our enemy, or both; and you can't Belong with us unless you Believe what we Believe. Maybe not even then, but it certainly helps. Our religion, our party, our tribe, our town, our school, our race, our nation. Believe. Belong. Behave. Or Be damned."

"But human beings have—"

"A need to belong somewhere, to believe in something? Yeah, Sister—if I may still call you that—they seem to. It's virtually genetic. I'm on guard against it, and it still overtakes me. The concern is that we may annihilate ourselves before we can evolve, or mutate, beyond it; but you may rest assured that, even if we survive, as long as we're driven to Belong and Believe, we'll never be at peace, and we'll never be free."

"Ooh-la-la! That's crazy. A human who belongs to no group or believes in nothing? What kind of robot, what lost animal? No longer human at all."

"In the sense that a frog is no longer a tadpole, you may be right. And it may never come to pass, or have to. We just might learn enough tolerance, and jettison enough fear and ego, to compensate. The neutral angels could prevail: *neutral victory* being a particularly intriguing oxymoron. In the meantime, though, Sister—if I may still call you that—can't you hear them buzzing? Listen to the swarm that Be-lief and Be-longing have Be-got. B-boundaries. B-borderlines. B-blood B-bonds. B-blood B-brothers. B-bloodlust. B-bloodbath. B-bloody B-bloody. B-bang B-bang. B-boom B-boom. B-blast. B-bludgeon. B-batter. B-blow up. B-bomb. B-butcher. B-break. B-blindside. B-bushwack. Be-head. B-blackball. Be-tray. B-bullets. B-blades. B-booby traps. B-bazookas. B-bayonets. B-brute force. B-barbarism. B-babylon. B-babel. Be-elzebub. Be-etlejuice. B-bureaucracy. B-bagpipes. B-beanie B-babies."

"Beanie Babies? The kiddie stuffed toys?"

"Uh, sorry, that just slipped in. And, obviously, there're good things that begin with B, too. Bee-r, for example. B-biscuits. The Beatles. B-Broadway. *B-beinas.*"

"Bei——?"

He wasn't about to explain that *beina* was the Catalonian for, as Audubon Poe put it, a woman's treasure. So, he threw in triumphantly, as if he'd been saving it for last, "The B-ible."

"So, you do think the Bible a good thing?"

"Umm. Well. To be-labor my apiarian analogy: the honey that's dipped from that busy hive can be sweet and nourishing, or it can be hallucinogenic and deadly. All too frequently, the latter is confused with the former. Dip with caution. Reader be-ware."

Domino studied him, but he couldn't tell if it was with appreciation or contempt. To break the silence, and perhaps to win favor, he revealed that less than a year before, he had been considering joining the Catholic Church. He didn't mention Suzy.

"What?! Are you mad? How could you possibly be a member of the Church and yet not belong or believe?"

"Easy. It's the best way. To practice a religion can be lovely, to believe in one is almost always disastrous."

Understanding him to mean that to practice Christ's teachings and not believe in them was a finer thing than to fervently believe in them but never put them into practice, she had to nod in tenuous agreement. He was standing hypocrisy on its head. "Is that the way you managed to work for the CIA?"

"Yeah, probably, now that you mention it. It's called participation without attachment."

"But I don't . . ."

"Because the CIA is an extremist organization that has the unusual ability to function outside the compromising channels of normal political and commercial restraint, it has the potential to kick out the blocks here and there and help the world to happen. The original teachings of Jesus and Mohammed et al are also extreme. If a person can participate in those extreme systems without identifying with the humbug they've spawned, without becoming attached to, say, patriotism in the case of the CIA, or moralistic zeal, in the case of the Church, then that throbbing nerve that runs from the hypothalamus to the trigger finger might be sedated, minds might be liberated, and—who knows?—the logjam of orthodoxy and certitude might be broken, allowing the—what shall we call it?—river of human affairs to gurgle off freely in new and unexpected directions. Something like that. Cha-cha-cha."

"Is that your faith then? Freedom and unpredictability?"

He finished off his tea. "My faith is whatever makes me feel good about being alive. If your religion doesn't make you feel good to be alive, what the hell is the point of it?"

For a moment, she seemed taken aback. Then she snapped, "Comfort."

"Heh!" He sounded so much like Maestra he almost gave himself a bracelet.

"Hope."

"I can't do the math, but wouldn't x amount of hope cancel out x amount of faith? I mean, if you have faith the sun's going to rise in the morning, you don't have to hope it will."

"Solace."

"Solace? That's why God made fermented beverages and the blues."

"Salvation."

"From what? Aren't you talking about some form of long-term, no-premium, afterworldly fire insurance?"

Domino didn't respond, and he worried that he might have gone too far. "Of course," he said, "I've also never seen the point of chicken wings. Either for the chicken, who doesn't fly, or for the diner, who doesn't get enough meat to justify all the grease it takes to make them halfway edible."

A sudden blink of wistfulness caused her eyes to grow even softer than usual. "Tell me, do they still have the Philly cheese steak?"

"You bet they do. There *are* some things a person can count on."

She smiled, and it was, he thought, like a cross between the Taj Mahal and a jukebox. "Is there anything right now that is making you feel glad about being alive?"

"As a matter of fact, yes. I'm in a foreign country, illegally, in a mysterious convent, inappropriately, and in conversation with the blue nude's niece, improbably. What's not to enjoy?"

Briefly, very briefly, she closed her palms and fingers around the fists he'd rested on the armrests. "And in a wheelchair, unfortunately." She stood. "Okay. I must go now and visit my auntie. The excommunication has hit Masked Beauty quite hard. Hit all of us, really. But we will go forward." She straightened the sweet-smelling sprig behind her ear. She moved away.

Near the door, she paused. "Now that the patriarchal authorities have found our tiny band of desert nuns unfit to be in their Church, we're having to redefine our relationship to our religion. In addition to that, we have been trying for some years now to redefine our relationship to Christ, to Mary, to God. God is a fixed point, naturally, God is eternal and absolute, God doesn't change. But man's concept of God, man's interpretation of God, the way we view God has changed many times over history. Sometimes we think of him as more intimate, other times more impersonal and aloof; in some centuries he was seen to be primarily angry and judgmental and vengeful; in others, more loving and accepting. Our image of God evolves. Yes? And what would our ideas of God, of religion, be like if they had come to us through the minds of women? Ever think of that? We concentrate on such matters here, and for that reason I very much appreciate my talk with you, for while I may disagree with many of your absurd notions, you show me how it's possible to think freely, without constraints or limitations or preconceptions. That's helpful."

"We absurdists are always pleased to be of service."

"I also appreciate getting to tell you our own story. Because even though you refer to our convent as 'mysterious,' you now can see that our ceremony at the bonfire was a logical, pragmatic thing, like all of our activities. We are as simple as a candle, Mr. Switters. There's no magic here, no mystery."

"No, I guess not," he conceded. "Except, of course, for the document."

Domino blanched. "Ah, yes," she sighed, after a time. "The document. The Serpent in our Eden."

Maria Une delivered his lunch, and after it had been absorbed by that ball of mystic white light that he imagined to occupy his lower torso, its nutrients reconverted into photons, the chaff transformed into what he was prone to label "dark matter," as if bodily waste were the ash from a dead star, he e-mailed Maestra an account of the curious blue nude coincidence. Then, hating it all the while, he exercised for well over an hour, turning his cot into a gym mat, a platform upon which he performed sit-ups, push-ups, crunches, and other forms of self-torture as required by the tyranny of maintenance.

So exhausted was he by the strenuous workout that he fell asleep after reading less than a page of *Finnegans Wake*. When he finally awoke, it was dark. His dinner tray had been left on the bedside stool, and alongside the cornucopiate pita sandwich, there was a large glass of red wine (tea, eat your heart out!) and a sprig of orange blossoms.

He wouldn't see Domino until morning, but when morning finally came (he had read most of the night), he seemed so hale and fit (the workout had paid a dividend) that she proposed a tour of the oasis. For the next hour, she pushed his chair around the grounds.

Against the thick mud walls of the various buildings, yellow roses bloomed, and in the willows that surrounded the large spring that was the centerpiece and lifeblood of the compound, cuckoos sang. Irrigation troughs funneled water from the spring to gardens dense with tomatoes, cucumbers, chickpeas, and eggplants. In groves scattered throughout the oasis, there were trees that each in its own season bore figs, almonds, oranges, pomegranates, walnuts, dates, and lemons. Chickens scratched beneath jasmine bushes, as if doing a kind of archaic arithmetic; a solitary donkey swished its tail with such regular cadence that it might have been a pendulum for keeping the time of the world; and a few runty black goats bleated and chewed, bleated and chewed, in a manner that suggested they were eating their own voices. A great peace and a floral fragrance hovered about the place: it probably was at least a low-rent approximation of Eden.

"The Syrian government doesn't object to your being here?" Switters asked, recalling that no country on earth with the possible exception of Israel had experienced historically as many religious massacres as Syria.

"*Au contraire.* Damascus loves us. It can point to our token convent as an example of its tolerance and diversity. We're good, how do you say, PR for Syria. Damascus likes us better than Rome does."

Outside the arched and latticed doorway that led into the dining hall, Domino formally introduced him to each of the sisters. Each, that is, except for the one he most desired to meet. They ranged from Maria Une—the oldest, save for the elusive Masked Beauty—to Fannie, the youngest at thirty-four, and the most overtly friendly. In between, there was Maria Deux, taciturn and pinch-faced; ZuZu, who resembled the wine-jolly hostess of a TV cooking show; frizzy, foxy-eyed Bob, who might have been Einstein's twin sister; Pippi, who was cinnamon-haired, heavily freckled, and wore a carpenter's belt; and Mustang Sally, petite, plantain-nosed, and festooned with the kind of spit curls that hadn't been seen on a Frenchwoman since Brassaï photographed Paris's backstreet bar girls in the 1930s. In their identical ankle-length Syrian gowns, they might have been a culture club, a Greek sorority, perhaps, organized by mildly eccentric middle-aged Ohio housewives in a chronic pang of misplaced aesthetic longing. On the other hand, they were poised, tranquil, earnest, and highly industrious. They nodded politely when Domino informed them that their guest was fully recovered from fever, thanks to God and Pachomian charity, and would be departing their company on the supply truck the following day or the day after. His presence must have been a novelty, though whether welcomed or resented he couldn't tell. Certainly, with the notable exception of Fannie, the women appeared anxious to return to their labors.

Domino resumed the tour, pushing him out past the grape arbor, generator shed, burn barrel, and compost heaps, out to, and then around, the parameters of the high, solid wall that separated her gentle green island from the harsh sandy vastness that surrounded it. Eventually they arrived back at the great gate, and it was there, as she slowed to impart some fact or other (she seemed to enjoy wheeling him around: women love these fierce invalids home from hot climates?), that he noticed on the ground to the right of the gate a pair of wooden poles that had wedges attached to them about eighteen to twenty inches from the bottom.

Switters pointed. "What are those?" he asked.

"Those? Uh, in French they're called *les échasses*. I can't remember the English. The nuns use them to be tall enough to look through the hole in the gate."

"Stilts," he whispered. "I'll be double damned." He swatted his brow smartly with the palm of his hand. "Stilts! Of course! Why haven't *I* thought of that?"

To Domino's astonishment, he stood on the seat of his Invacare 9000 XT and had her, protesting all the while, lean against the upright stilts to steady them while he climbed onto their footrests. At his signal, she stepped aside, and off he clumped, moving the right stilt forward and then the left—before he went sprawling onto his face. He'd covered less than a yard.

But he insisted on trying it again. And again. Covering a greater distance each time before he fell. Domino was beside herself. "You'll break an arm! You're ruining your nice suit! How can you stand on these cotton-pick . . . , on these damn stilts when you can't stand on the ground?"

"Don't worry about it. I'll explain later. Let's go. I can do this. I did it when I was a kid in Redwood City."

She couldn't restrain him. He was like a puncture in a high-pressure hose, spurting in all directions, spuming with an irrepressible puissance. The longer he remained upright, the more excited he became. Soon—well, whether or not it was soon depended upon one's perspective: to Domino it seemed longer than a journey across purgatory on a lawn tractor—he was staying up for two or three minutes at a time. He wobbled, he lurched, he teetered and toddled and sprinted. He scattered goats and chickens, crashed into a date palm, got entangled in a laundry line (Oh, those ancient bloomers!), and, through it all, cackled like a lunatic.

Disturbed at their agricultural and domestic chores, the defrocked nuns gawked at him in disbelief and, perhaps, something close to alarm. Domino, running along behind him, pushing his empty chair, urged them breathlessly to ignore the spectacle. As if they could. Fannie, though, gave him an encouraging wink, and once, when he'd adroitly sidestepped a panicked nanny goat, Sister Pippi actually applauded.

In the Gascony region of southwestern France, where Pippi was reared, stiltwalking was somewhat of a tradition. Gascony farmers had once used stilts to wade in marshlands and cross the numerous streams, and were said to be able to run on stilts with amazing speed and ease.

Asked to build a set of portable stairs to enable the sisters to see through the sliding peephole in the gate, Pippi, in a fit of fun and nostalgia, had made these stilts instead.

Struck by Switters's persistence—he kept at it literally for hours—and delighted by his improvement—by late afternoon he was stilting with authority, if not exactly grace—Pippi beckoned him over to the roofed but open-air area at the rear of the storehouse where she maintained a small carpentry shop. "I've been saving these for a special occasion," she said in her Gascogne French, and as Domino squealed "*Non, non, non!*" Pippi produced from beneath a lumber pile a pair of stilts more than twice as tall as the ones on which Switters had been practicing.

"Wow!" said Switters.

"*Non!*" said Domino.

"You strap these to your legs," said Pippi, "so that you don't need to hold on to poles. But it takes good balance."

"My balance is unequaled," boasted Switters, and he used the shorter stilts to boost himself onto the low rear end of the carpentry shop's slanted roof. With Pippi and Domino holding the superstilts steady, he climbed aboard—and for a few breathtaking seconds, he jiggled, tilted, leaned, and swayed in slow motion, like a dynamited tower so in love with gravity it couldn't decide which way to fall. After he took a few steps, however, he gained stability, and Domino removed her hands from her eyes. For her part, Pippi shouted instructions and beamed with approval as, over and over again, he circled the carpentry shop. Confident now, he was about to strike out across the compound when Pippi stopped him. Seemed she had another surprise.

A couple of years before, Domino had purchased cheaply in Damascus a bolt of red-and-white checkered fabric. The idea had been to make tablecloths for "Italian night," the once-a-month occasion when the sisters enjoyed spaghetti and wine as a festive break from their plain Middle Eastern fare. For some reason, the cloth had been shelved and forgotten—by all, that is, except Pippi, who'd snipped off a substantial portion of the bolt and stitched from it a ridiculous pair of skinny trousers whose legs were a good seven feet in length. "*Voilà!*" she exclaimed, and Switters instantly recognized and approved her intent.

Once the checkered pants had been pulled over the stilts and fastened about his waist, and a tin funnel appropriated as a hat, he set off, head higher in the air than a streetlamp. It was so much like a one-man circus parade that he had little choice but to break into a booming, uptempo rendition of "Send in the Clowns."

The sisters abandoned their duties to line up and cheer the funny giant. Even dour Maria Deux had to grin. And each time he staggered past the chapel, he glanced down to see a face pressed to an uncolored pane in the stained-glass window.

Switters paraded. He pranced. He teetered. He waved. He sang. And everyone seemed enchanted. Everyone, that is, except Domino Thiry.

By the time Switters relinquished the stilts, dusk was settling onto the oasis like a purple hairnet through which a few stray strands of blondish daylight curled. After Pippi congratulated him on his performance, she hurried off to crank up the generator. Domino pushed him back to his room, through an archaic pastoral gloaming: cuckoos cooing themselves to sleep in the willows, chickens marching dumbly to the roost (one young hen lingering behind as if wanting to stay up past her bedtime and watch chicken MTV); the comforting, almost touching sight of people quietly performing their evening chores; the pappy air quickened by the fairgrounds smell of frying onions; everywhere a winding down, an innocence, a rhythm, a timelessness, an anticipation of stars, a secret fear of midnight.

The pair didn't speak. Switters was exhausted, undoubtedly, and Domino seemed in a bit of a pique. In silence they let themselves be swabbed by the curative sheep tail of bucolic twilight. Were they a normal couple in such a setting, they might be looking ahead to supper and wine and parenting and sex and prayers and dreams. As it was, Switters was imagining the possibilities that stilt walking might hold for him (between then and the autumn when he would return to Amazonia), and Domino was wondering how the hell he could walk on stilts in the first place.

That was the very question she fired at him—arms tightly folded, face all aglower—once she had shoved his chair across the threshold with just enough extra force so that he'd been obliged to brake to keep from crashing into the opposite wall. He turned slowly to stare at her, fatigue and just a touch of merriment tempering the fierceness that might otherwise have kindled his eyes. *"Un moment,"* he croaked, so parched and hungry he could scarcely speak. He tipped the water pitcher, drinking from it directly and not stopping until it was dry. Then he rolled to the crocodile valise, from which he withdrew a half-stale Health Valley energy bar, which he devoured in four mighty chomps. During the time he took to refresh himself, she changed neither position nor expression.

Wiping his mouth with the torn sleeve of his jacket, he turned to her once more. "Okay, Sister—if I may still call you that. . . ."

"Oh, for Christ's sake! Can't you just say *Domino!?*" She must have surprised herself with the heat in her voice because she immediately softened her face and her tone. "In the Middle Ages, a *domino* was a black-and-white mask that people wore during carnival. So, you see, my name connects me to my aunt in still another way."

"Okay. Cool. Did you notice, *Domino,* that each and every time I fell off the stilts, no matter how hard I fell or in what position I landed, I managed to bend my legs so that my feet never touched the ground? No? Yes? You're not quite sure? Well, I did, and they didn't. You are now about to find out why."

After the painful experience with Suzy, it was unthinkable that he would lie to Domino. (Maybe he couldn't lie to the Devil *or* God.) Nor was he inclined to offer her the abridged version that he'd related to Maestra and Mayflower Cabot Fitzgerald. No, he gave her, as she stood transfixed in the doorway, the full account, complete with Sailor Boy stew and penis-jab, although he did first warn her, much as he had Bad Bobby, that what she was about to hear was so unbelievable that he scarcely believed it himself. And he left purposefully vague the precise outlines of Today Is Tomorrow's head: there would be limits to her credulousness.

The telling took the better part of an hour, and when at last he slapped his now permanently soiled trouser legs as if to punctuate the end of the story, Domino seemed, well, not so much perplexed as hypnotized, not so much stunned as drunk, her customary radiance restored, even intensified, like the sultan's chronically sick wife who was miraculously restored to health by the stinking beggar's fairy tales. She said little, however; just looked kind of goofy in a dignified way and then excused herself to try to digest the strange and perhaps tainted ambrosias he'd just fed her.

"I'll be packed," he called after her. "In case the truck to Deir ez-Zur comes in the morning." And to himself: *But I'll be damned if I'll blow this falafel stand without having a peek at Masked Beauty.*

As it turned out, however, by 7:30 A.M., when Domino knocked with his breakfast tray, something had happened that put a spin—positive or negative, he honestly couldn't say which—on his desire to meet the once blue nude. Life was *Finnegans Wake,* to be sure, except for those times when it was Marvel Comics.

"Look at this," Switters muttered, barely glancing up from the computer over which he was hunkered, and on the screen of which a message from Maestra dully shimmered in a state of inkless, bloodless, ephemeral, somehow untrustworthy electronic quiddity. Squinting, Domino read over his shoulder, slowly extracting the salient facts from the hard-nosed rococo of Maestra's prose.

It appeared that the Matisse oil that had hung for so many years over Maestra's living room mantel; the painting that had enlivened certain of Switters's boyhood fantasies and that briefly had seemed destined to become his own; the ace up his grandmother's filmy financial sleeve; the innovative razzmatazz ramble of flattened pigment inspired by the naked body of Domino's aunt, was, in a word—in two words, to be exact—stolen property.

And when the painting was reproduced in the auction house catalog, its rightful owner had come forth.

In January 1944, five months before Allied troops landed at Normandy, the last prominent Jewish family left in the south of France had been finally discovered and arrested. Their hiding place, an abandoned mill, was comfortably, even elegantly furnished, and among articles confiscated there by the Nazis were artworks that the cultivated fugitives had continued to accumulate, even in their time of peril. A few weeks later, Matisse's *Blue Nude 1943* was loaded aboard a train that departed Nice, bound, presumably, for Berlin. That was the last that the family, imprisoned and tortured, or Matisse, aging and forgetful, was to hear of it. Until, that is, it turned up at Sotheby's just now, where it attracted the attention of the lone surviving member of that persecuted family, who immediately laid claim to it.

The good news for Maestra was that the grateful owner was presenting her with a two-hundred-thousand-dollar reward (a fraction of its worth) for having "protected" the painting for all those years and for surrendering it without a legal battle. The interesting news for Switters was that the owner turned out to be Audubon Poe's patron, the Beirut-based businessman, Sol Glissant.

"That is interesting to me, as well," said Domino. "Not only because of the picture and its connection to my aunt but because Sol Glissant happens to be the benefactor who donated to the Pachomian Order this oasis!"

"Are you jiving me? Enough, already! If the world gets any smaller, I'll end up living next door to myself."

"Oh, but I am beginning to find these . . . these coincidences involving you and Masked Beauty and the painting and all of us to be exciting, to be meaningful. Suppose they are omens? Operating instructions from the Almighty? This news from your grandmother, it only makes me more confident that what I am about to propose to you is the correct decision."

She had his full attention then. Clicking off the computer, he gazed at her directly, finding her at that instant more than usually vivacious.

"We spoke of you last night after dinner and again this morning, all of us, including Masked Beauty, and we have decided to ask you to stay on with us here at—at the convent. If I may still call it that."

Switters felt something subtle slither out of his nether regions and up his spine, but he would have been hesitant to label it kundalini. Even before she revealed the reasoning behind this surprising request, he could sense his vision of getting Seattle's Art Girls involved with stilts—stilt-making, stilt-racing, stilts for stilts' sake—fading into vacancy.

Domino's reasons were both practical and philosophical.

Switters excelled at languages. He had advanced computer equipment and a satellite telephone. He was adept in their use. Isolated more than ever from the world at large, the sisterhood would benefit in numerous ways from establishing electronic and telecommunicative links with those it wished to influence, assist, save, or solicit for funds. Because of his experience in the CIA, he might also be helpful in dealing with Middle Eastern political situations and the never-ending whirlpool of Vatican intrigue. He would become their communications expert, office manager, and security chief. He'd put the thorn on their rose and the skin on their drum.

Quite aside from that was his gender. The nine Eves had judged that it might be a good idea, after all, to admit an Adam to their little Eden. No longer bound, except by choice, to their vows, some among them had suggested that it was not merely elitist but cowardly to shun all masculine contact. What were they afraid of? Did they lack confidence in their choices? They were feminists of a sort, but well aware that reviling half the human race was a component neither of true feminism nor the Christian faith. Wasn't Jesus a man? (They weren't so sure about God.) Hadn't men (St. Pachomius, their fathers) begat them, figuratively and literally? They were in general agreement that they could use a dose of healthy male energy in their lives. It had to be said that Domino, for one, was not entirely convinced that Switters was a *healthy* manifestation of male energy, but that question would resolve itself in time.

Meanwhile, she, personally, was fascinated by his Amazonian escapade, by the so-called curse upon him. She believed that she, through prayer, Christian ritual, and modern psychology could break the spell he believed himself to be under. Jesus was known to have cast out *beaucoup* demons, and over the centuries quite a few priests had followed his example. She saw no need for Switters to venture back into that dark, damp, teeming jungle—he was at heart a desert person, just like her. She was sure she could help him. It was her duty.

Switters tugged repeatedly at one of the more springy of his barley-colored curls, as if it were a cheap plastic ripcord and he in Mexican freefall. "How long do I have to think it over?"

"Oh, somewhere between twenty-four hours and twenty-four minutes. It depends upon the truck."

He tugged some more, he furrowed his brow. The small scars on his face seemed to furl into nodes. "Do you suppose I might lubricate my cognitive apparatus with some squeezings from your swell vineyard?"

"But you haven't eaten your breakfast. It's not yet eight o'clock in the morning."

"The wine doesn't know that. Wine only recognizes two temporal states: fermentation time and party time."

"Yes, but you must eat your omelet. The sausage in it is from chicken."

"Fine. I like chicken. Tastes just like parrot."

Without further protest, she went off to fetch a bottle of red, leaving him to ponder her unexpected proposal and—because his mind, even when unlubricated, was disposed toward extrapolatory zigzag—some advice given him years earlier concerning middle-aged palm trees.

It was in the South Seas, on one of those sweet little coconut isles where the word for *vagina* has a preposterous number of vowels. (On second thought, maybe the vowels aren't excessive, considering that vowels do possess a decidedly yonic quality, particularly when contrasted with the testosterone flavor of most consonants.) He was sitting at the end of a dock in the company of an American-born professional diver who, for an annual stipend from Langley, kept an eye on French activities in that part of Polynesia. Switters had come down from Bangkok to pass to him some new cryptography software. The delivery completed, they were sipping rum and gazing out to sea.

"Man," said Switters, "that's a nasty-looking crowd of clouds over there, all rough and raggedy-assed and milling about, like a herd of white-trash shoppers just crawled out of shacks and sheds and trailer homes for the end-of-winter sale at Wal-Mart."

"Storm's coming," the diver predicted. "A big 'un."

"Not a typhoon, I hope," said Switters, glancing over his shoulder at the small, casually built wood-frame houses that dotted the unprotected shore. "I don't think I'd want to be frolicking about this paradisiacal poker chip if a real typhoon bore down on it."

"Nothing quite like that today," the diver assured him. "But do you know what to do if you're ever caught on a beach like this during a typhoon or a hurricane? The company not teach you that? Well, you tie yourself halfway up the trunk of a middle-aged palm tree."

"Why so, pal?"

"Elementary. An older palm tree will be dry inside and stiff and brittle. In a big gust, it'll snap right off and drop you in the raging flood with a couple hundred pounds of tree trunk strapped to your back. A youngish tree may be graceful and slim and easy to climb, but ultimately it's too springy, too lithe, too pliable: it'll bend nearly double in the gale and dip you underwater and drown you dead. Your middle-aged palm, though, is just right. Solid, but still has enough sap in it to be somewhat limber. Neither break nor flop. It'll give you the strong, flexible support you need to keep from being carried off or blown away."

"I'll bear that in mind," Switters promised, and sliced another lime for their drinks. In truth, he gave it no further thought whatsoever until that morning in the Syrian desert, far from any ocean, awaiting his hostess's return from the convent wine pantry; and then he was only partially serious when he asked himself if a woman such as Domino might not be the human equivalent of the middle-aged palm, the personified tree to which the tempest-tossed might emotionally attach themselves without fear of being undone by, say, naive Suzylike whimsicality or crotchety Maestralike recalcitrance. Not that he viewed himself as any orphan of the storm, exactly, but he was at rather loose ends until his planned return to Peru in the autumn, and barring another assignment from Poe, Domino's offer was perhaps his most interesting prospect and certainly the most substantial.

In any case, upon her return with the bottle, Domino did nothing to discredit the arboreal comparison, so, for better or worse, he might as well entertain it. At the very least, he was learning that for some Western women—even pious ones—middle age needn't necessarily mean dowdiness, torpor, or capitulation.

"Now," said Switters, after swirling the first big gulp of wine around in his mouth and swallowing it with satisfaction, "don't get the idea I'm a boozer. Setting out deliberately to get drunk is pathological. I like to drink just enough to change the temperature in the brain room. I'll turn to less mainstream substances if I want to rearrange the furniture."

Since there was a finite amount of wine on the premises and the nearest liquor store was days away, Domino wasn't particularly worried about his drinking habits. She had other concerns.

"Should you decide to remain with us," she said, "you may become very homesick for America."

"Oh, I don't know about that. Haven't spent much time there in the past ten years." He drew in a long, hard breath of wine. "America," he mused. "America's pretty violent and repressive these days. But as my pal Skeeter Washington might put it, it's a 'bouncy' violence, a 'bouncy' repression, often ribboned with exuberance and cheer. Believe it or not, America's a very insecure country. It's been scared into a kind of self-imposed subjugation first by the imagined threat of Communism and then by the imagined threat of drugs. Maestra calls us an 'abusive democracy,' one in which everybody wants to control everybody else. Lately, even tolerance, itself, has been usurped by the sanctimonious and the opportunistic, and turned into an instrument for intimidation, bullying, and extortion. Yet the U. S. continues to pound its sternum and boast that it's the home of the brave and the land of the free. If that's brazen chutzpah rather than blind naiveté, then I guess I can't help but admire it."

The wine had wasted no time greasing the pistons of his tongue, and he probably would have gone on to expound upon his observation that in the late 1960s, everything in America—art, sports, cinema, journalism, politics, religion, education, the justice system, law enforcement, health care, clothing, food, romance, even nature: *everything*—had devolved into forms of entertainment, and how, by the nineties, most of those forms of entertainment had become almost exclusively about merchandising. However, Domino aborted his rant by stating, with just a flicker of accusation, "You worked for perhaps the most notorious fearmongering institution in your fearful America."

"Mmm. That's right, I did. It's called 'riding the dragon.' "

"It can also be called 'seeking sensation.' I think you have a need to be always stimulated, to be the action man. How do they call it now? A *player*. Yes?"

"Only an errand boy," he protested, refilling his glass with wine as dark as a monster's gore. "Only an errand boy."

"Describe it however you wish, I still think you crave to work close to the bull. Or the dragon, if you prefer. But in Spain they say that the matador in time becomes the bull. Is not he who rides the dragon part of the dragon?"

"Not if he's fully conscious."

"Perhaps not. But I believe there is much to be said for active withdrawal. Not apathy, you understand, not acquiescence or inertia. Ah! My English vocabulary is coming back like the swallows to Cappuccino. No, what I am speaking of is a refusal to participate. A choice to live in a kind of voluntary exile. To observe the dragon from a distance, to study its strengths and weaknesses but to reject it, resist it, by refusing to engage it and give it energy. For example, we Pachomians, after our excommunication, debated going off, one by one, to Third World villages, where we would try to convince a few native women of the wisdom and urgency of limiting procreation. Our successes probably would have been small, our psychic expenditures great. Instead, we decided to stay here in the wilderness, secluded in holy shadow, shooting sometimes our tiny arrows from concealment but mainly working on the growth of our souls, and guarding . . . that which is ours to guard. So, Mr. Switters, what do you think of active withdrawal? Is it selfish? Is it cowardly? Irresponsible?"

"Nope," he said between sips. "Not if you're fully conscious."

From the way in which she tilted her head, leaning toward him ever so slightly while the flabby razor of incomprehension carved a little crease in her brow, it was obvious Domino was unsure what he meant exactly by "fully conscious." He ought to have been able to explain, to inform her that *full consciousness* referred not so much to a state in which a person always behaved in a manner he or she knew to be just, regardless of public opinion, though that was important; nor even to an awareness so keen that the person never allowed fear, ego, desire, or convenience to delude him or her into believing their behavior was more just than it actually was, though that was nearer the point; but rather, to the clear and persistent realization that at bottom, all human activity was cosmic theater: a grand and goofy and epic and ephemeral show, in which an individual's behavior, good or bad, was simply the acting out of a role, the crucial thing being to stand back and observe one's performance even as one was immersed in it. Switters ought to have been able to elucidate for the simple reason that this definition of "fully conscious" closely resembled the unwritten, unspoken creed of the CIA angels. However, Bobby Case had warned him that it was always a mistake to attempt to define terms such as *full consciousness.* "Even iffen you do a good job of it," Bobby said, "you'll end up sounding like a checkbook mystic or some New Age mynah bird, and most folks won't get it anyhow." According to Bobby, a person got it—*bingo!*—or they didn't; no amount of spelling it out or scholarly discourse was going to peel the peach. And, come to think of it, had Sailor Boy, after issuing his concise counsel, ever felt the need to add anything more? Not once. That settled it. Switters lowered his lids, blanking out Domino's not quite comprehending gaze. He smacked his lips. "Mmm. A most accommodating vintage. Makes my palate feel like the jewel in the lotus, like a taxfree investment, like a pocket street-map of Hollywood, like Lincoln's doctor's dog, like—"

"A mediocre wine and you know it," she corrected him, though a certain glint in her eye indicated that she, influenced now, might be incubating a thirst of her own. "Well," she said, "even if you don't object philosophically to active withdrawal, that doesn't mean you are personally suited for it. For example, we are very orderly here."

"So? Nothing wrong with that—as long as you don't deceive yourself into believing your order is superior to somebody else's disorder."

"But, disorder is—"

"Often just the price that's charged for freedom. Order, so-called, has claimed more victims historically than disorder, so-called; and besides, if properly employed, language can provide all of the order a person might ever need in life. Language—"

"You're throwing me off track. Save language for later." She nodded at the wine. "All right. I'll have one sip." Accepting the glass from him (there was only the one), she went on. "What I'm trying to say is, I worry—all of the sisters worry—that should you accept our invitation, you will find the necessary routines of the Pachomian oasis to be boring and dull." Rather abruptly, she raised the glass to her mouth and drained it.

A ruby droplet, at once as authentic as blood and as artificial as a bauble of carnival paste, glistened on her upper lip like an Aphrodite love boil, and Switters felt a bewildering urge to expunge it with his tongue. *Easy, big fella.* "A legitimate concern," he agreed, "although I've generally managed to find a modicum of what we childish Americans call 'fun' and you more refined Europeans term 'pleasure' any place the bus has dropped me off."

"That is a talent," she said, sighing. "Unless you can count Italian nights at the dining hall or romping in rainwater in Vatican bikinis—which is what the sisters were doing at the moment you passed by with your nomads and heard them laughing—we nuns have never placed much emphasis on pleasure. Joy, perhaps, but certainly not fun. So, that is something else you could do for us here: teach us how one might remain sensitive and compassionate, yet still enjoy oneself in such a defiled, destructive age."

"Oh, I don't know. . . ."

"But, you see, we must not be thinking only of ourselves, we must not be unfair. You, Mr. Switters, must find pleasure at our Eden, as well, or else you will be dissatisfied here. So. That is where Fannie comes in." She poured the last of the wine into the glass and passed it back to him.

He frowned. "Fannie?"

"Why, yes. Fannie." And at that point, the middle-aged palm tree, without so much as swaying, dropped a coconut onto his skull. "Fannie wants to fuck your brains out," she said.

He jounced a spatter of *vin rouge* onto the knee of his last clean trousers. And if that wasn't embarrassing enough, he blushed. He knew he blushed because he could feel himself blushing, which caused him to blush all the pinker. Blushing did not suit a man such as Switters any more than sheep's lingerie suited a wolf. Domino was surprised by his shock but was also more than a trifle amused.

"What's the matter?" she asked coyly. "Have I made another passé remark? Doesn't anyone say 'fuck your brains out' anymore? Has it followed 'cotton-picking' into the vernacular dustbin?"

"Caught me off guard, that's all," Switters muttered. "Didn't expect—"

"And well you shouldn't expect such talk from me. I don't even like to think about these matters. So let's get it over with quickly." She took the glass from him and wiped it with a handkerchief before drinking. "It is not unusual for a novice in a nunnery to indulge in what the Church terms the 'self-abuse.' You know what I mean. It is discouraged, even punished, but to a certain extent expected and tolerated. Fannie, however, was incorrigible. She played with herself in chapel, at Holy Communion; she diddled in the confessional even as she was asking forgiveness for diddling. It's reported she masturbated with one hand while counting her rosary prayers with the other. In every additional respect, she was the model novice, hard-working and devout, so the mother superior believed Fannie to be in the grips of an Asmodeus, a demon that is said to possess young nuns to make them lustful. Every exorcist priest in Ireland had a go at her, and when exorcism failed, the Irish shipped her off to a convent in France, where her behavior might be better understood. Why do so many people believe that the French are the sex race, the world leaders in eroticism? Why?"

"Because they've never been to Thailand."

"Really? The Thai are better at sex than us?" Switters thought he detected a soupçon of wounded national pride. "In any case, Fannie ended up with the Pachomians, and now she's released from vows and is hot to trot: another obsolete expression, I suppose. She likes you. She's still young and attractive. I find it degrading to pimp like this, but as it may be the only way to assure that both of you are content to remain at the oasis. . . ."

"Well, you can stop it right now. As far as I'm concerned, Fannie can stick with her finger."

"Why? Don't you find her appealing?"

"She's not so bad." He was about to add, "For a woman of her age," when it occurred to him that such a sentiment could be both undiplomatic and self-incriminating. What he said instead, however, was worse. He didn't intend to say it, wasn't sure he meant it. It contradicted, in fact, the very comment he had so prudently suppressed, a remark that for all of its insensitivity had at least been truthful. He felt ventriloquized, as if the imp in him, for reasons that it alone understood, was throwing its voice. "I guess I thought maybe you and I might . . ."

"Ooh-la-la! No, no, no. You and I? That is ridiculous."

"Why? Don't you find me appealing?"

"You're not so bad," she said, giving it right back to him (or to the trouble-making bugger who had hijacked his larynx). "For a man of your age." Had she read his mind? Her tone became more serious. "I lost my virginity when I was sixteen." (An image of Suzy went zinging through his brain like a hot pink bullet.) "It took me years to get it back. If I ever lose it again, which is rather unlikely, it will be to a man with whom I'm united in Christ. That wouldn't be you, would it, Mr. Switters?"

"Offhand, I'd say the odds are against it. But stranger things have happened." (*Shut up, you little bastard!*)

"No. I doubt if you could meet my standards. You haven't found maturity yet, and you haven't found peace."

He wanted to say, "If you're referring to that pre-senile stagnation that passes for maturity these days and that hypocritical obsequiousness that passes for peace, I'd rather have shingles than the one and scurvy than the other." What emerged from his mouth, however, was, "Damn! You sure know how to break a guy's heart."

"Nonsense. Even though you told me you loved me the moment you laid eyes on me . . ."

"I did?!" He came within half a hue of blushing again. (While he had lain in helpless delirium, his evil elf must have had a field day.)

". . . we both know you do not. It was just your usual line of—how do you call it?"

"Flapdoodle?" he suggested helpfully, regaining some control.

"Besides," she went on, "the pain of love does not break hearts, it merely seasons them. The disappointed heart revives itself and grows meaty and piquant. Sorrow expands it and makes it pithy. The spirit, on the other hand, can snap like a bone and may never fully knit. In the Order of St. Pachomius, we have always worked to build strong spirits. Spirits that can never be broken. Not even by the things that are to come."

"What things?"

Domino stood. She was light on her feet, yet firmly planted. (Like a palm tree of a certain vintage?) "Your own spirit, for all of its— flapdoodie?—is very stout, I think, and would not be so badly out of place here. Perhaps it's even needed. But you mustn't feel pressured. We'll get along without you. Even Fannie will. And cursed and mis- guided and lost to Christ as you are, you may actually need us more than we need you. So, you decide. I'll go away now and let you mull it over. Just remember that the supply truck could arrive at any hour."

"Wait." He caught her wrist. It felt as if he'd grabbed the neck of a swan.

"Yes?"

"The truck. From Deir ez-Zur won't it go back to Damascus?"

"Eventually, but along a different route. It returns to Damascus by way of Palmyra, the oasis town about a hundred kilometers to the south of us."

Somewhat reluctantly he released her arm. Sister Domino's flesh was as pure, and as forbidden, to him as Suzy's always was, and thus had the capacity to make him dizzy. "Hmm. Well. Ah. What's the date today? Around the first of June, isn't it? I'll tell you what. Let's cut a deal. In the fall, I've got to bop down to Peru to see a man about a taboo. But I'll stay until then. How's that? I'll stay through Sep- tember, providing my grandmother is healthy, and for those—what is it?—four months, I'll give you my absolute best, although I'm mak- ing no promises regarding Fannie. I'll stay—but there are a couple of conditions."

Eyes narrowing, she stiffened, turning her cheeks into something resembling toy igloos for Eskimo action figures. She was thinking that Switters was going to insist on being shown Cardinal Thiry's secret document. He knew she was thinking precisely that, and it made him smile. If that dusty old paper really was the Serpent in their Eden, it undoubtedly would reveal itself to him in time. And if not, he didn't give a good goddamn. He had other wants.

"First, I want to meet Masked Beauty."

"*Mais oui.* Of course you will. That goes without saying."

"And I want Sister Pippi to build another pair of stilts for me. A shorter pair. A pair whose footrests—this is essential, so listen up—a pair whose footrests are exactly two inches above the ground."

bobby case thought it was hilarious. Hilarious. Switters, the scourge of Iraq, the brave-hearted bane of the pickle factory, the poetry-spouting libertine who raised eyebrows at the C.R.A.F.T. Club, even; Switters, operative's operative and erstwhile stalwart defender of the erotic rights of the young, now a flunky at a convent, performing mundane clerical services for a gaggle of over-the-hill nuns! Hilarious.

When Bobby learned that the nuns had been recently defrocked, were holed up in a private oasis in the Syrian desert, and answered to an abbess who, in 1943, had been the model for the Matisse nude that graced Maestra's living room wall, he had to admit that the situation had a novel flavor, a certain cachet. But it was still pretty funny. Bobby had to laugh, despite the fact that Switters could not now accept the assignment in Kosovo that was about to be offered by Audubon Poe. And he undoubtedly would have laughed all the harder had he, like the cuckoos in the willow trees, had a bird's-eye view of Switters clomping and hopping around the convent grounds on a pair of under-size stilts.

The new stilts hadn't been long in coming, and, as requested, hadn't been long in length. The soles of his feet—as smooth and pink as a babe's—were held off the ground at the barely perceptible height of two inches and not a centimeter less or more, and from that modest elevation he scanned the terrestrial and the astral, inspected the commonplace and the rare, as though he were revolving apace with the axle that turned the Wheel of Things. What cosmic insight was afforded by the two-inch perspective? The only advantage as far as he could tell—perhaps because he cloddishly clumped rather than mystically levitated—was that everything seemed a bit less serious when observed from an ambulatory loge. Of course, that might have been the master's point. And Today Is Tomorrow's, as well. A similar thought had even occurred to him in his Invacare 9000. At any rate, he certainly didn't look like an enlightened being as, ungainly and stiff-legged, he negotiated the oasis's shady paths. He walked the way furniture might have walked. Or a stick beetle on its journey along a twig.

It wasn't that he was slow. After a week or ten days of practice, Switters, on stilts, could have beaten any of the nuns in a footrace. Moreover, his movements were entirely devoid of the strain, deliberation, and self-pitying sloth that one sometimes noticed in the physically impaired. On the contrary, he stilted with a reckless ebullience, so glad was he to be free of the wheelchair and its sickly associations. Still, there was something comical about him, like a crow blundering across a pavement grate or a boy in his mother's high heels (Domino, in fact, wondered why he didn't simply wear clogs, to which he explained that his survival depended upon there being space, air—oxygen, nitrogen, argon, plus traces of helium, hydrogen, ozone, krypton, xenon, neon, carbon monoxide, and methane—between his feet and the earth), and the sisters never reached a point where they could watch him without some amusement. Bobby, for better or worse, was deprived of the spectacle, but as has been noted, he found the whole business in Syria quite funny, including, once he was let in on it, the business of Sister Fannie. His mirth didn't prevent him, however, from offering Switters sincere and well-reasoned advice. His e-mail read thusly:

```
> Whether or not you're man enough to admit it, podner,
> you're attracted to innocence like mildew to strawberries.
> But just because that little Irish rosary wrangler is a tech-
> nical virgin, that don't mean she's pure. From what you tell
> me, Fannie's less innocent than your average Patpong skivvy
> girl, intact cherry and a million damn Hail Marys notwith-
> standing. That don't mean squat lessen you want it to, but
> I'd be remiss if I failed to point it out.
> It strikes me that the one you really want is the older one
> (not that Fannie ain't Methuselah's eldest daughter by your
> and my usual standards), and I have to say I find that both
> touching and troublesome, like when that nice aunt of mine
> near Hondo used to bake me cookies but always shaped and
> colored them so that they looked like ladybugs, which meant
> I could only eat the damn things alone in the root cellar or
> out back of the garage. Well, maybe that there is an imper-
> fect analogy. But you listen to Captain Case, this is your cap-
> tain speaking: if you really do have a heartfelt hankering for
> the older one with the name that cannot help but evoke
```

> memories of Antoine better known as Fats, whose rendition
> of "Blueberry Hill" was so frigging awesome and definitive
> that in nearly fifty years hardly any other singer has had the
> balls to try to cover it, then you should not lay a paw on
> Fannie, no matter how sweetly Domino may sanction it or
> swear it's copacetic. Because once you do the deed with
> Fannie, any chance for romance with Domino will have flown
> out the window like a pigeon who just noticed the rotisserie
> was on.
> Objectively speaking, you might be better off with the older
> one (Forty-six? Are you kidding me? Jesus, boy!) for the
> reason that there ain't as likely to be COMPLICATIONS that
> might interfere with your rumble in the jungle come
> October.

How did Switters react to Bobby's advice? Well, he said to himself: *I'd eat ladybug cookies in broad daylight in the middle of downtown Hondo or Dallas or any precious place else, including the end-zone bleachers at the Texas-Oklahoma game, and any redneck cracker unevolved atavistic possum-lipped hooligans who were wont to harangue me about it could damn well. . . .* Then, suddenly he remembered the album of Broadway show tunes so cautiously concealed in the secret compartment of his crocodile valise, and his bravado dissolved in a hot flush of shame.

That evening, he set up the computer in the dining hall and played the CD throughout dinner. It eased his private guilt only marginally: they were middle-aged French nuns, after all, not a pack of testosteronies, and they, moreover, enjoyed the concert thoroughly, although Mustang Sally did mention during coffee that she preferred rock 'n' roll.

After the last romantic swell had subsided, he took Fannie by her callused little hand, led her to his room, undressed her, and lay down with her on the tracks before the conjunctional freight train.

Why?

Because "Stranger in Paradise" from *Kismet* always made him feel . . . libidinous.

Because he refused to believe that he might have a "heartfelt hankering" for Sister Domino.

Because he was not the sort of man to be compromised by rational advice.

Because he was Switters.

Having slept through breakfast the next morning, he arrived, yawning and reeking, at the office they had established for him in the main building to find a note taped to his computer screen. It summoned him to an immediate conference with Masked Beauty.

He had been introduced to the abbess nearly a fortnight earlier, when Domino had escorted him to her quarters, and had had only fleeting glimpses of her since. That initial meeting was memorable, however.

Her apartment was small, no more than double the size of his own room, and sparsely but opulently furnished, which is to say it contained only a tiny table, a cane-bottomed chair, a wooden settee, a chest of drawers, and a corner shrine encircled by wooden candlesticks, yet there were marvelously rich carpets underfoot, the pillows on the settee (which apparently doubled as her bed) were boisterously patterned and could have been stolen from an oriental harem as imagined (or actually visited in Morocco) by Matisse, and the tassel-roped curtains that draped both the windows and doors were of such heavy brocade that they would have strained the back of the stoutest camel and defied the claws of the meanest housecat. Masked Beauty had stood at one of the windows, peering through a narrow part in the brocade, her back turned to Switters as the candles flickered and a cloud of incense smoke seemed to overload with oily perfumes every molecule in the space.

When her tall, erectly held figure slowly pivoted to face him, he saw that she was veiled. The sensation he had was that of being received by a Bedouin matriarch (were there such a thing) or the wife of a minor pasha (were such a reception permitted). Despite the crucifix that hung above the shrine and the image of Mary that dominated its nave, the atmosphere in the apartment was decidedly more Levantine than Roman. Lines from Baudelaire's *"L'Invitation au Voyage,"* the very first poem he'd studied at Berkeley, drifted through his mind, lines such as, "In that amber-scented calm" and "Walls with eastern splendour hung," and, waiting to be introduced, he spontaneously blurted out in French the poem's refrain: *"Là, tout n'est qu'ordre et beauté / Luxe, calme et volupté."*

Domino and Masked Beauty exchanged glances. Both sets of eyes seemed to be smiling. The abbess, in a flat, childish voice, bade Switters sit beside her on the couch while Domino arranged for tea. Then, without excess of preamble, and still under veil, she engaged him in a dialogue about *beauté*. He told her that in America, socio-political dullards had chopped up beauty and fed it to the dogs sometime in the late 1980s on grounds ranging from its lack of pragmatic social application to the notion that it was somehow unfair to that and those who were, by beauty's standards, ugly.

The abbess asked if it wasn't true that beauty was, indeed, useless, to which he responded with an enthusiastic, *"Mais oui!"* He proclaimed that beauty's great purpose was always to be purposeless, that its use to society lay in its very uselessness, that its lack of function was precisely what lent it the power to scoop us out of context, especially political and economic context, and provide experiences available in no other area of our lives, not even the spiritual. He likened those philistines who would banish the beautiful from art, architecture, dress, and language in order to free us from frivolous and expensive distractions to those scientists who proposed blowing up the moon in order to free us, psychologically and commercially, from the effects of the tides.

The abbess agreed that a world *sans lune* would be a poorer world indeed—in the desert, especially, moonlight was the magic frosting that slathered delectability onto the scorched hard torte of the earth— but surely those critics were correct when they complained that ideas and ideals of physical beauty tended, at worst, to oppress the plain in appearance, and, at best, to make them feel inadequate; while giving those graced with comeliness, through no particular effort of their own, a false sense of superiority. "Yeah," Switters blurted in English, "but so what?" Then, in his halting French, he argued that the two positions were equally egocentric and thus equally inane. Moreover, given the unpleasant option of having to associate with either the self-satisfied beautiful or the self-pitying plain, he'd choose the former every time because beauty could sometimes transcend smugness whereas self-pity just made ugliness all the more unattractive. He was willing to concede, though, that the plastic crown of glamor could bear down as heavily on its wearers as the dung corona of plainness could upon its, and that frequently the difference between the two was merely a matter of fashion, rather than any objective, universal aesthetic indices.

During this banter, which persisted for nearly half an hour, Domino remained silently attentive. She busied herself with refilling their teacups and to his pronouncements outwardly reacted only twice. At one point, he had nodded toward the plaster Virgin in the shrine and wondered why those who had been allegedly visited by Mary at places such as Fatima and Lourdes (homely young girls in both instances) had been moved to dwell upon her physical beauty, comparing her to film stars or pageant queens, when, historically in all probability, she was an average-looking teenager from a dusty backwater *shtetl*. Both Domino and her aunt had started a bit at that, exchanging meaningful blinks, before the abbess suggested that the girls naturally would have had a limited frame of reference with which to attempt to describe Mary's holy radiance.

Later, as Domino bent over to pour tea, her chestnut hair had fallen over her face, and the easy grace with which she'd employed her left hand to sweep it back prompted Switters to declare that that gesture, itself, was an unconsciously choreographed act of intense beauty, and of more value, ultimately, to the human race than, say, the sixty new jobs created in a depressed suburb by the opening of a Wal-Mart store. As she straightened up, Domino whispered near his ear, "You're out of your cotton-picking mind."

For her part, Masked Beauty had clucked and compared Switters to Matisse, who, she professed, identified the female form with beauty to such a degree that for Henri, it was the perfect symbol of love, truth, and charity; both a garden of sensual delights and a link (more so than prayer) to the divine. "It's flattering to be adored, I suppose, but that is a terrible burden to load on the backs of women." She clucked again. "Henri was an old fool, and if you are not careful, you will end up the same." She laughed. "But Domino was right. You are an *interesting* fool."

Now that the subject of Matisse had been broached, Switters wanted to ask the abbess all about the circumstances surrounding the painting of *Blue Nude 1943*. Before he could facilitate the segue, however, his hostess stood, seeming to indicate that the visit was at an end. Switters rose to face her. She would have been only a couple of inches shorter than he, were he not now back on his stilts, and he found himself checking out her feet to see if she wore some sort of platform shoes. She did not. When he lifted his gaze from her sandals, he saw to his delight that she was loosening her veil. He supposed he was prepared for anything, but he was wrong.

The septuagenarian's face, when the veil fell away, proved to be nearly as round as her niece's, yet without a trace of a double chin. She had large but elegant ears, a voluptuous mouth that became frank and impatient at its corners; a nose longer, more bony than Domino's, though no less perfectly formed; eyes that were the same odd mixture of gray, green, and brown, but whereas Domino's orbs invited comparisons to, for example, diamond-dusted napalm, amphetamined fireflies, or hot jalapeño ginseng spritzer, Masked Beauty's, no longer isolated above the veil, seemed to be paling, waxing transparent, as if agate cinders were cooling into a watery ash. In contrast to her thick, wavy, elephant-colored hair, the abbess's complexion was rosy and youthful, so smooth, in fact, that her skin might have been her most memorable attribute—were it not for that other thing.

That other thing—the thing that cut short any impulse to exclaim, "My God, she must have been gorgeous in her day!"—was
a wart. On her nose. Near the tip of her nose. And not just any
common, everyday wart. Hers was a singular wart, a wart among warts,
the rotten ruby jewel in the crown of wartdom, the evil empress, the
burning witch, the tragic diva of the wart world.

Very nearly the circumference of a dime, reddish umber in hue, it
appeared spongy in texture, irregular in outline, resembling nothing so
much as a speck of hamburger, a crumb of rare ground beef that might
have spilled out of a taco. Even as she stood stationary, the wart
appeared to shudder, like the tiny heart of a shrew, and to radiate, as if
a fungus that grew on raw uranium was practicing for fission. Simultaneously feathery and lumpish, like a squashed raspberry, a pinch of dry
snuff, a tuft of moss that a wounded robin had bled upon, or the butt
end of an exploded firecracker, it caught the candlelight and in so
doing, seemed to enlarge before his eyes.

The really astonishing feature of the protuberance was neither its
size nor its color, its brim nor its woof, but the fact, not immediately
registered, that it was two-tiered: a second, smaller wart sat atop the
first, piggybacking, as it were, like a pencil eraser with a spinal hump,
or a little foam-rubber pagoda.

Switters didn't know what to say. Few did. Which is why, Domino
told him later, that her aunt had finally taken up the veil and also why
the aunt, herself, had been the one to break the silence. "It's a gift from
God," she said.

"Are you sure?" asked Switters.

"Positively. My uncle, Cardinal Thiry, gave me no peace about my
sexy appearance. Everywhere I went, men, including priests, stared or
made remarks. Even novices, other nuns, would eye me lasciviously.
My beauty was a distraction for others and an onus for myself. I shaved
my head and wore loose clothing, but it made scant difference. So, I
began to pray to the Almighty that if he wanted me to do his work, he
would grant me a blemish, a physical fault so unappealing that others
would be affected only by my deeds rather than my looks. I prayed
and prayed, often out in the Algerian desert alone, and—*voilà!*—one
morning I awoke with a honeycombed spot on my nose. The more I
prayed—I was the diametric opposite of Lady Macbeth—the more
glaring the spot became, but I wouldn't quit; and, in my thoughtless
avidity, obviously, I went too far. Even my wart grew a wart. We must
be careful what we pray for. In my old age, I'm left to wonder whether
God had not intended me to be a model all along. He gave me the gift
of beauty—which in your opinion can make the world a finer place—

and I rejected it, exchanged it for this other gift, this organic speckle that is more effective than any mask. Nowadays, I often mask the mask and imagine that I hear God's laughter in the wind."

"There's always cosmetic surgery," Switters suggested brightly.

She shook her head. The wart, like a plug of hairy gelatin, shook with it. "I've scorned one divine gift, I shan't scorn another."

After they'd taken their leave of her, Domino said, "Poor auntie. But you see, Mr. Switters, what prayer can do?" For days Domino had been urging him to pray with her for the removal of the shaman's curse.

"Exactly. If this curse is lifted, it could be replaced with something worse."

"Oh, but your affliction is not a gift from God. It was levied by the Devil."

He'd grinned. "I wouldn't be too sure about that," he said, half-stepping on his stilts so that she might keep up with him, and from somewhere faraway, he thought he heard a rustle of psychic foliage.

All that had occurred two weeks ago. Now, he was rapping at the apartment door for his second audience with the twice-masked beauty, an encounter that, due to his romp with Fannie, promised to be of a different tenor.

Switters was relieved to find Masked Beauty alone, that she wore her veil (the wart having struck him as pathological), and that her quarters were once again clouded with incense: he'd awakened too late to bathe properly, and Cupid's briny chlorines clung to him like clamskin britches. No sooner had he hopped off his stilts and onto the settee, however, than Domino breezed in, her bright eyes dancing, her cheeks ablaze. The pair of them, niece and auntie, stood facing him—apparently there was to be no tea—in their long cotton gowns. He switched on his best simper but sensed that the wattage was weak.

"What happened last night?" the abbess asked abruptly.

"Last night? Happened?" If innocence was toilet tissue, Godzilla could have wiped his butt with Switters's smile. "Why, uh, I took the liberty of providing a dollop of dinner music. Hope it didn't unduly impinge on anyone's digestion, or—"

"With Fannie."

"Oh? With Fannie." He shrugged. "The usual."

Domino rolled her eyes, a beautifully seriocomic gesture in a woman that neither Matisse nor his rival, Picasso, neither Modigliani nor Andrew Wyeth, had ever captured. "Usual for you, perhaps. How did it go for Fannie?"

Switters glanced around the room, as if searching for assistance or inspiration. Mute and motionless in her shrine, the shiksa-like Mary offered neither. "Why don't you ask Fannie?" he said finally and a little defiantly. What was this all about?

"We can't," Domino replied, after translating his response for the abbess. "She has gone."

"Gone? What do you mean?"

"A Syrian surveying team came by very early this morning. Had you arisen at a decent hour you might have noticed. We feared they were police hunting for you, but they only wanted to fill their water casks. When they left, Fannie left with them."

He scowled. "Voluntarily?"

"It would seem so. She took her belongings."

"No note?"

"Rien," said Masked Beauty.

"Nothing," said Domino.

"Well, dash my dumplings," said Switters.

The next half hour ranked among the most uncomfortable he'd ever spent. It made him long for the minefields along the Iraqi-Iranian border. As delicately as possible considering the nature of the previous night's activities, even waxing poetic when circumstance and élan allowed, he attempted to give the women an overview, from his perspective, of how it had gone for Sister Fannie.

He'd rather expected that Fannie would be a scratcher, a screamer, a biter, one of those bedroom banshees whose veneer of civilization was involuntarily ripped away by the claws of Eros. To his surprise, her volcano lay dormant, and no shifting of plates that his undulations engendered could precipitate a measurable eruption. The first time, she had grimaced and whimpered a little, because as gentle as he was, he had hurt her. The second time, she was more relaxed, and the third, in the dawn's early light, she'd actually cooed a couple of times with pleasure. For the most part, however, she'd been a quietly interested, curious, almost studious participant, eager enough but not in the least demonstrative.

And now she had decamped, leaving him to wonder if losing her virginity at thirty-four mightn't have been anticlimactic for her, a big disappointment, and, suspecting that it must have been his fault (which, alas, it might have been), and spurred on by her Asmodeus, she'd gone in search of a man or men who might better live up to her long-held expectations. Or, casting himself in a more favorable light, he considered that it might have been so overpoweringly wonderful for her that she'd been unable to speak or move out of sheer awe, and afterward she'd run off to sample a variety of partners in order to make comparisons. (Somehow, that seemed less feasible.) On the other hand, the experience—good, bad, or mediocre—might have buried her beneath such an unexpected avalanche of conditioned Catholic detritus that a spirit-bruising guilt had sent her scurrying home to Ireland to beg refuge as a lay sister in an orthodox nunnery.

"Je ne comprends pas." He shrugged. "I don't understand." Indeed, he didn't understand, and it would ruffle his masculine feathers for months to come, because Fannie neither returned nor sent any word.

Strangely enough, once he completed his full account of the deeds that had nearly demolished his narrow cot, Domino sighed, smiled sympathetically, and said that Fannie's exodus, as long as she came to no harm, was probably for the best. For her part, Masked Beauty said nothing more on the subject whatsoever, but instead inquired if Switters would mind teaching her how to operate a computer.

Beginning tomorrow morning, he e-mailed Bobby Case, *Matisse's blue nude will be sitting beside me at this very keyboard.*

Far out, Bobby wrote back. *Next thing I know, you'll be knitting socks with "Whistler's Mother."*

It's true, I suppose: I am learning to appreciate older women to whom I'm not related. But you needn't put Whistler's mother in quotes. The actual title of the painting to which you refer is "Arrangement in Gray and Black."

Thanks for correcting me. You're a true friend. I could have made a fucking fool of myself at any number of swell soirees.

"I wish I didn't," Switters told his pupil, "but when I leave at the end of September, I have to take this vampire with me."

Masked Beauty said she understood but that she had reason to believe that God would eventually provide the Pachomians with a computer of their own.

Right, thought Switters. *God going under the name of Sol Glissant.* Aloud, he explained that it wouldn't be quite the same, that the sisters would require a server, one with satellite capabilities since there were no telephone lines into the oasis, and should they obtain one, there would be hook-up charges and a monthly fee. When the old abbess asked who his server was, she was surprised to hear him answer, "The CIA." She'd thought he had severed his ties to that organization. He explained that officially he had, but that he still had friends at the pickle factory, clever angel boys who saw to it that he remained on-line.

"This research you're going to be doing—and the Langley search engine is the best that exists—will all be paid for by the CIA. No, no, it's not a problem. Even when it isn't bribing dictators and financing right-wing revolutions, the company's got so much money stashed under its mattress it can't sleep at night for the lumps. The CIA doesn't submit its accounts to Congress as specifically required by our Constitution, which means it's an illegal arm of government to begin with. So, even if we're stealing, we're stealing from outlaws."

"I'm unsure that that makes it more virtuous."

"Maybe not, but it certainly makes it more fun." At that point, Domino, who'd stopped in to see how the lesson was going and if Switters's French was up to the task, gave a light little laugh. He grinned back at her and neglected to inform either of them of the high probability that Langley was allowing him to remain on-line so that it could keep tabs on his activities, those, at least, to which he gave electronic voice.

He went on to warn Masked Beauty that the computer would tax her Christian patience, for while the machine was developed as a time-saving device, it frequently ate up far more time than telephone calls or physical trips to the library. "Some of the Web sites you may want to visit will be getting so many hits you'll have to queue up like a Chihuahua waiting for its turn at the world's last bone. There's nothing intrinsically wrong with the Internet, there're just too damn many people using it. Too damn many people using the roads, using energy, using parks and trees and beaches and cows and sewers and planes, using everything except good taste and birth control, although I suppose those two may be the same thing. I mean, did you get a look at the parents of the American septuplets? And did you think of geometric progression and shudder in horror? That one couple's one tasteless test-tube tumble could dork down the entire gene pool?"

Neither of the Frenchwomen was familiar with the "little miracle in Iowa," but, as he well knew, overpopulation and its myriad foul consequences was a paramount interest of theirs, so his rantlette garnered a favorable response. He was mistaken, however, in his supposition that Masked Beauty's travels on the Internet would be limited to sites either directly concerned with family issues or ones that provided the occasional forum for those who were. She would, with his assistance, visit such sites from time to time, but the primary focus of the Pachomian abbess's investigations proved to be on a different subject altogether. Fortuitously, perhaps, it was a subject to which Switters, the previous year, had devoted a modicum of attention.

June. July. August. September. Summer in the Northern Hemisphere—
which included, naturally and, as a matter of fact, emphatically, the
Syrian desert. The sun was as red as a baboon's backside. Relentless,
it rose each and every morning and like a malicious baboon climbing a staircase, treated those trapped on the ground floor to a rude
display.

Serrated with heat, abuzz with wind-whipped sand, the air outside
the compound was like a bouquet of hacksaws. Within the walls, plenteous pools of shade made life bearable, though it was far from cool. At
odd moments, orchard trees would quiver, as if trying to shake themselves free of the heat, or would tilt ever so slightly, as if longing to lie
down in their own shade. Then, all would grow still again until the
next brimstone breeze wafted with a gritty obduracy out of the great
oven door. It was an oven that knew well the stern exertions of soda
and salt, but not at all the puffy gaieties of yeast.

The pace inside the oasis was slow, and summer seemed to drone
on like a filibuster, even to Switters, who was one of those who believed that time in general was gathering speed. When he wasn't asleep
on his Fannie-crippled cot, perusing the odd paragraph of *Finnegans
Wake*, or exchanging the infrequent correspondence with Bobby or
Maestra, he was interacting, in various, particular, and for the most
part lackadaisical ways, with the eight pious pariahs with whom he
shared the outpost.

Where most of the ex-nuns were concerned, interaction was fairly
minimal. He joined them for simple meals at one or the other of
two rude wooden tables; and complaining that "Italian nights" were
too few and far between, he instigated thrice weekly "music nights,"
meaning that on Tuesdays, Thursdays, and Saturdays (the sisters fasted
on Sundays, and Switters was forced to steal into the garden then
and eat cucumbers off the vine), he'd lug his equipment into the dining
hall and play during supper a CD from his limited collection. It
goes without saying that he wished wine to flow on those occasions
("Let us be festive!" he'd cry, or "Let the good times roll!") but
succeeded in getting it served only on Saturdays. Saturday became
"blues night," for the women had rather taken to his two Big Mama
Thornton recordings; on Thursdays he treated them to the Mekons (about whom they were lukewarm), Frank Zappa (whom they
actively disliked), or Laurie Anderson (they were baffled but fascinated); while on Tuesdays, never without a tinge of concealed embarrassment, he'd spin Broadway show tunes (nearly everybody's
favorite).

In his self-appointed role as recreation director, he tried to get
them involved in making toy boats and racing them in the irrigation

troughs, but the Pachomians were not the Art Girls. Only Pippi exhibited either inclination or aptitude. The racing program quickly petered out, though not before Maria Deux scolded him in front of everyone for christening his stupid slat of wood *The Little Blessed Virgin*.

Speaking of Pippi's aptitude, the fact that her role as the convent's handyperson was never challenged by Switters disappointed those who had believed that in inviting him to stay, they would be getting "a man around the house," a Mr. Fix-It but his serious lack of dexterity didn't bother Pippi. Proud of her minor skills in carpentry and simple mechanics, she was protective of her domain. The Marias, however, were appalled, and Bob muttered once that it was no wonder that Fannie had fled. Not everybody got Bob's meaning.

Bob had taken over Fannie's duties as goatherd and chicken mistress, which left Maria Une a bit shorthanded in the kitchen. ZuZu mopped his room once a week, and either she or Mustang Sally delivered the pitchers of water with which he must constantly rehydrate himself in the Syrian summer, and the pails of water he must use to bathe. Since he elected not to attend chapel, he saw the six undernuns primarily at meals, although, of course, he glimpsed them going about their various chores as he stilted to and from his office. Beneath their placid, reverent, industrious exteriors, he began to sense an undercurrent of skittishness, almost a controlled hysteria, but he reasoned, correctly as it turned out, that it had nothing to do with him.

Despite his shortcomings in the areas of maintenance and religion, they seemed generally unresentful of his presence among them, finding him, well, novel, if not actually entertaining. At least, he didn't exacerbate their ingrained fear of maleness. (Was it not just such a fear that had led them to marry the mild and distant Christ, the one male figure who never would threaten them with brutish strength or callous sexuality?) Masked Beauty once referred to Switters as their *monstre sacré*, and among themselves that had become their pet name for him. When Mustang Sally ventured that as far as she could tell, he was neither monstrous nor sacred, Domino, in perfect imitation of his tone and his demeanor, had grinned and said, "I wouldn't be too sure about that."

As for Domino, his relationship with her had changed since the Fannie affair, but it was a subtle change. Had Fannie not fled, things might have gone more as Bobby had predicted, there might have been in her attitude a discernible measure of jealousy or scorn. As it was, she was aloof from him to such a smallish degree that he was forced periodically to suspect that he only imagined it. At no time was she unfriendly. On the other hand, at no time did she show up at his door again with flowers behind her ear.

During the first month of his residency, Domino had prayed over him quite a bit. A few times she succeeded in coaxing him to pray with her. He was sincere and respectful during their prayerful duets but also noticeably ill at ease. By late June, the exorcism instructions she'd requested from Sicilian Catholic sources had arrived via e-mail. On three successive Sunday evenings, after fasting all day, she had positioned and lit the prescribed number of candles, laid her hands on his head in the prescribed manner, and chanted the prescribed incantations. They were impressive little ceremonies (his favorite part was when she took his head in her hands), but since at their conclusion he refused to test the results, they were destined to be inconclusive. Goodness knows he wanted to please her, almost as much as he wanted the taboo dispelled, yet he had only to aim a trembling toe toward the ground than the stricken image of R. Potney Smithe flooded his brainpan, prompting a hasty, apologetic withdrawal. Frustrated, though sympathetic, Domino canceled further exorcisms and soon broke off the prayer sessions as well. He saw less of her after that.

His summer was spent most often in the company of Masked Beauty. For hours each morning, the abbess joined him in his baked little office, where they cooled themselves with tea and palm-frond fans, where he regained a level of fluency in French, and where the two of them gradually reached a level of comfort with the mask beneath the veil. It was such a nuisance raising the veil every time she took a sip of tea that after a week she'd asked his permission to bare her face. Of course, he assured her that it was fine, yet if "fine" meant that the wart was incapable of distracting him, that he was oblivious to it, or that he would ever become really used to it, then he had misspoken. Every Tuesday night, when the song, "I've Grown Accustomed to Your Face" from *My Fair Lady* resounded in the dining hall, he couldn't help but think, *Henry Higgins would be singing a different tune if he'd hooked up with Masked Beauty.*

Considering that in every other aspect she was as handsome as a person of her advanced age might hope to be, one would think that her little gift from God could be overlooked. It could not. *It* was the *monstre sacré*, a magical beast. He tried to compare it to the third eye of an Asian saint, but the wart was as blind as a mole rat and twice as ugly. Both repelling and compelling, it was charged with the grisly charisma of a serial killer. In its globby piled-on redness, it was a scarlet letter embroidered by an obsessive compulsive. And it was too damn vivid.

Nevertheless, they each made a certain peace with its imposition. He refused to allow the wart to unsettle him, she refused to brood over whether he might possibly be unsettled. Thus, they proceeded with their objectives.

"This little bastard operates on solar batteries, the likes of which are unknown to the civilian population. When you get your conventional desktop PC—and I wish we had one now because it'd be a lot easier to teach you on—you'll either have to run your generator during daylight hours or else, if you choose to go DC, charge its batteries almost every night. Burn more fossil fuel, in any case, I'm afraid. The dinosaurs died so that chat rooms might flourish."

Masked Beauty nodded. She didn't exactly take to cyberspace like a duck to orange sauce. Switters attributed this to her background rather than to her age. Look at Maestra, after all. As the weeks dragged dryly by, the abbess learned little more than how to boot up and shut down. One problem was that she could barely type. When there was a lengthy e-mail to transmit, Switters functioned as a stenographer, taking her dictation directly on the keyboard. A couple of things prevented him from becoming so bored that he unleashed his imp: one, the realization that it was Matisse's blue nude for whom he was clerking; and two, the delight he took in imagining the look on Mayflower Cabot Fitzgerald's steely face every time Langley intercepted another missive from Switters's address clamoring for papal reforms and advocating global birth control. And, ha-ha, what about those exorcism instructions?

Soon, however, it seemed that less and less of their time was devoted to e-mail and more and more to searching the Internet. The subject of their search was Mary aka Miriam aka Maria aka Marian aka the Blessed Holy Virgin Mother of God, the legendary Jewess whose maidenhead was alleged to have remained unpopped, sound as a dollar, even after she gave birth to a seven-pound baby boy.

In one of their earliest conversations, Domino had disclosed to Switters that the Pachomians were busily redefining their relationship to their religion: to Jesus, to Mary, and to God. Working now with Masked Beauty, it was clear to him that, for the present, their central focus was on Mary. Since Mary was mentioned in the Bible no more than a dozen times, and then mostly in passing, and since she was paid little or no attention in the first four hundred years of the Church's existence, any material upon which one might base a reevaluation of her was comparatively recent. That didn't mean that such material was scarce. Oh, no. Enough had been written about her—an astonishingly

huge amount in the late twentieth century—to fill every boxcar on the
Bethlehem, Golgotha & Santa Fe Railroad. If one aspect of the material
interested the abbess more than any other, she did not let on.

It was slow going. For reasons of both portability and government
security, the sophisticated little computer lacked a printer. Switters
read aloud the data off the screen—often struggling to translate as he
read, for the majority of it was in English or Italian—and Masked
Beauty wrote it down in French and by hand. Following their afternoon siestas, she and Domino would go over the longhand "printouts,"
and several evenings a week, the entire sisterhood would gather for
group discussions centered around the gleaned information. Switters
would have liked to have been included in those discussions, if for no
other reason than to blow the gunk out of his intellectual carburetor
and to keep his discursive spark plugs clean. It was a long, long way
from the C.R.A.F.T. Club, but, hey, a fully conscious man was an
adaptable man.

When the Mary material concerned, as it increasingly did, one or
more of the Virgin's alleged modern apparitions, he was especially
keen on joining the conversations. For better or worse, he'd trod the
electronic road to Fatima before, and he very well might have something to contribute. (Remembering that Suzy had not even sent him a
copy of her paper, a thin sheen of hurt lacquered his so-called fierce,
hypnotic green eyes, only to instantly evaporate in the arid air. He
couldn't blame her. Suzy's generation was unforgiving of dishonesty,
and rightly so. Alas, it remained rather blissfully unaware that it was
being lied to by corporate America—through the movies, TV shows,
and magazines it so adored—a hundred times a day, but that's another
story.) Alas, again, no invitation to participate in the dialogues
appeared forthcoming. Whether out of their exclusiveness or consideration for his own privacy, the doors to their meetings were closed
to him.

Then, late one night at the burnt end of August, as the happy
ghosts of long-deceased Bedouins rode the gritty desert winds (because they in life possessed the wisdom of physical nonattachment,
nomads enjoyed an unusually smooth transition into death and made
the world's most contented ghosts), he discovered himself in unexpected and unusual discourse, the consequences of which were to be
considerable.

It was well past midnight when he heard the bell. The bell ding-
donged him out of a dream in which red-eye gravy played a promi-

nent role. (Could it be that he'd munched one too many cucumbers, chewed a few too many chickpeas?) After the first four or five rings, he was alert; after the next four or five, he was on his stilts. He stood at the door, which had been left ajar to facilitate a nighttime stirring of day-parched air. There was more ringing, followed by male voices from outside the compound, followed by female voices from within. The male voices sounded angry, the female voices alarmed. Switters unzipped the crocodile valise. *Mr. Beretta! Rise and shine!*

Before he could pull on his trousers, there was a burst of automatic gunfire. In a flash, he was through the door, stilt-sprinting along a moonlit path in his boxer shorts. The ones with the baby ducks on them.

Something brighter than blood sang in his arteries. It climbed up his spine like the high notes of an anthem, clarifying his lungs, teasing his muscles and making them brisk. It wasn't a syrup of wahoo, really: it wasn't pure enough for that. Mostly, it was good old retro primal adrenaline, concocted in the fight-or-flight kitchen, the reptile house of the brain. But there were drops of wahoo in it. Had he said otherwise, he would have been untruthful.

He hadn't gotten far before he met Domino. She'd been running to his room to get him. "For the gate," she gasped. "They are demanding it open."

"Yeah, I can hear that. Although their French really sucks." He resumed his sprint. "And I have to say your English isn't much better."

"Switters! . . ." She was trying to keep up with him.

"It's okay, darling. It's just because you're excited."

Domino looked at him as if he were completely demented. "This is serious!" she cried.

"Ah, yes," he agreed. She could have sworn his tone was sarcastic, or at least facetious.

By then, they had reached the gate. All of the sisters, with the exception of Masked Beauty, were gathered there. A couple of them had their hands clasped, apparently in prayer, but they were amazingly calm and composed. On the other side of the thick mud wall, men were shouting in broken French. They were saying that the oasis was a holy garden of Allah that had been desecrated by handmaidens of the great Western Satan. "Ah, yes," muttered Switters again. This time, his voice had overtones of boredom and weariness. "Infidels!" the men screamed repeatedly. There was another savage spurt of gunfire. Switters yelled to the women to take cover, although he realized that the bullets, for the moment, were being sprayed in the air.

"They're drunk," whispered Domino, who was crouched at his side.

"Yeah, but not on arrack. Help me onto these stilts." He was transferring to the taller pair that Pippi kept at the gate.

"Killer-B stuff?" she suggested, steadying the poles.

He grinned at her approvingly and nodded. "That's some toxic honey. Blind a man and make him crazy."

"Do be careful."

Leaning the stilts and his body against the gate so that his hands would be free, he slid open the grate and stared down on the men, who raised their rifles and stepped back a few feet to stare up at him. There were only three of them. They had sounded like more. Dressed in cheap civilian khakis and those red-and-white checkered headdresses that always looked as if they'd been yanked off tabletops in a suburban spaghetti parlor ("They've copped our Italian night!" he wanted to yell to Pippi), the men had arrived in a dented old Peugeot sedan.

He greeted them in polite Arabic, and it would have been difficult to determine which had surprised them more, his language (it was an extended greeting and as flowery as the finest Arabic often can be) or his sex. The fact that the moon was illuminating—and the grate framing—a grin spiked with strife-torn teeth, a pair of gleaming f.h.g. eyes, and the barrel of a most capable-looking revolver, must also have contributed to their astonishment.

After a period of rather stunned silence, the men all began to clamor at the same time. Speaking Arabic now, one asked what kind of man would live in a nest of unclean women, another demanded to know what a foreigner was doing speaking in the tongue of great Allah, and the third inquired if Switters was prepared for death.

To the first question, he replied, "A *lucky* man"; to the second, "It's as stupidly ethnocentric to think God's language is Arabic as it is to believe Jesus spoke King James English"; and to the last, "Everybody on earth, unfortunately, is prepared for death, but very damn few are prepared for life." The eloquence of his Arabic surprised even him: he must have chipped the rust off when traveling with the Kurds and Bedouins. While the attackers were quietly jabbering among themselves about his replies, he interrupted to ask if they might tell him a joke.

His request bewildered them—and rekindled their hostility. "Tell you a joke? Do you think this is a funny matter?"

"Hey, it's written in the Koran that the gates of Paradise open wide for he who can make his companions laugh." He quoted the chapter and verse, challenging them to look it up. "I was wondering if you boys might be among those favored by Heaven."

That threw them into a state of consternation. For a good three or four minutes, they conferred with one another, occasionally scratching their kaffiyehs with their rifles, as if trying to remember a punch line. Finally, the eldest of the trio (all under thirty) stepped forward and announced, "It is irrelevant to Heaven whether or not we can make you laugh because you are not our companion."

Well, that was reasonable enough, and he told them so. "You fellows aren't as dumb as I originally believed." At this, they seemed oddly pleased. Then, again listing chapter and verse, he brought up Mohammed's prohibition against priests, asking them why, since the Koran clearly stated that each individual must approach God singularly and alone, had modern Islam spawned such an authoritarian hierarchy of ayatollahs, imams, and mullahs.

This time, their consultation was more brief. "These exalted authorities to whom you refer," the spokesman said, "are not priests but scholars." He stepped back rather smugly, confident that he'd had the final word, unaware that he was dealing with Switters.

Though Switters didn't know the Arabic for *semantics*, he, nevertheless, got his point across. "They can call themselves 'scholars' until the camels come home," he said, "but the truth is, they function as priests and bishops and cardinals, and you know they do. They intercede between a man and Allah."

All four of them bantered about that for a while, making a lot of fuss but getting nowhere, until Switters eventually said, "Show me, if you can, where it says in the Koran that a devout Muslim has the duty or the right to kill those who don't believe as he does. Show me where Mohammed sanctions the murder of those of another faith—or no faith at all—and I'll unbolt this gate and let you in to bravely slaughter these unarmed women." When there was no immediate response, he added, "It is not the Prophet who advocates violent behavior but ambitious ayatollahs, and the politicians who share their vested interests."

Of course, the men could not refute him with scripture, as the Koran was on Switters's side, but they argued with him, bringing up such things as the Israeli displacement of Palestinians and the murderous legacy of the Christian Crusaders, neither of which he was wont to defend in the slightest. In fact, he seconded everything they said about the Crusades, plainly exhibiting his own disgust and revulsion, yet refusing to accept any residual guilt, claiming that it had nothing to do with him *or* them. He understood, however, that Arabic peoples had a different sense of time, of history, than a Westerner such as himself; had, like the Kandakandero, a different relationship with the past and their ancestors.

After that, the discussion cooled down. The night was cooling down as well, and on the ground behind him, the ex-nuns were beginning to shiver in their thin cotton gowns. The talk continued, though,

for at least another two hours, during which many cross-cultural theological issues were fairly evenly debated. In the end, the attackers,
drained and a trifle flabbergasted by the encounter, made as if to depart. Just to make sure, to cap the melting sundae with a tangy cherry,
Switters announced that the compound was under the personal aegis
of President Hafez al-Assad, Audubon Poe, and Pee-wee Herman, and
if any harm came to its occupants, heads would roll all the way to
Mecca. "Take it up with those worthy gentlemen if you have any
doubts. Tell them Switters sent you."

The men nodded gravely. Then, following an exchange of formal,
fairly cordial farewells, they climbed into the Peugeot, which, sus-
pensefully, took as long to start as a barrio limo, and drove off into the
sands.

"Oh, goody! My trusty starship."

At some juncture during the seemingly interminable bull session,
Domino had slipped away to his room and fetched his wheelchair.
Now, he dropped onto it. Once he was seated, the sisters, cold, fraz-
zled, some very nearly asleep on their feet, crowded around him as if
he were a conquering hero. Women love these fierce invalids home
from hot climates?

"Magnifique!" exclaimed Masked Beauty. The abbess had shown up
at the gate soon after the engagement began and, having acquired a
rudimentary familiarity with Arabic as long ago as her service in
Algeria, translated for the others, as best she could, the highlights of
the debate. She had arrived veiled, in the event that she had to confront strangers, but had removed the cloth now, and it dangled from
her fingers. A ray of moonlight striking her double-decker wart made
the growth resemble a dab of ketchup-coated curds. *Cottage cheese with
ketchup,* he thought. *Richard Nixon's favorite meal. Probably got the recipe from
John Foster Dulles. Patooie!*

"How do you know so well Islam?" the abbess asked.

"Oh, I used to flip through the Koran—and the Bible—and the
Talmud—occasionally," he said. "Before I discovered *Finnegans Wake.*"

Thanking and congratulating him again, Masked Beauty patted his
curly top. Then, shooing her charges ahead of her like geese, she, and
they, went off to bed. Domino stayed behind, however, intent on
pushing his chair. "I don't believe I can sleep," she said, "but you must
be exhausted." He claimed that he was as buzzed as a June bug up a
maypole, so they repaired to his room for a spot of cold tea. It was the

first time she had visited him there since the Fannie affair at the beginning of summer. She stood with her back to him while he pulled on a
shirt and trousers. Baby ducks, *adieu*.

When they were settled, he in his Invacare, she on the stool (the
cot was avoided as deliberately, as warily, as if it were an altar upon
which certain arcane, unmentionable rituals were known to have occurred), she told him how grateful she was that the incident at the gate
had concluded without bloodshed. He said that no self-respecting
cowboy would have let such a splendid opportunity to fire his gun
pass him by, but that he supposed a peaceful solution was best for all
concerned. "Those agitated stooges probably have innocent kids to
support."

"It's their religion," she said accusingly.

He corrected her. "It's their religion plus *your* religion."

"Our lives were threatened, and you are saying that my religion
must share the blame? What have we done?"

He sighed. "You've tried to own God," he said. "Just like them."

Domino looked puzzled. Then she nodded. "Okay, I think I see
what you mean. The Moslems and the Christians are each insisting
that their way to God is the only way, so if only one side is right, then
those on the other side . . ."

"Having hocked their lives, are left to face death without the pawn
ticket. That smarts. And remember: there're three sides to every story,
including the monotheism story."

She curtly dismissed the Jews, however, stating that Judaism's
Killer B's wouldn't figure into the final equation. Before he could challenge that assertion—and, really, all he was wanting to do was to settle
back and unwind—she asked what the name *Fatima* meant to him.

"It's the podunk burg in Portugal where that most profoundly
splendid of oxymorons, the Virgin Mother, supposedly yo-yoed the
sun in 1917." One didn't play cyberspace errand boy for Marian enthu-
siasts of all ages without picking up a tidbit or two. "Fatima, Lourdes,
Bosnia; Knock, Ireland; Tepeyac, Mexico. Isn't it fascinating how Mary
usually seems to turn up in ugly, boring, economically depressed
locales in dire need of a tourist attraction? Projecting, we could forecast that she'll show up next—where? Western Oklahoma, probably.
Middle of Saskatchewan. Except that those places don't have enough
Catholics on site to organize a fish fry."

Ignoring his sarcasm, she said, "*Fatima* was also the name of
Mohammed's daughter."

"Yeah, you're right. The Prophet's favored offspring. That hadn't
occurred to me."

"So, the question is: are they connected? These two Fatimas?"

"Everything is connected. But the links can sometimes be hard to uncover." He took a gulp of tea. She took a sip. Outside, a rooster crowed. It sounded like a spastic adolescent trying to imitate Tarzan. "Too bad roosters aren't more like parrots," he said. "We could train them to crow inspiring things like, 'People of the world, relax!' instead of kicking off our day with a lot of cock-a-doodle-do."

Domino smiled in spite of herself. "Oh, you Switters. I don't know whether you are a virtue or a vice."

"Neither do I, but why does it have to be one or the other? Why, for that matter, can't we be simultaneously monotheistic *and* polytheistic?"

"Ugh! Polytheism? Ooh-la-la! All that noisy jumble of gods hiding in tree trunks and chimney hearths, with necklaces of skulls and more arms than a granddaddy spider. Abominable!"

"They tend to teem, all right, but overlooking the fact that some of them are too damn vivid, couldn't we just accept them as various aspects of the one God, who's an eternal, absolute mystery and can never be pinned down or accurately described, anyway?" He gulped the last of the tea. "If a person is truly devout, why couldn't they be both a Christian *and* a Moslem? And a Jew? Don't look at me like I'm a naive ninny. They all rolled out of the same pasture. Ol' Abraham and his peevish herdsmen buddies—cowboys, now that I think of it— inventing the one-god-our-god-and-he-be-a-bruiser concept as a response to and a rebellion against the sexual superiority of women."

"I might have known you'd bring sex into it sooner or later."

"If you have a problem with the sexual complexion of the universe, take it up with Mother Nature. I'm just one of her baby boys."

The rooster sang an encore. Then, another. But so far no single photon of dawnlight had squirmed through the curtain threads. "If women had played an active role in shaping our relationship to God, everything might be different," she said. "There might not be a conflict between the Church and Islam."

"There might not *be* any Church and Islam," he interjected. "Women wouldn't have seen the need for them."

"As it is. . . ." She sighed and shrugged. After a pause, she said, "Despite what I know and you do not, I'm unwilling to concede defeat—or switch sides." She rose and smoothed out her dress. Evidently she'd pulled it on in a hurry when the disturbance had awakened her: he could tell she was bereft of underwear. Her nipples pushed against the cotton like urchins pressing their noses against a candy store window. In the candleshine, her pubis was faintly outlined, like a map of a phantom peninsula. He considered it wise that she leave, but since the conversation had taken the turn that it had, he felt he simply had to ask:

"Have you never heard of the neutral angels?"

Suppose the neutral angels were able to talk Yahweh and Lucifer— God and Satan, to use their popular titles—into settling out of court. What would be the terms of the compromise? Specifically, how would they divide the assets of their earthly kingdom?

Would God be satisfied to take loaves and fishes and itty-bitty thimbles of Communion wine, while allowing Satan to have the red-eye gravy, eighteen-ounce New York steaks, and buckets of chilled champagne? Would God really accept twice-a-month lovemaking for procreative purposes and give Satan the all-night, no-holds-barred, nasty "can't-get-enough-of-you" hot-as-hell fucks?

Think about it. Would Satan get New Orleans, Bangkok, and the French Riviera and God get Salt Lake City? Satan get ice hockey, God get horseshoes? God get bingo; Satan, stud poker? Satan get LSD; God, Prozac? God get Neil Simon; Satan, Oscar Wilde?

Can anyone see Satan taking pirate radio stations and God being happy with the likes of CBS? God getting twin beds; Satan, waterbeds; God, Minnie Mouse, John Wayne, and Shirley Temple; Satan, Betty Boop, Peter Lorre, and Mae West; God, Billy Graham; Satan, the Dalai Lama? Would Satan get Harley motorcycles; God, Honda golf carts? Satan get blue jeans and fish-net stockings; God, polyester suits and pantyhose? Satan get electric guitars; God, pipe organs; Satan get Andy Warhol and James Joyce; God, Andrew Wyeth and James Michener; God, the 700 Club; Satan, the C.R.A.F.T. Club; Satan, oriental rugs; God, shag carpeting? Would God settle for cash and let Satan leave town with Mr. Plastic? Would Satan mambo and God waltz?

Would Almighty God be that dorky? Or would he see rather quickly that Satan was making off with most of the really interesting stuff? More than likely he would. More than likely, God would holler, "Whoa! Wait just a minute here, Lucifer. I'll take the pool halls and juke joints, *you* take the church basements and Boy Scout jamborees. You handle content for a change, pal. I'm going to take—*style!*"

Because Bobby Case had convinced him that any neutral angel worthy of the name would have recognized that Yahweh and Lucifer could no more be truly separated than the two sides of a coin (they needed each other for balance, for completion, for their identity, for their survival—which may have been why the more reflective of the angels had elected to remain neutral in the first place), Switters reserved speculative rants such as the preceding for his private entertainment (except, of course, when circumstance and/or magnitude of substance abuse dictated otherwise). Therefore, he treated Domino to a factual, relatively straightforward presentation of the neutral angel information as it had survived in Levantine folklore and biblical allusion (often the same thing) for four thousand years. Domino was incredulous, but rather than dismissing the story out of hand, agreed to ponder it and to investigate it with what resources she had at her disposal. "That's funny," she said, and she smiled that special smile of hers that was such a perfect blend of unintentional cynicism and warmest charity. "Not long ago, I would have said that I would pray over it." She paused. She wrinkled her brow in a way that caused a third of it to disappear. "Switters, are you ever, on your own, inclined toward prayer?"

He barely hesitated. "When I feel I'm in need of shark repellent, I try to pray. When I feel I'm in need of smelling salts, I try to meditate. I'm not saying that one's necessarily superior to the other—both are capable of being reduced to a kind of metaphysical panhandling—but if more people smelled the salts and woke the hell up, they'd find they wouldn't need to be fretting about sharks all the time."

"And what about Serpents?"

He grinned. "You mean the Snake in the garden? The Snake is good, Domino. The Snake is smelling salts on a rope."

Before either of them could prepare for it, she stepped to his wheelchair, bent over—loose breasts bobbing like turtles on a buckboard, hair swinging around to eclipse her moonish cheeks—and kissed him quite emphatically on the bridge of his nose.

"I like you in a way that is too unusual," she whispered.

"The feeling is mutual," he said.

Then the rooster crowed her out the door. As he listened to her footsteps disappearing, crunchily, down the sandy path, he thought he overheard the slick voice of Satan. And Satan, in this aural hallucination, was saying, "Okay, Yahweh, here's a proposition for you: why don't you take the world's bargirls under your wing and let me have a turn with the nuns?"

In the annals of Switters lore, the diurnal interval following the aborted terrorist attack would be forever known as the Day of the Hiccuping Jackass.

It may or may not have been an omen, but the day began with Switters awakening late to discover that he had the wrong pair of stilts by his cot. Domino had placed the poles across his lap prior to wheeling him back to his room, and at the time neither he nor she had noticed (the moon had set, and they were both a bit groggy) that it was Pippi's original, tall pair she'd retrieved and not the customized, two-inches-above-the-ground stilts, the ones he'd designed to provide an ambulatory state of ersatz enlightenment. *Oh, well,* he thought, *these might be fun for a change,* so he stork-walked to the office on stilts that put his unbreakfasted mouth at fig level, higher than the ripe lemons that dangled from their branches like bare lightbulbs in a nineteenth-century shoe factory.

Masked Beauty had slept late, as well, and she arrived at the office only moments before Switters. She greeted him with fresh tea and fresh compliments on his handling of the previous night's situation. Then she announced that she had had quite enough Marian material for the time being and she wanted him to begin searching the Net for information about Islam. It wasn't mainstream Islam in which she was interested, she was well versed in that, but the more esoteric doctrines.

Switters studied her, fighting to keep his focus off the wart. "Expecting more trouble?" he asked.

"No, no. The nearest village is in the hills, thirty kilometers away over rough terrain. Men do not come here easily. The Syrians in general are sympathetic people, nice people. It is only the Muslim Brotherhood that makes the problem for Christians, but, then, fundamentalists are the same everywhere, are they not?"

"Yeah. Their desperate craving for simplicity sure can create complications. And their pitiful longing for certainty sure can make things unsteady."

"I imagine that word somehow has spread about our excommunication, and that has inflamed those who are already disposed toward fanatical piety."

"Maybe, but I saw on the Net that the U.S. military recently retaliated against terrorist operations in Sudan and Afghanistan, and you can bet that's put a bee up many a djellabah. Good thing our visitors mistook me for a Frenchman."

"A mistake no Frenchman would ever make," she said, referring both to his accent and his grammar. "Now, what I wish to investigate is—"

The abbess was interrupted by a knock, and they glanced up to see Bob standing in the open doorway, wearing an expression that was almost as fritzed as her hair. Generally, Bob appeared as if she'd been sired by one of the Marx Brothers—perhaps all four—and now she was alternating between looks of sheepish contrition, like Harpo after striking a sour note on his instrument of choice; popeyed incredulity, like Chico watching the diva disgorge the aria in *A Night at the Opera*; waggy disgust, like Groucho learning that his best jokes had once again been eviscerated by network censors; and peevish indignation, like Zeppo sensing that it was his fate to be perpetually upstaged by his three siblings.

Bob apologized profusely for the interruption, but, *mon Dieu*, she hadn't asked to be put in charge of livestock, she wasn't a farmgirl, if only Fannie had fared better at the hands of some she could name; but Fannie had fled, and what was she, Bob, supposed to do in such a crisis, et cetera, et cetera. Masked Beauty calmed her with reassuring clucks and waves of her veil, and eventually they drew from Bob the source of her fluster. It seemed that the donkey had hiccups. Had had them for forty-eight hours, give or take an hour. Bob kept thinking they'd go away, as her own hiccuping always had, but they'd persisted, maybe even worsened, and the poor dumb creature couldn't eat, couldn't sleep, was becoming unsteady and weak, and if something wasn't done, surely it would hiccup itself to death.

As Bob appealed to Masked Beauty, Masked Beauty appealed to Switters, and Switters, without stopping to consider how it might come across in French, said, "People of the world, relax. I'll give it a shot."

First, he stilted over to the little stableyard, where the donkey was tethered. Sure enough, the beast was racked with spasms. They were occurring about every other second, and each time its diaphragm contracted, its skinny sides would inflate and deflate, as if it had strayed into the product inspection line at a whoopee cushion factory, forcing from its epiglottis a jerky sound somewhere between a cough, a sneeze, a fairy choking on fairy dust, and a socially prominent dowager trying to stifle a belch. Repeatedly the donkey's donkey larynx was issuing the first quarter-note of a bray, a hee-haw from which the *haw* and most of the *hee* had been scrunched and extinguished.

"Pathological," muttered Switters, surveying the scene with a mixture of pity and revulsion. Then, gathering his wits, he sent Bob to the kitchen for sugar. "Tell Maria Une I want . . ." He surveyed the animal. "Tell her I'll need most of a small sack. You know: at least a kilo." Next, he dispatched Pippi (who'd come over from her shop to see what was the matter) to fetch a pail of water.

When the sisters returned (Bob was followed by Maria Une, who was demanding to know what was to become of her precious sweetener), Switters spilled the sugar into the water bucket and stirred it with a rake handle. He set the solution under the donkey's convulsive muzzle, but the beast was too distressed to take more than a few laps of it. They waited. The donkey hicced, then lapped again. It obviously liked the taste but simply couldn't consume the mixture with enough speed or in sufficient quantity for it to be therapeutically effective. "Okay, Bob, you restrain the noble jackass. Pippi, prepare to pour."

With that, Switters destilted onto the scrawny back, straddling it as though he were Don Quixote about to ride into war. "Bring on the windmills!" he yelled, as he grasped the slobbery muzzle, top and bottom, and pried the greenish-yellow teeth apart. "Whew! I'm a model of dental elegance compared to you, buckaroo. Come on, Pippi, pour. Pour!"

"*Assez?*"

"No. More. The whole damn bucket. But not so fast, you don't want to drown the thing."

The donkey was struggling mightily, causing Switters, atop it, to resemble a rodeo clown, but they eventually succeeded in emptying most of the sugar water down the creature's gullet. Masked Beauty held the stilts for Switters, and, with considerable difficulty, he transferred onto them. The little ass was braying now, genuinely braying, and retching as if it might spew out every drop with which they'd flooded its tank. In a minute or two, however, it settled down, seeming dimly to notice that its demon had been exorcised. The humans, too, noticed that the hiccuping had ceased, and as the healed patient squeezed its head into the bucket to lick up residual sugar, they applauded.

Joining in the applause was Domino, who had come upon the scene about the time that Switters was mounting his spasmodic steed.

"*Incroyable!*" she called. "Do your talents have no end?" She was abeam with mock adulation.

Shuffling the poles, he hopped awkwardly around to face her. "Switters," he growled, as if, with gruff modesty, introducing himself. "Errand boy, acquired taste; roving goodwill ambassador for the Redhook Brewing Company, Seattle, Washington; and"—doffing his hat, he attempted a courtly bow, an exercise not easily performed on stilts—"large-animal veterinarian."

(Sometime, perhaps that evening at dinner, he would confess that his grandmother had taught him the hiccup remedy. Was it before or after she taught him to cure childhood moodiness with Bessie Smith, Muddy Waters, and Big Mama Thornton? He couldn't remember.)

Whether disposed to savor the passing moment or with a view toward advancing himself further in Domino's good graces, he swept his hat in an ironic parody of a knightly gesture, as though, with ostentatious ceremony, he was dedicating his triumph to her, his lady. His backside happened to be to the donkey—rather too close to the donkey for the donkey's liking—and at that exact, fastuous instant, the ungrateful creature lashed out with its hind legs, one of its hooves kicking thin air but the other dealing Switters's right stilt a blow that sent him flying.

Domino dove forward to catch him. She underestimated his momentum, however, and they both ended up on the ground, he on top of her. She was flat on her back. He lay facedown, his manly jut of a chin resting just above her darling little jut of a nose. In that uneven alignment, their eyes could not meet, so he stared for a few seconds, while recovering his wind, at the rocky soil just beyond the crown of her head. "Are you okay?" he asked, afraid to move a muscle.

"Oui. Yeah. Ooh-la-la!" She laughed nervously. "I was trying to keep your feet from touching the earth."

And she had. The toes of his sneakers rested upon her shins.

"So!" he said. "You do believe in the curse."

Still not moving, he could feel her half-face flushing beneath his half-face. He could also feel her body, flattened and yet somehow buoyant, under the weight of his body. She was as soft as a marshmallow bunny, he thought, yet simultaneously as firm as a futon. Most of the words that she stammered about her action being intended only for his peace of mind were lost in the folds of his throat—and in the concerned chatter of those Pachomians who'd clustered around them.

It was at about that point—and no more than ten seconds had passed—that he became aware of his pen of regeneration and of the red ink rushing into its inkwell. It was positioned against her belly, not far from where the concave yolk of her umbilicus simmered in its downy poacher, and an equal distance, more or less, from that vital area and favored masculine destination that is known in the Basque language (Switters could verify this) as the *emabide* and sometimes as the *ematutu*. Whatever the proximities, and no matter what *it* was called in Basque, Switters's rod of engenderment was growing more rigid, more perpendicular, by the moment; was behaving, in fact, like a hydraulic jack, threatening, he imagined, to lift him right off her, suspending him above her prone body as if he were a plate on a shaft, a bobbin balanced on a spindle.

Domino had round cheeks. She had the kind of nice round cheeks that made a person want to press one of their own cheeks against one of hers, to hold it there, slide it around a bit, the way an affectionate mother might lay a cheek against her baby's bare bottom, or a boy put his cheek to a cold, ripe cantaloupe, sniffing its lush, musky fruitiness out of the corner of his nostrils. Domino had those kind of cheeks, and Switters admittedly had sometimes had that kind of reaction to them, but, naturally, had never yielded to the temptation, nor, alas, could he really yield to it now, despite this unusual opportunity, for his cheeks had landed a few inches to the north of her cheeks, and cheek-to-cheek congruency could be attained only were he to slide downward, a southerly migration that, to phrase it crudely, would have put the carrot dangerously close to the rabbit hole.

As it was, he was pronged against her lower abdomen in such a spring-loaded fashion that he could feature himself, without use of hands or feet, vaulting over the henhouse. Undoubtedly, she was aware of the protuberance—she was practically run through by it: nun on a stick—and that awareness must account for the fact that she was silent, tense, and seemed to be holding her breath. As his own embarrassment turned gradually to panic, he rejected the notion of trying to collapse the bulb by mentally picturing radically anti-erotic images (his mother with the stomach flu, for example, or a Pomeranian humping a sofa leg) and, instead, dug the heels of his hands into the earth and flipped himself off her, onto his back. His talents had no end?

Gasping slightly from the effort, he lay there beside her with his feet in the air, looking like an advertisement for an aerosol insecticide. (Of course, a dead bug wouldn't be sporting an erection. Or would it? Hanged men are reputed to be so affected, why not a zapped beetle? Perhaps there was a reason why they were called "cockroaches." And think of the Spanish fly.)

The sisters assisted Domino to an upright position, whereupon she brusquely brushed off her blue chador (which is what Syrian women called their long cotton gowns), and retreated, muttering that there were important matters that required her immediate attention. The others then attempted to hoist Switters back onto his stilts, but the ex-linebacker's bulk was too much for them. Bob, understandably grateful, and seemingly oblivious to the accidental subtext of his topple onto Domino, volunteered to go fetch his wheelchair. "Merci, Madame Bob," he said weakly.

For the nearly ten minutes that it took Bob to return with the chair, he lay there like a yogi in the dead-bug asana, growing slowly flaccid; shielding his eyes from the pulsating radiation of a sun, now directly overhead, that resembled a phoenix egg laid in a campfire and impaled on a laser; and talking to his abnormally elevated feet. "Be patient, ol' pals," he whispered to his feet. "Please. Another month, that's all. Then we're hot-footing it—that's just a figure of speech—to South-goddamn-America. And one way or another, feets, I'm gonna set you free."

For the next couple of weeks, Domino and Switters were shy around each other. In fact, without it being overly obvious, even to themselves, and without going to any great lengths to achieve it, they were in avoidance of each other. Cloistered in the confines of an eight-acre oasis, it was, of course, impossible that their paths wouldn't cross several times daily, but when such encounters occurred, they'd smile, exchange a polite nod or two, fidget, squirm, and hasten on their separate ways before the headless chicken—the totem bird of discomposure—could find hemorrhage space in their cheeks. Inevitably, one or the other would steal a backward glance. Switters, having been trained as a sneak, was more adept at this than she.

Their lone conversation during this period concerned the round, mud tower that rose above the compound like a silo for a Scud of manna, a missile with a warhead of milk and honey. He'd been stilting past the decrepit wooden door in the tower's base when Domino and ZuZu exited through it, carrying pails, brooms, and mops. "Oh, hi," said Domino, straining to sound casual. "Uh, now that we've finally given the tower room a cleaning, you might want to spend some time up there."

"Why would I want to do that?"

"Your feet are forbidden to touch the ground."

"That's the story."

"And that would include the ground floor of a building."

"The way I interpret it."

"Yes, but what about the floors above ground level? The third floor or the twenty-third? Wouldn't they be safe? The same as the floor of the car or of the airplane flying above the earth."

He tugged at his hair, which, having been trimmed by Mustang Sally that very afternoon was, for the first time in weeks, shorter in length than her own. "Good question. I've asked it myself on countless occasions. The answer's in the fine print. But I can't read the fine print, because . . ." His voice trailed off.

"Because," she said, "there isn't any fine print. There isn't any large print, either."

"It's an unusual contract in that respect. However, I plan on renegotiating it in the very near future."

At this reference to his impending departure, there was a slight but perceptible shift in Domino's body language. Apparently caught somewhere between relief and regret, and wishing to display neither, she excused herself. As she marched off with her mop, she gestured at the tower top, tilting her head toward it in such a manner as to suggest without words that he at least ought to have a look up there.

Oh, yeah? Climb stairs on stilts? That would certainly promote my blood into active circulation. In the process of mentally rejecting her suggestion, he peered inside, where, as he soon noticed, there didn't happen to be any stairs. Rather, there was a ladder: wooden, old (much too old to have been built by Pippi), barely angled, and probably thirty feet in height. Despite the fact that it looked like something devised by prehistoric pueblo daredevils, it seemed sturdy enough, and, moreover, he felt confident he could plant his feet on its rungs with impunity as far as the taboo was concerned. Nevertheless, Switters did not climb the ladder. Not that day.

Through the dry biblical whisper of the groves—past twiggy branches adangle with seed-stuffed pomegranates and under the toad-tongued leaves of almond trees—he clumped back to the office at a pace that precluded any prolonged enjoyment of arboreal shade. He was bent on reading one more time the e-mail he'd received from his grandmother that morning, the note that informed him that Suzy, having "gotten into a speck of trouble" in Sacramento, had been sent to live with Maestra for a year and would be attending the Helen Bush School in Seattle. What perplexed Switters about the note, what prompted him to keep rereading it, was that he couldn't ascertain from its ambiguous flavor whether Maestra was encouraging him to be sure to stop by on his way to Peru or warning him to stay away from her door at all costs.

"**so,**" **said masked** Beauty. "You will be leaving us in a fortnight."

"More or less," Switters concurred. "The exact day depends on when the supply truck shows up." He had the feeling that sometime during the eighteen hours since he'd happened upon Domino at the tower, the niece and her aunt had discussed the fact that his stay among them was drawing to a close.

Masked Beauty was pouring tea, the ritual with which their morning routine began. He'd already booted up and was stealing a quick glance at Maestra's e-mail, as if overnight it might have undergone a syntagmatic rearrangement, or he, after a night's rest, might find in it a nugget of information that had escaped his earlier scrutiny. She bent by his chair, smelling, as always, of incense and rough soap; her skin scoured, her chador as crisp as if it were a habit. She was laundered, she was regal, she was immortalized by Matisse, of whom she would seldom speak, and bewarted by God, of whom she spoke frequently, though often in a tone of bewilderment.

"Yes, the supply truck." She sighed. "If Almighty God is not blessing soon our treasury, that truck won't be bringing us much more petrol." She shrugged then and smiled, and it would have been considered a smile worth admiring had it been situated at a greater distance from the mutated mushroom cap on her nose. "Ah, but dear St. Pachomius got along just fine without a generator, did he not?" It was a rhetorical question, and the abbess, in that unmodulated, childish voice of hers that was at such odds with both her brittle majesty and her brazen defect, went on to say, "In any case, Mr. Switters, I do hope your sojourn here has been in some tiny measure agreeable."

His mood was languid, tongue still slack from the wordless joy of awakening to cuckoo calls in a sunlit cubicle far from any confines that conceivably might be labeled *home*, so the approval rating that she seemed to be seeking—the testimony to adequacy if not the rave review—failed to gush forth from him. Later that evening, when he had taken on as much wine as he could quietly accommodate, he would become downright gassy in his tribute, but at that lackadaisical moment, with his ears adjusting to her French, he yawned, stretched, and said only, "Beats Club Med all to hell."

Having finished tea, they got down to business, the first order of which was the posting of e-mail to several United Nations agencies on the subject of birth control. "Now that I've been excommunicated, my protests lack the authority they once had," she said. "On the other hand, I am at liberty to show less restraint." She debated whether it was worthwhile to also e-mail Western heads of state. "The greater the population grows and the more threatening the social and environmental problems that that growth causes, it seems the more reluctant our leaders are to address the issue. Crazy, no?"

"Ever wonder," Switters asked, "why people get so worked up over whale hunts, yet object very little to the killing of cattle? It's because whales are rare and intelligent and untamed, whereas cows are commonplace and stupid and domesticated." Presumably he was referring to the manner in which the powers that be, with the greedy compliance of the media and the eager assistance of evangelicals, were busily bovinizing humanity, seeking to produce a vast herd of homogenized consumers, individually expendable, docile, and, beyond basic job skills, not too smart; two-legged cows that could be easily milked and, when necessary, guiltlessly slaughtered. If that was his meaning, however, he did not belabor her with it.

"You failed to mention *beautiful*," said the abbess.

"Pardon?"

"Beautiful. You, such a champion of beauty: I imagined you would claim that the whale is more revered than the cow because the whale is the more beautiful."

"That's, indeed, the case," he said. "But if they weren't so damned ubiquitous, cows also might be considered beautiful."

"Familiarity breeds contempt?"

"Breeding breeds contempt. Beyond a certain point. The dignity of any species diminishes in direct ratio to its compulsion to teem, or to the extent that it allows teeming to be foisted upon it."

Masked Beauty sighed another of her curtain-rustling French sighs and suggested that they commence their clicking and browsing. Obediently, he brought up *Islam*, then clicked on *esoteric*. "This morning," she declared, "I wish to see what they have to say about the pyramids."

"Pyramids?"

"Yes."

"In connection to Islam? I mean, I'm sure there's a Web site for pyramids, but . . ."

"In connection to Islam," she insisted.

"Yeah, but I don't believe there *is* a connection." (Isn't everything connected, Switters?)

"The pyramids are in Egypt. Egypt is an Islamic country."

He chuckled, a bit patronizingly. "The pyramids were constructed— when?—around twenty-seven hundred B.C. Mohammed didn't stick his nose through the fence until three thousand years later. I don't believe—"

"Click it," she ordered. He clicked it. And was as astonished to find himself scrolling up Islamic references to pyramids as he had been, days earlier, to discover that esoteric Islam, in opposition to the adamantly patriarchal mainstream, was decidedly feminine in character and foundation.

Islamic accounts, it turned out, gave credit for the building of the pyramids to a Levantine king called Hermanos, a name, Switters immediately reasoned, that must be a corrupted spelling of "Hermes," the tricky Greek god of travel, speed, and esoteric adventure; the Speedy Gonzales of the ancient world, whose function was to journey beyond boundaries and frontiers, both physical and psychological; to explore the unknown and bring back to the sedentary, material and spiritual wealth. In the latter regard, Hermes was the prototype of the shaman, the precursor of Today Is Tomorrow. He was also, this inveterate voyager and con artist, a bit of a sex symbol, and crude phallic images of him were often erected at borders and crossroads. (Women love these fierce invalids home from hot climates?)

In any case, King Hermanos was said to have had the original two pyramids built as mystic vaults to house the revelations and secrets of the ancient sages, a place to shelter their mysterious sciences, as well as their bodies after death. The principal treasure hidden in the underground galleries consisted of fourteen gold tablets, on seven of which were inscribed invocations to the planets, whereas on the other seven there was written a love story, a telling of the star-crossed romance between the king's son, Salàmàn, and a teenage girl many years Salàmàn's junior. The love story may have been symbolic, the data suggested; a kind of spiritual allegory, but it wouldn't be incorrect to say that this material suddenly had Switters's full attention.

Masked Beauty, on the other hand, was puzzled by their findings, disappointed, and even a bit annoyed. Switters could detect her face darkening (the wart set against it like Mars against a thick winter sky) as he read to her from the monitor how Plato had learned of the gold tablets, the Hermetic Writings so-called, and had made a pilgrimage to study them, but was prevented by the prevailing Egyptian ruler from entering the pyramids. Plato then bequeathed to his pupil, Aristotle, the task of gaining access to the secret teachings, and years later, Aristotle took advantage of Alexander the Great's Egyptian campaign to visit a pyramid and slip inside it, using maps and codes passed on to him by Plato, but he succeeded in bringing out only one of the tablets (one on which a segment of the love story was inscribed) before "the doors were closed to him." Masked Beauty fumed. "Ooh-la-la," she said. "Now, I suppose I'll have to read that damned Aristotle. Oh, I know St. Thomas Aquinas ranked him second only to Christ, but those pagan know-it-alls only give me an ache in the head."

It's not Aristotle that's bugging you, thought Switters. He wondered, and not for the first time, whether she had once been enamored of old Matisse. Perhaps she didn't relish May–December love stories barging into her theological research, uncorking memories. And/or, it could be that she was expecting more definitive results from that research.

At any rate, by the time the abbess had copied down in her kitty-whisker script all that cyberspace had coughed up regarding pyramids and esoteric Islam, she was overdue for a nap. As she gathered her notebooks and pencils, her tea things, and her veil, she announced that dinner that evening would be served a half hour later than usual. "We are first holding a special vespers," she said. "To commemorate the birthday of Sister Domino. You are welcome to attend."

Swiveling from the computer, where he was about to take yet another peek at the e-mail from Maestra (Suzy in "a speck of trouble"? What kind of trouble?), Switters blurted, "Today's her birthday? September fifteenth? I wish somebody had told me. Will there be a party?"

"No, no," Masked Beauty assured him. "Only the prayer service. Around here, a natal anniversary is an opportunity to give thanks for the gift of life, not an excuse to indulge in frivolous pleasures."

A prohibition against birthday parties, mused Switters, who was growing a trifle weary of prohibitions. *Well, well. A little something may have to be done about that.*

Since, out there in the wilds, he could conceive of nothing else to give her, Switters spent the afternoon trying to compose a poem for Domino. After numerous false starts, he finally finished one, folded it, and concealed it in his breast pocket, thinking it highly improbable that he would actually present it to her. The poetic effort, in fact, so outwitted him that when it was over he felt compelled to flee the compound, slipping through the mammoth gate to stilt precariously for more than an hour over stone and sand in the ancient, clean, open desert, where the air was wavy and the sun rays strong, where everything smelled of infinity, star-ash, and ozone, and occasional gusts of scorpion-breath almost blew him off his stilts.

As he stiffly negotiated the ruined sodiums and hardened salts, he managed to step back mentally (he prided himself on periodic full consciousness) and watch himself negotiate; watch himself frankenstein along, one rigid step at a time, in the mineral heat; watch himself fret over a silly sonnet written to a nun for whom he had feelings that might not bear examination; watch himself try to interpret the Maestra-Suzy alliance and its potential implications (if any); watch himself speculate on how he was going to get out of Syria and into the Amazon so that he might petition a pointy-headed witchman to lift a taboo—and as he watched he said to himself, "Switters, methinks you may have successfully realized at least one of your childhood ambitions." That ambition, he recalled with a dry-throated chuckle, was to avoid in every way possible an ordained and narrow life. Were he as given to self-analysis as he was to self-observation, he might have seen fit to ask if he hadn't overshot the mark in that regard, but since, despite everything, he was feeling pretty good about being alive, the question of excess was never addressed.

Broiled pink and abraded still pinker, as if lightly chewed by the invisible teeth of eternity, he returned, panting, leg muscles aching, to the oasis, quaffed a whole pitcher of water, enjoyed a sponge bath (a washing that transcended maintenance), and then a snooze. When, refreshed and cologne splashed, he set off at last through the violet tingle—the smokeless smoke—of Syrian dusk, he was bound for supper but primed for party.

The sisters were already at table. He could hear Maria Deux's dour voice saying grace as he approached the dining hall door. He passed the hall without entering, going instead around back to the kitchen, where in a small attached shed, a kind of pantry annex, he knew the order's wine to be stored. The pantry door was padlocked, causing him to wonder if it had always been secured in that fashion or if special precautions had been taken as a result of his residency at the oasis.

Had he patience, a simple tool or two (a hairpin or nail file would have sufficed), and a lower ebb of spirit, he surely could have picked the lock, for, despite his imperfect dexterity, he had successfully completed the burglary course at Langley. In his present mood, however, he summarily rejected that option, returning, instead, to his room to wrest the Beretta from its crocodile-hide cocoon. Back at the pantry, he aimed the weapon at the padlock, and with a little grunt of enthusiasm (a truncated wahoo, one might reasonably categorize it), he squeezed off the rounds necessary to blow apart the lock, adding one or two more for good measure. For a split second, tiny burrs and shards of steel whizzed angrily in all directions, like metallic bees in a bug riot.

Alas, the pantry proved to contain but six bottles of wine. It was his own fault, the increased frequency of festivities from monthly Italian nights to weekly blues nights having depleted the stock. "One must make do," he muttered philosophically, and after jamming the pistol in his waistband, he gathered up the sextet of dusty green bottles and with difficulty, due to the manner in which a burden of almost any size could create an imbalance for a stiltwalker, tottered off to the dining hall.

The sisters had left the table and were bunched in the doorway, Domino out in front like the leader of the pack. He realized then that the gunshots had frightened them: they probably imagined themselves under another terrorist attack. "Sorry," he said. "Didn't mean to give you a scare. Firearms are to Americans what fine food and drink are to the French: can't hold a proper celebration without them." He treated the women to his sweetest, most luminous grin. "And we do, I understand, have something to celebrate this evening." He swung the grin like a searchlight, narrowing its beam on Domino. "Pippi, please relieve me of this libationary freight—and uncork it, if you would, so that it might inhale, to salubrious effect, nature's precious oxygens." Nearly toppling over in the process, he thrust the bottles upon the redhead and then clomped off to fetch his computer cum disk player. "Don't lament," he called. "Our separation will be most endurably brief."

True to his word, he was back momentarily, though he did not sit with them until he had unleashed Frank Zappa's atonal, polyphonic rendition of "Happy Birthday" upon the gathering. Deliberately shunning Domino's table (she shared it, as usual, with Bob, Pippi, and ZuZu), he took a seat (his feet planted carefully upon a chair rung) with those four diners—a relatively older group—presided over by Masked Beauty. To appease him, perhaps, there was an open bottle of wine on each table. The other bottles had disappeared. "One must make do," he mumbled, dividing his table's wine into four glasses (Maria Deux declined on the grounds of a troubled liver), and persuading, with forceful gestures, the other table to follow suit.

Gazing at Domino along a line of sight that bisected the wad of bubblegum that God, not wishing to defile his golden throne, had deposited on Masked Beauty's compliant proboscis, Switters raised his glass. All present held their breath. To their relief, he said only, "To Simone 'Domino' Thiry! Long may she brighten this ball of clay with her grace!" Everyone uttered an assent of some sort, as she was cherished by her colleagues, and Domino reddened rather charmingly.

After the toast, things settled down to normal for a while, although Zappa's contorted instrumentals kept a slight edge on the proceedings. However, as the wine receded—and it had completely vanished long before the eggplant-and-feta pie and the salad of chopped tomato and cucumber had been properly dispatched, the reverend sisters being thoughtful eaters—social intercourse attained a degree of animation typically seen only on blues nights and not always then. There was lively conversation and even a titter or two.

"Maria, O Maria, blessed lady of the tender repast, our genius engineer of endless culinary triumphs, please show us again the gastronomic mercy for which you are rightly renowned and allow the assembled celebrants to refill their cups, for though we be unworthy of the grape, any unsated thirst might be construed as an insult to the occasion. The birthday girl must be feted, and for that, naught but your prime-time vintage will do." Switters was guessing that the extra wine had been stashed with Maria Une's provisions. The hunch proved correct, for Masked Beauty, somewhat hesitantly, gave a nod of assent to the flustered old cook, whereupon Maria Une shuffled back to the kitchen and retrieved a pair of the missing bottles. When the vessels had been decorked and their contents distributed—both Marias this time abstained, leaving Switters little choice but to assume their allotment—a warm atmosphere enveloped the dining hall. Or, perhaps, Switters only imagined it.

Pippi lit candles at each table, as it was past the hour for her to turn off the power, and Switters withdrew the poem from his pocket, unfolded it, and read it to himself in the flickering glow while awaiting Pippi's return from the generator shed. The poem was about some golden tablets, inscribed with secrets of the soul and heart and hidden in the pyramids, and how a wise Egyptian king had refused to allow Plato to mooch the tablets on the grounds that the Greek—weakened by his priggish philosophy of asexual love—mightn't be able to bear up under the weight of so much robust passion. Clearly, the implication (he could imagine the poem being analyzed by his professor at Berkeley) was that the divine secrets are withheld from those who lack the courage to accept and explore their own sensual natures. *An accurate enough sentiment,* he heard his inner voice agreeing. *But I can't palm off this piece of anti-Platonic propaganda on Domino as a birthday present. What could I have been thinking?*

In a move to outflank his imp, he thrust a corner of the page into the nearest candle flame. The paper instantly ignited, and he held on to the burning poem until the fire reached his fingertips, whereupon he dropped the last smoldering corner of it onto the wooden tabletop. (Good thing Pippi had never gotten around to sewing those pseudo-Italian tablecloths.) All conversation ceased at the onset of this little pyromaniacal display, and he sensed himself the object of apprehensive surveillance. In the middle of the burning, however, he overheard Domino say dismissively, "Mr. Switters is a CIA agent," as if that explained everything; and he could tell that the sisters were conjuring images of him in a Moscow attic, on a secluded Cuban beach, or in a dim café in Casablanca, setting fire to coded instructions, plans for a deadly new weapon, or a single mysterious word scrawled in blood, in order that he might save a democratic government or a brave double agent, who happened to be, in her spare time, a beautiful contessa who'd donated her fortune to Catholic orphanages; and they, the Pachomian sisters, were reveling in these images. Reveling in them.

Inspired, Switters scooped up the poetry ashes and ate them. Then, lips all black and flaky, he raised his glass as if for another toast. His glass, alas, was empty. Registering his predicament, Masked Beauty handed him her wine, which was largely untouched. He smiled his appreciation. He took a gulp to wash down the lingering black snow of charred paper, and he said, "To nuns! On the occasion of Sister Domino's birthday, I salute all nuns, for nuns are the most romantic people on earth."

That seemed to go down pretty well with the assembly (although Domino was rolling her eyes a bit), so he elucidated. "Each nun gives her heart completely to a man from a distant place and a distant time, a legendary husband she loves beyond everything else, though he comes to her only in her prayers and her dreams. Every true romantic lives a life of idealized otherness, but it is the nun who lives it most purely and with the least self-serving compromise."

At this, the sisters applauded. Even Domino clapped, although her clapping seemed watered down with politeness. Switters bowed and was about to continue, was about, in fact, to launch into a diatribe against Church fathers for relegating nuns to subservient positions, was about to go so far as to accuse their beloved old St. Pachomius of actually establishing nunneries as a devious means of getting devout women out of the way, neutralizing their sexuality, and exploiting their unpaid labor. Fortunately, perhaps, the three elder sisters at his table chose that moment to stand and excuse themselves, Maria Une to soak her varicose shanks, Maria Deux because she sensed her liver trying to turn itself into pâté (if only she could envision a ball of mystic white light in its stead!), and Masked Beauty to get her masked beauty sleep.

Leaping onto his chair, Switters waved off their departure. "Please, sisters, grant me a moment more. I'll be leaving you soon, and before I go, I'd like to say. . . . Mmm, you know I could speak my piece with ever so much more, uh, ease and, uh, precision, were my tonsils frescoed with another light coat of the cardinal pigment: Maria, you flesh-bound instrument of numinous nurturance, I know you harbor two more bottles in your cupboard, and while I'd never be so rapacious as to covet them both . . ." At that point, ZuZu, who was weaving a bit and looking rather ruddy, filled his glass to the brim from a bottle she'd apparently retrieved from the kitchen when no one was looking. "Oh, thank you, my dear! God bless. Now. Mmm. Delicious. Now." He cleared his throat.

"I've spent the greater part of my adult life in the company of men. Yes. And men that no honest, plainspoken, hard-working, God-fearing folk would want to be around for eleven seconds: wild-eyed, restless, and often dangerous men; fellows who could not drink this fine *vin rouge* of yours without losing control; rebels and dreamers and lunatics, soldiers-of-fortune, out-of-work mercenaries, vagabond scholars, expat journalists, gamesters, bohemians, and failed international speculators; irresponsible men who insist that something interesting must be happening pretty much at all times—or else, watch out! Men who'd enthusiastically stay up for days arguing over the nuances of a book even its own author couldn't completely understand, yet refuse to devote half a minute to an insurance policy, a mortgage, or a marriage contract; men . . . well, I think you see the kind of fellows, bless their poor doomed butts, who I'm talking about here, and I mention them only to underscore the contrast between such men and the wholesome feminine companionship I've enjoyed these past nearly four months. Yes. Mmm."

Following a big swig that nearly exhausted his libation, he, gazing at the ceiling, went on to laud the women for their devotion to simple tasks and for practicing stability without stagnation, although, as the tribute lengthened, he began referring to them in such overheated terms as "sunstruck outcasts," "desert zealots" and "wilderness saints." Eventually, as lines from Thomas Gray's *Elegy Written in a Country Churchyard* ("Full many a flower is born to blush unseen / And waste its sweetness on the desert air") commenced to stray into the monologue, he realized that he'd lost his French and had been prattling away in English. *Good God! Not this!* he thought, as he suddenly imagined he heard himself crooning "Send in the Clowns." But it wasn't he. Someone had slipped his album of Broadway show tunes into the disk player.

As candle flames swayed to the haunting, bittersweet Sondheim refrain (part of the song's appeal was that it was impossible to tell whether it was cynically ironic or sentimentally self-pitying), Switters glanced around the dining hall and discovered that his audience had abandoned him. Only three of the ex-nuns remained. Bob and ZuZu were dancing. Slow dancing. Dancing cheek to cheek, fairly clinging to each other, the circus frizz (somehow musically appropriate) of the one almost engulfing the practical Julia Child crop of the other. *My, my,* he thought. *Am I responsible for this, or has it been going on for some time?* The only other remaining diner was Domino, who sat at the next table, her arms folded across her chest, regarding him with an amused, sympathetic smile.

He seemed momentarily dazed but quickly recovered. "A man must get carried away with himself from time to time," he said, "or run the risk of his juices drying up." Domino nodded, still smiling, and the laser finished with Sondheim and moved on to the next cut, which happened to be the terminally romantic "Stranger in Paradise." Indicating the blissfully gliding ZuZu and Bob, he inquired if she wouldn't like to dance. She replied that while his talents were numberless, she really didn't believe he could dance on stilts. "Push your table over here," he said, and when she had coupled the two tables, he hopped up onto the combined surface, bidding her to follow. "I've frequented Asian nightclubs with smaller dance floors than this," he said.

At first, they danced awkwardly, Domino keeping a discreet distance, but as she grew more accustomed to the novelty of the situation and as the music in her ears and the wine in her blood took over, she relaxed into his light embrace. "Can you believe?" she asked. "I haven't danced since my junior prom in Philadelphia."

"Well, then," he said, dipping her gingerly, then pausing as "Stranger in Paradise" faded out and "If I Loved You" from *Carousel* came on, "consider this your present. Happy birthday."

"Thank you. Thank you very, very much." Her appreciation struck him as touchingly genuine. "When is *your* birthday?"

"It was back in July."

"And you didn't celebrate?"

"Lost track of the calendar and forgot all about it—until sometime in the middle of the night. Then I got up and went out in the desert and tried to count the stars. Astronomers claim the human eye can see no more than five thousand stars at any one time, but I swear I counted nineteen thousand. Not including asteroids and major planets. Of course, I may have counted some black holes by mistake. But it was a splendid celebration."

Domino squeezed his hand and folded against him, moving in his arms like a pendulum moving in a grandfather clock. "I should like to have done that for my birthday: counting stars." She sighed close to his ear. "Better than vespers, maybe."

"Unless I'm mistaken, they're still up there. Sirius, Arcturus, Alpha Centauri, the Big Dipper, Orion, neutron stars, pulsars, novas, super-novas, red giants, white dwarfs, purple people-eaters, the whole twinkly-assed crew. We could. . . ." He motioned toward the door.

"No," she whispered. "Not tonight. I must go soon." Her voice brightened without rising. "But tomorrow night? We could, if you want, count stars tomorrow night."

"Sure. I'm free. I'll meet you around ten. At the gate."

"No. It'll be cold and windy out there in the open. We'll meet in the tower. You know? At the top of—what do you call it? The ladder."

"As long as it isn't the corporate ladder, I'll be happy to climb it."

They, in their dancing, had kicked over all but one of the candles. The dining hall was so faintly illuminated they could no longer ascertain if Bob and ZuZu were still in the room, yet Domino's eyes seemed luminous, even though partially closed. If it was the wine that was responsible, either on her part or his own, he would ever be wine's loyal friend. He swore it.

"My grandmother," he said, "confessed to me once that before she'd ever let herself become deeply involved with a man, she'd make sure to get him drunk. Maestra claims you can never know who a person really is unless you've seen how they behave when under the spell of Bacchus. It's a hard and fast rule with no exceptions: a bad drunk will make a bad husband. Or wife, for that matter. Sobriety, for some people, is a thin and temporary disguise."

"Sounds not quite a proper method to me. Are *you* drunk, Switters?"

"Certainly not. But it's a state that might be beneficially attained were I to gain access to that last bottle back in the kitchen. In the interest of knowledge, of course. We could see if I pass Maestra's test."

"You've rearranged enough furniture for one night." She smiled, glancing at the combined tabletops over which they'd been (at times, precariously) skimming. The ballad from *Carousel* had ended and a lively, up-tempo tune from *South Pacific* was intruding on the mood. She pulled away from him. "See you at the tower. Bring your calculator." She was going, and he was prepared to let her go, but, abruptly, before either of them could step aside, each of their faces moved forward, as if attracted by a sudden mutual activation of atomic dipoles or else shoved together by formless relatives of the Asmodeus. And they kissed. They surprised themselves utterly by kissing.

It wasn't a lengthy kiss, as kisses go, yet neither was it a friendly peck. (As the Egyptians knew full well, Platonism never stood a chance in this world.) It was a kiss of moderate duration, devoid of all but the sweetest hint of tongue, yet a kiss fraught with pressure, irrigated with mouth moisture, and animated by some force that transcended the mere contracting and relaxing of oral musculature. It possessed a muscular rhythm, however, as well as a kinetic inquisitiveness, and a systemwide excitation was somehow synergistically precipitated by the crude, unsanitary, and yet glorious co-mingling of lip meats.

How could anything as commonplace—and in their pink, fatty, babyish way, *dumb*—as human lips produce such mysterious pleasure? Accompanied by tiny noises like carp feeding or rubber stretching or fallen kumquats returning to the branch? Fusing one pair of lips to another must be akin to attaching an ordinary prefix such as *re* or *a* or *ex* to an ordinary (and rather harsh) verb such as *ward* or *rouse* or *cite*. Looking at it from another angle, their kiss was like a paper airplane landing on the moon.

When at last they began to pull apart, a thread of spittle as slender and silky as a spider's wire connected them for another second or two, as if they were continents linked by a single transoceanic cable. Then, with an inaudible pop, they were disconnected, staring at each other from opposite shores.

"À *demain*," she said, a little breathless but not rattled in the least. "Tomorrow night."

"The stars."

"Count them."

"Every damn one of them."

"Okay."

The following night, and every night thereafter for seven months, they lay on a Bedouin carpet in the roofless tower and looked up at the cat-black sky. Not many stars got counted. On the other hand, lest one jump to conclusions, not many carnal apples got bobbed, either—at least not in the sense of conventional sexual intercourse. What transpired nightly in the room at the top of the tower was at once more uneventful and more extraordinary than routine copulation and sidereal enumeration. And, no, that wasn't a typographical error back there: it persisted for seven months.

the first night that they met in the tower and lay on the rug (Switters never dared to test that floor with his feet), admiring a moon that looked as if it had been oiled by a Kurdish rifleman and pointing at the satellites that skittered from sky-edge to sky-edge like water-bugs crossing a cow creek, Domino confessed, with a minimum of embarrassment and no shame at all, that she had "a big crash" on him. Switters, ever the language man, was on the verge of correcting her English when it occurred to him that being infatuated with the likes of himself was, indeed, probably more akin to a "crash" than a "crush."

He reminded her, as she had once reminded him, that the very first time he laid eyes on her he'd blurted out that he loved her. He now had, he said, nothing to add to that declaration nor nothing to sub-tract. In all likelihood, he had been, as charged, out of his cotton-picking mind back then, and whether or not that condition had improved he was in no position to say. However—*however*—whatever he felt for her (and he could only describe the emotion as being as sat-isfyingly poignant as it was pesteringly agreeable), or she felt for him, it had been established—had it not?—that he was not her type, since he was a dollar short when it came to maturity and a day late when it came to peace.

"I may have been wrong about that," she conceded. "You are a complicated man, but *happily* complicated. You have found a way to be at home with the world's confusion, a way to embrace the chaos rather than struggle to reduce it or become its victim. It's all part of the game to you, and you are delighted to play. In that regard, you may have reached a more elevated plateau of harmony than . . . ummph."

Although shutting her up was probably not his sole or even primary motive, he kissed her before she could define him further. He kissed her hard—and soft and long and deep and dreamily and urgently, and she kissed him back. In a sense, Domino's kisses were rather like Suzy's, which is to say, they were both eager and shy, adventurous and uncertain, yet there was a strength in them (or immediately behind them), a solidity that made him feel that this simple, oddish act of osculation, was somehow supported by and connected to each and every one of what Bobby Case's ol' Chinese boys called "The Ten Thousand Things." Indeed, there was a sense in which a kiss was a thing as well as an act, and Domino's kiss, inexperienced in terms of execution but seasoned in terms of foundation, might be compared to new spring growth on a venerable tree, or (despite Switters's disrespect for pethood) a puppy with a pedigree. Moreover, being a thing in and of itself, her kiss, while undeniably a concretized expression of an emotional state, was not necessarily a mere prelude to other activity, the leading edge of a larger biological urge. He liked that about it: the self-contained, concentrated *isness* or *kissness* of it, though he would have been the last to maintain that it failed to encourage larger biological urges.

As a matter of fact, he worked her chador off her shoulders, unhooked her bra, and bared her breasts. She didn't object, though the breasts themselves, livid and alert, seemed almost to blink in astonishment at their exposure. He kissed them, licked and sucked them, rolled them in his palms, and squeezed their nipples between thumb and forefinger as if testing berries for ripeness or turning the knobs of a particularly delicate scientific instrument—and, actually, when he gently twisted the rosebud dials, it pumped up the volume of her breathing to a virtually orgasmic level. When he advanced his explorations and adorations to the lower half of her body, however, he was rebuffed. And, in truth, he didn't mind. He had his hands full—and his mouth full, too—and he was content with that largess.

After a while, they paused to see if the stars were still there. Domino fingered her own nipples, perhaps to calculate the difference between his touch and hers; or, just as likely, to facilitate a conversational segue. "Have you noticed," she inquired, "that the grapes are becoming full on the vine?" She wondered if he might be persuaded to stick around for the harvest and for the winemaking that would follow. She thought it only fair, she said, that he help replenish their pantry since he had done so much to reduce it. Of course, she knew how anxious he was to get down to Peru, no doubt with good reason. . . .

He interrupted to reveal that he'd always wanted to participate in a grape-stomping, longed to jump up and down on tubs of the fruit until his feet, including the spaces between his toes, were as purple as eggplants or 2-balls, and that he could never fully trust a person who didn't find the prospect of squashing grapes in their bare feet irresistible; but, alas, he feared that stomping grapes on stilts would be neither very enjoyable nor very effective.

"Silly," she said. "We are not old shoeless peasants. We use a press." Then, as if there was some doubt that he fully understood the meaning of the word *press*, as applied to separating articles from their juices, she unzipped his fly and reached into his pants. When she touched active flesh, she drew back, startled, as though, reaching for a rope, she'd grabbed a snake by mistake. Switters appreciated this, in that it mitigated her boldness and reestablished her innocence, but he also appreciated it when, more cautiously this time, she returned her fingers to the surrogate grape-bunch and gradually tightened her grip. They kissed. Domino squeezed. She squeezed rhythmically (instinctively?), relaxing and then increasing tension. And it wasn't long before the winepress demonstration produced graphic results. Needless to say, nobody thought to bottle the Château de Switters Beaujolais Nouveau, but few would have disagreed that it was a vintage pressing.

They spent the night in each other's arms, sleeping only intermittently due to the novelty, the shock, of their romantic union. And sometime before the sun reclaimed their patch of Syrian sky, he agreed to stay on at the oasis until the end of October. They both knew full well that neither her request that he stay nor his consent to do so had anything especially to do with the actual harvesting of grapes.

The supply truck came, bringing gasoline, flour, soap, cooking oil, sugar, toothpaste, and salt. It also brought magazines and mail. Included in the mail was a statement from the Damascus bank with which the Pachomians did business, and the bottom line was not encouraging. So few contributions had been deposited in their account (widows in Chicago and Madrid each sent them a hundred dollars, Sol Glissant appeared to have forgotten them altogether) that Domino instructed the driver to reduce their usual petrol order by half next trip and to deliver no toothpaste or cooking oil at all. They'd clean their teeth with salt and attempt to make their own oil from the walnuts that would be ripening soon. She also canceled magazines and papers: they could get their news from the Internet. She did order, on behalf of Switters and paid for with his deutsche marks, a five-pack of cigars, a ten-pack of razor blades, and a six-pack of beer. The driver, who had no idea that there was a man residing at the convent, gave her a funny look.

Later, when the truck had gone and he'd come out of hiding, Switters said, "First purchases I've made in more than five months, and in that time not one person has tried to hypnotize, charm, cajole, mislead, or frighten me into buying their goods or services. You can't appreciate how clean that feels." No, having lived so long in an ad-free zone, she couldn't really appreciate it, and she wondered if maybe he was not a bit of a tightwad. On the other hand, he had offered to pay what she considered an exorbitant sum for a pinch of hashish if only she would approach the driver about it. She refused.

The mail delivery also contained an unsigned postcard, addressed to Abbess Croetine and postmarked Lisbon. Everybody guessed it was from Fannie, though they couldn't remember ever having seen a sample of her handwriting. Its message read, in badly misspelled French, *Your secret is safe with me. For now!*

Something was sorely troubling Masked Beauty, and it very well could have been that mysterious postcard. Or, it could have been that their dedicated daily tours of Net sites simply were not bearing fruit or producing results to her liking. More than likely, she was upset both by the card and the unsatisfactory data. In any case, she began gradually curtailing her appearances beside the computer and seemed, during that October, to have initiated an acceleration of the aging process. Her complexion, which heretofore had been unnaturally smooth, showed signs of cracking. Her pale eyes faded further, and her posture, formerly as upright with natural dignity as a flagpole with pompous sentiment, commenced to slump, giving the impression that, like Skeeter Washington, she'd spent too many nights hunched over a piano. Switters suspected that computers themselves could cause premature aging; and, obviously, the abbess had long been subjected to the tugs of earthly gravity, but something else was weighing on her, wrinkling her and pulling her down. Only her wart seemed unchanged and unaffected, a clod of red mud from the mean fields of Mars.

As second-in-command at the convent, Domino must have shared Masked Beauty's every concern, yet she struck Switters as more radiant, more vivacious than ever. It would be easy to credit love, and maybe that's where credit was due, but neither she nor Switters was the type to let themselves be made over by Cupid. Undoubtedly, they were delighted, even thrilled by their amorous bonding, each thoroughly intrigued with the other, yet they were suspicious of the affair as well, and tended to regard it with a skeptical, sometimes mocking eye.

While they displayed no affection in public, their affair was quickly common knowledge, and some of the sisters, most particularly the two Marias, were more than a little disapproving. As for Bobby Case, he was informed only that Switters had postponed for a month his return to the Amazon. Nevertheless, Bobby ventured a fairly accurate guess as to the reason for the delay, and he chided Switters for thinking with his little head instead of his big one. Bobby also chose that moment to transmit a photograph of his current girlfriend, an Okinawan cutie who looked not a day over fifteen. The fact that Domino was old enough to be the girl's mother (almost, under the right circumstances, her grandmother), seemed not to faze Switters, if it registered on him at all.

Every night between nine and ten, he leaned his stilts against the tower's adobe wall and climbed the long ladder to what he had christened the Rapunzel Suite. There, he rolled onto the carpet, propped his feet on a cylindrical pillow, and, watching the stars slide by like lighted portholes in a luxury liner, awaited Domino's arrival. She would appear promptly at ten, never out of breath from the climb, pull her chador over her head, and snuggle in naked beside him. Unlike some women he'd known, she could shed her clothing without shedding her mystery.

It had been his experience that women of a certain age often tended to let themselves go. They became lax and dowdy. Switters supposed he couldn't blame them: nobody had a greater disdain for maintenance than he. Undoubtedly, some of their frumpiness could be attributed to sheer laziness, to frustration, and to capitulation: they had given up on themselves, given up on life. All too often, however, they had simply been worn down, exhausted by having to serve too many children in addition to the helpless golfing goobers to whom they were bound by law. Was it because she'd been neither a harried wife and mother nor a steely career-chasing spinster that Domino's spark continued to glow? Was it because she'd never compromised herself in the desperate, always illusional quest for security? He didn't know. He didn't very much care. "Never look a gift shoppe in the mouth" was his motto. Whatever she'd been like as a young woman, he suspected she had grown increasingly mysterious and alluring with age. She referred to herself as a "born-again virgin," and one night near the end of his October extension, he learned that she meant it literally.

She asked him if he celebrated Christmas, and he answered that there were very few days on the calendar that he wouldn't celebrate, if given half a reason. She protested that Christmas was special, it being the presumed birthday of Jesus Christ—or was that one more thing in which he didn't believe?

"Um, well, it's like this, Domino: I've always assumed that every time a child is born, the Divine reenters the world. Okay? That's the meaning of the Christmas story. And every time that child's purity is corrupted by society, that's the meaning of the Crucifixion story. Your man Jesus stands for that child, that pure spirit, and as its surrogate, he's being born and put to death again and again, over and over, every time we inhale and exhale, not just at the vernal equinox and on the twenty-fifth of December."

She pondered that for a good long while, then eventually changed the subject. Soon after that, they were kissing, as was their custom, and when she turned aside his efforts to open her legs, a rejection that also had become routine, she—again, as usual—seized hold of the bulge in his panda-bear shorts. By this time, their behavior seemed almost scripted.

Obviously, he wanted something more, but he neither pressured her nor complained. The French say that the best part of an affair is going up the stairs. Desire is almost always more thrilling than fulfillment. In all likelihood, he was caught up in the drawn-out yearning, in the kind of innocent nasty intimacy, the Suzyness, if you will, of their gropings, so when she inquired if he was content with her manual manipulations, he replied only that she was amazingly adept at them. "I feel like a baton in a homecoming parade," he said.

"I probably should not admit this to you," she said, lowering her long lashes, "but in high school in Philadelphia, I was—"

"A drum majorette?"

"A *what*? Oh? No, not that. I was a one-woman petting zoo. Every boy in school was crazy to stick their fingers in the sexy French pie, and I cheerfully accommodated a great many of them. It did not take me long to learn how to please them without—how do they call it?— going all the way. Only Mr. Frederick, my basketball teacher, ever fucked me. Just once. I felt so guilty about it, this married man twice my age, that I—"

He kissed her eyelids. "You don't need to spill these kind of beans." Something about it was making him uncomfortable, even as it titillated him.

"But you've been so patient. I really must explain. When we moved back to France, I threw myself with whole heart into the arms of the Church. It was not just from girlish guilt, I want you to know. All my life I had loved Christ. And Mary. Especially Mary. I won't bore you with details, but one thing led to another, and about the time that I decided to take up the cloth, I learned how my aunt came to have that wart on her nose. That gave me my own idea. I began to pray for the reinstatement of my virginity. Crazy, no? Such a silly girl. But I prayed and prayed. For years. And after a long while—it grew back."

"Grew back? You mean your maidenhead?"

"My hymen. Yes. God gave it back to me. It is not an illusion. I have medical proof. More than one doctor has examined me and pronounced me complete. Okay, big cotton-picking deal! It's nothing but a fold of mucous membrane . . ."

"A thin sliver of sashimi."

"But as slight and expendable as it may be, it is my tangible link to Mary. And because of Mary's unique oneness with humanity, which is her greatest attribute and appeal, it is a physical link, also, to the loving humanism that she represents. And that—that tiny tab of tissue . . ."

"That petal from a salty rose."

". . . is further proof of the power of prayer. To lose it for a second time, to squander a miracle, would be a major, dramatic thing for me. To permit that—that little . . ."

"Nub of translucent bacon."

". . . that petite . . ."

"Paper tiger that guards the pearl pot."

". . . to be pierced by even the finger of a man less important to me than my sacred vocation . . . well, it would be unacceptable."

In the unlikely event that Switters needed a reminder that the world was a woo-woo place, Domino's story of cherry resurrection would have filled the requirement. After taking a moment or two to absorb it, and thinking it wise not to ask what kind of man might possibly be as important to her as her sacred vocation, he clasped the hand that continued to clasp his now somewhat droopy member and asked, "This, however, is acceptable?"

"I don't believe Almighty God is coincé. A prude. Didn't he design these bodies for us to enjoy? Mary is said to have remained always celibate, a virgin *in partu;* yet she and Joseph lived together in wedlock. She would have had to do *something* to relieve his sexual tension."

The image of Blessed Mother Mary as a hand-job artist, to use the coarse vernacular, was a bit startling, yet he was willing to expand the notion. Again, he squeezed her grip. "There are other options, you know; other, uh, practices in which they could have indulged." He was pleased to observe that he could still lobster her up.

Domino admitted that there were said to be other, uh, practices. Especially in the Middle East. Then, after a short pause, she returned to the subject of Christmas.

"Just like Masked Beauty, I love and respect the desert. It's the place where I feel closest to my breath and to the breath of God. The only time I'm discontent out here in the wilderness is at Christmas. I miss then so much the lights and the families and the cheer and the snow." She talked about annual trips into the Alleghenies to cut a tree for their Pennsylvania house, about window displays in Philadelphia and Paris, the crowds, chocolate shops, candlelight masses at Notre Dame, and ice skating at Place de l'Hôtel-de-Ville. There was something, Switters noticed, very childlike about her as she reflected upon the joys of past Noëls.

For some reason, she expected the coming holiday, the Christmas that was eight weeks away, to be particularly lonely and glum. Masked Beauty would arrange a lovely service, she always did, but this year even she seemed drained of energy and joy. Maybe it was the excommunication, maybe their financial situation, or maybe age had simply caught up with the blue nude, for she seemed in a blue funk. The Marias were getting old, too; Fannie was gone, and up to who knows what, and ZuZu and Bob were in a world of their own. Ah, but if Switters were at the oasis! If he were there, Domino knew he would find a way to make their bare desert Christmas as festive as the Champs-Élysées. For all of them, but especially for her. Certainly, he had his own agenda, he needed quite literally to get back on his feet, she appreciated that, but hadn't Masked Beauty's experience, as well as Domino's own holy "wart," shown him what prayer could accomplish? And anyway, it was only eight more weeks. Of course, he might be intent on spending the season with his grandmother, and . . .

She was getting slightly worked up, and Switters was enjoying listening to her tizzy. Misinterpreting his silence, she thought the moment had come to play her ace. "If you will spend the Noël with me," she whispered conspiratorially, as if the stars had ears, "I will do something special for you."

Misinterpreting her offer, he said, "Are you trying to bribe me?"

She smiled. "I will open up for you something only thirteen people on the earth—"

"Thirteen? That's quite a lot. Listen, honey cake, if you wanted to open the pearly gates for me out of affection, or even out of wanton lust, I'd gratefully accept. But as payment for helping you fend off holiday depression . . ."

"You imbecile!" She rolled away from him. *"Imbécile.* You think for to have a Bing Crosby Christmas I would sacrifice my—I forget all your poetic names for it. No, jerko, I was talking about something altogether else."

"Calm down. You're losing your English."

She did calm down. She even laughed. Sailor Boy would have approved. "It's true, I suppose, that if you delay your departure, I might eventually find myself willing to experiment with one or more of those 'other practices' about which you were referring, but my bribe happens to be just this: on Christmas Eve, I will open up for your eyes the secret document that it has been the Pachomians' fate to conceal and protect."

"All right, I get it. You're offering to trot out the Snake. Forgive me. My rooster brain jumped the conclusion fence. But, Domino, think about it: I used to be in the CIA. I ate secret documents for breakfast. I've handled more secret documents than Maria Une has handled chickpeas. What gives you the idea that I might drool on the Persian at the prospect of seeing another one?"

She sighed. "I, also, must be guilty of the wishful thinking." She sighed again. "It's just that you appeared to have at least a small bit of interest in the matter."

"What matter is that?"

"The matter of the lost prophecy of Our Lady of Fatima. It isn't lost, you see. We have it."

As October picked up speed, dragging its grape skins behind it, daytime temperatures had become marginally less sizzling, the nights increasingly chilly. Switters, who hated the sight of gooseflesh (had found it pathological even prior to being subjected to the old crone's naked parrot in Lima), pulled a wool rug up to his chin as he propped himself against the tower-room wall and lit the last of the five cigars that had come in the most recent Damascus delivery. "Mmm," he hummed. "Mmm. Yes. A cigar is a banana for the monkey of the soul."

Domino was the only lover he'd ever had who didn't giggle almost automatically at his pronouncements. He wasn't sure if that was a character flaw on her part or further evidence of her good sense and substance. More naked than any parrot could ever hope to be, even if plucked and singed, even if boiled and eaten, she stood in a far corner, washing her hands in a ceramic jar kept there for the purpose. He blew a series of smoke rings in her direction, jabbing an index finger through the center of each one as it floated away. "The Zen art of goosing butterflies," he said.

It was too dark in the room to ascertain if she smiled, but she definitely didn't giggle. "Think about my proposition," she said.

He *had* thought about it. He was *still* thinking about it. He could smoke a cigar, make oblique remarks, admire her silhouette, and think about her proposition all at the same time. It was easy. Who did she think he was? Gerald Ford? John Foster Dulles? *Pbthbt!*

In truth, Switters was not overwhelmingly interested in the third and final prophecy of the Fatima apparition. He was curious about most of life's tics, quirks, mysteries, unreasonable passions, aberrations, fetishes, enduring enigmas, and odd-duck jive, and his encounter with the Fatima legend a year earlier in Sacramento certainly had piqued that curiosity, but it would have been difficult if not impossible to separate clearly his interest in things Fatiman from his interest in things Suzian. Had his little stepsister not been so keen on the subject, he doubtlessly would have rolled the Fatima story about in his brain tumbler a few times and then let it pass. On the other hand, in a universe he knew to be founded on paradox and characterized by the interpenetration of sundry realities, he didn't believe in coincidence. Although it was an era of resurgent Marianism, a recent survey had found that 90 percent of Roman Catholics remained unfamiliar with this Fatima business, and the fact that it had resurfaced so dramatically in his own life—in a setting occupied by Matisse's live blue nude and provided, at least in the beginning, by Audubon Poe's provider, Sol Glissant, well, these compounding synchronisms left him scant choice but to take it seriously.

Speaking of blue nudes, Switters couldn't help being struck at that moment by the similarity between the remembered figure in the painting, with its sapphire domes and midnight naves (a rambling plastic Gaudi cathedral pumped so full of huckleberry cream that its stained-glass windows were bulging out), and Domino's bluish silhouette as it loomed now in that tower lit only by starlight. In shadowy profile, bereft of flaw and detail, the ex-nun's body could have belonged to the queen bee of one of those North African harems that had set Matisse's thyroid and brushes to throbbing—although it could just as easily, he supposed, have stepped down from a 1940s jungle movie poster: an untamed, thunder-titted She who ruled tribes of awestruck warriors and consorted with panthers.

The minimalist spectacle of Domino's maximalist contours was enough to justify his decision to tarry at the oasis awhile longer. But there were other reasons (or excuses), as well. Chief among them was the trouble then brewing between Syria and Turkey. Having protested for a long time that Syria was arming and financing PUK separatists who were seeking to carve an autonomous Kurdish state out of sections of Turkey and Iraq, an angry Turkish government had finally dispatched troops to the Syrian border. Syria responded in kind. Now, according to the Net, armies were massed along both sides of the Turkish-Syrian frontier, and the border was closed tighter than a young girl's diary. Since Turkey was the only country from which he could legally fly home, Switters was rather trapped. Normally, the situation would have turned his crank—there were few things he loved more than that sort of challenge—but in a wheelchair or on stilts? . . . He could be reckless, but he wasn't stupid.

Any hope that Poe might pick him up somewhere along the Mediterranean coast was dispelled when Bobby informed him (in their personal Langley-proof e-mail code) that *The Banality of Evil* was plying the Adriatic and was likely to remain in those waters as long as the Balkan horror show shrieked on unabated.

What the hell? Switters had no great reason to rush his departure, did he? Suppose he actually could locate Today Is Tomorrow again and convince him to cancel the taboo: what then? He lacked prospect for gainful employment anywhere on the planet, and out here under the vast desert sky, where primitive equalities prevailed, the notion of completing his doctoral thesis had come to seem downright silly. That the human species was apparently evolving beyond the civilized limitations of analogic perceptions, heading toward a *Finnegans Wake* state in which its thinking and acting would manifest in terms of perpetually interfacing digital clusters—well, that phenomenon continued to fascinate him, but he could ponder it without interruption beneath the pomegranate trees at the oasis; he didn't require academic sanction or societal reward: "Having played for many years by our rules, Mr. Switters, you may henceforth call yourself *Doctor*, though please bear in mind the title is solely meant to massage your ego and does not qualify you to take Wednesday afternoons off or practice gynecology."

Moreover, although he couldn't begin to explain why or how exactly, he still believed he was gaining some special insights into existence by observing it from two inches above the ground. If nothing else, a man on stilts was a man apart. So what if he was noticed only by a gaggle of aging ex-nuns?

Thanks to President Hafez al-Assad's cordial relations with Fidel Castro, fine Havana cigars were available in Damascus—but only at the luxury hotels. Transdesert truckers did not shop at luxury hotels. Switters had been brought cheroots manufactured in the Canary Islands. Like all machine-rolled cigars, they were in a hurry to burn themselves up, a kind of vegetative death wish, a plant-world version of self-destructive rock stars. Still, like those fey rockers, they had talent while they lasted. Switters spewed a stream of richly flavored suspended carbon particles toward the Milky Way, obscuring about three thousand of those five thousand stars to which human vision was said to be limited. And he said, "So, how soon can I peruse the Fatima Lady's climactic fortune cookie?"

Domino was drying her hands. "How soon? Were you not listening to me? I said, Christmas Eve. If you stay, I will give you the Virgin's message on Christmas Eve. It will be apropos, you know, a kind of—"

"Yeah, I see. A gift for the man who has everything." Exaggerating his pucker, he blew a smoke ring so large a Chihuahua could have jumped through it. "Very well. I'll Adam this Eden for eight more weeks. And you'll guarantee you'll show me the goods?"

"I promise on the Holy Bible." Then she added for his benefit, "And on *Finnegans Wake*."

They sealed the bargain with a purposeful kiss, at the conclusion of which he gloated, "I outwitted you on that one, Sister, my love. I would have agreed to stay and celebrate Christmas with you even if you hadn't promised to show me the prophecy."

"No, you big imbecile, *I* outwitted *you*. I would have shown you the prophecy even if you had not consented to make me a happy holiday. I would have shown it to you tomorrow or the next day. Now, you have to wait until Christmas."

He pretended to be miffed. "How typical of you mackerel-snapping snafflers. I should have known better than to deal with a tricky theophanist. I've become yet another sad victim of simony." She ignored his ostentatious flaunting of vocabulary, and he became sincere. "But why, Domino? Why would you want to share your big holy secret with a virtuoso sinner like me?"

After a long pause, she answered, "Because the nature of Mother Mary's last words at Fatima has troubled us. We've never been quite sure if we interpret them correctly. Your—how do you call it?—*input* might be helpful. You look at religious issues in a most unique— What are you doing?"

Switters was pretending to write on an imaginary notepad with an invisible pencil. "I may have been fired by the CIA, but I still moonlight for the Grammar Police. *Unique* is a unique word, and Madison Avenue illiterates to the contrary, it is not a pumped-up synonym for *unusual.* There's no such thing as 'most unique' or 'very unique' or 'rather unique'; something is either unique or it isn't, and damn few things are. Here!" He mimed tearing a page from the pad and thrust it at her. "Since English is not your first language, I'm letting you off with a warning ticket. Next time, you can expect a fine. And a black mark on your record."

Domino pretended to take the imaginary citation. Then, miming every bit as well as he, she "tore" it into shreds. As she tossed the nonexistent confetti into his face, he had to fight to conceal his admiration.

True to her word, she would not show him the fabled third prophecy until Christmas. Why? Not because of peer pressure. The Pachomian sisterhood was far from unanimous in its enthusiasm to grant to its unruly male guest the privilege of handling, reading, and discussing the transcription around which their order had coalesced (ultimately, their custodianship of the Fatima revelations had knit them together more tightly than their advocacy of women's rights or even their devotion to St. Pachomius), yet there was none among them who would oppose the will of Domino and the abbess. After all, if it wasn't for Masked Beauty, there would be no transcript, no oasis, no Pachomian Order. Privately, some feared that their much adored Sister Domino had fallen prey to Fannie's demon, but they'd respect her wishes, Asmodeus or no Asmodeus.

Nor did Domino hold off out of mistrust. As inexperienced as she was in the area of romance, she knew in her bones that, for better or for worse, Switters cared too much to deceive her. He would never read the prophecy and then skip out.

In fact, twice during November she offered to go ahead and show him the prophecy; she was becoming a bit anxious to get his reaction. Switters, however, insisted on waiting. He reminded her that they had made a pact. They must honor that pact, he told her, they must honor it even if it was frustrating, unnecessary, or outright senseless to honor it, because not to honor it would create more quaggy willy-nilliness in the world. They had to honor it because in honoring it, there was a certain purity.

That was what had convinced her to wait. That was what had touched her. That was what had made her want to want what he wanted. It was the way that he said "purity."

She would not show him the prophecy until Christmas, but she felt free to provide some background, and he felt free to receive it. She told it to him the way that Masked Beauty had told it to her.

Sometime during 1960, Pope John XXIII summoned the bishop of Leiria to the Vatican. The Portuguese bishop, whose diocese included Fatima, was barely off the flight from Lisbon when the supreme prelate drew him aside and whispered his intentions to open the envelope in which Lucia Santos (then Sister Mary dos Dores) had sealed Our Lady of Fatima's final prophecy. Assuming that Lucia had written down the prophecy in Portuguese, Pope John was going to need the bishop's assistance.

That afternoon, following an austere private lunch, the two men retired to the papal study, prayed to God and to Mary, and slit open the envelope (which had been held for three years in the study wall safe) with a jewel-encrusted blade. The contents, surprisingly brief, were, indeed, handwritten in Lucia's native tongue. At that point, the bishop confessed what the pope already had deduced from their unsteady lunchtime conversation: his Italian was more than a little rusty. The pope had no Portuguese at all.

It was imperative that the translation be exact, every particular fully rendered, no subtlety or shade of meaning glossed over or ignored. The bishop had a suggestion. He was fluent in French, could read it as precisely as he read Portuguese. Suppose he translated the prophecy into French? His Holiness grumbled that that was a start, then left the study briefly to make a telephone call.

Working with extreme care, the bishop of Leiria spent approximately two hours translating the few lines of neat, if childlike, script. No sooner was the task completed to his satisfaction than there was a discreet rap at the door, and a third man joined them in the study. The newcomer was Pierre Cardinal Thiry.

Unsure of his own French, Pope John had decided to entrust the

Parisian red hat, whose Italian he knew to be *eccellente*, with the job of moving the text perfectly from French into Italian.

With the bishop looking over his shoulder, Cardinal Thiry went to work. The pope went next door to his bedchamber to rest his nerves. In less than an hour, Thiry had produced a translation that, while mystifying and somewhat disturbing, nonetheless satisfied both him and the bishop with its accuracy. On the page, however, it was aesthetically displeasing, so Thiry made a fresh, tidier copy for Pope John, absentmindedly folding the messy copy and inserting it between the pages of his Italian dictionary.

John XXIII, roused by a tiny silver bell, returned to the study, where he shambled to the tall, leaded window to read at last the notorious Marian prophecy by the fading light of the sun. Moments later, he rotated slowly to face his subordinates with the look of a man who had just learned that he had eaten his grandmother's parrot. No, it was worse than that. It was the look of a man who had just learned that he had eaten his grandmother.

After being repeatedly assured by the bishop and the cardinal that nothing, not a trace nor a tense nor a tinge, not a prefix, a suffix, nor an inflection had been lost in translation, Pope John again left the study, commanding the others to wait there. They did. They waited all night, dozing in the voluminous leather armchairs that were said to have been a gift to an earlier pope from Mussolini. A good twelve hours passed before John burst into the room, as haggard and red-eyed as a Shanghai rat. The pope obviously had not slept. The salt of dried tearwater streaked his cheeks. A flunky followed him in and lit a fire in the fireplace before departing.

John crumpled up Thiry's Italian translation and dropped it into the flames. He ordered the bishop's French translation burned as well. Then, with some apparent misgiving, glancing sorrowfully, almost appealingly, about the study, as if hoping the others might dissuade him, he fed, with trembling white hands, Lucia Santos's original to the indifferent fire.

The bishop must have felt that a portion of Portuguese history was going up in smoke, but he did not vocally object. In a few minutes, after the ashes had been scattered in the grate, he followed Cardinal Thiry out of the apartment. Pope John returned to his bed, where, according to Vatican gossip, he wept for several days.

At that juncture, the alleged third and final prophecy of Our Lady of Fatima existed in just two places: in the memory of Sister Mary dos Dores (then aged fifty-three and cloistered in Spain), and in a French translation concealed inside Pierre Cardinal Thiry's dog-eared old Italian dictionary. Whether the cardinal deliberately smuggled the document out of the Vatican for reasons of his own, whether he acted on sudden impulse, or whether he simply forgot about the extra copy in the swirl of the moment, discovering it when he got home, Masked Beauty was never to learn.

What *was* apparent was that the cardinal had decided the Virgin's words, as upsetting as they may have been, needed to be preserved. He did not want them in his possession, however, preferring that they be held outside of Europe altogether. Thus, he sealed the sheet of papal stationery inside a heavy manila envelope and placed it in the care of his Jordan-bound, headstrong but trustworthy, disturbingly pretty ("Get thee behind me, Satan!"), young niece. For twenty-one years, Croetine hid the envelope, unaware of its contents. Upon her uncle's death in 1981, she thought she ought to have a peek.

Quite probably, Croetine was stunned—she never described her initial reaction—but a couple of years later, under fire from Rome and having changed her name to Masked Beauty, she called her renegade sisters, one by one, into her quarters, read to them the cardinal's account of how he came to obtain Mary's prophecy, and then let each nun read the message for herself. Now their shared and sacred secret, they bore it like a cross and protected it like a covenant, to what end they didn't really know. What they did recognize was that it pasted them, all nine of them, inseparably one to another, a miraculous Marian mucilage—until Fannie had pried herself loose.

"You were never completely taken with our Fannie," Domino asserted. Naked, she lay sprawled on her side like a shipwrecked cello. As far as he could tell, there was neither accusation nor rivalry in her remark.

"Not especially. Cute, but . . ."

"She was chaste, but she wasn't pure?" Domino thought she was starting to figure him out.

"She was strange, but she wasn't inexplicable."

"Oh? *Du vrai?* So, then you can explain why she ran away."

"I cannot."

"Then Fannie *is* inexplicable."

He shook his head. "There's an explanation for her exodus. We just aren't privy to it. Ignorance of the facts is no more synonymous with inexplicability than technical chastity is synonymous with purity."

"Ooh-la-la. Does this mean you're going to write me another ticket?"

"No, my subjective semantic opinions are not to be confused with the uniform rules impartially enforced by the brave men and women of the Grammar Police." He stroked her smooth, voluptuous rump. "By the way, have I ever told you about the time Captain Case and I were strip-searched at a roadblock inside Burma? Rubber gloves were unavailable there, you see, and the militiamen, understandably not wishing to foul their fingers in our . . . what you French sometimes call *l'entrée de artistes*, had a pet monkey they'd trained to do the job for them. He was a smart little fellow with tiny paws as red as valentine candy, and—"

"Switters! Why are you telling me this thing?"

Good question. He was damned if he knew. Was it because that day in Burma he'd been harboring a secret document (though hardly a prophetic one) in his *entrée de artistes*? Or was it because the proximity of Domino's exposed fundament—as dreadfully inviting as the entrance to an unexplored Egyptian tomb—was reminding him both of the jitter-fingered monkey's electrifying probe and the request he'd squeamishly denied that uninhibited young woman down in Lima?

Dissatisfied with their exchange of e-mail, Bobby Case finally took the risk of calling Switters on the satellite phone. The date was November 22, 1998, which, incidentally, happened to be the thirty-fifth anniversary of the death of Aldous Huxley. It was also the thirty-fifth anniversary of what, in a more perfect world, would have been the secondary and less newsworthy of the two events, the assassination of President John F. Kennedy.

In truth, the call probably wasn't all that risky. The CIA liked to keep tabs on its former employees, particularly those disemployed in an uncordial atmosphere, and even more particularly those it suspected of continued unfavorable attitudes and activities (if for no other reason, Switters's association with Audubon Poe qualified him as a person of interest), but as it scrambled to establish a new identity, scrambled, indeed, to justify its existence in a so-called post-Cold-War world, the agency would have assigned Switters an insultingly low priority. Still, like every intelligence organization, the CIA was fueled by paranoia, and one never knew when a cowboy might sprout a wild hair.

Bobby weighed those things, for his own sake as well as his friend's. Then, he made the call. Langley would have pinpointed the Swit's location months ago, he reasoned, and, besides, this conversation was to be of a decidedly personal nature. Wasn't it?

As it turned out, it wasn't quite as personal as Bobby might have liked. So evasive was Switters about his reasons for postponing his return to the Amazon that Capt. Case began to imagine all sorts of goings-on—political, mystical, and sexual—at the Syrian oasis. He began to wonder if he hadn't ought to be at the convent himself, joining in the fun. In the end, however, he began to conclude, from things said and unsaid, that Switters might actually have lost his head over one of the molting French penguins or "some unhappy shit like that."

So Bobby, who was well trained in the art of firing rockets, let one fly. He mentioned that he'd contacted Maestra recently from Hawaii, where he'd gone for a few days of R and R, just to see if she had any insight into why her damn fool grandson wasn't tending to business (i.e., getting his legs back, in order that he might walk the Switters walk as well as talk the Switters talk). Suzy had answered the phone. "Yep, son, I knew the instant she said 'hello' it was your Suzy. Her voice was so hot and sweet I damn near had to open a window and send out for insulin." Bobby paused, and in the silence he could picture Switters pinkening around the edges of what he styled his "dueling scars," could virtually hear, all the way from Okinawa, the clenching of those teeth that Norman Rockwell might have loved (in an eight-year-old boy; in a man Switters's age, they would have scared the corny illustrator half out of his smock).

After an effective interval, Bobby continued. "We had us a nice little chat. She told me she'd been upset and confused for a spell but that she was older now—she's turned seventeen, you know: where does the time go?—and she'd got a better handle on things. 'I miss him a lot,' she said, and I could hear it in her voice like an upholsterer who's swallowed one too many tacks. She says she dreams about you—there's folks that'd consider that a bona fide nightmare—and worries about you, you being off unsafe somewhere in a damn wheelchair.

"Of course, I informed her that you'd soon be doing what was necessary to get up on your hind legs again like a man. And that then you'd surely come and take her for a stroll downtown. She was so pleased she near about squealed like a monkey. Say, do you remember that time in Burma when—"

"Forget it, Bobby!"

"Listen, I put in for leave last month so I could go down to Peru with you to fix things with your witch doctor, and then had to cancel it. I'm putting in for another one, and I aim to take it. Thirty days is too long to spend in Texas now that the golfers have got ahold of the place, so iffen I'm not gonna be cruising the Amazon with you, guess I'll have to fall by Seattle, see what I can do for Maestra and Suzy in your unexplained absence."

Switters knew he was being manipulated, but he didn't hesitate. "Right after Christmas," he said firmly. "Ere the needles have browned upon the tree. Ere the reindeer dung has rolled off the roof. Ere the egg has gone rancid in the last of the nog. Ere Baby Jesus has been crammed back in the box."

"I'm banking on it, podner," said Capt. Case.

But that afternoon, even as he fondled the old rag of a training bra for the first time in nearly a year, Switters had an eerie sensation that he'd made a pledge that couldn't be kept.

damascus is said to be the oldest continuously inhabited city in the world.

It was on the road to Damascus (then already six thousand years old) that the apostle Paul (formerly Saul) suffered an epileptic seizure. Pounded to his knees by the relentless strobe of the sun, an egg-white mousse of spittle sudsing from his baked lips, Paul imagined he heard the big boom-boom voice of God (formerly Yahweh) admonishing him to scorn sensuality, snub women, and subdue nature, instructions that he subsequently incorporated into the foundation of the early Church (what came to be called "Christianity" was really Paulinism).

It was on the road to Damascus, now a paved highway lined with pizza parlors, car lots, and ice cream stands, that Switters, too, experienced a painful pulsation of lights behind his eyes, knocked sideways by his first migraine in eight months. Switters did not hear God's basso profundo. Above the horns, shouts, canned Arabic music, amplified prayers, and ubiquitous unmuffled motors—the cacophony thickened dramatically as they neared the city—he registered not a whisper of heavenly guidance, although at that point he might have welcomed some succor if not some actual advice.

If Switters's head ached twice as badly as usual, it may have been because he was of two minds.

Having rejected Deir ez-Zur as being too close to the Turkish border troubles, and Palmyra as being too far from anyplace useful, he had elected to ride the supply truck cum desert taxi all the way to Damascus. From there, he would have to negotiate a stealthy entry into Lebanon. (Maybe he'd drop in on Sol Glissant, take a dip in one of his pools, have one last gander at Matisse's *Blue Nude 1943*.) From Lebanon, he figured it ought to be easy enough to scoot into Turkey. So—ahead of him, somewhere down the line, there was Redhook ale and red-eye gravy; there was air-conditioning and beaches, there were libraries and galleries and forests and skylines, there were Maestra and Bobby and Today Is Tomorrow and the thing that had always seduced him and pulled him forward: the promise of new adventure. There might even have been—dare he consider it?—Suzy. Those things and more waited at the farthest end of the Damascus road, and they put the wahoo in him. But back at the other end, behind him, receding quickly now, there was a compact little Eden, where the almonds were toasting and the cuckoos were crooning. Back there was the infamous last prophecy of Our Lady of Fatima. Back there was a magic wart and a magic hymen. Back there was Domino Thiry.

Thus, as through the intermingling smokes of falafel fires and lunatic traffic he entered the city where the alphabet was born and zero invented, Switters was of two minds. Each of them was agleam. Both of them were hurting.

To report that he was of two minds is not to imply, exactly, that he was torn by dilemma. Though hardly a stranger to contrariety, Switters had always seemed to take a both/and approach to life, as opposed to the more conventional and restrictive either/or. (To say that he took *both* a both/and *and* an either/or approach may be overstating the extent of his yin/yanginess.) Wasn't he friend to both God and the Devil? Moreover, there had never been any question about whether or not he would leave the Pachomian convent: his eventual departure was written in every little star that ever burped its hydrogen and farted its helium in the void above the roofless roof of the Rapunzel Suite. In fact, something had been revealed (*suggested* may be the more accurate word) at the convent that had propelled him from the place as unstoppably as if he, himself, were a belch of sidereal gas.

Nevertheless, Switters could be said to be of two minds for the simple reason that, on the outskirts of Damascus, his synaptic electric bill was being split, fifty-fifty, by the process of anticipation and the process of memory, the former yanking his thoughts onward, the latter drawing them back.

In the end, the migraine proved no match for those two processes. As vicious as the headache was, it barely blunted his vague but exciting mental foretaste of South America via Seattle, while his memory of Christmas in Domino's tower was too acute to be overridden at all.

on christmas eve, Switters had attended vespers. He went expecting to be bored in a nostalgic and not altogether displeasing way. Those expectations were met. Afterward, roast lemon chicken with garlic sausage stuffing was served in the dining hall. There were walnut cookies and hot date tarts. The last remaining bottle of old wine—the sole survivor from the Domino birthday bash—was uncorked, and he led the sisters in a toast to the rebirth of the Divine in the world.

"And to the kings and wise men who arrived from the East," he said in French. In English he added, "Bearing gifts of frank incest and mirth."

Masked Beauty, who hadn't comprehended the English, asked earnestly if Egypt was by any chance east of Bethlehem. Domino, who'd caught the pun, asked him to please refrain from sacrilege. She wagged a scolding-mother finger at him, with an expression that seemed to say, "Just wait until I get you home, young man!"

He didn't have long to wait. Following a brief songfest in front of the rather goofy Christmas tree that he had fashioned from date palm fronds and snowed with puffs of shaving cream, a caroling during which everybody sang "Silent Night" in French, English, and the original German, and Switters performed solo a paraphrase of "Jingle Bells" in a tootered-up chipmunk voice ("Jingle bells / Batman smells / Robin laid an egg"), the gathering broke up. He and Domino retired to the tower.

In one corner she had made a smaller version of his dining-hall tree, substituting satin ribbons for the aerosol foam. Beneath it, on a brass tray, she'd placed three items:

A bottle of arrack.

A jar of petroleum jelly.

A manila envelope with rumpled edges and an aura around it.

Before the silent night, holy night was through, they'd investigate all three.

The wine that Switters had helped press in October (from grapes that, on stilts, he'd helped to pick) was too young to be agreeably consumed. Domino had ordered the potent date liquor from Damascus as a holiday treat. He thanked her for her thoughtfulness, but, concerned that she might still be under the impression that he was a man who required alcohol's flame to light the fuse of his zest, he attempted to assure her that arrack was a nonessential perk.

"Alcohol," he said, "is like one of those beasts that devours its own young." He told her that strong drink, early on, gave birth to whole litters of insights and ideas and joyful japes. But if you didn't round up those bright and witty cubs and whisk them away from her, if you allowed them to remain in her lair as the postpartum depression set in (if you kept drinking, in other words, beyond a certain point), she'd whirl on them and chew them up or swallow them alive, and in her dark maw she'd turn them to shit. He held out his cup. "I'll have just one," he said, secretly wishing she had bought him hashish, instead. (Wasn't it ever thus with Christmas gifts?)

Of course, he had more than one. More than two. But he didn't overdo it, at least not by C.R.A.F.T. Club standards. Anyway, it turned out that the arrack was primarily for her own benefit. It prepared her for the other items on the tray. Starting with the petroleum jelly.

"Are you sure you want to do this?" he asked. Following an extended barrage of arrack-scented kisses, during which each of her sumptuous bulges had been lovingly measured and stroked; during which his lingam had been symbolically peeled and repeeled as if it were the principal effigy of a bacchantic banana cult, she had presented herself for lubrication.

"Why not? If I am to live like a desert woman, I should love like a desert woman." But she *wasn't* sure. Wasn't this one of the sins that had brought down Sodom?

(The squish of the jelly. The socket that formed around his finger. The suction of the mouth that never eats. The flutter of the lashless eye. A pink noise that traveled up the spine like the whistle of a toy train. A troll burrow commandeered for a royal wedding. The bride stripped bare by her bachelors, even. The groom, in purple helmet, yet to arrive.)

"*Et tu?*" she asked breathily. "And you? Are you sure?"

"I'm sure I want every youness of you," he answered, adding somewhat cryptically, "Ah, that road I've never traveled, where the oyster meets the fig!"

But *he* wasn't sure, either. Feeling that remote part of her anatomy commence to dilate, to grow, as it were, hospitable, it occurred to him—ominously, perhaps—that he knew the word for it in only four or five languages.

(The bridegroom muscling through the cellar door. The rattle of the plumbing. The furnace's roar. Ceiling plaster cracking. Cans falling off the shelves. Basement flooding. Cat escaping up the chimney with a banshee yowl and its tail on fire. 'Twas the night before Christmas and all through the house, everything was stirring and God save the mouse.)

Afterward, they lay quietly in each other's arms, exhausted, awed, a little stunned; bonded the way people are who have shared an experience about which others can never be told, and which, they intuit, will be forever remembered yet rarely referred to between themselves.

Nearly an hour passed before Domino got up, lit several extra candles, poured them each another half-cup of arrack, and returned to their carpets, envelope in hand.

"Every girl who enters a convent," she began, by way of a preamble, "does so for two reasons, only one of which is religious. The secondary reasons vary from the girl to the girl, though you are correct when you are thinking—I know how the Switters mind works—that the reasons frequently involve some aspect of sexual fear, sexual guilt, or compensation for rejection by the opposite sex. It is true that there are few physically attractive nuns. But then there is the case of Masked Beauty, who became a nun for the same reason she generated that escargot on her nose: she was sick and tired of always being stared at by men."

Switters gulped the arrack. He was not a sipper. Domino didn't notice. Her eyes were fixed on the envelope.

"Some novices hear the call to serve humanity, to teach or to nurse. Those who enter closed convents, cloisters, choose to serve by being rather than by doing. That was what I chose. For my God, I would be instead of do, believing that the penance and reparations of the few can effect the salvation of the many. But I had, I must confess, other, less admirable motives. I wanted, you see, to belong to a special group, to be a member of a secret society that stood apart from the world, that operated closer to the bone, closer to the truth, closer to God's mysteries than the rest of humankind. Perhaps it was due to the way I was spurned by the girls in my American school, the ones who kept me out of their clubs and called me 'French whore' and so forth. It doesn't matter why, I still was guilty of elitist aspirations."

"Good for you. The right kind of elitism can restore the butterfat to a homogenized society. It multiplies nuance and expands the range of cultural motion." He started to recount for her Maestra's views on the virtues of true elitism, but Domino waved him off.

"I'm not looking for justification or approval, but I was sure you would understand, because in a sense it must be similar to your decision to belong to the CIA. I've come to suspect that we are somewhat alike in that way, having a desire not for power but for a status that lies beyond the consciousness of those who are merely powerful. Now, however, let me tell you that while I loved the stark sanctity of the cloister, it failed to entirely satisfy me. The secrets there were not especially secret, for one thing. The Christian select had essentially the same—how do you say it?—*scoop* as the Christian masses. They simply ritualized it differently and concentrated on it more exclusively. So, silly Simone was disappointed and by 1981 had decided to leave the nunhood. Really. I was set to turn in my wimple. That's when my aunt showed me the contents of this envelope." She patted the scruffy packet.

"It isn't that what is inside here is so amazing. You may well regard the last prophecy of Fatima as anticlimactic or even outright nonsense. The intriguing thing for me, silly sinner that I am, has always been the very secrecy of it, the fact that I have had access to holy information that not even the College of Cardinals, not even the present pope is privy to. By luck or design, our little maverick order was charged with the safekeeping of a . . . a *unique* message—ha! no grammar ticket!— that the Blessed Mother deemed vitally important. I've found that situation exciting. It's put me in league with Mary somehow, and it's made me feel a part of something singular, momentous, and . . . I don't know . . ."

"Fun?"

"No, no. For all of the consternation it's caused us here, it has been thrilling for me, as I've shamefully admitted, but I would draw the line at calling it 'fun.' How could I when there is nothing the least bit funny or, from the Western point of view, even hopeful about the third prophecy. In fact, it's all quite horrible. Quite horrible."

Her eyes suddenly became tight and intense. "But see for yourself. *Voilà.*" She thrust the envelope into his hands.

It was sturdy, the old envelope, but scuffed and flaky, and might have felt to him like the dried skin of a sidewinder had not his fingertips been slick with petroleum jelly.

Switters offered a brief preamble of his own.

"Etymologically," he said, clearing that part of his throat that hadn't been cleared by the arrack, "a prophet is somebody who 'speaks for' somebody else, so I take prophecy (from the Greek, *prophētēs*) with about the same amount of salt as I take press releases from a corporate shill. A prophet is just a self-proclaimed mouthpiece for invisible taciturn forces that allegedly control our destiny, and prophecy buffs tend to be either neurotically absorbed with their own salvation or morbidly fascinated by the prospect of impending catastrophe. Or both. A death wish on the one hand, a desperate, unrealistic hope for some kind of supernatural rescue operation on the other."

As he undid the clasp on the envelope, she informed him that the roots of the word notwithstanding, the prophet in this case was not speaking on behalf of a higher power, was hardly God's publicist but rather, in a sense, a whistleblower, warning her beloved humanity what the Almighty had in store for it if it didn't shape up. Our Lady of Fatima, then, was a kind of spy, a mole, an operative, working behind the scenes to delay if not forestall divine retribution, scheming to buy more time for her earthly brood. Domino thought that Agent Switters, of all people, would be sympathetic.

He responded that any feeling of occupational bond with the Virgin Mary was regrettably beyond him at the moment, but he promised to keep his mind as open to Marian ideas as a convenience store was to hold-up men. Nevertheless, he believed it only fair to advise her up front that he was as leery of those who predicted the future as he was disdainful of those for whom the future always promised to be real in ways that the present was not. "It's here. Today. Right now," he said.

"What is?"

"All of it."

"Today is tomorrow?"

"There you go." He flashed her a grin that could housebreak a walrus. Then, he opened the envelope.

Inside the envelope were not one but four sheets of paper. On two of them, Domino had provided complete English translations of the first and second Fatima prophecies. The crowning item, obviously, was the page of personal papal stationery, now dog-eared and yellowed, upon which Cardinal Thiry had written down his French version of the controversial third prophecy nearly forty years earlier. In addition, there was included an English translation—rendered, presumably, by Domino—of the third prophecy.

Since he had read them largely in bits and pieces or paraphrase, while assisting Suzy and Masked Beauty with their individual research projects, and since Domino was of the opinion that the trio of predictions was ultimately inseparable, Switters decided to refamiliarize himself with One and Two before tackling the pièce de résistance.

the first prophecy

You have seen Hell, where the souls of poor sinners go. To save them, God wishes to establish in the world devotion to My Immaculate Heart. If what I say to you is done, many souls will be saved and there will be peace. The war is going to end soon, but if people do not cease offending God, a worse one will break out during the reign of Pius XI. When you see a night illuminated by an unknown light, know that this is the great sign given to you by God that He is about to punish the World for its crimes, by means of war, famine and persecutions of the Church and the Holy Father.

Okay, then. And next—

the second prophecy

To prevent World punishment, I have come to ask for the consecration of Russia to My Immaculate Heart and the Communion of Reparation on the first Saturdays (of each month). If my requests are heeded, Russia will be converted and there will be peace; if not, she will spread her errors throughout the World, causing wars and persecutions of the Church. The good will be martyred, the Holy Father will have much to suffer, and various nations will be annihilated.

Already sedated by dinner, arrack, and the act of love most naughty, Switters could barely read those prognostications without yawning. They struck him as vague, bland, generalized, incongruous, and overly concerned with the fate of the Church, its dogma, and its leader. Had he heard them related by a starry-eyed ten-year-old Portuguese peasant girl in 1917, they might possibly have spun the propeller on his intellectual beanie, but now he just stretched and sighed like a hockey coach at a tea dance before proceeding to the ballyhooed main event: that legendary ultrasecret time-release pope onion,

the third prophecy of fatima

Before this century draws to a close, there are to be unimaginable advances in all sciences. These achievements will bring about a great physical ease but little intelligence or happiness. Everywhere, communication and education will flourish, yet men, deprived of My Immaculate Heart, will sink ever further into stupidity. Anguish and violence will increase apace with material wealth, and many will be lost to fiery death and sickness of spirit. In the century after this one, however, a certain unexpected wisdom and joy will come upon a segment of the population that has survived the earlier sorrows, but, alas, the Word that brings about this healing will be delivered to mankind neither from Rome's basilica nor from a converted Russia, but from the direction of a pyramid. Whether it is by design of God or the Evil One, even I do not know, yet the World must not fail to pay it close attention, for Heaven and Hell hang in the balance.

That was how it went. Switters read both the English and French versions, and as far as his sleepy mind could tell, they were in perfect agreement. In the next to last sentence, the French *mot* had been translated as "word" when he supposed it could have been rendered, as it often was in French, as "cue" (something said or signed in order to elicit a particular action onstage), but the meaning here was virtually the same, and he was scarcely in a mood to quibble. In fact, he yawned like a pigeonhole before conceding that "This little augury is more intriguing than the first two. Definitely more intriguing. But I honestly can't see what all the furor is about, why you'd find it so horrifying or ol' John the Twenty-third would go through a ream and a half of Kleenex."

"You don't see why?"

"No, sister love, I don't. I mean, it's hardly headline news that the corporate state and its media are using the latest gadget-com and gimmick-tech to dumb us down as steadily as if they were standing on a stool and pounding our brains with a frozen ham. Or that an abundance of information can exacerbate ignorance, if the information is of poor quality. Or that people can be lavishly entertained right around the clock and still feel empty and disconnected. Fatima slam-dunked the crystal ball in that regard, I have to give her credit, whoever she was. All that stuff is on us like a bad suit, and she called it in 1917. But, hey, there's a flip side to it, ways to profit from it, ways to get around it, and—"

"Yes, yes," Domino broke in impatiently. "The remedy is Her Immaculate Heart. But what about the rest of the prophecy?"

"You mean the nice part about unexpected joy and wisdom heading our way in the next century? Sounds bloody jolly to me, to quote the late Potney Smithe, Esquire. Bloody jolly. Assuming that you and I will be among the survivors."

"Yes, but this so-called wisdom and joy, this healing, will not be brought about by the Church."

"So? Who gives a damn whether the Church brings it about as long as it's brought about?"

She frowned so hard her cheeks nearly doubled. "Don't you see? The enlightening doctrine is to come from the direction of the pyramids. From the Middle East. That means Islam. Mary's inference is that Islam will succeed where Christianity has failed. Who gives a damn? Everyone in the Western world *ought* to give a damn! The implications are almost too disturbing to be contemplated."

"Well now, this wouldn't happen to be the whining of a poor loser, would it?" A herd of sarcastic remarks was set to stampede out of his voice box, but he bit his tongue and turned them back. He didn't want to hurt her, and he was too drowsy to covet prolonged conversation. "Listen," he said, "these prophecies leave a lot of room for interpretation, and there's a possibility you may have missed—"

"Don't you think we haven't—"

"Yeah, I know you and Masked Beauty have been kicking this gong around for years, but you still may have misinterpreted some point or other. Isn't that why you wanted me to cast my unflinching bloodshot beam on it? I, who have left speechless entire roomfuls of itinerant journalists and shadowy international entrepreneurs with my unprecedented unravelings of certain passages of *Finnegans Wake*? Just let me sleep on it, sister love. Do please let me sleep on it."

With that, he blew out the closest candle, kissed the disappointed nun, and snuggled down between the rugs. "Have you noticed," he asked in a faint, sweet voice just before he began to snore, "that nobody talks about the sandman anymore?"

Our hero must have received a heavy dusting of the sandman's sedative grit because when he finally awoke, the sky was full of blue and the bed empty of Domino. The secret envelope and the telltale Vaseline were gone as well, though the English translation of the third prophecy could be seen protruding from his left tennis shoe. It was eight according to his watch, which meant it would have been eleven, Christmas Eve, in Seattle. He'd intended to ring his grandmother at an earlier hour, but even though it was now past her bedtime, he decided to call her. He held his breath as he punched in the numbers, fearful that Suzy might answer the phone, discouraged that she probably would not.

"This had better be good," a sleepy voice grumbled.

"It's a holiday greeting, full of love, warmth, and good cheer," piped Switters.

"You!" Maestra growled. "I might have known. You think an old woman doesn't need her rest just because it's Santa Claus's birthday? Next thing I know you'll be calling me up at midnight on the Fourth of July to pledge allegiance to what's left of the flag." Then she softened and inquired as to his health and whereabouts—"Not that you'd be truthful about it"—and complained that he was off in some flea-bitten land somewhere, ignoring her, risking his hide and lying about it, when it was no longer of any necessity. "You can take the boy out of the CIA but you can't take the CIA out of—"

"Merry X-mas, Maestra."

"Heh! Merry X-mas, you no-good scamp. I miss you. Little Suzy misses you, too, for some unfathomable reason. It was you who put dirty ideas in the poor child's head and led her astray. She's gone to Sacramento for the holidays. What time is it, for God's sake? That cute Captain Case checks up on us every now and then. *He* doesn't wait until the middle of the night on Christmas. Okay, there's just one thing I have to know. Are you still scooting yourself around in that pathetic dodge-'em chair?"

"No. I'm not. I'm on stilts."

There was prolonged silence on the other end of the line, although he could tell from her breathing that she definitely hadn't dozed off.

Maestra's silence must have been contagious, for the oasis was unusually quiet that morning. He was soon to learn from a note pinned to
the door of his room that Masked Beauty, rather abruptly, had decreed
it a day of private devotion, during which the sisterhood would neither
eat nor speak. *That's fine,* Switters reasoned. *It'll create an atmosphere con-
ducive to my contemplation of the Fatima folderol.*

But was it folderol? Rilke, the poet whose verses had helped him
get out of bed mornings in Berkeley, wrote, "The future enters into
us in order to transform itself in us long before it happens." And Today
Is Tomorrow, with his vision root, had offered the Swit an actual
glimpse of the interpenetration of realities and chronologies. He
could not with conviction deny that prophecy was theoretically possible. It was just that so much of it reeked of hysteria, esoterica,
naiveté, and humbug—and Fatima's forewarnings were hardly free of
that shrill cloy. Nevertheless . . .

Nevertheless, a fair amount of what she (be she Divine Mother or
schizophrenic pasture girl) had predicted in her three-pronged prog-
nosis had indisputedly come to pass. It wasn't much, really, but it
was enough to merit serious consideration of the remainder of her
declarations.

The part that Switters found encouraging (though he would never
admit to a need for encouragement), and the part that seemed to hurt
Domino deep in her heart, was the business about a happy transformation of humanity (or, rather, a portion of humanity, an elite, perhaps)
that would be cued not from the Church or the Kremlin but from
pyramid territory. Domino believed this a foretelling of the triumph of
the Islamic point of view, a victory of Mohammed's metaphysical
system over the institutions and metaphysics of Jesus Christ. Switters
was not so sure. He kept harkening back to the material he'd pulled off
the Net for Masked Beauty, the stuff about King Hermanos con-
structing the pyramids as vaults in which to shelter the revelations and
secrets of the ancient sages. He'd wager neither his Beretta nor his
Broadway show tunes on it, but he had an inkling that it was in those
mystical, astrological, and alchemical texts known as the Hermetic
Writings, rather than in the teachings of the Koran (and the dogma
into which those teachings had been subsequently corrupted), that
modern survivors would locate their cue as to how to attain and sustain
a wise and joyful existence. After all, the Hermetic Writings were from
the pyramids, were, in effect, *responsible* for the pyramids, whereas any

connection between pyramids and Islam was of the most tenuous and after-the-fact geographical nature.

Thus it was that on Christmas Day, Switters had sat in the shade of a lemon tree and, while nibbling on leftover falafel that he'd stolen from Maria Une's deserted kitchen, sump-pumped into his frontal lobe everything that he could remember about the Hermetic tradition.

Chickpea in his mouth, dry heat in his nostrils, papery leaf rustle and narcotic hen cluck in his ears, grainy wind on his skin, distant shimmer (like a flutter of god beards, a pulse of muslin-wrapped phosphorus) in his eyes, thirst never far from his throat: it was, in terms of the senses, a perfect situation in which to try to summon his faint knowledge of that series of writings (like the Bible, it was a disjointed, fragmented collection rather than a unified canon) known as the *Corpus Hermeticum*. The tradition, while popularized in ancient Greece, had originated in still older Egypt, in places probably not wildly different from this one.

Hermetic teachings, as best as he could recall, did not constitute a theology, but, rather, were designed as a practical guide to a sane and peaceful life of natural science, contemplation, and self-refinement. They did, however, in their effort to define and celebrate humanity's place in the grand scheme of things, analyze at great length our relationship to the cosmos, before and after death. Their purpose, though, was to educate and improve; to enlarge the soul rather than to save it.

Well and good, Switters supposed. There was much to admire about a belief system that refused to proselytize or to water itself down to attract converts, that was nature friendly, body friendly (references abounded in the writings to various forms of sex magic), tolerant, respectful, and innocent of any recorded act of repression or bloodshed. A belief system that didn't insist on belief? That did more good than harm? He'd award it six stars out of five and tell it to keep the change—bearing in mind all the while that a committee of dullards (who but the dull had time or patience to serve on committees?), a small infusion of earnest missing links, could pull it down to their squeaky level and enfeeble it almost overnight.

Still, the Hermetic tradition had deeper roots than any of our religions (though not as deep as shamanism), and was rumored to be preserved to this day by adepts who honored it without banging any pots and pans. On the other hand, those adepts (sometimes called the Invisible College) were few in number, weak in influence. Even in its heyday, Hermeticism had never—so far as anybody knew—turned a single tide of history. Was there any sound reason to reckon that there would occur a resurgence of Hermetic interest in the near next century (the millennial page was so close to flipping one could feel its latent breeze), and that it would thus inspire or instruct a significant minority of the corporate-molded populace to tune its cells to a higher frequency? No, there was something about such a scenario that just didn't pitch. Granted, he wasn't much of a consumer, but if this was what Fatima was selling, he was keeping Mr. Plastic in his wallet, at least until he kicked a few more tires and drove around the block.

Using one of the stilts, he swatted a winter lemon loose from a bough, catching it as it fell, a feat that filled him with immense pleasure. He reamed the fruit with a stiff finger, and for some perverse reason, thought of Domino and the intimacies of the previous night. Then, squeezing lemon juice onto a patty of cold falafel, smelling its citric aliveness, rolling its fresh solar acids—yellow, dynamic, and changeless—along the bronco spine of his tongue, he turned back to the curious prophecy.

What possible impetus could there be for a Hermetic renaissance? An unearthing, perhaps, of the fourteen golden tablets? He tried to imagine a team of Egyptologists brushing the sands of centuries from the plates, scanning their magnifying glasses along the columns of glyphs, suggesting, months or years later, during an announcement on CNN, that if beleaguered viewers were only to heed the oblique instructions so quaintly encoded in those ancient alchemical symbols, they might develop techniques and practices for overcoming their human limitations, and, in the process, a way to understand—and function smoothly within—an immutable cosmic order. But try as he might, he couldn't envision the impact of such information lasting much beyond the cheeseburger and minivan commercials that would follow it. Hermeticism had its merits, certainly, but it lacked immediacy. It seemed so stereotypically occult as to be fusty and inane, like the wizard hat that Mickey Mouse wore when he played the Sorcerer's Apprentice. In his gut (where the ball of white light was spritzing the acerbic droplets of lemon juice), he sensed that a neo-Hermetic utopia was even less likely than an Islamic one.

Pausing then, brushing the last falafel crumbs from his lips, he thought of the old trickster who'd given his name to those Greco-Egyptian mysteries: old Hermes, god of transitions, runner of errands between the two worlds, patron of explorers and thieves. Setting up his three-card monte stand on the frontiers of knowledge, Hermes was neither a suffering savior deity nor a loving father deity, but a brash bringer of new ideas and practical solutions to those who were quick enough to grasp them, strong enough to accept them. Hermes could be regarded as the immortal prototype of the mortal shaman, and like shamans everywhere, he was a revered practitioner of folk medicine, conversant on every level with plants, constellations, and minerals. He could heal, but he also could—and would—play outlandish pranks. Rather similar, as Switters had earlier noted, to Today Is Tomorrow, damn his parrot-boiling hide.

In the Aegean and eastern Mediterranean regions, Hermes had been identified originally as one of the Great Mother's primal serpent-consorts, an aspect still alluded to by the pair of snakes entwined around a rod in the Hermetic logo of the American Medical Association. Levantine lore went so far as to view Hermes as a personification of the World Snake, the ruler of time, and in dragging that arcane tidbit from his memory pond, Switters's mind again scrolled to the Amazonian shaman. When Switters had asked R. Potney Smithe if the Kandakandero religion (if it could even be loosely described as a religion), had a name, the anthropologist had replied that when the tribal elders referred to anything remotely resembling a belief system, it was with a phrase that translated as something like, the Cult of the Great Snake. ("That's bloody damned epic, isn't it? Eh? Mind you, I haven't the foggiest notion what it infers.") Switters hadn't a clear notion, either, but there in the Syrian bake, he experienced a tiny chill as he remembered that other character, the crafty, multilingual, ex-Marxist mestizo who, though not a Kadak (not one of the "Real People"), appeared to be working toward becoming Today Is Tomorrow's disciple, if not his lieutenant or rival; and how the dude had renamed himself Fer-de-lance and sported a constrictor-skin ensemble (except for gold teeth and Nike basketball shoes). Fer-de-lance radiated some spooky, transcultural, reptilian charisma, which was not unenhanced by the buzz that he supposedly had an ongoing relationship—a totemic dialogue, a Moby Dickian fixation, a vendetta, or a marketing ploy: who could even guess?—with a forty-foot-long anaconda. Hale fellow, well met.

As near as Switters could recollect, Today Is Tomorrow, himself, expressed no direct interest in any kind of serpent magic, not in regard to time or anything else. However, this circuitous reminiscing about the witchman had brought his image fully to mind, and, abruptly, at that instant—wham! bam!—a thought hit Switters like a stockyard paddle smacking a porker's backside. Could it possibly? . . . Yes! Of course! How obvious! That was it! He felt the validity of it in every gob of his marrow. And in a sudden rush of eureka, he forgot himself, taboowise, and very nearly sprang to his feet.

He had caught himself, steadied himself, realigned his heels on the loaf of red rock where they'd been carefully propped, and leaned back against the spindly trunk. Overhead, the lemons swung like papier-mâché stars in a cheesy planetarium. It was a totally bizarre theory, he supposed, this connection he was entertaining, but the Fatima phenomenon was pretty crazy, too, and the mere fact that it had been accredited by a major mainstream institution didn't render it any less so. Switters was, well, if not thoroughly emotionally excited, at least intellectually stimulated, and he was anxious to share his "discovery" with Domino. Much as she had shared the secret prophecy with him? Had drawn him into the pudding? Irrationally, perhaps, he thought of Eve introducing the consciousness-expanding snake fruit to her partner in Eden. The sharing of certain kinds of knowledge is seldom without consequences.

For better or for worse, however, his desire to apprise Domino was thwarted. She remained in seclusion the whole of Christmas Day, thickly cocooned in prayer, though whether to please Baby Jesus, the Virgin Mary, or Masked Beauty was never evident. Frustrated, Switters had brainstormed awhile longer under the furniture-scented tree, then stilted off to the office to e-mail a holiday greeting to Bobby Case. To his surprise, his friend had returned the sentiment immediately. *Massive merriment to you, son. Here on Oki, we got us raw octopus with all the trimmings. How you spending your day?*

There being no way to truthfully explain, Switters replied that he had to leave right away to attend a performance of *The Nutcracker.*

Hope it's the one with Tonya Harding, wired Bobby. And that was that.

In his room, having retrieved the remainder of the arrack from the tower, Switters drank, pondered, drank some more, pondered some more. Within an hour, both the drinking and the thinking petered out, and he turned to *Finnegans Wake,* though he got no further than a line in the preface, where Stan Gebler Davies wrote of Joyce, "The man had an interesting life, which most men do who have an abiding interest in women, drink, high art, and the operation of their own genius." Stopping to consider that statement—wondering why it seemed so tricky, so difficult, to lead simultaneously an interesting life and a convention-ally moral life (it was as if some pathology of dualism conspired to make them mutually exclusive)—he fell asleep and did not wake until morning, when there was an urgent rapping at his door.

"Monsieur Switters! Le camion! Le camion!"

"Pippi?" It had to be Pippi, for even the voice sounded freckled and red-haired. "What? The truck? *Le camion? Pourquoi?"*

It was true. The supply truck had arrived. It hadn't been expected for another couple of days. Switters was tempted to kiss it off, to catch it the next time it came through, which would be only two or three weeks. But then he remembered his "discovery" and rushed to get out of bed and throw his things together.

"*Dépêchez-vous!*"

"I'm hurrying. *Où est* Sister Domino?"

Pippi assured him that Domino would meet him at the gate. And she did. Had it not been so abrupt, she probably wouldn't have cried, but she had no time to prepare herself, and teardrops, one after the other, rolled like dead bees down the overturned hives of her cheeks as she explained to the astonished driver that the white-suited male (A man? Here?) in the wheelchair would be needing passage to Deir ez-Zur.

The trucker insisted that Switters ride in the front with him and his assistant, undoubtedly as much out of curiosity—he wanted to question him—as politeness or respect. He fired up the engine and waited, with impatience and disbelief, while the crippled American and the French nun embraced.

Domino's smile cut like a prow through the cascading tears. "I should have no complaints," she said with a brightness that was only half false. "I've known the full strong love of a man of the world and yet emerged with my maidenhood immaculate. A virgin *in partu*." She tried to laugh, but there was a chirpy lump in her throat.

"Cake and eat it," said Switters approvingly, noticing that his own voice sounded as if it were being run along the pickets in a fence. "Listen. We never got time to talk. About the third prophecy, I mean."

"I know. I know. This is happening too fast. You must write me about it as soon as you can. The truck still brings our mail." She glanced nervously at the driver.

"No. Listen. You have to hear this. It's not Islam."

"Not Islam?"

"The word, the message that can transform the future. It isn't going to come from Islam. It's coming from Today Is Tomorrow."

"What are you talking about?" Was this dear man a nut case, after all?

"The prophecy says the cue will be delivered from the direction of *une pyramide*. Not *les* but *une*. Singular. The direction of one pyramid. Don't you recall that Today Is Tomorrow has this head . . . the man's a living pyramid! Whatever comes out of his mouth comes from the direction of a—"

"Ooh-la-la! This is crazy."

The driver sounded his horn. The assistant, standing by to help Switters into the cab and fold up his wheelchair, clapped his hands. Switters quieted them both by snarling something in colloquial Arabic, the equivalent of "Hold your fucking camels."

"You'd better go, my dearest," said Domino.

"Think about it," Switters insisted. "The guy's a pyramid with legs."

"So? He's a savage. He's an illiterate witch doctor. A wild primitive who lives in the forest, incommunicado."

"True enough. But he's got a kind of philosophy. I'm serious. He's got a concept. A vision. And it's out of a pyramid, not that a pyramid per se is any—"

"What kind of 'philosophy'? What could he have that would—"

"I'm not sure. I mean, it's *unique*, but I only know the general outline. I'll find out, though. If there are pertinent details, I'll find them out when I'm there. Okay?"

"Okay," she sighed, unsure as to what she was agreeing to. She made a little furrow in her chin, which the tear runoff filled like rainwater in a ditch.

The other Pachomians, one by one, had gathered at the gate to see him off. ZuZu, Pippi, Mustang Sally, both Marias, Bob. Masked Beauty was last to arrive. She wore her veil, of course, but he could detect her beauty-buster behind it, glowing like a holographic hush puppy, a glob of ghost grease in the morning sun. Holding her old body erect, august as an abbess ought to be, proud as a Matisse nude, she clasped his hand. "Tell them to limit their procreation," she said in her flat, childish French. "Wherever you go, tell them."

Switters squeezed her bony fingers. He promised. Then, as the burly assistant lifted him bodily into the truck, he blew the sisterhood a round of kisses and yelled, "Save my stilts!" He yelled it again, wedged between the two truckers, as they drove away. *"Au revoir!* Save my stilts!"

In the deep velvet radish of his heart, he must have realized that it was highly unlikely that he would ever see those Pippi-made stilts again, yet had he been unwilling to lie to himself, he would have been a very poor romantic, indeed. Why, he might have asked, did it seem so tricky, so difficult, to lead simultaneously a romantic life and a fully conscious one?

During the long, rough drive—east-northeast to Deir ez-Zur (where they passed the night), south-southwest to Palmyra (where they again slept over), and on southwestward to the capital—Switters was compressed like anchovy paste in a living sandwich. The assistant, on his right, rarely spoke, but Toufic, the driver, encouraged by Switters's earlier display of Arabic, questioned him relentlessly. A squat man, about thirty, with a lath basket of tight black curls, and soft brown eyes that leaked soul by the ounce, Toufic was a Christian (Eastern Orthodox, of course, not Roman), and as such, demanded to know what his passenger had been doing in a convent. Toufic also had relatives in the rug trade in Louisville, Kentucky, and while he himself had often dreamed of emigrating there, he was incensed over America's recent air attacks on the innocent people of Iraq and wanted from his rider a full accounting for those bully-boy atrocities.

Switters's answers must have pleased him, for by the time they got to Deir ez-Zur they were conversing agreeably, and by the time they departed Palmyra they were behaving like schoolyard buddies.

They entered Damascus (about 7 P.M., December 28) on An-Nassirah Avenue, proceeding at a slow, noisy pace to the walled old city and the Via Recta, mentioned in the Bible as the "Street of Straight," though its straightness, like many another biblical reference, could hardly have been meant to be taken literally. The Via Recta marked the boundary of the city's Christian quarter, and it was into that quarter that Toufic drove Switters after the other passengers and ten crates of dates had been offloaded. "For your comfort and safety," he said, reminding Switters that they were in the middle of Ramadan, the holy month of fasting. Between sunrise and dusk, he would find nothing to eat outside the Christian quarter, and even there only in a private home. Moreover, the sacred rigors of Ramadan had intensified anti-American passions in Syria (the Iraqi bombing raids having occurred only ten days earlier), and in some parts of Damascus there were blades that would relish the wicked white butter of a Yankee throat. Luckily, Toufic and his family had a spare room to let.

With a cough—half leaded exhaust fumes, half brazier kabob smoke—Switters accepted the offer. He trusted Toufic but regretted that Mr. Beretta lay unattended in the crocodile valise in the rear of the truck. The ex-operative was getting a wee careless in his retirement. He sighed, disgusted but not really surprised that Clinton had fallen in with the cowboys. It was an all too familiar story.

Toufic stopped the truck, an aging deuce-and-a-half Mercedes with a canvas canopy, on a coiling side street and sounded the horn four times. With squeaks and rattles, a rickety corrugated tin door was raised, and Toufic backed the vehicle into a deep, narrow garage. Dimly lit by a pair of raw forty-watt bulbs that dangled from the stucco ceiling like polished anklebones on strings, the space smelled of motor oil, solvent, sour metals, musky rubber, and burnt gunk. Off to the right, more brightly illuminated, was a small glassed-in office occupied by three men: two standing, one seated at a cluttered wooden desk. Toufic had to go to the office to complete some paperwork. He suggested that Switters wait where he was. "I'll be needing my valise," said Switters, fairly pointedly.

The assistant fetched the bag. Then he fetched brushes, rags, and a tub of soapy water and began vigorously to wash the peeling paint of the sand-and-sun-tortured truck. Through the veil of scrub water that coursed down the windshield, the naked lightbulbs reminded Switters of the lemons of St. Pachomius. Their yellow blaze aggravated his headache. He shifted his gaze to the office, where Toufic was now in conversation with the others: the man at the desk, who was an older, fatter version of Toufic, and the two standing men, who, Switters noticed, wore suits and ties and European faces. Something about the pair tightened Switters's Langley-trained eye. He squinted through the sudsy stream. He patted his valise.

After nearly a half hour, Toufic returned, scolding the assistant for killing his truck with cleanliness. "Go home to your family," he ordered, shooing the busy washer out the door. "We go, too," he told Switters, and he unfolded the chair. Puzzled at how nimbly his passenger leapt from the cab into the Invacare 9000, he asked, "What did you say again was the trouble with you?"

"Walking pneumonia." The phrase did not translate well into Arabic.

Toufic lived several blocks from the garage. Switters rolled along beside him through the streets of the oldest continuously inhabited city on earth. It was in this very neighborhood that the misogynist, Paul, had taken refuge after his fit on the Damascus road and formulated the structure and stricture of what would become known as Christianity. The Street of Straight, indeed. As they bumped along over the worn paving stones, Toufic, a bit embarrassed, informed Switters that he could only offer his room until early the following morning. Toufic had been assigned an unexpected driving job, and, of course, he could not leave Switters alone in his home with his wife.

Of course not. Toufic may have been Christian, but he was nonetheless Arabic and thus subject to the sexual insecurities that among men of the Middle East achieved titanic, even earth-changing proportions; insecurities that had spawned veils, shaven heads, clitoridectomies, house arrest, segregation, macho posturing, and three major religions. *The women hereabouts must have really been something!* thought Switters. They must have had loins of fire, pussies of gold; their libidos must have brayed like wild asses and loomed like desert dunes. Inexhaustible, inextinguishable, inextricable, they had turned the weaker sexual animal inside out and drove him to build cultural, political, and religious walls in order to contain their deep, roiling juices, walls so steep and rigid they still stood. The Levant had no monopoly on penile insecurity: two of the world's most magnificent creatures, the tiger and the rhinoceros, were going extinct in 1998 because Asian males believed they needed to consume the body parts of those beasts to shore their precious peckers up; and dangerously excessive population growth in many nations was due to a husbandly compulsion to publicly demonstrate virility by keeping their poor wives pregnant. Yet, it was in the Middle East that the perception of pussy whippery had manifested itself most dramatically and with the longest-lasting consequences, and Switters (who had, himself, experienced a tinge of coital frailty after Sister Fannie bolted his cot) wished he might have visited the tents of some of those lusty Semitic and pre-Semitic lasses. Had the men been ego-wounded crybabies and scaredy-cats, or were the women actually that free, that hot? In any event, you can bet he would have learned the name for their intimidating treasure in every tribal dialect.

His reverie, his fanciful yearning for a time machine that might set back his presence on that Damascus street by five thousand years, was punctured by Toufic's resumed apologies. Apparently the driver imagined that his guest was sulking. "I am very sorry, my friend, but I must drive again come the dawn. I had not thought it so."

"No problem," Switters assured him. "Will you be going anywhere near the Lebanese border? I could use a ride."

"Oh, no. As a matter of fact"—he laughed—"I must drive again back to the convent oasis."

The wheelchair skidded to a stop. "Why? What do you mean?" The migraine shot out of his ears like squirt from a clam. He hadn't felt so alert in months.

Toufic looked worried, as if he were again offending the American. "Those two foreign gentlemen at the garage. They wish to be taken there tomorrow."

Switters remained stationary. "What for?"

"Why, business of the Church, most assuredly. One of them is a religious scholar from Lisbon in Portugal, and the other is a lawyer in the employ of the Vatican."

"They told you this?"

"They told my boss. I will transport them in his car with the four-wheel drive. No need for the truck, naturally. The gentlemen could not hire a car from the airport because the drivers there are under Ramadan."

En route to Deir ez-Zur, they'd discussed Ramadan, and Switters had wondered why, if a people were at one with the Divine, was not *every* month holy; why this setting apart of dates and places, shouldn't Tuesday be as glorious as Sunday or Saturday, shouldn't one's water closet be as sanctified as Mecca, Lourdes, or Benares? If Toufic imagined such thoughts in his guest's mind at this moment, however, he was badly mistaken.

The foreign gentlemen at the garage . . . The younger, thinner one (late thirties, probably, and lithe as a bean vine) had a face like the instruction sheet that came with an unassembled toy: it looked simple at first and ordinary and frank, but the longer you studied it, the more incomprehensible it became. It was his body language that was troublesome, however. From his receding ebony hair to the points of his hand-tooled shoes, the Italian carried himself with the self-conscious grace of a commercially oriented martial artist. He feigned an attitude of disinterest, of relaxation, yet every muscle was spring-wound and tense, ready to pop into furious action. Switters had observed a similar look in many a street-level operative, in many a hitman. There was a time when he had observed the look in his own mirror.

The older man (well over sixty) had wispy gray hair and the ruddy complexion of a whiskey priest. His mouth was babyish and weak, a mouth meant for sucking a sugar tit; but behind his gold-rimmed spectacles, his eyes were as hard and unfeeling as petrified scat. Although he seemed highly intelligent, Switters could detect that his was an intellect of the shrewd variety, the kind that grasped facts and figures and understood virtually nothing of genuine importance; a well-oiled brain dedicated to the defense, perpetuation, and exploitation of every cliché and superstition in the saddlebags of institutionalized reality. *This cookie is the spitting image of John Foster Dulles*, thought Switters, and immediately he dispatched a sample of his oral fluids to mingle with the dust of the oldest continuously inhabited city on earth.

Switters turned to the somewhat bewildered Toufic. "Beginning tomorrow, pal," he said, "you're going to have a new assistant. I hope your employer's jalopy seats four comfortably." He fixed the slack-jawed Syrian with what the unoriginal have described as his fierce, hypnotic green eyes. "I'll be going back to the oasis with you."

He unzipped his valise and, tossing aside C.R.A.F.T. Club T-shirts and socks with little cartoon squid on them, went straight for the false bottom. "First," he said, "you've got to help me install this device in the rear seat of that car we'll be driving. In English, we call it a *bug*."

Switters grinned. Toufic looked numb. Above them, the third-quarter crescent of the Ramadan moon was itself a numb smile, perfectly suited, perhaps, for the human activities upon which its dry silvery drool seemed ever destined to fall.

part 4

You only live twice:
once after you're born
and once before you die.
　　　　　—Bashō

once upon a time, four nuns boarded a jetliner bound from Damascus to Rome. Alitalia Flight 023 took off to the northeast and flew out over twenty or so land miles of the arid Syrian plain before banking with an avian grace and turning back toward the Mediterranean. From the air, the desert appeared a loose, lumpy weave of red and yellow strands, like a potholder made in the craft shack at a summer camp for retarded children. The nuns were sweating like mares, and as they . . .

Sorry. It's no big deal, really; nothing major, not anything that wholly justifies this interruption. And yet despite the fact that the truths in narration are all relative truths (perhaps the truths in life, as well), despite the sovereign authority of poetic license, this report, claiming no kinship to Finnegan, has, in the interest of both clarity and expediency, endeavored never to indulge in the sort of literary trickery that actively encourages readers to jump to false conclusions. So, while it may be overreactive in this instance, while it may even smack of the kind of self-righteous puritanism that is to genuine purity what a two-bit dictator is to a philosopher king, let us reach into the inkwell jewel box and withdraw two sets of exquisite superscript signs— " for the right ear, " for the left—and hang them from the lobes on either side of the word *nuns*. Like so: "nuns." This, of course, is not for purposes of ornamentation, although these apostrophic clusters possess an understated, overlooked beauty that transcends the merely chic. (Do they not resemble, say, the windblown teardrops of fairy folk, commas on a trampoline, tadpoles with stomach cramps, or human fetuses in the first days following conception?) No, a stern word such as *nuns* is undemanding of decorative trinket. We so adorn it here only to set it apart from other words in the sentence for reasons of scrupulous verisimilitude.

It was reported above that once upon a time in Damascus, four nuns boarded an airliner bound for Rome. To be absolutely factual, while they may have looked like ordinary holy sisters to their fellow passengers, three of those "nuns" had been long-since defrocked and the fourth "nun," the one rolled aboard in a wheelchair, was a man.

The part about them sweating, however, was completely accurate. They perspired because it was a warm day in May, and they were dressed in dark, heavy winter habits that had been dug out of a trunk in the abbess's storeroom, their lighter habits, customary in that area of the world, having been ceremoniously incinerated approximately one year before. They also perspired because they were nerve-racked, because their ability to board the flight had been in question to the very last moment; because recent history, already somewhat of a trial for them, had really gotten out of hand after the evening when that "nun" most deserving of apostrophic disclaimer—the imposter, the man—had reappeared at their convent.

The supply truck, when en route from Damascus to Deir ez-Zur, always stopped for the night in a hill village about thirty kilometers west of the Pachomian oasis. That was why it would arrive at the compound early of a morning. The car, an Audi sedan with reinforced suspension, heavy-duty shock absorbers, and four-wheel drive, traveled faster than the truck, even across that rude terrain; there were no deliveries to be made in the village, and the European clients would brook no delay. So, Toufic drove through the settlement with only a honk and a wave, and pressed on to the convent. They arrived just before sunset.

Ordering Toufic and his suspect "assistant" (again, the earrings of qualification) to wait in the car, the two men walked up to the great wooden gate. As they read its sign, Switters listened with interest to hear how many times they'd ring the bell. He watched even more intently to see which of the sisters would eventually admit them. He knew that in time the pair would be admitted. He knew their business. Their quiet conversation in the backseat had resounded in his ear chip like dialogue in a Verdi opera, and although his Italian was hardly *perfetto*, he had scant difficulty in piecing together their intentions.

Not surprisingly, it was Domino Thiry who finally let them in. She couldn't see him, and Switters caught only the briefest glimpse of her, but it was enough to set his pulses syncopating the way they used to do when Suzy entered the room. He wondered if Suzy would still affect him like that—and could think of no reason why she would not. He lit a cigar. There was little cause to rush. The churchmen were undoubtedly ruthless, but they would prefer negotiation to intimidation, intimidation to violence. There would be protocol to follow. On both sides. Right now, he imagined that tea was being served.

"Back there on the other side of Jebel ash-Shawmarīyah," said Toufic, referring to the central mountain range, "when we passed that band of Bedouins, you almost broke your eyeballs looking at them. I thought you were going to leap from the car and join them."

"I almost did. But I didn't see anyone I recognized."

Scoffing, Toufic pulled the lever that allowed his seat to recline. He had driven for nearly nine hours, a lot of it spent dodging rocks and potholes in the roadless road. He lay back and lit a cigarette. If he was aware that his cigarette, any cigarette, was to Switters's cigar what a two-bit dictator was to a philosopher king, he did not let on. "You may have been better off intruding on Bedouins instead of getting mixed up in the internal affairs of a church to which you don't even belong."

"I expect you're right."

"You Americans!"

"Always butting into other people's business?"

"We are told that America is the land of the free."

Switters might have brought up video surveillance in public places, police microphones on neighborhood street corners, sniffer dogs in airports, blue codes, urine testing, DNA data banks, Internet censorship, helmet laws, tobacco laws, seat belt laws, liquor laws, persecution for joking, prosecution for flirting, litigation over everything under the sun, and the telling statistic that in the U.S., 645 out of every 100,000 citizens were locked up in prisons, as opposed to an average of 80 per 100,000 in the rest of the world. However, it was just too difficult to put those things into Arabic. And anyhow, he would have had to end by suggesting that maybe those outrages were a small price to pay, America being so bouncy, and all.

Switters switched to French, in which Toufic, like many Damascenes, was modestly conversant. "If *land* is taken to mean *nation*, then 'land of the free' is an oxymoron. You know this word? An oxymoron is a faux paradox, an incongruity that arises not out of the pervasively contradictory nature of the universe but out of a clumsy or deceptive misuse of language. Our oxymorons are more dangerous than our missiles, pal. Back when the mendacious phrase 'genuine imitation leather' was accepted by the populace without violent protest, it paved the way for all the bigger, more sophisticated lies that were to follow. But, hey, don't get me wrong, Toufic, I'm no seditious malcontent. After eight months of living high on the chickpea, I'd just love to sink down into one of those American fried ham suppers with gravy, a meal so greasy you have to tie it to your teeth to chew it. Afterward, a Baby Ruth candy bar, an hour of Pee-wee Herman. And if the truth be told, I'm nearly as admiring of the audacious hustler who had the sheer gall to promote a 'genuine imitation' as I am disappointed in the public that neglected to lynch him for it. P. T. Barnum, Joseph Goebbels, John Foster Dulles." He spat out of the window. "The 'genuine imitation leather' bastard could rub shoulders with the worst of them."

Switters turned to see if Toufic had followed any of this babble and found him sound asleep. Well, okay, this was as good a time as any to bring on Mr. Beretta. He removed the handgun from crocodilian confinement and stuck it in the waistband of his trousers. He was convinced that the Vatican attorney (perhaps earrings— " " —are needed here, perhaps not) was armed. He pictured the fellow curling a finger around a teacup handle or a sugared date much as it might close around a trigger. The longer he pictured this, the more uneasy he became. At last, he shook Toufic gently awake.

"You were dreaming of Louisville, Kentucky, weren't you? Dreaming of the Yankee dollar. I could tell by the way you were grinning. Sorry to interrupt, pal, but I'm in requirement of strategic relocation."

Toufic was groggy and irritable, but he followed instructions, driving without headlamps around to the rear of the convent and parking close to the mud wall. Grunting, Switters slithered backward through the window, then scrambled up onto the roof of the car. From there, it was an easy matter to hoist himself to the top of the wall. Seated on the wall, he waved Toufic back to the gate and wondered what to do next. He wasn't particularly worried because the electricity wasn't on in the compound yet, and he knew that any minute now Pippi would have to— Yes, perfect, there she was!

There commenced a low voltaic drone, like Thomas Edison's spiritual mantra or the romantic humming of ogres in love. Toward the center of the oasis, a few lights flickered on. Pippi backed away from the generator shed and broke into a trot, pigtails swinging, as if in a great hurry to resume unfinished business elsewhere on the premises. Then, out of the corner of her eye, she saw him. Obviously she didn't know it was he. From the way she screeched, she might have been transported for a second back to Notre Dame—and the way he squatted there atop the wall, the tip of his cigar glowing red in the thickening dark, well, to mistake him for a gargoyle was by no means ridiculous. He called her name, which no horrid gargoyle had ever done, even in her nightmares, but still she trembled, one freckled hand over her mouth. Perhaps, she imagined him to be the ghost of Cardinal Thiry, come to punish the Pachomians for having failed him. She was delusional enough to fear such a thing. The deeply religious are by definition superstitious. As she slowly crossed herself, Switters observed, not for the first time, how much she resembled a middle-aged version of Audubon Poe's daughter, Anna. Oh, that succulent sprig, Anna! To think he might have. . . . But why was he thinking of such things now?

"Pippi! *C'est moi. Les échasses, s'il vous plaît.* The stilts. *Dépêchez-vous. C'est moi, bébé.* The fucking circus is back in town!"

When she realized it was he, she shrieked anew. She hopped around in a circle squealing before composing herself and dashing to fetch him the nearest pair of stilts. They were the outsized stilts, the Barnum & Bailey stilts, the absurdly tall pair, for his customized two-inch walkers had been left in his old room, and the regular pair was at the front gate where it was always kept. What the hell. He'd called it, hadn't he? Send in the clowns.

If the stilts that had held him two inches above the ground were analogous to enlightenment, this extra-elevated pair must have represented Nirvana. It was not surprising, then, that so few aspirants ever attained the Nirvanic state. Switters, by now an accomplished stiltsman, was nearly as ungainly on the exaggerated numbers as he had been the first and only time he'd ever strapped them on. He teetered, staggered, and dangerously swayed, but he set off, anyway, following behind Pippi, only too glad that his hands were free. For the present, he busied his hands with the task of brushing foliage aside as they traversed the various orchards. At one point, his head banged against a high branch in a willow tree, startling a pair of roosting cuckoos and causing them to rocket from their untidy nest, their normal sweetly mournful song taking on an angry, hysterical edge. He grabbed a limb to keep from falling and sent yet another of the slender white-and-olive birds flapping noisily into the night air. "Oh, stop your bitching," he scolded them. "It isn't that late. You remind me of my grandmother."

Governing her pace so that she would be close enough to break his fall should he topple, Pippi—in staccato, over-the-shoulder bursts—tried to fill him in. "From the Vatican. They want it. The prophecy. The Church knows about it. Fannie told. Watch your head. They want it now. I think Masked Beauty will not give it up."

By the time Pippi and Switters reached the main building, the meeting had lost any semblance of civility. In fact, the participants had erupted from the conference room and were grouped outside by the jasmine bushes, arguing heatedly. So much for sneaking up on them. A ten-foot Switters came weaving and wobbling through the eggplant patch just as the older churchman, the scholar from Lisbon, reached out and ripped off the abbess's veil. She slapped his face, a light blow that did not stun him half as much as the sudden sight of her two-story wart. He was gawking at the growth as if transfixed when his gaze was diverted by the arrival of the careening colossus, its throat full of wahoo, its hair full of leaves.

After that, the scene became a tad chaotic. Switters circled the group (he had to keep moving, otherwise he would fall), demanding to know if the rights of property owners were being violated, if trespass had occurred, and if the gentlemen present were cognizant of certain provisions of the Geneva Convention. He waggled a finger at the professor. "That ain't no way to treat a lady," he cautioned, although it was hard to tell if it was menace or merriment in his voice. The sisters were jabbering excitedly to one another, pointing accusing fingers at the professor, who, once he recovered from the shock of Switters's intrusion, began berating Masked Beauty for the inappropriate state of affairs. Several goats, awakened by the disturbance, were bleating, the donkey brayed, and irate cuckoos made passes overhead. Only Sister Domino and the so-called attorney remained calm; Domino because . . . well, because she was Domino, and the attorney because he recognized Switters from their day-long drive and realized that there was more to this farcical turn of events than met the eye. It was unthinkable that he would become flustered. He was a professional and wore no expression at all as his gaze followed the antics of the maniac stilter.

Dr. Goncalves, for that was the Fatima scholar's name, insisted, in French, that he would not leave the compound without the document he had come to secure. Obviously, he had made that same assertion several times before, although more politely, under less clamorous conditions. For her part, Masked Beauty was firm in maintaining that the paper in question was the private property of the Pachomian Order, to which Dr. Goncalves, his face growing more scarlet by the moment, replied that no such order was recognized by the Church and therefore did not exist. "What do you call this, then?" the abbess wanted to know, gesturing with the remains of her veil at the women and the grounds around her. "I was inclined to call it a misguided violation of the covenant with God," Goncalves answered, "but now I call it a madhouse, as well." He removed his straw hat and swatted at Switters with it as he came stumbling by. Switters laughed and then remarked to Scanlani, for that proved to be the younger man's name, "Nice threads, pal." Scanlani was wearing a snail-colored suit with a signature

Armani cut. At the compliment, his upper lip twitched in an almost imperceptible hint of a snarl.

Masked Beauty attempted to refasten her torn veil, an action that for some reason infuriated Professor Goncalves. He snatched the filmy cloth from her hand and lashed her with it. Drawing back to strike him with a kind of roundhouse wallop, the old woman's body went akimbo in a manner that mimicked the way Matisse had liked to paint her. *Interesting*, mused Switters, for he could detect in the arrangement of cubes, spheres, cylinders, and cones that formed her body, in the planes these shapes flattened into when he narrowed his eyes, the foundation of Analytic Cubism. In paintings such as *Blue Nude 1943*, had Matisse humanized Cubism, restored it to a natural, less formalistic state without relinquishing its inner dynamic, rescued the female form from Picasso's wood chipper, and put it back together as a whole slab of juicy color?

As he was pondering that notion, Domino acted. She stepped between the professor and her aunt as if they were silly, quarreling children. "Enough," she announced evenly. "You gentlemen must leave here at once. This is an official request, and if it is not honored, then matters will be turned over to our chief of security." With a nod of her head, a toss of her glossy brown hair, she indicated the joker on stilts—and it was then that she and Switters made eye contact for the first time that evening. Something went leaping between them, something intimate and lively, but also quizzical, wary, and a wee bit weird.

Acknowledging his role, Switters bellowed at the men in his rudest Italian. "*Sparisca! Sparisca!* Get lost!"

As if activated by a switch, Scanlani sprang. He took five lateral steps with the quickness of an NBA point guard and thrust out his right leg with the force of a Thai kickboxer. The leather sole of his expensive Milano-cobbled boot smashed into one of Switters's stilt poles. Instantly losing his already precarious balance, Switters tumbled wildly backward. With a splintering crash, he landed in a jasmine bush. Broken twigs dug into his back like daggers, but what was left of the shrub served as a buffer between him and the earth. His feet had not touched. A trickle of blood ran from a deep scratch on his cheek. "Another damn scar," he lamented. "I tell you, the gods are jealous of my good looks." Two or three fragrant petals were plastered to the wound. He sniffed. "It smells like the junior prom in here," he said.

Scanlani's generic expression was unchanged, but Dr. Goncalves laughed derisively. "Your chief of security?" he asked with a smirk. Pippi and ZuZu made an effort to help Switters out of the shattered bush, but he waved them off. "Go get my starship," he whispered to Pippi. "It's in the car parked at the gate."

Domino glared at the professor. "If he's injured," she said, indicating Switters, "you will *never* be given the prophecy."

"Oh?" Goncalves raised his eyebrows. "So you are saying that we may be given it?"

"That depends. Our order will have to discuss various—"

"Over my dead body!" exclaimed Masked Beauty.

"Now, aunt, let's keep an open mind. At some future date, after certain conditions have been met, certain concessions granted, it may be in everyone's best interest to—"

"It is in everyone's best interest that you surrender the stolen document immediately," Goncalves said. His tone was as threatening as a green sheen on mayonnaise. He shoved Domino aside in order to confront Masked Beauty directly. "Look at you!" He forced the words through clenched dentures. "Just look at you. How can the likes of you think to defy the authority of the Holy Father?" The old abbess blinked. Had she any lingering worry about still being beautiful, it was all gone now.

"I defy the authority of the Holy Father!" came a loud cry from the bush. "I defy the authority of the Holy Authority! I defy the authority of the unholy authority! Fuck authority and the Polish sausage it rode in on!" Then he added, because his back was being painfully gouged and because he was on a roll, "Fuck the Dallas Cowboys!"

"Oh, do watch your tongue, Mr. Switters," chimed in Maria Deux. "All is lost through sacrilege."

"Silence that heathen oaf," commanded Goncalves. He said it to Masked Beauty, upon whose rococo rhino polyp his beady eyes remained fixed, but it was Scanlani who moved catlike toward the busted bush, not walking so much as gliding. The jurist hadn't gotten far, however, before three shots rang out in rapid succession.

Mr. Beretta had spoken. Mr. Beretta had barked at the stars.

Disturbed again, the cuckoos took flight with a fluttering of feathers and shrieks of protest and alarm. The sound of scrabbling goat hooves was heard, and from the henhouse a great chorus of nervous clucking suddenly ensued. Scanlani froze. Switters leveled the gun at him. He fully expected Scanlani to whisk a pistol of his own from inside his fine jacket. He imagined the move would be as slick as a magician's. It would be pretty to watch. Even his stance—well-shod feet wide apart, both hands on the gun—would be instinctive and classic. So, Switters was actually disappointed when Scanlani made no move.

Switters's position was awkward and uncomfortable, laid out as he was on a bed of organic nails, but he held the 9-mm steady. His intent was to try to shoot the gun out of Scanlani's hand without hitting him. He'd accomplished that feat once in Kuwait City, blasting a Czech-made CZ-85 apart in the fist of a double agent. Particles of metal had flown off it like cold black sparks. Dropping what was left of the pistol, the man had whimpered. He'd held up his vibrating hands to watch their hue redden, his fingers already swelling like microwaved frank-furters. But, as they say, "That was then and this is now." (What would Today Is Tomorrow make of such a maxim?) Switters was not at all convinced he could duplicate the marksmanship, even if he was on his feet. He steadied the barrel and waited. For whatever reason, Scanlani failed to act.

"Throw down your gun," Switters ordered. He wasn't sure he'd gotten it right in Italian, so he repeated the command in French and English. Scanlani shrugged, a big arrogant Neapolitan shrug. "Okay, pal, have it your way," said Switters. "Remove your jacket." The alleged attorney understood, for he slipped out of his suit coat, folded it care-fully, and placed it on the ground. The shoulder holster Switters had expected to be exposed was nowhere in sight. "Damn!" he swore. He couldn't lie in that position much longer.

Waving the Beretta, he had Scanlani remove his shirt and twirl like a fashion model. There was no handgun stuck in his waistband, front or back. "Okay, clever boy, take off your pants." The man refused. For the first time, he displayed emotion, and the emotion was outrage and disgust. Switters's back felt like the time clock in an anthill. This was becoming unbearable. "Remove your damn pants!" he repeated vexa-tiously. Dr. Goncalves and the sisters looked dumbfounded.

Again, Scanlani refused to comply. Switters squeezed off a volley of shots at the dirt alongside the handsome calfskin boots. Everyone shrieked. Scanlani hastened to unbuckle his belt. And several moments passed before Switters realized three things:

1. Scanlani was unarmed.

2. Inadvertently, he had asked the fellow not to remove his trousers but, rather, to pull down his panties, a linguistic gaffe that could be traced to certain nights in Taormina and Venice, when he'd desired a clearer view of what the Italians, speaking clinically, referred to as *la vagina* (the same as in America), but informally (and sweetly) tended to call *la pesca* (the peach) or *la fica* (the fig).

3. One of the bullets fired at Scanlani's feet had ricocheted off a rock and struck Masked Beauty in the face.

"It was an honest mistake," said Switters, referring to the gunpoint dis-
robing of Scanlani: he hadn't yet noticed that Masked Beauty was
bleeding. "I gave you credit for being something more than just
another scumbag lawyer. Please accept my apology. And my condo-
lences." Domino, who likewise was oblivious to her aunt's wound,
rushed over to add her apologies. Switters's heart seemed to liquefy
when he witnessed the characteristic and irrepressible compassion in
her concern. Nevertheless, he called out, "Keep your distance, sister
love. The man may be unarmed, but his manners are deplorable."

He thought he heard her mutter, "No worse than your own," but
he couldn't be sure, for about that time Pippi had barged onto the
scene, pushing his wheelchair. Toufic was with her. Together, they
lifted him out of the tangle of twigs (it resembled an oversize cuckoo's
nest) and onto the "contour plus" cushion that still adorned the "drop-
hook, solid-folding" seat. Continuing to brandish the automatic pistol,
he waved it at the rapidly dressing Scanlani and at Goncalves, who was
one big eel-mouthed gash of petulance. "Toufic, ol' buddy, our guests
were just saying their good-byes. You're supposed to chauffeur them
to Deir ez-Zur for their overnight lodging, as I recall. In the dark, no
road, a good sixty kilometers as the camel flies: I suggest that you organize an expeditious departure." It was then that he—and Domino—
had noticed the Pachomians huddled around the abbess.

Once it was ascertained that Masked Beauty was not gravely
injured, he ushered the Italian and the Portuguese to the gate. The
former was mutely furious, the latter loudly vocal with accusations and
threats. As Switters was removing his belongings from the car,
Domino rushed up and insisted that he give the Vatican delegation his
satellite phone number and e-mail address. She told them she was
sorry that things had gotten out of hand—both sides were at fault, she
said—and she urged them to contact her and the abbess when tempers
had cooled. Perhaps, she said, something could be worked out.

When the Audi pulled away, she glared at Switters, and not
because she'd overheard him lobbying a somewhat bewildered Toufic
to include a pinch of hashish in his next scheduled delivery to the convent. "You reckless maniac," she scolded. "Your irresponsible macho
gunplay has disfigured my aunt."

Horrified that he might have caused Masked Beauty permanent
harm, he rolled himself rapidly to the infirmary, where his guilt and
sorrow subsided slightly after he learned the extent of the so-called
disfiguration. It seemed that the ricocheting bullet had grazed the old
woman's nose, neatly slicing off at the base the tiny Chinese mountain
of horn flesh, the violet viral cauliflowerette, the double-dipped God-
wart that for many decades had been protuberating there.

Nobody at the oasis got much sleep that night. Even the animals were restless and jumpy. The sisterhood was atwitter with agitation, and Masked Beauty, although surprisingly free of pain, was in a state of shock following her abrupt and artless amputation. "You'll just have to get used to being desirable again," Switters told the abbess. "Is it not a fine thing to be rebeautified on a planet that's being systematically trashed? You know, my mother always wanted me to become a plastic surgeon. It would have saved her a fortune in lifts and tucks."

For her part, even as she swabbed his own scratched cheek with iodine, Domino remained in a huff. True, she and her sisters had not merely accepted but actively solicited his protection, yet she found it brutal and anti-Pachomian that he would assault an official party from the Vatican (no matter that the party was belligerently authoritarian) with a deadly weapon. He replied that "assault" was a bit of an exaggeration. And then he told her a story.

The story had been passed on to him by Bobby Case, who had learned it from one of his "wise ol' boys." It seemed that long ago, a holy man, a bodhisattva, was walking through the Indian countryside when he came upon a band of poor, troubled herdsmen and their emaciated flock. The herdsmen were moaning and gnashing and wringing their hands, and when the bodhisattva asked them what was the matter, they pointed to a range of nearby mountains. To drive their flock to fresh green pasture on the other side of the hills, they had to traverse a narrow pass. In the pass, however, a huge cobra had established a den, and each time they went by it, the snake attacked, stabbing its long venomous fangs into animals and humans alike. "We can't get through the pass," the herders complained, "and as a result, our cattle and goats are starving, and so are we."

"Worry not," said the bodhisattva, "I will take care of it." He then proceeded to climb up to the pass, where he rapped on the entrance to the den with his staff and gave the cobra a lecture it would not soon forget. Thoroughly shamed and chastised, the big serpent promised that it would never, ever bite the herders or their charges again. The holy man thanked it. "I believe you when you vow that in the future you will refrain from the biting of any passerby," he said, and went on his way.

About a year later, Bodhisattva came that way again. From a distance, he saw the herdsmen. They appeared content, their animals hardy and fat. Bodhisattva decided to look in on the cobra and compliment it on its good behavior, but although he repeatedly rapped his staff on the rocks, he received no response. *Perhaps it moved away*, thought Bodhi, and he made to leave. Just then, however, he heard a weak groan from deep inside the cave. Bodhi crawled inside, where he found the snake in pitiful condition. Skinny as a drawstring and battered as a tow rope, it lay on its side, fairly close to death.

"What on earth is the matter?" asked the guru, moved nearly to tears.

"Well," said the cobra in a barely audible voice, "you made me promise not to bite anyone. So, now, everybody who comes over the pass hits me with sticks and throws stones at me. My body is cut and bruised, and I can no longer leave the den to find food or water. I'm miserable and sick, but, alas, there is nothing to be done to protect myself, because you proclaimed that I shouldn't bite."

Bodhisattva patted the poor creature's head. "Yes," he agreed. "But I didn't say you couldn't *hiss*."

The meaning of the story was not lost on Domino. She soon forgave Switters for his hissing. She continued to believe that he had hissed excessively and had taken an unseemly amount of pleasure in hissing, but she was not one to linger in the stale cellars of resentment. Nevertheless, her attitude toward him had changed. While he could have attributed the change to his cavalier gunplay or to the accidental shearing off of Masked Beauty's growth (if he could divest the abbess of the shield behind which she'd taken refuge—her supernatural wart—mightn't he likewise flush Domino from behind the convenient cover of her supernatural hymen?), he realized that she had seemed different, somehow, even before the shooting started. Thus, he was not entirely surprised when she announced that their tower-room petting sessions were at an end.

"I've had my fling," she said, "and escaped relatively unscathed. I believe I can safely state that should I ever enjoy such acts again, it will be under the auspices of matrimony."

"And I'm not a candidate to share your marriage bed?"

In spite of herself, she smiled. "If that is a proposal, I will give it due consideration."

Perhaps fearful of arousing his imp, he elected not to pursue the matter, and that seemed okay with her. They had a great many other things to talk about, and over the next four months—during which lengthy and, at times, acrimonious negotiations with the Vatican took place almost weekly via e-mail—they talked as fervently as they once had kissed. If either or both of them regarded conversation an unsatis-factory substitute, they did not let on.

The talking had begun the morning after the incident, when, in the shade of one of the walnut trees, she had briefed him on the rea-sons why the Church had sent Dr. Goncalves and Scanlani to retrieve the Fatima prophecy in the first place.

A lot of the briefing was pure conjecture—the piecing together of tid-bits of information that Goncalves had let slip, combined with an intu-itive feel for the situation—but in weeks to come, when more facts became available, Domino's assessment proved quite accurate, although it should be noted that the full story unfolded slowly over time and may never be completely known.

For whatever reason, Fannie, after she fled the oasis, had made a pilgrimage to Fatima in rural Portugal. There, under the spell of the very place where the Virgin Mother had allegedly made her most dra-matic historical appearances, Fannie had requested an audience with the nearby bishop of Leiria. Eventually, an interview was granted. The bishop was aware of his predecessor's involvement with the Lady's third prophecy, how he had concealed it in his safe from 1940 until 1957, when, under the direction of Pope Pius XII, he'd hand-carried it to Rome; and then, three years later, how he'd gone to assist Pope John XXIII with its translation. What the current bishop didn't know was why the Vatican powers had never revealed the contents of the prophecy. He'd heard the rumors, but felt it was none of his busi-ness. Still, he was intrigued by the defrocked Irish nun's story, allowing that it was at least feasible that the Church believed the prophecy destroyed, and even that the infamous Pachomian abbess, Croetine Thiry, might, through her late uncle, have ended up with the only extant copy.

It was one thing to be intrigued, quite another to take action. If Pope John had, indeed, burned the prophecy and what he believed to be the only copies thereof, he must have done so for a very sound reason. The Vatican undoubtedly would concur with that reason-ing. The news that Cardinal Thiry's translation had escaped the flames might hold a minimum of delight for it. And Rome had a long tradi-tion of killing, literally or figuratively, the messenger. On the other hand, if a surviving copy did exist, wouldn't it want to be apprised? Especially if the copy was in the possession of a loose cannon such as Abbess Croetine?

In the end, the bishop nervously telephoned that cardinal in Rome whose duties included the investigation of miracles and visitations. He relayed Fannie's story and awaited official reaction. It was not long in coming. Less than a week after the phone call, the cardinal rang up the bishop and instructed him that Fannie's tale was a blasphemous hoax and should be dismissed as such and forgotten.

Feisty Fannie, however, was not so easily deterred. She went to see Sister Lucia, now nearly ninety-two years old and living again in Portugal. To the surprise of those around her, the normally reclusive Lucia received the Irishwoman. In private, Fannie told her story, and as she recited the words of the third prophecy (over the years, all of the Pachomians had unintentionally memorized it), cerebral calcification cracked, rust flaked away from axon terminals of mnemonic neurons, and in the old woman's brain, synapses that hadn't fired in years—decades, perhaps—commenced to shudder, sputter, and send off sparks. They shook hands with other synapses, and the crone found herself recycling each and every word of that fateful prognostication that she'd received over miraculous meadowland airwaves in 1917 and written down for presumed posterity in 1940, the words that she had cautioned would "bring joy to some and sorrow to others."

On a couple of occasions in the past, Sister Lucia had voiced polite disappointment that the Church had not even attempted to consecrate Russia, as the Lady of Fatima had directed in the second prophecy, and that the third prophecy hadn't been acknowledged at all. But Lucia was nothing if not an obedient handmaiden. She had always submitted docilely, thoroughly, to the authority of Vatican fathers. Even in her advanced age, however, she was not unaware of the worldwide resurgence of Marianism in general, and of interest in the Fatima Virgin in particular. Like Switters, moreover, she was susceptible to Fannie's Irish charm. It hadn't taken the fugitive Pachomian more than an afternoon sipping watered-down port in a sunny Portuguese garden to convince the nonagenarian nun that the time had come to honor the Holy Virgin's wishes, to present her exhortations and warnings to humankind, with or without Vatican cooperation.

Both Fannie and Lucia were aware that a significant conference was scheduled for early June in Amsterdam. Entitled "New Catholic Women," it was to be a gathering of nuns, laywomen, teachers, writers, and concerned parishioners who had in common a growing spirit of resistance toward the repressively sexist practices and attitudes that persisted within their church. It was the premise of conference organizers that the Church's continued hostility toward women threatened both their religious lives and, due to its intractable ban on artificial birth control, their physical lives. Representatives of the Blue Army, the largest and best known of the contemporary Fatima cults, had announced their intentions to attend the gathering, and Fannie experienced little difficulty in persuading Lucia that Amsterdam in June was the ideal place and time to disclose the contents of the secret third prophecy to the masses for whom Mother Mary had intended it. For reasons as political as spiritual, regular conferees would be receptive to an airing of Marian information that had been supposedly suppressed by the patriarchs. They would be receptive to the airing whether or not they as individuals believed Mary had actually appeared at Fatima, and the Blue Army would be overjoyed, since it regarded the long-reticent Sister Lucia as only slightly less saintly than Mary herself. The frosting on the Communion wafer was that the conference was bound to attract global media coverage.

Some media members were, as early as December, already paying attention, for when word leaked out of the "New Catholic Women" organization office that the legendary Sister Lucia would surface in Amsterdam to personally unveil the third prophecy of Fatima, the news popped up in papers and on broadcast stations around the world. As is often the case, buzz begat buzzsaw. The phone calls and faxes that the bishop of Leiria began suddenly to receive from Rome were uniformly lacking in any shade of tickled pink.

Within seventy-two hours of the leak, a helicopter deposited a Vatican cardinal in Leiria. The red hat was accompanied by his secretary and two members of the Holy See's legal affairs team, one of whom, not surprisingly, was the mysterious Scanlani. Portugal's foremost Fatima expert, the scholarly theologian and fascist apologist, Dr. Antonio Goncalves, also joined the discussions in the bishop's study. The following day, Goncalves, the bishop, and the cardinal descended on Sister Lucia and browbeat the frail old nun into publicly announcing that she would not under any circumstances appear at the Amsterdam confab, that she was not at all certain that any text of Fatima's third prophecy existed, and that if one did exist, it rightfully was in safekeeping at the Vatican.

As for Fannie, she slipped out of Portugal as stealthily as she had slipped out of the Pachomian oasis. No matter. The Vatican team was not particularly worried about her. Not only was the defrocked Irishwoman deficient in ecclesiastical cachet, she was a known sexual deviant, having, as a matter of record, undergone a number of exorcisms in an attempt to purge her of the Asmodeus that had continued to corrupt her well into her thirties. It would be easy to denounce and discredit her, particularly since she did not possess the copy of the prophecy but only claimed to have read it and memorized it under dubious circumstances somewhere in Syria. Given the facts, the Amsterdam conference quite probably would not even allow her a forum.

So much for that. But suppose, Dr. Goncalves asked, that a copy of the third prophecy was, indeed, held in a maverick desert convent; suppose it was in Cardinal Thiry's verifiable handwriting; and suppose, just suppose, it did, as the wench Fannie had intimated, call the future of Roman Catholic influence into question? Shouldn't an effort be made to secure the document and turn it over to the Holy Father, the single personage with the authority to determine its fate? What if, inspired by Fannie's efforts, that troublesome Abbess Croetine should decide to carry her uncle's translation to Amsterdam in June?

The cardinal was a practical man. "I hear the desert is pleasant this time of year," he said. He winked at Scanlani. He winked so hard it jiggled his velvet cap.

january. february. march. It was a period of flat suspense. Alfred Hitchcock on a grapefruit diet. A clock that ticked but did not advance: every time you looked, it said five minutes to midnight. A bomb with a damp fuse. The other shoe that drops and drops and keeps on dropping. Ice fishing as an Olympic sport. The tension was so steady, the pressure so uniform, there were weeks when it might have been boring were it not on the verge of being desperate.

It was the threat of serious danger that kept Switters in Syria. True, the sisters relied on his computer, but he could have left it with them and gone on to South America adequately served by his flip phone. They would have accepted the computer, all right, but they wanted no part of the government-customized Beretta Cougar 8040G, no matter how he Tom Clancyed its light weight, negligible recoil, side-mounted magazine release button, and all-around athleticism. ("I'm not gun-happy by any means," he assured Masked Beauty, "but we angels can't let the cowboys have all the fun.") So, he remained at the oasis, committed to its protection until matters were somehow resolved. He had a sense of responsibility, of loyalty, Switters did, but it must be mentioned that he was also motivated by simple curiosity.

Not that Switters would have deemed curiosity an inferior or even ordinary motive. *Au contraire.* On his very first field assignment for the CIA, he had, undercover, accompanied a champion high-school marching band from New Richmond, Wisconsin, on a trip to Moscow. There had never been anything in Russia even remotely resembling the eighty-piece, high-stepping, plume-bedecked ensemble that, fronted by a baton-twirling, short-skirted, white-booted drum majorette, paraded from Gorky Park to Red Square, booming a brassy, sassy rendition of "Jesus Christ, Superstar"; and Switters, when he could pry his gaze off the majorette (any hope on his part to get in her pants was ruthlessly squashed by a sizable phalanx of mother hens from the New Richmond PTA), couldn't help but notice how many Russians simply turned their backs on the spectacle and went about their dreary business in the streets. *Even if you were fiercely anti-American*, he thought, *wouldn't you at least be curious?* In later years, when he would find himself the only outsider, the first Caucasian, in a remote African or Asian village, he would notice that some inhabitants gaped openly, grinning at him with itch and relish, while others looked right past him or turned away, expressionless. And so he came to recognize that there were two kinds of people: those who were curious about the world and those whose shallow attentions were pretty much limited to those things that pertained to their own personal well-being. He concluded further that Curiosity might have to be added to that list of traits—Humor, Imagination, Eroticism, Spirituality, Rebelliousness, and Aesthetics— that, according to his grandmother, separated full-fledged humans from the less evolved. Of course, curiosity was not entirely lacking among four-footed beasts, as many a dying cat would attest, and Maestra's narrow-focused "missing links" were occasionally capable of being intrigued by trifles like the domestic affairs of film stars and royalty; but such displays of interest were feeble, even pathetic, when compared to the inquisitive marveling of the wonderstruck, the obsessive questing of scientists and artists, or even to the all but squealy speculations of those who could barely wait to see what was going to happen next.

In that regard, the Vatican also could be assumed to be partially motivated by curiosity. The pope, naturally, was curious about the augury that had set his predecessor to throwing off tears like an ice sculpture in a wind tunnel. Dr. Goncalves was curious for academic reasons. Even the blandly arrogant Scanlani must have been curious. The Church undoubtedly wanted possession of the Fatima prophecy because it worried that it might encourage the feminist bent of the new Marianism and because of the rumor that the Virgin had foretold of a spiritual renaissance in which the Christian establishment, unthinkably, was not a major player. Every bit as much as it feared and resented the prophecy, however, the Church was curious about it. Domino, with the help of Switters, both stoked and thwarted that curiosity. And they and the sisterhood lived with the consequences.

January. February. The Ides of March. A sky-lidded night plain. A starloaded sky. A moon without a pond to primp in. A wind without a leaf to tease. A nighthawk without a wire to rest on. A couple without a corner to turn. Her sandals, his wheels, made a popcorn-eating sound in the sand.

He watched as she squatted to pee. She was matter-of-fact. He whistled a show tune. Although they never touched, theirs was the radiating, maddening-to-others intimacy of longtime easy lovers. If she made enough water, the moon might glimpse itself, after all.

Now that they no longer rendezvoused in the tower room, Domino and Switters often strolled together at night. Rather, she strolled, he rolled. (Stilting in tandem with a companion on foot produced ridiculous rhythms.) Switters usually preferred to stroll and roll outside of the compound, out in the desert, both because they could speak more freely there and because he could check the perimeters for possible intruders. By March, the Vatican had apparently given up on trying to pressure Syria to deport the Pachomians: thanks to Sol Glissant, they held clear legal title to their land. Army helicopters no longer buzzed the oasis, and the last police raid, in early February, had failed for the third time to find an alien American male on the premises. ("Just one pretty nun," reported the officer-in-charge, "and nine ugly ones, including an old abbess who can't stop rubbing her nose and a big burly mute one, confined to her bed.") Still, it paid to be alert. Switters remembered those Islamic militants from the closest village, and it would not have surprised him if Roman agents incited them to spy on, or even attack, the convent.

For more than two months, while the abbess paced in her chambers, absentmindedly but compulsively polishing the unfamiliar regularities of her newly planed proboscis, Domino had bargained hard with Rome. Scanlani, who proved as verbose electronically as he was taciturn in person, spoke for the Church. Initially, starting about a fortnight after Switters had run him and Goncalves off the compound, his on-line communiqués consisted of the kind of insidious intimidation—bully-boy menace couched in oblique legalistic formalities—for which lawyers were universally despised. When Domino failed to back down, when she intimated and then flatly stated that her aunt might, indeed, attend the "New Catholic Women" conference, disputed document in hand, Scanlani became gradually, reluctantly, more conciliatory. Of course, at that time, Masked Beauty, still wary of its presumed Islamic overtones, had absolutely no intention of publicizing the Virgin's message in Amsterdam or anywhere else, but she came to appreciate her niece's strategy: "If the Holy Father agrees to reinstate the Order of St. Pachomius," Domino would write again and again, "then the Order of St. Pachomius will consent to turn over to the Vatican the sole extant text of the third prophecy of Fatima."

Eventually an industrial-strength votive candle had flared in the old abbess's mind. She chuckled. She stroked her shockingly sleek snout. *"Chantage,"* she said.

"Yes." Domino grinned back. "Blackmail."

They laughed. They bit their lips, their tongues, the pulpy lining of their cheeks—and went right on laughing. They were disgusted with themselves, guilt-ridden, ashamed; but they were, momentarily, at least, forced into giggles by the very idea of it. Blackmailing the pope!

And there had come a day, just past the middle of March, when the pope blinked. Scanlani signaled that, in exchange for the return of certain Church property, the Holy Father would officially accept the Pachomian sisters back into the fold. There was a catch, naturally, and it was the terms of the Roman offer that had occupied Domino and Switters on their stroll and roll that night in the parched but cooling grit, where the moon, as anticipated, had indeed examined its acne in the puddle that Domino straddled like the primordial Mother of Oceans.

Because of her youth in Philadelphia, perhaps, she'd never acquired the French habit of dabbing herself with the hem of her skirt, so she squatted there, panties down, for a while, as if waiting for the wind to dry her. To distract his thoughts, Switters tried to spin his chair, but it was no use: you couldn't pop a wheelie in the sand. Finally she stood, affording him just a flash of what, in South Africa, the whites called the *poes* and the *moer*, the coloreds called the *koek*, and many blacks knew as *indlela eya esizalweni* (a mouthful any way you looked at it): the cultural information latent in the different ways those neighbors referred to the same commonplace and yet everlastingly mysterious organ was fodder for a fascinating sociological thesis, though not from our man Switters, who was happy just to have learned the names, in case an occasion ever arose to address the thing in question in its proper local idiom. At any rate, Domino was beside him again now, repeating the conditions of the Vatican proposal.

"They'll readmit us to the cloth, but they won't support us financially, which is okay, because we're used to poverty and we can take care of ourselves. However, they also demand that we stay out of Church politics, keep our mouths shut, don't rock any boats."

"And you absolutely will not agree to that?"

"Mais non! We have to speak out. It's our duty to life. Putting a stop to this rampant, irresponsible procreation is like finding the cure for cancer. The 'breeders,' as you call them, are rather similar to cancers,

actually; tumors with legs. A cell becomes malignant when it misinterprets or mishandles information from the DNA, and then all it cares about is replication—at least that's what I've read—and it will go on blindly, selfishly replicating itself even though it smothers the innocent, healthy cells around it. And, of course, it eventually dies itself because it has destroyed its environment. Everything dies then. Yes? So, the egotistical breeders misinterpret God's word, or cultural definitions of manhood, and they—"

"Yeah, I get the analogy, sister love." Moreover, he agreed with it, although it seemed harsh coming from her. He wondered if some of his own cheerful cynicism had rubbed off on her. He wondered, too, to what degree, if any, she'd ever entertained the fantasy of bearing children of her own.

Now and again, one could detect in a childless woman of a certain age the various characteristics of all the children she had never issued. Her body was haunted by the ghosts of souls who hadn't lived yet. Premature ghosts. Half-ghosts. X's without Y's. Y's without X's. They applied at her womb and were denied, but, meant for her and no one else, they wouldn't go away. Like tiny ectoplasmic gophers, they hunkered in her tear ducts. They shone through her sighs. Often to her chagrin, they would soften the voice she used in the marketplace. When she spilled wine, it was their playful antics that jostled the glass. They called out her name in the bath or when she passed real children in the street. The spirit babies were everywhere her companions, and everywhere they left her lonesome—yet they no more bore her resentment than a seed resents the uneaten fruit. Like pet gnats, like a phosphorescence, like sighs on a string, they would follow her into eternity.

Not every childless woman was so accompanied—it may have been only those who at least partially, on some level, wanted the girls and boys that they, for whatever reason, chose not to conceive—but when Switters looked hard at Domino, as he did now, he saw her saturated with other lives. He wondered if she was aware of her phantom brood, but he wasn't about to ask. If he broached that subject, his imp might start messing with his coconut, and the next thing he knew, he could be inquiring about what she thought of his potential as a father. He liked children and children liked him, better than most adults liked him, but men such as Switters didn't breed in captivity. Oh, no. What he *was* going to ask, and not for the first time, was why she and Masked Beauty, having slowly, steadily moved away from much of the old patriarchal doctrine, still desired to be a part of the traditional Church. The reasons she gave were never very clear, though he surmised that they were not dissimilar to the emotions that caused him to sometimes muse wistfully about the CIA.

Before he could raise the question, however, they were distracted by a noise. It came from close to the compound, there where the bud-weighted boughs of an orange tree overhung the wall. The sound was that species of muffled hack related to an inverse yap, as if someone were trying to suppress a cough. Switters exposed Mr. Beretta to the light of the moon. In a whisper he asked Domino to push his chair toward the noise, and she complied, tensely but calmly.

As they drew nearer, a form stirred in the shadows. Grasping the pistol with both hands, Switters yelled something in Arabic, wondering as he did so why he hadn't chosen Italian. Instantly two figures darted from the wall. Two short figures. Two small figures. Two dog-like figures. Loping off into the dunes, they unraveled a ribbon of musk behind them.

Domino smiled with relief. "I—I don't know the English," she said.

"Jackals," Switters informed her. "Rare to see one these days. We've had ourselves a lucky little nature ramble."

His nose was turned up at the jackal smell. Her nose was turned up at his pistol. She stood scowling at its beautiful ugliness. She shook her head, and moonbeams exposed the underlying red in her hair. "When you were a secret agent," she asked, "did you have a double-oh seven? License to kill?"

"Me? Double-oh seven?" He laughed. "Negative, darling. I had a double-oh oh. License to wahoo."

She knew that by wahoo he was referring to a cry of exhilaration, an exclamation of nonsensical joy, and she knew, also, that it had a basis in Scripture—"Make a joyful noise unto the Lord"—but she was not so sure she could distinguish between that kind of defiant exuberance and mere childish bravado. She continued to fix him with a half-frown of affectionate disapproval.

Meanwhile, Switters's attention was focused long and hard in the direction of the fleeing jackals. After a while, Domino said, "I didn't know you were so interested in wildlife." He might have rejoined that wildlife was the only life that did interest him, but he just kept looking and listening, saying nothing. Those jackals concerned him. They gave him an evil feeling. He was aware that while few people kept jackals as pets because of their odor, the animals were easily tamed. Conceivably, some party could have trained the jackals to skulk around outside the compound walls. A bug could have been concealed in the fur of one or both of them, a listening device that would record any voice within fifty yards spoken above a whisper. Vatican security might neither possess equipment that sophisticated nor a mentality that ingenious or perverse, but the black-bag tekkies at the pickle factory were capable of that and more. Much more.

If Mayflower Cabot Fitzgerald had been interested enough in him to have him tailed in Seattle, he quite likely had had his name put on satellite. That meant that anytime anyone typed the name Switters into an on-line computer or spoke the name Switters into a telephone—anywhere in the world—it would be recorded and pinpointed geographically and chronologically, by one of the covert satellites that the company had had put in orbit around the planet.

As he considered that possibility, sitting there beneath a granary of stars that were not all stars, he was struck by the thought that the giant bulbs, the shiny black and copper pods that he'd seen circling the globe when his consciousness was massively enlarged by yopo and ayahuasca; the bulbs that called themselves our overlords and boasted that they ran the show; the pods that the shaman dismissed as a bunch of big blowhards . . . well, what if the master bulbs were just a more evolved generation of intelligence satellites? The fact that Amazonian Indians had apparently been familiar with them for decades, if not centuries, meant little in a realm where the past was today and today was tomorrow: the connectedness of electronic technology and primal mythology seemed not only plausible but inevitable when one accepted the scientific theory and mystical principle of the interpenetration of realities. Wasn't advanced cybernetics a hell of a lot closer to meditative and psychedelic states than to the meat-and-potatoes commerce of everyday life?

"Hey! Where have you gone?" Domino shook him, though rather timidly, for he still clasped the weapon that she now called his "hisser."

Switters cleared his thoughts. He decided not to share his concerns about the jackals. It was probably silly, anyway. So far, there had been no inkling that the company was involved in or even interested in this dispute over the Fatima prophecy. Sure, the Vatican and the CIA sometimes cooperated—after all, they both believed they had a huge stake in controlling human behavior and maintaining the status quo—but, more than likely, the Church would prefer to keep the Fatima fracas under its own steeple. He reminded himself that it was easy to grow paranoid in the desert. The absence of shadows caused the mind to invent them. History had proven this a hundred times over in a landscape where one man's mirage was another man's divine revelation.

No, he couldn't permit himself to start hallucinating company spooks with obedience-school jackals. One thing he knew for certain, however, was that Scanlani and his bosses were going to be infuriated when the Pachomians refused their offer. That meant he wasn't going to be leaving Syria anytime soon. And in the skeleton-dry wind, he could hear the rift widening between him and three of the four human beings he cared about most.

When, in the fortnight following Christmas, he had failed to show up in Seattle, Maestra had e-mailed him and Bobby had phoned. Their frustration with him was almost explosive. Then, about a week later, an e-mail had arrived from Suzy. The first two communiqués had been anticipated, but Suzy's caught him off guard, and while its tone was very different, it was no less affecting.

When you were just a sprout, wrote his grandmother, *I advised you never to trust anybody who didn't have secrets. Even though it's sound advice, I could kick myself for impressing it so firmly on your soft little brain. I've created a damn monster.* Maestra wanted him home, wanted him out of that wheelchair or off of "those crazy damn sticks," and if her requests weren't promptly honored, she wanted a detailed explanation of why they were not. His clandestine ways had become intolerable. She intimated that she was on her last breath and if he was to see her alive, he'd better not tarry. He was fairly sure the deathbed bit was an act, and he wrote back to remind her that she'd also taught him that guilt was a useless emotion. It didn't prevent him from worrying, however, especially when, undoubtedly piqued by his flip attitude and lack of candor, she'd not written back.

As for Bobby, he'd practically shouted into the phone. "Where the hell are you, podner?! Are you still *there?*"

"You mean *here?* I'm afraid so."

"With *her?*"

"Not necessarily."

"*What,* then?"

After a pause, Switters had answered, "Not your need to know." There was a modicum of sweet revenge in that reply, but any pleasure he took from it was short-lived. Well aware that Switters was working neither for the company nor Audubon Poe, Case was not, as he put it, "buying one Texas ounce of that 'need-to-know' horseshit."

Dehydrating Okinawan rice paddies with the heat of his frustration, Bobby said that he'd always considered Switters a cut above the other loose cannons, jumping beans, jackrabbits, flakes, wild cards, and hot potatoes with whom, due to his own shortcomings as a responsible citizen, he'd been doomed to associate, but he, Switters, had turned out to be the worst of the lot. "It come upon me one night in Bangkok, actually, that if you didn't back offen that fucking James Joyce, it was one day gonna drive you over the lip—and now it's went and done it."

Bobby said he had leave coming up and he was going to use it to take matters in his own hands. He threatened to blow into Syria like a twister out of Hondo. Switters had half believed him. But Bobby hadn't appeared. Neither had he e-mailed or called.

The letter from his stepsister arrived later in January, arrived soundlessly, spectrally, no wood fibers to give it substance, no ink to ferry its essence to the eyes the way blood ferries oxygen to the brain; arrived as a standardized arrangement of backlit glyphs upon a cold glass panel; unscented with Suzy's perfume, unlicked by her wet tongue, devoid not merely of tearstains but of pizza or lipstick traces; an aseptic transmission whose ephemerality was all the more pronounced due to the fact that his computer was programmed to trashcan after six hours any and all messages for reasons of security (that contemptible word!). With a quaint old low-tech pencil, Switters had copied it onto the flyleaf of *Finnegans Wake* (talk about your stained paper: wine, beer, cigar ash, soy sauce, fish sauce, gravy, blood, unspeakable and indefinable vegetable-animal-and-mineral deposits, the kind of splotches that might enliven the bedsheets of a Third World beach motel). He reread it once a week. No more, no less.

Hi,
   Guess you weren't expecting to hear from me after so long a time, huh? There's a whole lot I've been wanting to talk to you about and I'd been saving it until I saw you again. Everyone was so disappointed when you didn't come home at New Years. This really isn't your home though is it? And I know you have a good reason for doing whatever it is you're doing now. And Switters I also understand that you must have had good reasons for behaving how you did in Sacramento. I'm very very sorry I tripped out that night. I should of trusted you more instead of thinking you were a big liar or had gone crazy or something. I guess I was just confused. I was such a baby back then, such a child. I think about what a spank girl I was back then and it's like I want to hurl my breakfast or something. I can't believe it was only a little over a year ago! I'm 17 now, as you ought to know, and a lot has changed with me. Time is a funny thing isn't it? A planet made out of rock and water takes a few turns in space or whatever and suddenly you're a different person than you were before. It's a weird system if you ask me. Anyway I'm here in Seattle now and enjoying the rain. Ha ha. There's some pretty

cool kids at my new school but Maestra won't let me hang with them much. She's really great though, and when I get bummed she plays me old blues records and stuff. Reads to me out of Shakespeare who I totally love! I don't want to bore you with my life but this socked-in morning finds me in a whirl of questions bubbling up from the unseen below or from somewhere over the rainbow maybe. You're way far the wisest man I've ever known and you could always make anything in life seem not just okay but funny and grand. You did hit on me a lot but I know it came from a place of passion and love and I know you're a person with deep feelings that you hide behind your crazy antics and I also know that you'd protect me with your life from anything or anybody that ever tried to hurt me. Now that I'm older and more "experienced" you would find me a horse of a different color as they say. Please forgive me for being such a clueless brat in the past. And please keep a little bit of me in your heart. There's a piece of you in mine and it grows as I grow.

I miss you,
Suzy

On at least one occasion when he read over her letter, Switters had unlocked the hidden compartment in his famous crocodile valise, retrieved a particular nylon and cotton vesture (stained almost as colorfully as the flyleaf of *Finnegans*), and dangled it in the candlelight, its twin cups, though as empty as potholes, mirroring the atmospheres as well as the hemispheres of his brain. Perhaps not surprisingly, Switters, as an erstwhile cyberneticist, had some theories about the bicameral brain, its fractile reflection of a universe steeped in paradox: how, simultaneously and inseparably, it functioned both as a computer running programs and as a program being run, how its mastery of pre-emphasis often failed to protect it against random signals, viruses, or the meddling of "imps." That sort of thing. Of course, when it's taken into account that Switters was a fellow who liked to pretend that his corporeal being was energized and regulated by a ball of mystic white light—a kind of luminous coconut—it's understandable that reservations might arise regarding the trustworthiness of his views.

In any case, when he went on-line to compose a reply to Suzy's letter, he resisted any impulse to refer to the brain's tendencies—dramatically pronounced in schizophrenics, virtually nonexistent in many "missing links"—toward ambivalent or contradictory states. The example of her bra notwithstanding, such theorizing would have come across as esoteric if not entirely irrelevant, and, worse, might have veered dangerously close to self-analysis.

Neither could he consider writing to Suzy in the roguish manner he'd favored in the past, telling her, for example, that between her honey thighs she was "as tight as a plastic doll, as squeaky as a Styrofoam sandwich, as soft and sweet and salty as periwinkle pie." No, as accurate as such comparisons still might be, he no longer felt impelled or entitled to make them.

Instead, after deleting about a dozen different approaches, he limited his response to a simple declaration of affectionate appreciation. He was grateful for her words, he said, and would not forget them or take them lightly. " *'The men don't know,'* " he concluded, quoting a line from Willie Dixon, a bluesman he was sure was in Maestra's record collection, " *'but the little girls understand.'* "

Of all of mankind's inventions, the helicopter was the most totalitarian. Barbarically invasive, it used its vertical maneuverability—its capacity to climb, descend, hover, and whirl—as a means of raucously raiding life's tender corners, scattering to the rats and dogs the last sweet crumbs of human privacy. Peasants in their paddies, Humboldt hippies in their pot patches, happy revelers at inner-city block parties, drivers on freeways, sunbathers lazing nude on deserted beaches, all were prey, sitting ducks for those angry gunships with their authoritarian voices and prying eyes. The sound of the rotary blades—*cop cop cop cop cop!!*—was entirely appropriate for a craft that had come to symbolize police-state potentiality and to mechanically embody every libertarian's nightmare.

Any winged aircraft, from the smallest Cessna prop puppy to the biggest Boeing behemoth, was a romantic artifact, a swoozy sculpture, a sailing thing of irresistible appeal; but a helicopter . . . a helicopter was like a funky old shoetree that a witch had caused to levitate. Chunky and uncouth, it was as if some weird kid had planted a homemade whirligig in the fat of a turd.

Switters hated helicopters. Even though twice—once in Burma, once on the Kuwaiti-Iraqi border—they had John Wayned down to lift him out of dire situations, he never saw one without fantasizing about shooting it out of the air (the fact that they sometimes could be used for good, and thus win the approval of the naive masses, served only to make their evil more insidious). When, on March 20, a whirlybird (cute nickname for such a hellish machine) dropped from the new spring upon the oasis, its needling motor sewing stitches in the sky, its blades chopping ozone into bluish kindling, whipping the first blossoms off the orange trees, stirring up dust and chicken feathers, turning leaves inside out like pocketknives, coughing smoke in the faces of frantic cuckoos, Switters barely could restrain himself from trying to make his fantasy a reality.

The helicopter hadn't landed. Neither had it fired upon them. It buzzed the compound, low and loud, a half-dozen times and then *whump-whump*ed off in the direction of Damascus. However, its intrusion, coming less than seventy-two hours after Domino had e-mailed Scanlani to reject the Church's offer, left little doubt in Switters's mind about the mood in Rome. Domino wasn't as convinced as he of the connection, but he'd warned her all along that the Vatican wouldn't suffer her rejection with mercy or charity.

Switters was especially concerned because this helicopter, unlike the ones that had flown over them back in January, did not bear the insignia of Syrian military. It bore, in fact, no insignia at all, an omission with uncomfortable implications. Once again he had to wonder if Langley might not be involved in this religious rumpus, an eerie feeling that intensified when, on two more occasions, he discovered jackals lurking beneath the walls of the paper-snaked Eden. Domino scoffed at the notion of eavesdropping jackals until he told her about the several hundred espionage dolphins that regularly plied the world's bays and harbors for their handlers in the CIA. His former colleagues were hardly uningenious.

"It's likely to get ugly from now on, sister love. I don't want to alarm anybody, but I smell smoke in the cabin, and the exits are not clearly marked."

As stubborn as Domino was, he eventually convinced her to call an emergency meeting to formulate a defense strategy. The helicopter, which had torn down her clothesline and mussed her hair, provided a bit of an impetus.

That evening in the conference room, Switters was the last to arrive. He entered wearing a shabby suit (a year of crude laundry had taken its toll) and a sheepish grin. His laptop, it seemed, had just received an e-mail from Rome in which, much to his astonishment, the Church had backed down, agreeing, in exchange for the Fatima prophecy, to refrock the Pachomians without any undue restrictions on their rights of free speech.

If Switters thought that that was the end of it, that he could quit the convent now with an easy mind and swivel his attentions to the furtherance of his personal agenda, the fleshing out of the film script of his life, including a scene in which he, with the hard rubber charm of Bogart, would persuade a picturesque Amazonian medicine man to lift a quaint taboo, well, if that's what he thought, he was mistaken. Because the very next day, Domino contacted Scanlani and brazenly upped the ante.

Although it was completely against his best interest—and probably hers as well—Switters couldn't help but be delighted by her rash action.

Dawn's last cock-a-doodle was still aquiver in the red rooster's craw when she knocked at his door. Unfazed by the nakedness obvious beneath his thin muslin sheet, she plopped her plumping bottom (time's dung beetle was rolling her buttocks into lush round balls) onto his bedside stool and shared her intentions. If the Vatican fathers wanted the Fatima document, she told him, they were going to have to meet yet another demand. To wit: they would have to agree to disclose to the public the full text of the third prophecy within six months of its receipt, to disseminate its contents and make them widely known.

"A stipulation guaranteed to ferment patriarchal peevishness, I would venture," said Switters.

She shrugged. She smiled. She said, "*C'est la vie.*"

"But what about Masked Beauty? I've been under the impression that she's always insisted on keeping the prophecy secret because of the doubt and pessimism it could generate among earth's happy Christians."

"Precisely. That's why I've come to you. My aunt has never really heard your interpretation of the Virgin's pyramid reference. She still suspects it's an admission of the superior truth of Islam. I need you to explain, to convince her otherwise." She paused. Her eyes seemed to stop and savor a particular bulge in the bedclothes. "*Peut-être* convince me, as well," she mumbled.

They agreed to meet in Masked Beauty's quarters in an hour. Domino appeared reluctant to leave his company, and when she did, he had the distinct feeling that she was going to her room to indulge in the covert delicious shame that dogged not merely Fannie but most in her vocation.

Aroused by the image, Switters considered a similar, perhaps synchronous indulgence but decided instead to review the prophecies, about which he maintained, not altogether uncharacteristically,

ambivalent feelings. Obviously, the predictions, whether Marian or
Lucian in origin, had correctly called some shots. (Was it mere coincidence? Did it matter?) Moreover, certain aspects of them about which
he'd held reservations had, over time, been elucidated by Domino to
his general satisfaction. For example, regarding the first prophecy,
where the Virgin was alleged to have warned that "a night illuminated
by an unknown light" would be the sign that God was ready to punish
his misbehaving lookalikes with war and famine, Domino had contended that that was an accurate foretelling of a unique (she used the
word with trepidation, worrying that she should have said "unusual"
instead) meteorological event. On January 25, 1938, much of the
Northern Hemisphere was dazzled and panicked by what has been
described as the most dramatic and bizarre display of the aurora bore-
alis in recorded history. Undulating bands of vivid color, wide, violent,
and continuous throughout the night, were accompanied by snapping
and crackling sounds, causing thousands to believe that the world was
ablaze and doomsday was on the front burner. Less than ninety days
after that awesome atmospheric laser circus, Hitler marched into Aus-
tria, and the great war that Fatima had predicted was off and running.
Switters searched "northern lights" on the Internet and soon found that
Domino's facts were accurate.

In the second prophecy, he'd been put off by all that "consecration
of Russia" business. As near as he could figure, Fatima's command was,
at best, Red-baiting and, at worst, a modern example of misguided
evangelical zeal being used to justify Roman Catholic imperialism. It
hadn't worked in this case, but it conjured up images of black-robed
priests walking arm in arm with genocidal conquistadors, adminis-
tering absolutions while the loot—and the bodies—piled up. True,
Fatima hadn't advocated a forced conversion of Russia, and to consecrate, i.e., to declare or make sacred, was in and of itself a noble gesture. Yet, it smacked somehow of self-serving expansionism or, at least,
condescension.

Not so, argued Domino. She pointed out that the Virgin had
spoken of "the error of Russia," and Switters had to concur that no
honest, intelligent person could claim any longer that Communism,
however well-intentioned, was anything less than a wretched economic and psychological mistake. However, that was not quite the
point, according to Domino. While it had been popular in reactionary
circles to paint the Fatima Virgin as a sort of cold warrior, prodding
the holy armies of capitalism to subdue the godless Commies, Our
Lady was actually saying something quite different. She was, in fact,
promoting a revitalization of the Christian faith, a return to the original teachings of Jesus, the rebel rabbi who so vigorously scorned the

kind of worldly pursuits that had come, a few centuries after his death, to preoccupy a corrupt and power-mad Church. If the Vatican fathers were proud and foolish and materialistic, and though it pained her to admit it, Domino believed they were; if Rome was spiritually broken beyond repair, and this, too, she'd come to believe; then where could the spiritual center go to fix itself, to reestablish itself on those principles of Jesus that mankind had generally found just too damn difficult to follow?

"To the individual heart," replied Switters. "The only church that ever was."

His answer startled Domino, caught her by such surprise that after jerking upright, she slowly drooped forward in her chair, like a sunflower that could no longer bear the weight of its crown; and for thirty seconds or so, she was so lost in thought that her orbs were kind of an inky smear. He squeezed her knee (one of those familiarities in which he rarely anymore indulged) and the eyes winked back on, like modem lights after a power surge. "I meant geographically," she said. "Where could Christ's renewed Church recenter itself in the physical world?"

Switters thought: *Wall Street? Disneyland? Devil's Island?* To him, the location of Catholic world headquarters was so irrelevant to anything remotely significant that he didn't bother to venture a serious guess.

"There was nowhere in Western Europe that was any improvement over Rome, and the United States of America was not Jesus's style."

"Too bouncy," agreed Switters.

"Christ always shunned the high and mighty; so we are told. He preferred to mingle with the whores and publicans and sinners, he directed his message to the wayward and downtrodden. Is this not so? Well, in Russia there was a vast population of materially and spiritually impoverished souls, lost and longing for change. It would have been a clean slate, a fertile field. What better way to deal with an unholy land than to thrust upon it the mantle of holiness? Yes? *Oui?* To replace a bad king with an honest peasant, to replace our imperious pope with a converted Bolshevik, wouldn't this be an action true to the stark spirit of Jesus? Perhaps equally as important, shifting the cornerstone of Christianity to Russia would have served to heal the tragic schism between the Western and Eastern Orthodox faiths and to reunite their rites. So much suffering on so many levels might have been avoided if the Church had had the grace to heed its Mother's words. In the stillness of her Immaculate Heart, the hurly-burly antics of Stalin would have seemed like some cruel slapstick, comic and stupid, and few would have supported him. That was in 1917, remember, when there was time."

Reviewing Domino's words on that spring morning, he repeated

the phrase to himself: "when there was time." Did the fact—and it certainly appeared to be a fact—that history was accelerating mean that
there was less time? Or more? Were there fewer beans in the jar, or
were the beans simply pouring in at such a furious pace that they were
creating a vortex? He knew that at the center of every cyclone there
was a calm circle, a space into which time's tentacles did not seem to
reach. Was that tondo of stillness what was meant, then, by the odd
phrase, "my Immaculate Heart"?

Intrigued, he sat *zazen* on his cot for thirty minutes—thirty minutes
as measured by those dials and digits that seemed to have so little to
do with that void into which meditative stillness always transported
him. (He supposed *Immaculate Heart* was as good a label for it as any
other.)

Centered now, he felt he was properly prepared to hypothesize
about Today Is Tomorrow. However, on the way to Masked Beauty's
chambers, he stilted by the pantry shed and picked up a bottle of wine.
Maria Une protested that it was still too young to drink, but he
responded that in the Immaculate Heart, terms such as "too young"
were relative if not inapplicable. The old cook was uncertain how to
take that reference, and while she studied him for signs of sacrilege, he
pushed aside the thoughts of Suzy that the remark had unintentionally
engendered.

Then, as he was badgering Maria Une for a corkscrew, he believed
he heard the jackals again, yapping just beyond the wall in broad daylight. It took him a minute to realize that it was only Bob and Mustang
Sally chortling over some private joke down by the onion beds. Was
he becoming paranoid? No, at least not when compared to Skeeter
Washington, who, admiring the stars one evening on the deck of Poe's
boat, was heard to say, "If the universe be expanding, they gotta be
something chasing it."

There was a faint lilac smudge where the wart used to stand. A visual
whisper had replaced the visual cackle, the seeable caw. When candlelight struck it, it seemed a dot of bluish fog, a nail scar from an ancient
crucifixion, a pinpoint of shadow cast by a migratory moth. Three
months after separation from her divine wad of tissue, Masked Beauty
continued to mark its absence by compulsively rubbing and pulling
at her nose, like one of those compassionate zoo apes that openly
toys with its genitals in order to relieve the guilt of visiting school-
children.

Caressing her snout, Masked Beauty glanced from the wine bottle to Domino and back again. Pushing her hair from her face, Domino glanced from the wine bottle to Masked Beauty and back again. Switters smiled weakly. "All those sponges in the ocean," he said, "it's a wonder there's any water left." Ah, the power of the non sequitur! Not knowing how to respond, the two women put away the tea things and wiped the dust from a set of wineglasses. Domino was a bit nervous about how her aunt would react to Switters's interpretation of the pyramid prediction, Masked Beauty was clearly uncomfortable without a veil—or rather, she was uncomfortable without a mask to mask—but once they grew accustomed to the idea, they both welcomed a glass of early morning wine. The women sipped, and Switters, as was his practice, gulped. They were mostly silent; he, with each swallow, became more verbose.

Testing limits of credibility, he told the abbess everything he knew about the Kandakandero shaman with the pyramid-shaped head: his origins, his potents and powders, his fatalistic despair over the white man's invasion of his forest, his discovery of humor and his attempts to appropriate its magic, his theory that laughter was a physical force that could be used both as a shield and as a spirit canoe in which the wisest and bravest—the Real People—could navigate the river that separated and connected the Two Worlds.

"Which two worlds? Why, Heaven and earth, if you please. Life and death. Nature and technology. Yin and yang."

"You mean the female and the male?" asked the abbess.

"In a sense. More precisely, more fundamentally, it's light and darkness. Light and darkness without any moral implications. Good and evil exist only in the biomolecular realm. In the atomic realm, such notions become useless, and in the electronic realm, they disappear altogether."

Switters talked briefly about particle physics and the search for ever smaller elementary particles. "Recently physicists have started to conclude that in the entire universe there may be only two particles. Not two *kinds* of particles, mind you, but two particles, period. One with a positive charge, one with a negative. And listen to this: the two particles can *exchange* charges, the negative can trade off to become positive and vice versa. So, in a sense, there's only *one* particle in the universe, it being a pair whose attributes are interchangeable."

"What makes them decide to trade places?" asked Domino.

"Excellent question, sister love." Switters took a swig of wine. It was, indeed, very young, but it possessed a toddler's bashful bravado. "Maybe they get bored. I don't know. Figure that out and you can go eat lunch with God. Twice a week. Make *him* wash the dishes."

Domino made an expression somewhere between a wince and a

smile. Masked Beauty's was closer to the wince. The abbess ran a finger along the length of her nose. Her nose resembled an inflated map of the Yucatán Peninsula, the bluish spot indicating the lost capital of the Mayas.

"It gets better," said Switters. "This is only theory, there's no empirical evidence, but the belief now is that when they crack the final nut, split the most minute particle—and we're talking about something smaller than a neutrino—what they'll find inside, at the absolute fundamental level of the universe, is an electrified vacuum, an energy field in which light and darkness intermingle. The dark is as black as a bogman's toejam, and the light is brighter than God's front teeth; and they spiral together, entwined like a couple of snakes. They coil around each other, the light and the darkness, and they *absorb* each other continuously, yet they never cancel each other out. You get the picture. Except there isn't any picture. It's more on the order of music. Except the ear can't hear it. So it's like feeling, emotion, some absolutely pristine feeling. It's like, uh, it's like . . . love."

He paused to drink, and Masked Beauty studied him. "Are you versed in matters of love, Mr. Switters?"

Switters shot Domino an embarrassed look. The look he got back had as much insolence as shyness in it. "I love *myself*," he said. "But it's unrequited."

Both women laughed at this. Then Domino said, "Mr. Switters is experienced in love, auntie, but not in pure love."

(Switters didn't argue, but had Bobby Case been present, the spy pilot would have objected, "Why, hell, ladies, pure love's the only kind of love this silly hombre knows at all.")

Rising to light another stick of incense, the abbess commented that while their discussion of advanced physics was certainly interesting, she failed to detect its bearing on the subject at hand.

"Well," said Switters, "this pyramid-headed *curandero* from deep in the Amazonian jungle seems to have concluded that light and darkness can merge in a similar fashion on the biomolecular plane, the social plane. He says it occurs during laughter. That a people who could move in the primal realm of laughter could live free of all of life's dualities. They would be the first since the original men, the ancestors of the Real People, to live in harmony with the fundamental essence of the universe. The essence our quantum physicists are talking about. Today Is Tomorrow says the civilized man can't perpetuate that state because he lacks the Kandakandero knowledge of the different levels of reality, he's become emotionally invested in one narrow, absurdly simplistic view of the nature of existence; and the Indians can't do it because they lack the buoyancy of the civilized man's humor. But the people strong and nimble enough to combine unlimited intellectual flexibility with the mysterious energy of the laugh, well, they would become . . ."

"Enlightened?" ventured the abbess.

"Enlightened and endarkened," Switters corrected her. "Enlightened *and* endarkened. The ultimate."

Masked Beauty wasn't convinced. "A sense of humor is a fine thing," she agreed, "but it is not a way of life, and it certainly is not a means of serving our Lord. This strange savage of yours does not even *know* our Lord."

"Why does that matter? Fatima said that in the next century— which pops out of the box in about nine months, by the way—the message that will bring unexpected joy and wisdom to a segment of humanity isn't going to be coming from the Church of your Lord. Am I right? She said it will come from the direction of a pyramid. Well, Today Is Tomorrow qualifies as a pyramid, as near as I can tell, and he's got a much fresher message than Islam, including esoteric Islam, with which, if you factor in the Hermetic tradition, it has a little bit in common." He gulped. "Mmm. This vintage possesses a rather touching innocence, don't you think?"

"Yes, and it is almost gone," the abbess noted. She'd never seen anyone drain a bottle of wine so wholeheartedly. "Perhaps I am just a stupid old woman, but I fail to understand how your shaman's ideas are at all practical or applicable. How can a mere sense of humor—"

"And a flexible, expansive definition of reality," Switters reminded her.

"Okay, that as well. But in a troubled world such as ours, one cannot walk around laughing at everything like a mindless magpie. Where is the hope in that?"

He didn't seem to have a ready response. Tugging at a curl, as if the pressure on his scalp might activate cerebration, he cleared his throat but said nothing. He was entertaining notions about how a radical and active sense of humor could puncture the sterile bubble of bourgeois respectability, how it could destroy smug illusions and in so doing, strengthen the soul; how if the essence could somehow be extracted from laughter, that essence might prove less like sound than like flavor, the flavor of the soul tasting itself at the raw bar of the absolute. Yet, he was neither informed enough (he hadn't previously given it much thought) or drunk enough to put such notions into words. What the hell? Since when was he the shaman's mouthpiece?

Observing his hesitation, Domino spoke up. "I don't believe Mr. Switters is advocating mindless laughter, auntie. I don't believe he is advocating anything. He's simply trying to solve the riddle of the third prophecy. And I must say, I find it an attractive alternative to our own interpretation."

"What? Laughing one's way into Heaven?"

"I think what is at issue here," Domino went on, "is a kind of mindful playfulness. I have observed it in Mr. Switters, and I suspect it could be extricated from Today Is Tomorrow's philosophy—a philosophy, by the way, that seems almost to have resulted from combining aspects of an archaic shamanic tradition with a kind of Zen nonattachment and an irreverent modern wit. Mr. Switters defeats melancholy by refusing to take things, including himself, too seriously."

"But many things *are*—"

"Are they? What I've learned from Mr. Switters is that no matter how valid, how vital, one's belief system might be, one undermines that system and ultimately negates it when one gets rigid and dogmatic in one's adherence to it."

Masked Beauty rubbed her scar as though trying to erase it. Or to stimulate new growth. "I realize that happiness is relative and often dependent upon or at least affected by external circumstances, whereas cheerfulness can be learned and consciously practiced. Both you and Mr. Switters seem to have a knack for practicing cheerfulness— oh, but I can see that our discussing Mr. Switters in this way is making him uncomfortable. Let us return to the ideas of his pyramid man. Assuming that a deliberate comic cheerfulness can evolve into a sustainable joy, where does the wisdom come from?"

Domino deferred to him, but he nodded for her to answer. "I would guess," she said, "that what might be extrapolated from Today Is Tomorrow's epiphany is that joy itself is a form of wisdom. Beyond that is the suggestion that if people are nimble enough to move freely between different perceptions of reality and if they maintain a relaxed, playful attitude well-seasoned with laughter, then they would live in harmony with the universe; they would connect with all matter, organic and inorganic, at its purest, most basic level. Could not that be our Lord's plan for us, his goal for his children? Now, auntie, don't make a face. Perhaps . . . perhaps that's even where God resides, there in that—how did Switters call it?—that energized void at the base of creation. It makes more sense than on some poof-poof Riviera among gold-plated clouds."

Pausing to let that sink in—to sink into her own consciousness as well as her aunt's—Domino took a Switters-sized swallow of wine. "Perhaps, too," she resumed, "Today Is Tomorrow's ideal is precisely what is needed to rescue the human race from its tragic flaw: prideful narcissism. Isn't that where all this 'seriousness' comes from? A dilated ego?"

Switters regarded her with amazement. He saw her in a whole new light. On the grease rack of his esteem, he jacked her up a few more notches. *What a stand-up girl!* he thought. *She gets it. Better than I get it, maybe.* He felt a spreading warmth toward her. He also felt a spreading need to urinate. The degree to which the wine had contributed to both of those sensations is not worth examining. It is enough to say that he reached for his stilts, blew kisses, presented the women as a parting gift his favorite word in all of earth's languages—an ancient Aztec utterance that meant *parrot, poet, interlocutor,* and *guide to the underworld;* all that stuffed into a single word; and a word, he assured them, that could not be properly pronounced unless one had had one's tongue surgically altered, preferably with an obsidian blade. He presented them with a spitty approximation of that word, and then, before anyone could say, "What? It doesn't mean *vagina?*", he weaved off to the nearest privy, leaving Domino to convince Masked Beauty that the third prophecy of Fatima referred not to a triumph of Islam but to the views of a capitate freak from the Amazonian forest; and to persuade her, further, that the prophecy, bizarre implications and all, should be made public by the institution most at risk from it.

Evidently, she did a pretty good job, for shortly after noon, she sought him out and had him e-mail Scanlani with the Pachomian demand for full disclosure.

If Domino could imagine that God occupied the fundamental subatomic particle, where did she think Satan lived? In the fundamental anti-particle? In a quarklette of dark matter? Wouldn't the presumed interweaving of light and darkness in that minutest of maws give her a clue that God and Satan might be codependent if not indivisible? The real question was where did the neutral angels reside, the ones who refused to take sides? There would be, of course, plenty of elbow room of a sort in that elementary space. Because the light waves therein would have been transformed into photons had they struck any matter, indications were that the space was infinitely empty. Which also would suggest that God and the Devil were energies in which, outflanking Einstein, mass dropped out of the equation.

By the time Domino arrived to have him e-mail Scanlani, the effects of the grape had worn off, and Switters was no longer bruising his brain with such thoughts. He felt bruised enough by the wine itself, its infantile character having left him with the kind of headache with which newborn babies leave sleepless dads. Any impulse he might have had to wonder aloud to her how it was that the microcosmic could not merely reflect but *contain* the macrocosmic, any desire to suggest that levity might actually be the hallmark of the sacred, had evaporated, and he was not unhappy to be thusly unburdened. He wished to concentrate on convincing Domino that her tactics with the Vatican would likely provoke strong reaction. He wanted the oasis to steel itself.

Once again, however, he was mistaken. Not three days had passed before word arrived from Rome that the Pachomian demand would gladly be met. According to Scanlani, the Holy Father had been planning all along to make public the third prophecy as soon as he was convinced of its authenticity.

Noticing Switters's frown, Domino asked if he smelled a rat. "Worse," he said. "I smell a jackal."

It did have a stink about it. It seemed much too easy, passing beyond the smooth into the slick. What worried him even more than Rome's newfound spirit of accommodation was the last line of Scanlani's communiqué, the line that advised that within the week, representatives of the Holy See would be arriving at the Syrian oasis to collect the Fatima transcript.

"You cannot allow that," Switters insisted.

"Why not?"

He then outlined several grisly scenarios, one in which all occupants of the compound were shot dead and the massacre blamed on religious fanatics (or, if Damascus was cooperating, on the troublesome Bedouins); another in which insidious chemicals were employed to make it look as if a deadly virus had swept through the order. They might paint the Pachomians as a suicide cult. They might even slaughter the sisters and blame it on him. "We're out here in the middle of nowhere, vulnerable, unprotected, naught but the wind and the cuckoos to witness our fate."

Domino scoffed. She proposed that his service in the CIA had lowered his reality orientations. "There would be no cause to murder us, nothing to gain. Suppose they renege on their promise and don't make public the prophecy, or else they edit it to their advantage; and suppose then that we protest and release our own version of the prophecy, Cardinal Thiry's version? How many will believe us? How many will care? In the end, we are no more to them than the nuisance fly."

"People swat flies," he said, but he knew that she was right.

Governments—and the armed agencies that served them—loathed intellectuals and artists and freethinkers of every stripe, but they didn't particularly fear them. Not anymore. They didn't fear them because in the modern corporate state, artists, intellectuals, and freethinkers wielded no political or economic power; had no real hold on the hearts and minds of the masses. Human societies have always defined themselves through narration, but nowadays corporations are telling man's stories for him. And the message, no matter how entertainingly couched, is invariably the same: to be special, you must conform; to be happy, you must consume. But though Switters was well aware of those conditions, he was also aware that they could be and ought to be subverted. Moreover, he was aware that cowboys periodically caught Hollywood fever, instigating ludicrous, horrendous capers out of sheer ennui, a smoldering appetite for thrill and domination. So he badgered Domino relentlessly until she at last gave in.

The Pachomians, she e-mailed Scanlani, would surrender the Fatima prophecy only to the Holy Father himself. It would be directly delivered to the pope and none other. "Do not waste your time traveling to Syria," she told him, at Switters's insistence. "We shall travel to Rome."

This time, the reaction was more typical, if not more reassuring. Hostility seethed from every glyph. Scanlani chided Domino for her presumptuousness, her audacity and insubordination in thinking she could order the Holy Father about, thinking she could force a papal audience. He reminded her that her superiors had gone out of their way to be accommodating, and for her ingratitude and impertinence he berated and belittled her as only a practiced lawyer could. His attack brought her close to tears. Contrite, she was ready to back off, but Switters wouldn't permit it. "The grand mackerels have given in before, and they may again. Stick to your—pardon the expression—guns."

Reluctantly she did. And a wicked war of words ensued, a dispute that raged for weeks. No Vatican representative came to Syria, but overheated electrons zinged eastward across the Mediterranean on a regular basis, and hard-boiled electrons often passed them, heading west. Several times Domino seemed to lose her stomach for the fight, but Switters, operating on not much more than a hunch, propped her up, girded her loins (though he might have preferred to ungird them), and pushed her back into the fray.

Toward the end of April, she prevailed.

She didn't know if she had simply worn them down or if they were getting nervous as June and the "New Catholic Women" conference approached, but quite abruptly one day in the weeks following Easter, the Church fathers relented, going so far as to issue a thoroughly polite formal invitation to meet with the Holy Father in a fortnight's time.

Hugging Switters, almost sobbing with relief, she said she was overjoyed that it was done and that, in the end, winning an audience with the pope was worth all the Sturm und Drang.

"Personally, I'd rather meet Pee-wee Herman," he said, "but if you're happy, I'm happy. And if you're *safe* and happy, I'm happier yet."

She suggested that he must be happy on his own account as well. He could leave now, leave at once, and start attending to his considerable personal agenda. "Not so fast," he said. "You may have won the compulsories, but you still have to skate the freestyles, and there ain't no way your coach is abandoning you until the last damn twirl is twirled. Oh, no! Not with *this* set of judges. Some way, somehow, I've got to escort you to Rome."

She told him he was out of his cotton-picking mind. She told him he was crazy and brave and sweet. He told her he was just curious.

the may moon looked like a bottlecap. More specifically, entering its last phase, the moon looked like a bottlecap that a fidgety beer-drinker had squashed double between macho thumb and forefinger. The moon was making Switters thirsty, and he said as much to Toufic, but the truck driver wasn't listening.

"I want to love America," Toufic lamented, "but America requires me to hate it."

Toufic had come to drive the Pachomian delegation to the airport at Damascus. He arrived on a Monday evening so that they might get a very early start on Tuesday morning. He arrived with a crumb of hashish for Switters, and they sat by the car now, smoking it in the faintly moon-painted desert. He also arrived with American offenses on his mind. Offenses in Iraq. Offenses in Yugoslavia. Those offenses made Toufic angry, but mostly they made him sad. His large brown eyes seemed saturated with a kind of molten chocolate grief.

"What is wrong with your great country?" Toufic lamented. "Why must it do these terrible things?"

Switters held a cloud of candied smoke in his lungs. "Because the cowboys wiped out the buffalo," Switters said.

"Everywhere a buffalo fell," said Switters, "a monster sprang up in its place."

Switters was going to list some of the monsters, but his mouth was dry, and he feared he couldn't expectorate.

"There's a direct link between the buffalo hunts and Vietnam," said Switters.

Straining to comprehend, Toufic sighed with his eyes.

"When Lee surrendered at Appomattox," said Switters, "it sealed once and for all Wall Street's power over the American people."

Switters said, "There's a direct link between Appomattox and genuine imitation leather."

"But," Toufic lamented, "your country has so *much*."

"Well," said Switters, "it has bounce. It has snap. It has flux."

"Americans are generous and funny, the ones I have met," Toufic lamented, "but I am compelled to oppose them."

"It's only natural," said Switters. "American foreign policy invites opposition. It invites terrorism."

Switters said, "Terrorism is the only imaginable logical response to America's foreign policy, just as street crime is the only imaginable logical response to America's drug policy."

Toufic wanted to pursue this in greater detail, but the hashish was kicking in, and Switters was rapidly losing whatever interest he had in politics. "Politics is where people pay somebody large sums of money to impose his or her will on them. Politics is sadomasochism. I don't want to talk about it anymore."

Switters said, between pursed lips, for he was holding in the last of the oily smoke, "Let's talk about . . . let's talk about . . . Little Red Riding Hood."

Switters told Toufic the story of Little Red Riding Hood. Toufic was puzzled but enthralled. He listened attentively, as if weighing every word. Then, Switters told Toufic the story of Goldilocks and the Three Bears. He did the voices. Switters did the big gruff bass Daddy Bear voice, he did the medium-sized nurturing domestic Mama Bear voice, and he did the little high-pitched squealy Baby Bear voice. Toufic was absolutely spellbound.

Toufic wanted more. So, next, Switters tried to describe *Finnegans Wake* to him. It was not a complete success. Obviously baffled, Toufic became disinterested, even slightly irritated; but Switters persisted in his "titley hi ti ti" talk and his "where, O where is me lickle dig done" talk, just as if he were back at the C.R.A.F.T. Club in Bangkok.

But Switters wasn't in Bangkok, he was in the Syrian desert, and the May moon, entering its last phase, appeared folded over on itself like a thin yellow omelet. It was making him hungry, and he said as much to Toufic, but the truck driver was no longer listening.

Six of them crowded into the Audi sedan long before dawn. Toufic, of course, was at the wheel, and there were Masked Beauty, Domino, Pippi, Mustang Sally—and Switters, dragged out in nun's habit, traveling (he hoped) on ZuZu's passport. As they lined up in the dark to pack themselves into the car, Masked Beauty turned and faced them. "We are going to Italy," she announced solemnly, perhaps unnecessarily. "You will find that it in no way resembles Italian nights in our dining hall."

"Italian nights? What are those?" asked Mustang Sally, referring sarcastically to the fact that the sisters had not enjoyed an Italian night since Switters had cleaned out their wine cellar back in September.

"Cock-a-doodle-doo!" crowed Switters, trusting that he'd turned the tables and awakened the rooster.

The drive was hot and hard. For fifteen or so miles around mid-morning, they were shadowed by a helicopter. This particularly angered Pippi, who badly needed a pit stop. Watching her squirm to hold her water, Switters was given yet another reason to despise choppers.

They arrived at the Damascus airport at half past one, believing themselves unfashionably early for a 5 P.M. flight. Such, alas, was not the case.

Switters had purchased their tickets over the Internet, courtesy of Mr. Plastic, and they picked these up at the Alitalia counter without a hitch. (When Domino inquired how he intended to pay for them, he said that was not an issue, since he'd charged them to his grandmother's attorney, whose credit information he'd had the foresight to hijack after the woman cheated him out of his cabin in the mountains.) Up to a point, clearing customs likewise had gone smoothly. Switters, wheelchaired and bewimpled, pushed by Pippi and fussed over by Mustang Sally (as though he were the most unfierce of invalids), was accepted as Sister Francine Boulod (ZuZu's real name) without question. Whenever an official looked him over, Switters would commence to drool, inspiring the *douanier* to shift his attentions elsewhere. The trouble came when the women were advised that while they were free to leave the country, or free to stay, once they left they could not return: the Syrian government would not be renewing their visas.

Lengthy protests and convoluted discussions followed. When the Frenchwomen objected that they could not possibly depart Syria under those circumstances, the customs agent-in-charge shrugged and said, in essence, "Fine. Don't go." Switters wasn't liking the implications of this at all, but he dared not open his lightly rouged, drool-bedewed mouth.

Having eventually exhausted her arguments with officials at the airport, none of whom could supply her with a reason for the visa restrictions, Masked Beauty began making frantic phone calls. Nobody appeared to be in that day at the Syrian Foreign Office. Every living soul at the French embassy seemed to be in a meeting. The abbess made call after call, to no avail. And now, Flight 023 was boarding.

At the last minute, just before the gate was closed, it was decided that Masked Beauty would remain in Damascus to attempt to resolve the visa problem. The rest of the party would proceed to Rome, where with any luck, the abbess would catch up with them in time for their papal audience on Thursday. They left her stewing, rubbing her nose as if it were a lamp whose genie had gone on coffee break. They barely made the flight.

the three former nuns and one quasi-nun (here's a way to avoid the "earrings") had reserved rooms, on Switters's recommendation, at the Hotel Senato. A smallish *albèrgo*, the Senato sat, modest cheek to pagan jowl, next door to the Pantheon in the Piazza della Rotonda, the loudest, most colorful, most, for that matter, *Italian* corner of Rome, and a favorite of Switters's, although he sometimes complained that the area bordered on being too damn vivid.

At the check-in desk, the clerk handed Domino a message. It was from Scanlani. He welcomed the Pachomians to Rome. He informed them that their audience with the Holy Father had been moved up to 14:30 hours on Wednesday, the following day. And he advised them that in Italy it was illegal to impersonate a nun, so all of them, most especially their "chief of security," ought to change into civilian clothes.

It was a rather stunned flock of penguins that lugged its bags (there were no bellmen at the Hotel Senato) into the dwarfish lift. Only two persons could fit at a time, and Domino and Switters elevated last. "I know you don't like the sound of this," she said, fluttering Scanlani's note, "but it's going to be okay. I only hope my aunt gets here in time. The prophecy is hers. I don't feel right about surrendering it without her."

After dropping off her bag in the room that she would share with Mustang Sally and Pippi, Domino came to Switters's room to help him off with his habit. "Hold still, ZuZu," she said playfully. "Only forty-six more buttons to go."

Beneath the heavy habit, he wore his undershorts. The boxer shorts with little snowmen on them and maple trees with buckets attached for collecting maple sap. With a sudden flourish that astonished them both, she yanked them down around his ankles.

She fondled him until he was as stiff as a tire iron. Then, cupping his testes in the palm of her hand, like a farmgirl weighing guinea eggs, she knelt before his Invacare 9000 and gave him a single lick; a long, slow, wet, pedestal to pinnacle lick. He laid his hands on her head, hoping to guide her into more of the same, but she stood and backed away from the chair. She was shaking.

"I want you so bad I could scream," she said. "I want you so bad I could yell and spit and scratch the flowers off this wallpaper. I want you so bad I could kick the furniture and pray to God and piss in my panties and weep."

"*But?*" he asked, as she took another step backward. It was only one word, but his mouth was so dry he could barely utter it. As a matter of fact, it came out in Baby Bear's voice. He was stiffer than before, if that was physiologically possible, and a fever had descended upon him like a satyric malaria.

"*But* I've made a vow to Mary and to myself and to that part of myself that is Mary and vice versa. Not until I am married."

"We cou-cou-could marry tomorrow," he stammered. "Hell, the *pope* could marry us." The imp had hold of him for certain.

Domino smiled. It was a smile that could have overturned three or four Vespas in the piazza beneath their window. "Silly goose," she said. "It would never work out between us. I'm too old and you're too . . . Anyway, you will make fun of this, but when I enter St. Peter's tomorrow, it is important to me to enter as a virgin. I may not have on my habit, but between my legs as in my heart, I will be a nun."

"The maidenhead Lazarus," he muttered, hoping that he didn't sound too sardonic. He did, after all, admire the sheer obstinacy of her commitment to the patriarchs' bogus notion of innocence. "The hymen that rose from the dead."

She frowned. But then she smiled again. "Yes," she said with an air of pride that was only partially feigned. "And it's the only one on the planet. It's unique."

"So far as we know." He was still so aroused his eyeballs were hard.

"Yes," she agreed, as she backed out of the room. "So far as we know."

the next day they lunched just off the piazza at the gastronomically glorious Da Fortunato al Pantheon, although only Switters and Mr. Plastic had much of an appetite. Thrilled to be out of the chickpea zone at last, Switters gobbled both grilled sea bass and spaghetti alle vongole veraci, washed down with a carafe of frascati. It was Italian asparagus season, and he ordered the *aspàrgi bianchi* in three different preparations, pausing between each to improvise asparagus poetry: "Erect as the white knight's lance, a flameless candle that lights the country ditch, pithy pen with a ruffled nib for writing love letters to his cousin, the lily; O asparagus! lean lord of spring" etc. etc., on and on, in Italian, French, and English, until the waiters joined Domino and Sally in rolling their eyes.

After dessert and grappa, they stopped back by the hotel to see if Masked Beauty had arrived. She had not, alas, so they split up and took two minicabs to Vatican City. Switters rode with Pippi, who was practically gnawing the freckles off her fingers with nervous excitement. Pippi was wild to see the Holy Father, of course, but she felt somehow that the timing was wrong. "This is supposed to be happening tomorrow," she whined.

"Today *is* tomorrow," said Switters. He took her hand and held it tightly until they reached the half-hidden service entrance off Via di Porta Angelica, where, as instructed, they were to meet Scanlani. Indeed, the Swiss Guardsman who answered Domino's ring ushered them inside immediately, and there Scanlani waited, expressionless, smartly dressed, looking as if the Exxon *Valdez* had run aground in his hair. He showed no surprise at seeing Switters.

The party was invited onto a minibus, not much more than an oversize golfcart, which, having no provision for the disabled, caused Switters a bit of difficulty. Apparently, Scanlani found this amusing,

although it was almost impossible to tell. Switters wanted to hold on
to the rear of the vehicle and be towed, but his host objected that it
would attract attention. Pippi and a Swiss Guardsman tipped him over
and more or less dumped him into the cart. His chair was folded and
plopped awkwardly and heavily in his lap. He patted the contraption.
"It's guaranteed fireproof," he said, and grinned at Scanlani.

Traveling the Vatican's back streets, out of sight of pilgrims and
tourists, they passed through two security checkpoints, at the second
of which they were taken into separate cubicles and searched so thoroughly that afterward Domino whispered in Switters's ear that she
might as well have lost her virginity to him the night before. The
guard captain was highly alarmed by Switters's pistol, but Scanlani said
it was okay, telling the captain that the crippled American "used to be
one of us" (a statement to which, under normal circumstances, Switters
would have strenuously objected). He was made to give up the
weapon, however. They locked it in a vault, assuring him that he could
retrieve it on his way out. Without the gun in his waistband, he had to
tighten his belt. "How to eat a huge lunch and still lose weight," he
mumbled.

"I warned you not to bring that thing in the first place," said
Domino.

The captain and three other Swiss Guards now accompanied them
to the large building that stood at the northwest of Piazzo San Pietro,
the ugly old gray castle in which the pope had his apartments. They
entered through a side door and in a wood-paneled vestibule were
greeted with practiced courtesy by a cardinal—robe, red beanie, and
all. He was the prelate in charge of investigating miracles. "Do you do
warts and hymens?" asked Switters. Neither the cardinal nor Domino
acknowledged his remark, but there was a throb of unspoken menace
in the almost imperceptible curl of Scanlani's upper lip.

With an air of aloof benevolence, such as one might find in
a kindergarten teacher whose interest in children was strictly professional, the cardinal led the group down a long, dim hallway to a
door that opened onto a garden of unexpectedly large dimensions.
Spring flowers and spring-green shrubs were everywhere, and there
were pines and chestnut trees and scattered broken hunks of ancient
columns that, relieved of their burden of porticoes, lay about in decorative retirement. Birds were singing, though with no more or no
less religiosity than if they'd been at a New Jersey landfill, while the
afternoon sun fuzzed everything in a lazy chartreuse haze. Gas of
asparagus.

At the far end of the garden, perhaps fifty yards' distant, there was
an ivy-covered pavilion, a raised gazebo of sorts, made of ivory-

painted latticed wood, and it was down a graveled path to that gazebo that the cardinal led them, single file, after first briefing them on the protocols of a papal reception.

Approximately five yards from the gazebo, the cardinal stopped them. When Switters, who'd been propelling himself, didn't brake quickly enough, his wheelchair was jerked to a halt from behind. He glanced over his shoulder to see the captain hovering there. "I thought the Swiss Guard were all young bucks," Switters said. "You look old enough to remember John Foster Dulles." His subsequent expectoration was subdued, even delicate, but the Guardsman shook his chair forcefully and laid a firm hand on his shoulder.

"The Holy Kielbasa witnessed not one speck of my secular sputum," Switters protested. He was correct. There was a throne inside the shadowy gazebo, but as best he could tell, peering through the ivy vines, it was presently unoccupied.

"You've been drinking alcohol, sir," the captain said.

"Merely boosting the ol' immune system," explained Switters.

The party had spread out a bit in front of the gazebo, and the ex-nuns were staring hard, straining to glimpse the patriarch whom they might resist but whom they could not help but revere: their conditioning would allow no other response. Not one papal blip had appeared on their radar screens, however. Switters could make out two figures in business suits to either side of the empty throne, but neither of them cast a popish shadow. Scanlani entered the gazebo then and joined them. The trio conversed briefly, then called to the cardinal. In turn, the cardinal beckoned to Domino. "You have the paper of interest? Good. Please come." He took her by the elbow and steered her up the four short steps that led into the gazebo. Mustang Sally and Pippi fell in behind her, bursting to genuflect, but a Guardsman blocked each of their paths, and even though Switters hadn't moved, he felt the captain tighten his grip on the wheelchair.

A pair of songbirds flew over, making songbird noises.

Domino paused at the top of the steps. Although her back was to Switters, he could tell she was riveted on the pavilion's rear entrance, searching for some sign of a little white monkey with china blue eyes and an aura of milky authority. She searched in vain, proceeding no farther, clutching the dog-eared Fatima envelope to her bosom. Gently the cardinal tried to nudge her inside, but she wouldn't budge. At that point, however, Scanlani and his two companions began, in a friendly, if deliberate, fashion to edge toward her.

As they inched out of the deeper shadows, into the confusing pattern of ivy leaf and sunlight, one of the men proved to be good Dr. Goncalves, Fatima scholar and author of a biography of Salazar, in which he portrayed the Portuguese dictator as a latter-day apostle. There was something familiar about the second man as well. In a few clicks of his biocomputer, Switters identified him as a company spook, a shrewd, rat-eyed cowboy by the name of Seward, who was run by Mayflower Cabot Fitzgerald and who apparently possessed some interest and expertise in religious affairs, having at one point petitioned Mayflower to allow him to smack the Dalai Lama, whose inner circle Seward had managed to penetrate. "The little sheet-wrapped bastard's promoting a destabilizing brand of happiness," Seward was said to have complained. Mayflower countered, "His emphasis on happiness is precisely why nobody takes him seriously."

Switters was taking Seward seriously. It would be a major understatement to say he did not like the looks of this, the sound of it, the smell of it.

Those in the gazebo were conversing now. Even in the sweet green hush of the garden, he could hear nothing of the men's side of things, but every now and then, he caught a word or two of Domino's. He heard her say "no" a lot. He heard her say, "This isn't right." He heard her say, "I can't do that." He heard her say, "I will have to consult the abbess." From the way her back muscles rippled under her best chador, he knew she was squeezing the prophecy to her breast, like the child she'd never borne. He glanced at Pippi. Her freckles were winking out like dying stars. He glanced at Mustang Sally. Plastered by sweat to her forehead, her spit curl formed an ominous question mark. "No," he heard Domino say. Her voice was as firm as cheddar. Then, "How will I know that it's . . ."

With one of those effortless, swift moves of his, Scanlani glided toward her. Something was clamped in his fist. Something about the length of a small flashlight. Something as shiny black as a licorice popsicle. Something obviously made from nonmetallic materials, perhaps in order that it might pass unnoticed through airport metal detectors. Like Switters's Beretta. The Beretta that was locked now in a Vatican vault, as though it were one of the Holy See's legendary treasures.

His arm extended, Scanlani leveled the sinister object at Domino's head, intending—there was no doubt—to shoot her point-blank, right between the eyes.

Switters screamed. "Stop, motherfucker! You!"

The captain attempted to restrain him, but the way Switters snapped the man's wrist in half, it might as well have been the wrist of a Barbie doll.

It is tempting to report that that whole past year with Sister Domino was unfolding now before him in a speed-parade of images—odd and endearing and frustrating; a hurricane of blurry memories that blew past his inner eye as if it were tied halfway up a middle-aged palm tree. In actual fact, there was nothing at all in his brain but a clear, clean hum: the cultivated signal that, in men of his background, transformed the primal siren of *wah-wah* panic into an articulated call to action.

Switters leapt from the chair.

His left foot hit the ground first. The instant it touched, it was as if an angry viper had sunk its fangs into the instep. A severe jolt shot through his body. There was a deafening *pop*, and a ball of white light—decidedly not a mystic coconut—exploded behind his eyes.

He staggered sideways.

He pitched forward onto his face.

Switters had once read somewhere that according to data accumulated from the black-box flight recorders of crashed aircraft, the last words spoken by pilots, upon realization that they were doomed, was most often, "Oh, shit!"

What did it say about human frailty, about the transparent peel of civilization, about the state of evolution, about the dominion of body over mind, when, at the moment of their imminent death, modern, educated, affluent men were moved to an evocation of excrement? That as the ax abruptly fell on their mortal lives, technologically sophisticated commanders of multimillion-dollar flying machines usually uttered no proclamation of sacred, familial, or romantic love; no patriotic sentiment, no cry for forgiveness, no expression of gratitude or regret, but rather, a scatological oath?

Quite likely, it said very little. Almost certainly, the word *shit* was issued without the slightest conscious regard for its literal meaning. On an unconscious level, the oath might be significant, but one would have to be a fairly fanatical Freudian to propose that it indicated the persistent domination of an infantile fixation on feces.

In any event, though he might imagine Bobby Case uttering something of the sort (Bobby was a Texan, after all), Switters, mildly appalled by the information, vowed that no such phrase would mark *his* final exit. "Oh, shit" lacked grace, lacked class, lacked charm, lacked imagination, lacked any indication of full consciousness. It was simply vulgar, simply crude, and while Switters appreciated profanity's occasional value as verbal punctuation, as a highly effective vehicle for

emphasis, he was scornful when louts swore as a substitute for vocabulary, youths as a substitute for rebellion, stand-up comics as a substitute for wit.

When his end came, Switters had always trusted that he would
improvise something original if not profound; something appropriate
to the specific situation, which was to say, something dramatically correct. If nothing else, should time be short and inspiration shorter, he
would, he had vowed, bellow *wahoo!*—one final, culminating, roller-
coaster-rider whoop of defiant exhilaration.

A noble ambition, perhaps. Yet when the earth viper bit, when the
internal fireball exploded, when he lost contact with the world and
went spiraling off into an electrified darkness, he hadn't cried *wahoo* or
anything remotely resembling a famous last word. And had there been
a black box in the cockpit of his Invacare starship, it would have
recorded his last words before he was sent spiraling into that electrified darkness as, "Stop, motherfucker." How very déclassé, how very
embarrassing.

Electrified darkness because it wasn't passive. And it wasn't really dark.
Or rather, it was dark and it wasn't dark. It was a darkness that behaved
like light. Or, maybe, it was light that behaved like darkness. How was
he supposed to know? Spiraling into it, out of control, he was in no
position to judge. The condition seemed, in a sense, *neutral*—yet, as
stated, it was far from static. Had he time to analyze it (which he did
not, being embedded in a trans-temporal state, where the linear pencil
of analysis had an eraser at both ends), he might have described it as
an interface. As an interface between darkness and light. As an imperceptibly thin crack between yin and yang. A reality between *that* which
is and *this* which is. A number between one and zero. Spiraling.

Switters realized then that he had passed that way before. The
Hallways of Always. Except now there were no botanical tryptamine
alkaloids churning in his belly. And so far, no pod things boasting that
they owned the business. There was, however, a faint glow in what
might be called the distance, a sort of end-of-the-tunnel luminosity,
and it was pulling him toward it. "No! I absolutely refuse to have some
trendy near-death experience," he heard himself exclaim. "Serve me
the real enchilada or let me—"

"Heh!"

"Maestra? Is that you? Are you . . . okay?"

There was no reply. He spiraled on through the tunnel. Or, the
tunnel spiraled on through him. Was he a toy boat in the gutter, or

was he the gutter—and where were the Art Girls? He drew closer to the glow. Or, it drew closer to him. It was proving to be not a light as such, but something more on the order of a pulsating membrane, feathery and multicolored, with lots of greens and reds. The membrane had no alter image, no counterpart, and he began to wonder if in that dichotomous void, there wasn't a singularity after all. Might this be the aura of the Ultimate? The medulla of the mandala? The Immaculate Heart made visible? A hyperspatial hymen? He became aware, then, of sound: not the music of the spheres, by any means, but a low, crusty, constricted noise, scrumbling harshly out of the membrane, almost as though it were clearing its throat.

Yes, that was it. Switters had the distinct feeling, moving into that polychrome pulsar, that it was preparing to speak to him; that, like the alleged prophets of old, he was about to hear the actual voice of that which men call *God*. He was, as the figure of speech would have it, all ears.

There was another spasm of hacking rasps. Then—it spoke.

"Peeple of zee wurl, relax!"

Was what it said.

The glow sputtered out.
Nothingness replaced it.
And that was that.

Send in the clowns.

at that instant, or so it seemed, Switters reentered the realm of ordinary consciousness. He knew it was the realm of ordinary consciousness because it hurt like hell. And because he sensed the presence of advertising.

Things did not come slowly into focus. He opened his eyes and, *bingo,* he took everything in sharply and at once: the pale yellow walls, the Chianti-colored curtains, the sleek chrome table at bedside (in Italy, even hospital rooms had style); the Marlboro cigarette billboard that dominated the view from the window; Pippi in a brand-new, contemporary, lightweight habit, Domino wearing her old Syrian chador, wearing her old marrow-melting smile, wearing her round cheeks and vivacious air.

"Where am I?" he asked. Immediately, he groaned and, unwisely, slapped his sore forehead. "Let me withdraw that question," he pleaded. He withdrew it because, within limits, he could guess where he was and, more important, because the question was so pathetically predictable. What a cliché.

"You've come back to life," said Domino. Her voice, even more than usual, was like a Red Cross doughnut wagon purring into earshot after a disaster.

"To where?"

"To life. *La vie.*"

"Right. To life. To the ol' bang and whimper show. You, as well, Domino! You're okay! Bless your heart! The bastard didn't . . . What happened? *Bonjour,* Pippi. I should say, *Sister* Pippi." He indicated her garb. "Man, that was fast. How long was I out?"

"This is the tenth day."

He sprang halfway up in bed, nearly severing the IV tube. *"Ten days?!!"* He was flabbergasted.

Gently Domino eased him back down onto the pillow. "Day before yesterday, you started mumbling in your sleep. The day before that, you fluttered your eyelids and wiggled your toes. The doctors were pretty sure you were going to come out of it. We've offered many, many prayers."

"But what. . . ?" He ran his hand over his bandaged head. "I wasn't shot, was I? It was the taboo."

Domino smiled sympathetically. "You fainted," she said.

By Domino's account, it happened like this:

When the empty throne caused her to pause at the gazebo entrance, she had been informed that the Holy Father's lunch had been unkind to him, and due to heartburn ("surely the breath of Satan"), he would be unable to keep his appointment. The pontiff sent blessings and regrets, and requested that she entrust "the paper of interest" to his aides.

Suspecting subterfuge, Domino refused. She asked for a postponement. She'd come back later with her abbess, she said. A small argument ensued. Eventually Scanlani took out his flip phone and punched in a number. He said that she could enjoy the rare privilege of speaking to the pope on the telephone. He said the pope would personally verify that he wished the envelope turned over to an aide. "How will I know it's really him?" she had asked. Scanlani fired a short burst of Italian into the mouthpiece. The lawyer listened, he nodded. "He'll wave to you," he said. "The Holy Father will wave to you from his bathroom window. You will be able to see him up there, on the phone, talking to you. What an honor."

As Domino, confused, was considering this, Scanlani held out the cell phone. "Go ahead. Speak to the Holy Father," he said, holding the phone to her head. It was then that Switters had gone berserk.

"You broke a man's arm. You yelled something obscene. You bounded out of your chair. But as soon as your feet touched the earth, you fainted."

"It was Today Is Tomorrow. His curse. Wham! Hit me like a poison hammer. All the way from the Amazon."

"I'm sorry," she said soothingly. "You fainted."

To keep himself from shouting, "Did not! Did not!", he gazed out the window at the Marlboro Man. There was a fucking cowboy for you. Corporate puppet, believing he was free; brain full of testosterone, heart full of loneliness, jeans full of hemorrhoids, lungs full of tar.

"When you fell," she said, "you hit your head on the edge of one of those old broken columns. Ooh-la-la! It was terrible. It sounded like a coconut cracking." She turned to the freckled nun. "Darling, we've been remiss. Would you please go alert the medical staff that Mr. Switters has awakened."

After Pippi left the room, Domino said, "We're here in Salvator Mundi because the Vatican hospital refused to admit you. In fact, the Swiss Guard has a warrant for your arrest. Now, be calm. That American, that Mr. Seward, promised he wouldn't let them touch you. And if he doesn't stop them, I shall."

The conviction with which she said this made him grin. And when he grinned, his head hurt. "So, I tanked and split my skull."

"Yes, you did." After a beat, she added, "You also chipped another tooth. I must tell you, I will not stand at the altar with you until you've spent some quality time with your dentist."

He was startled. "At the altar, Domino? The altar? Does this mean you've decided that I'm not too . . . after all?"

"By no means," she said. "You definitely are too. . . ." She lowered her lashes. She stared at the floor. When she smiled, it was as though a hurdy-gurdy ice cream truck, laden with thirty-one flavors, had followed that doughnut wagon into the scorched neighborhood. "But I think I might want to marry you anyway."

Switters looked out of the window. To the Marlboro Man, he said, winking, "Hear that? Rimbaud wasn't kidding, pal. Of course, it takes more than calluses and a cough to qualify as a fierce invalid."

A doctor arrived and shooed the women out. Brandishing a penlight, he spent an inordinately long time staring into what some have called Switters's fierce, hypnotic green eyes. He warned his patient that Italian immigration authorities were itching to get their hands on him, but, for the time being, the hospital would not permit it. He inquired if he was hungry, and Switters, licking his chops, commenced to recite the entire menu of Da Fortunato al Pantheon. Later, an orderly brought a covered bowl. Unlidded, it proved to contain a clear broth—but this being Italy, several meaty tortellinis bobbed in it like fat boys at the beach.

Early the next morning, the testing began, culminating in a 360-degree CAT scan. Considering what he'd experienced during his coma, maybe it ought to have been a parrot scan. A poet scan. An interlocutor scan. A guide-to-the-underworld scan. (Pronounce the Aztec word and win a free week at the Gene Simmons Tongue Clinic.)

Throughout the day, as he was being poked, probed, punctured, pricked, and positioned; even as he lay sweating in the claustrophobic culvert of the CAT scanner, Switters had one primary question on his mind. It wasn't, *What's going to happen to me next?* It wasn't, *Will I marry my nun and live happily ever after?* But, rather, *How did I survive the curse?*

Perhaps it was psychosomatic, a self-fulfilling prophecy, but he *had* felt a massive jolt when his foot touched the ground. It was like being struck by lightning. Yet, it hadn't killed him. Today Is Tomorrow wasn't the type to do things in a half-assed way, and there was evidence that he didn't make idle threats: consider poor Potney Smithe. Was this the shaman's first attempt at a joke? No, as Potney might have put it, not bloody likely. Nevertheless, Switters had broken the taboo and escaped retribution. Why? Why hadn't he died?

That evening, he got an answer.

Domino was allowed to visit him after dinner (risòtto con funghi and tiramisù). She gave him a big kiss. Then she gave him a big envelope.

"What's this? The prophecy?"

"No, no. The Vatican has the prophecy. I ended up giving it to them, even though I never got to see the pope at his bathroom window. What they will do with Fatima's words, who can guess? I advised Scanlani that we have an interesting interpretation. He said he'd get back to me." She smiled skeptically. "But they did reinstate us. Issued us new habits."

Switters started to say, "There could be a slow-acting, skin-absorbed poison in the fabric"—but he caught himself. Hadn't he subjected her to quite enough paranoia? Besides, she was still wearing a chador.

"The envelope is from your friend, Bobby Case. Oh, I forgot to tell you that Masked Beauty is in Rome. She came a week late. While she was attending to the visa problem in Damascus, she picked up our mail at Toufic's office. This was in our box. Yes, and Captain Case has telephoned twice, as well. He's very nice. *Très sympathique.*"

"Yeah," Switters growled. "Case can nice the damn birds out of the damn trees." Was that a twinge of jealousy he felt? He flipped over the envelope and recognized Bobby's surprisingly fine handwriting. "You say he called?"

"Perhaps it was forward of me, but I took the liberty of phoning your grandmother the night of the . . . the accident. She must have informed Captain Case because he called two days later. He called again yesterday shortly before you came out of the coma. I had brought your cell phone over from the hotel."

Switters examined the postage stamps. They were not Okinawan stamps. They were Peruvian stamps. They were stamps from South-too-goddamn-vivid-America.

He delayed opening the envelope until Domino had gone. An hour later, when the night nurse came in to take his temperature and update his chart, he was still staring at its contents.

It contained a single photograph, eight and a half by eleven. In the background of the picture, against a tangled wall of tropical forest, stood a group of twenty or so Indians, nearly naked, strangely painted. In the foreground was an object that he recognized almost immediately as Sailor Boy's old cage, made of wicker, shaped like a pyramid. "Well, what do you know?" he mumbled, though it was hardly unusual that the Kandakandero had kept the thing. Then, he noticed that the birdcage wasn't empty. There was something inside.

It was another pyramid.

A pyramid the size of a soccer ball.

A pyramid crowned with parrot feathers.

A pyramid with a human face.

The accompanying note, on Hotel Boquichicos stationery, was in Bobby's incongruously elegant script.

I knew you wouldn't believe it unless you saw it—so take a good look. Take two looks and call me in the morning.

Don't worry, podner, I didn't smack him. It wasn't necessary. They say a big snake got him. Forty-foot anaconda or some unhappy shit like that.

It's wild down here, ain't it? Man! No wonder you believed that curse. My guide is the new head shaman and he is one radical dude. Says he knows you. I'm bringing him back to the States with me, which ought to be a lark and a half. I'll fill you in soon. Meanwhile, have yourself a nice long walk. You've earned it.

In the photograph, the warriors were all grinning in razzle-dazzle unison, like the cast of a minstrel show.

Switters borrowed the nurse's penlight and examined the head in the birdcage. It was also smiling. It looked . . . relaxed.

the floor had felt strange at first: alien, almost threatening. Gradually, however, it became increasingly hospitable. Beneath his bare feet, the waxed linoleum turned into an orgy. He went from walking like Neil Armstrong to walking like Krishna. Both cool and warm, smooth and wavy, the floor felt like fruit skin. It felt like lettuce. Something invisible and pleasurable oozed up between his toes. Up and down the hallway he padded, slapping the floor with his soles to experience the floorness of it. Every now and then, when he was out of sight of the nurses' station, he did a little monkey dance. "I'm going to jump out the window and dance on grass," he told Domino. She reminded him that he was five stories up.

For much of the day, Domino walked with him, listening to him rant about large snakes, the World Serpent, the healing python of Apollo, the wiggly staff of Hermes, and so on; how, in his opinion, the Serpent hadn't seduced Eve into tasting the apple of forbidden knowledge, rather, the Serpent *was* the apple: watching the Serpent shed its skin and be reborn, Eve was introduced to the prospect of immortality; observing the Serpent on its forays underground, Eve was led to suspect that there was more to life than met the eye, that there were other, deeper, levels; a reality beneath the surface of reality, an unconscious mind. Hadn't the metaphoric Serpent in Domino's own little Eden, once it was viewed from a wider angle, blown open the gates—and angered the authorities? As for why serpent power killed Today Is Tomorrow, however, he had barely a clue. Supreme knowledge is supremely dangerous, ultimate mysteries remain ultimately mysterious. Beware the delusional rationalist who argues otherwise.

The walking was delicious, and the ranting was pretty good, too. He walked and ranted, ranted and walked, interrupted only by lunch and by Masked Beauty, who stopped in to squeeze his hand and say *adieu*. The abbess, Mustang Sally, and Pippi were returning to Syria that evening. She hoped to see him there again someday. She looked handsome in her new summer habit. The scar on her nose had darkened, he noticed. It was now the exact same shade of blue in which Matisse had immortalized her naked body in 1943.

Later, drained by the walking, and in bed early, Switters lay fantasizing future scenarios. Bobby Case was bringing Fer-de-lance to the Northern Hemisphere. To the white man's world. Fer-de-lance, with all his ancient magic and contemporary awareness; a half-breed in every sense of the word; equipped—linguistically, epistemologically, and physically—to flourish in more than one reality. Suppose Fer-de-lance were to throw in with them? With Switters, Bobby, Audubon Poe, and Skeeter Washington (who'd recently lost a hand defusing a land mine in Eritrea, but was said to play a hot five-finger-and-nub piano); with B. G. Woo and Dickie Dare and some other operatives and ex-operatives whom he ought not to name? Maybe even Domino would come aboard: hadn't she expressed a weakness for the idea of a purist elite? Suppose the lot of them were to combine forces? To organize. Sort of.

They probably wouldn't name it, this new organization of theirs. Cult of the Great Snake would be presumptuous and far-fetched; and he was getting pretty tired of *angels*, as Hollywood, gullible Christers, and New Age loopy-doodles had combined to give them a trite, fairygodfather image. Most definitely, the group would not have a creed. Unless it was something modest and non-doctrinaire, such as, "The house is on fire, but you can't beat our view."

They wouldn't even believe, especially, in their mission; not in any fervent way. If they believed too adamantly, then sooner or later they would be tempted to lie to protect those beliefs. It was a small step from lying to defend one's beliefs to killing to defend them.

Hey, they might not be fully cognizant of the nature of their mission. They'd contemplate it, to be sure, and argue over it, but it would be dynamic, a work in progress, ever subject to change. Only the weak and the dull of the world knew where they were going, and it was rarely worth the trip.

They'd use Poe's yacht, maybe, and Sol Glissant's funding. But they'd be more aggressive than Poe had been. Poe was treating the symptoms. They would attack the disease. They would fuck with the fuckers. Sabotage: physical, electronic, and psychic sabotage. Monkey wrenches. Computer viruses. Psychedelic alterations. Ridicule. Japes. Spells. Enchantments. Dadaisms. Reinformation. Meditational smart bombs. On the side, they might deface a few advertisements. Vandalize some golf courses.

Mostly, however, they'd follow Fer-de-lance's lead. See what he had up his snakeskin sleeve. See if he really was destined to bring Today Is Tomorrow's message into an unsuspecting new century. Determine if Our Blessed Lady of Fatima, in her role as feminine principle, employing her archaic code, had actually rematerialized to alert her children to a hard and wonderful truth about to stream in a helix of light and shadow from the direction of a pyramid.

Not quite asleep, not wholly awake, Switters was lying there fantasizing about all that when the cell phone suddenly beeped. "This had better be good," he growled into the mouthpiece.

Maestra actually wept at the sound of his voice. She quickly recovered, however, and proceeded to tell him how inconsiderate he was, and what a buffoon; no, something worse than a buffoon, because he was brilliant and therefore had no right to behave buffoonishly. He was also a pervert. She ordered him to come to her the instant they let him out of that "squalid Italian hospital," and never mind the bracelets: her arms were getting too damn scrawny to support them anymore.

Then, Suzy got on the line. Got on the phone with that double-tongued little voice of hers, her consonants straight-backed with the most demure sincerity, her vowels all lopsided with hormones. Suzy told him she loved him and wanted to be with him forever, in the way he used to talk about back when she was just a spank girl. She'd be eighteen in less than a year and could do as she pleased.

"You know, I had sex last summer, Switters, and now I'm so sorry. I'm devastated. Not because they got mad and sent me to Seattle, but because you weren't the first. You know? Well, I've been praying to Mother Mary that she'll restore my virginity. So that I can give it to you. Honestly. I really am praying for that. I know it's goofy, but miracles can happen, can't they?"

"They can, darling. They happen all the time."

There has got to be a way to have both of them, he thought. Domino and Suzy, too. He spent the entire night devising one delectable and improbable scheme after another, refusing to accept that the fates might force him to choose one or the other. He loved them both. He wanted them both. It was only natural. He was Switters.

early the next morning, he checked himself out of the hospital, and he and Mr. Plastic flew to Bangkok. To clear the coconut. To mull matters over.

There was a temple by the river, where he meditated every day. Nights, there were the girls of Patpong. Bless them. Bless every slink and wisp of them. There were refreshing, if timid, beers. Food so spicy it'd run a motor. A little stick now and then.

Cowboys were fond of saying, "If it ain't broke, don't fix it." Switters thought, *It's always broke, and we can never fix it. On the other hand, there's nothing to break, so what is it we imagine we're fixing?*

The baht was weak against the dollar. A back-alley tailor made him a new linen suit. He walked in it. Danced in it. Acknowledged the Tao. The seam in the Tao. At moments he felt as if he were at least an inch and a half off the ground.

He kept bumping into old acquaintances, and one midnight they took him to a meeting of the C.R.A.F.T. Club—where, legend has it, he got up and squawked like a parrot.

ACKNOWLEDGMENTS

The author wishes to lift a goblet of vintage ink to his agent, Phoebe Larmore; his editor, Christine Brooks; and his five-book line editor, Danelle McCafferty (who taught him south from north—or was it the other way around?). He also salutes his assistant, Barbara Barker; his former assistant, Jacqueline Trevillion (twelve years before the mast); his longtime typist, Wendy Chevalier; and the numerous other women (lucky dog!) who dominate his life, including, but definitely not limited to, his attorney, Margaret Christopher; his yoga teacher, Dunja Lingwood; his Patpong social directors, Little Opium Annie and Miss Pretty Woman; his anatomical researcher and mayonnaise scout, Koryn Rolstad; his French connection, Enid Smith-Becker; and, most emphatically, his eternal love dumpling, Alexa.